aloft

aloft

CHANG-RAE LEE

RIVERHEAD BOOKS

a member of Penguin Group (USA) Inc.

New York

2004

This is a work of fiction. Names, characters, places, and inci-
dents are either the product of the author's imagination or are
used fictitiously, and any resemblance to actual persons, living
or dead, business establishments, events, or locales is entirely
coincidental.

Riverhead Books
a member of
Penguin Group (USA) Inc.
375 Hudson Street
New York, NY 10014

Library of Congress Cataloging-in-Publication Data

Lee, Chang-rae.
Aloft / Chang-rae Lee.
p.   cm.
ISBN 1-57322-263-1
1. Middle class men—Fiction.   2. Suburban life—Fiction.
I. Title.

PS3562.E3347A79   2004   2003058630
813'.54—dc22

Printed in the United States of America
1   3   5   7   9   10   8   6   4   2

This book is printed on acid-free paper. ♾

Book design by Amanda Dewey

To Michelle,
for all the love

one

FROM UP HERE, a half mile above the Earth, everything looks perfect to me.

I am in my nifty little Skyhawk, banking her back into the sun, having nearly completed my usual fair-weather loop. Below is the eastern end of Long Island, and I'm flying just now over that part of the land where the two gnarly forks shoot out into the Atlantic. The town directly ahead, which is nothing special when you're on foot, looks pretty magnificent now, the late-summer sun casting upon the macadam of the streets a soft, ebonized sheen, its orangey light reflecting back at me, matching my direction and speed in the windows and bumpers of the parked cars and swimming pools of the simple, square houses set snugly in rows. There is a mysterious, runelike cipher to the newer, larger homes wagoning in their cul-de-sac hoops, and then, too, in the flat roofs of the shopping mall buildings, with their shiny metal circuitry of HVAC housings and tubes.

From up here, all the trees seem ideally formed and arranged, as if fretted over by a persnickety florist god, even the ones (no doubt volunteers) clumped along the fencing of the big scrap metal lot, their spindly, leggy uprush not just a pleasing garnish to the variegated piles of old hubcaps and washing machines, but then, for a stock guy like me, mere heartbeats shy of *sixty* (hard to even say that), the life signs of a positively priapic yearning. Just to the south, on the baseball diamond—our people's pattern supreme—the local Little League game is entering the late innings, the baby-blue-shirted players positioned straightaway and shallow, in the bleachers their parents only appearing to sit church-quiet and still, the sole perceivable movement a bounding golden-haired dog tracking down a Frisbee in deep, deep centerfield.

Go, boy, go.

And as I point my ship—*Donnie* is her name—to track alongside the broad arterial lanes of Route 495, the great and awful Long Island Expressway, and see the already-accrued jams of the Sunday Hamptons traffic inching back to the city, the grinding columns of which, from my seat, appear to constitute an orderly long march, I feel as if I'm going at a heady light speed, certainly moving too fast in relation to the rest, an imparity that should by any account invigorate but somehow unsettles all the same, and I veer a couple of degrees northwest to head over the remaining patchworks of farmland and scrubby forest and then soon enough the immense, uninterrupted stretch of older, densely built townships like mine, where beneath the obscuring canopy men like me are going about the last details of their weekend business, sweeping their front walks and dragging trash cans to the street and washing their cars just as they have since boyhood and youth, soaping from top to bottom and brushing the wheels of sooty brake dust, one spoke at a time.

And I know, too, from up here, that I can't see the messy rest, none of the pedestrian, sea-level flotsam that surely blemishes our good scene, the casually tossed super-size Slurpies and grubby confetti of a million cigarette butts, the ever-creeping sidewalk mosses and weeds; I can't see the tumbling faded newspaper circular page, or the dead, gassy possum beached at the foot of the curb, the why of its tight, yellow-toothed grin.

All of which, for the moment, is more than okay with me.

Is that okay?

Okay.

I bought this plane not for work or travel or the pure wondrous thrill of flight, which can and has, indeed, been scarily, transcendentally life-affirming and so on, but for the no doubt seriously unexamined reason of my just having to get out of the house.

That's certainly what my longtime (and recently ex-) girlfriend, Rita Reyes, was thinking about several years ago, when she gave me a flying lesson out at Islip for my birthday. Really, of course, she meant it as a diversionary excursion, just a hands-on plane ride, never intending it to lead to anything else.

At the time she was deeply worried about me, as I was a year into having early-retired from the family landscaping business and was by all indications mired in a black hole of a rut, basically moping around the house and snacking too much. On weekdays, after Rita left for her job as a home-care nurse (she now works the ER), I'd do my usual skim of the paper in front of the TV and then maybe watch a ladies' morning talk show and soon enough I'd feel this sharp nudge of ennui and I'd head to the nearby Walt Whitman Mall (the poet was born in a modest house right across the street, which is now something they call an "interpretive center" and is open for tours) for what I would always hope was the easeful company of like-minded people but would end up instead, depending on the selling season, to be frantic clawing hordes or else a ghost town of seniors sitting by the islands of potted ficus, depressing and diminishing instances both.

When Rita came back home, the breakfast dishes would still be clogging the table, and I'd be on the back patio nursing a third bottle of light beer or else napping in the den after leafing through my tattered *Baedeker's Italy* for the umpteenth time. She'd try to be helpful and patient but it was hard, as that's what she'd done all day long. More often than not we'd end up in a shouting match because she'd toss aside my guidebook a bit too casually and I'd say something loose and mean about her mother, and she'd retreat to the bedroom while I went to the car and revved the engine inside for a long minute before clicking open the garage door. I'd find myself at a run-down Chinese place on Jericho, chasing a too-sweet Mai Tai with wonton soup for dinner and then phoning Rita, to see if she wanted her usual pupu platter appetizer and shrimp with black beans, which she would, and which I'd bring back and duly serve to her, as the saying goes, with love and squalor.

All this began occurring too regularly and finally Rita told me I had better get into something to take up my time, even if it was totally useless and shallow. Immediately I thought maybe it was finally time I strapped myself into a convertible sports car or fast boat, some honeyed, wet-look motor that the neighbors would gape at and maybe snicker and whisper *micropenis* about and then pine after, too, but I wanted something else, not quite knowing what exactly until the moment I opened the gift certificate from Rita for Flaherty's Top Gun Flight School.

I must say I was nervous that day, even downright afraid, which was strange because I've flown in hundreds of planes, some of them single-engine like this one and certainly not as kept-up. I could hardly finish my breakfast toast and coffee. I kept trying and failing to pee, all the while thinking how it was that a person should die exactly on his birthday, how maudlin and rare, and so also a bit pathetic if it actually did happen, especially if you weren't someone famous, all of which Rita caught on to, fake eulogizing me all morning with hushed phrasings of "And he was *exactly* fifty-six. . . ."

But I could tell she was worried, too, for she wouldn't kiss me or even look me in the eye when I was leaving for the airfield, hardly glancing up from her cooking magazine as she murmured a casual, if all swallowed-up, goodbye. Sweet moment, potentially, as it should have been, with me supposed to drop my car keys back into the loose-change bowl and saunter over to Rita in my new aviator shades and cup her silky butterscotch breast through the opening of her robe and assure us both of the righteous tenure of our (then nearly twenty) years of devotion and love; but what did I do but mutter goodbye back and mention that I'd be home in time for lunch and could that osso buco she'd made two nights ago be heated up with extra orzo, or maybe even some couscous with snips of fresh mint? Rita, of course, responded with her usual "No problem," which anyone else even half-listening would think was a dirge of pure defeat and trouble but was long my favorite tune.

So I drove off with my sights set high again, for there's little else more inspiring to me than the promise of a hot savory meal prepared by a good woman. But the second I entered the private plane entrance at MacArthur Field and saw the spindly wing struts and narrow fuselages of the parked Pipers and Cessnas, my heart caved a little and I thought of my grown children, Theresa and Jack, and immediately speed-dialed them on my cell phone. I was ready to say to each the very same thing, that I was deeply proud of their accomplishments and their character and that I wished I could relive again those brief years of their infancy and childhood, and then add, too, that I would never burden them in my decline and that they should always call Rita on her birthday and holidays.

But then Theresa's English Department voice-mail picked up, not her voice but the ubiquitous female voice of Central Messaging, and all I could manage was to say I hadn't heard from her in a while and wondered if anything was wrong. Next I got Jack's voice-mail, this time Jack's voice, but he sounded so businesslike and remote that I left a message for him in the voice of Mr. T, all gruff and belligerent, threatening to open a big can of whoop-ass on him if he didn't lighten up.

This, too, didn't come out quite right, and as I was still early for the flying lesson, I called my father, who would certainly be in.

He answered, "Who the hell is this?"

"It's me, Pop. How you doing?"

"Oh. You. How do you think I'm doing?"

"Just fine, I'm betting."

"That's what you want to think. Anyway, come down and spring me out of here. I'm packed and ready to go."

"All right, Pop. The nurses treating you well?"

"They treat me like dog shit. But that's what I'm paying for. What I worked for all my stinking life, so I can wear a gown and eat airline food every meal and have a male nurse with tattooed palms wipe my ass."

"You don't need anybody to do that for you."

"You haven't been around lately, Jerome. You don't know. You don't know that this is the place where they make the world's boredom and isolation. This is where they purify it. It's monstrous. And what they're doing to Nonna over in the ladies' wing, I can't even mention."

Nonna was his wife, and my mother, and at that point she had been in the brass urn for five years. Pop is by most measures fine in the head, though it seemed around that period that anything having to do with mortality and time often got scrambled in the relevant lobes, a development that diminished only somewhat my feelings of filial betrayal and guilt for placing him via power of attorney into the Ivy Acres Life Care Center, where for $5500 per month he will live out the rest of his days in complete security and comfort and without a worldly care, which we know is simple solution and problem all in one, which we can do nothing about, which we do all to forget.

"I'm taking a flying lesson today, Pop."

"Oh yeah?"

"Have any words for me?"

"I never got to fly a plane," he growled, and not in response to me. "I never rode in a hot-air balloon. I never made love to two women at once."

"I'm sure that can be arranged."

"Aah, don't bother. I don't need any more examples of my sorry ass. Just do me one favor."

"You name it, Pop."

"If you're going down, try to make it over here. Top corner of the building, looking right over the parking lot. Aim at the old bag waving in the window."

"Forget it."

"You are not my son."

"Yeah, Pop. I'll see you."

"Whatever."

One of our usual goodbyes, from the thin catalogue of father-son biddings, thinner still for the time of life and circumstance and then, of course, for the players involved, who have never transgressed the terms of engagement, who have never even ridden the line. I then walked into the hangar office with a light-on-my-feet feeling, not like a giddiness or anxiety but an unnerving sense of being dangerously unmoored, as though I were some astronaut creeping out into the grand maw of space, eternities roiling in the background, with too much slack in my measly little line. And it occurred to me that in this new millennial life of instant and ubiquitous connection, you don't in fact communicate so much as leave messages for one another, these odd improvisational performances, often sorry bits and samplings of ourselves that can't help but seem out of context. And then when you do finally reach someone, everyone's so out of practice or too hopeful or else embittered that you wonder if it would be better not to attempt contact at all.

And yet I forgot all that when I finally got up off the deck, into the *Up here.* I won't go into the first blush of feelings and sensations but summarize to say only that my first thought when the instructor let me take the controls was that I wished he'd strapped a chute on himself, so he could jump the hell out. Nothing in the least was wrong with him—he was a nice, if alarmingly young, kid from an extended family of pilots, the Flahertys. But feeling the motor's buzz in my butt and legs, the shuddery lift of the wingtips in my hands, and gazing down just this middle distance on the world, this fetching, ever-mitigating length, I kept thinking that here was the little room, the little vessel, I was looking for, my private box seat in the world and completely outside of it, too.

After we landed and taxied toward the hangar I peppered the kid pilot for his opinion on what sort of plane I should buy and where I might find one. Through his big amber sunglasses (same as mine) he nodded to a three-seat Cessna with green stripes parked on the tarmac and told me it was for sale by a guy who had suffered a stroke on his last flight, though he had obviously weathered it and somehow brought himself in. It was an older plane, the kid said into his squawky microphone, in his clipped, mini–Chuck Yeager voice, but a reliable one and in good shape. It had been on the market for a while and I could probably get it at a good price. It wasn't the sort of plane I'd want if I was thinking about zipping back and forth across the country, but for shorter, leisure junkets it'd be ideal, which seemed just fine to me. Inside the hangar office the secretary gave me the guy's number, and it turned out he lived in the town next to mine, so on the drive back home I called and introduced myself to his friendly wife and we decided why shouldn't I come over right then and talk about it with her husband Hal?

Their house was an attractive cedar-shingled colonial, built in the 1960s like a lot of houses in this part of Long Island, including mine, when the area was still mostly potato fields and duck farms and unsullied stretches of low-slung trees and good scrubby nothingness. Now the land is filled with established developments and newer ones from the '80s, and with the last boom having catapulted everyone over the ramparts there's still earthmoving equipment to be seen on either side of the Expressway (eight lanes wide now), clearing the remaining natural tracts for the instant office parks and upscale condos and assisted living centers, and then the McMansions where young families like my son Jack's live, with their vaulted great rooms and multimedia rooms and wine and cigar *caves*. I should say I'm not against any of these things, per se, because it seems to me only right that people should play and work as they please in this so-called democratic life, and even as I'm damn proud of my son Jack's wholly climate-controlled existence (despite the fact that we don't really talk much anymore), there is another part of me that naturally wonders how this rush of prosperity is ruining him and Eunice and the kids and then everybody else who has money enough not to have to really think so deeply about money but does all the time anyway, wherever they are.

A national demography of which, I suppose, I've been an integral part, though in the past few years—since getting this plane, in fact—I've realized I have more than plenty, if plenty means I can ride out the next twenty or so years of my life expectancy not having to eat dried soup noodles if I don't want to or call one of Jack's employees instead of a real plumber or always remember to press my driver's license against the ticket window for the senior citizen rate at the multiplex. And though I've never had enough real surplus or the balls to invest in the stock market (an unexpiable sin in recent years, though now I'm a certified financial genius for socking away everything I have in Treasuries), unless I'm struck down by some ruinous long-term disability, I'll be okay. Oh you poor-mouthing owner of a private plane, you might be thinking, and rightly, for the Cessna did cost nearly as much as a big Mercedes, and isn't cheap to maintain. But in my defense, I still live in the same modest starter house I bought just before Jack was born, and never wore clothes I didn't buy at Alexander's and Ward's (now at Costco and Target—my longtime patronage clearly no help to the former defunct), or dined if I could help it in any restaurant, no matter how good, with menu prices spelled out in greeting card script. And if this plane is indeed my life's folly, well, at least I found one before it's too late, when the only juiced feeling of the day will be yet another heartbreakingly tragic History Channel biography on a nineteenth-century explorer or the *ring-ring* of some not-quite-as-old coot at the door delivering my day's foil-wrapped meal-on-wheels.

When I got to the stricken pilot's house his friendly wife, Shari, greeted me and then suddenly gave me a quick hug in the foyer, and so I hugged her back, as if I were an old war buddy of his and she and I had had our flirtations through the years, transgressions which I would not have minded, given her sturdy nice shape and pretty mouth. She showed me into the big, dark faux-walnut-paneled den, where a man in a baseball cap and crisp button-down shirt was sitting in an uncomfortable-looking wooden armchair with a plaid blanket spread over his legs. The place was freezing, as though they had the air set to 62 degrees. The cable was on but he was faced more toward the sliding glass door than the TV set, looking out on the covered deck, where they had propped a trio of silky-looking cardinals on the rim of an ornate plastic birdbath. The birds were amazingly realistic in detail, with shiny yellow beaks and black-masked faces, except perhaps that they were way too big, but I'd never been that close to such birds and I figured most things in the natural world were bigger than you thought, brighter and more vibrant and more real than real. As we approached, it was clear that he was dozing, and for a long almost parental second we stood over him, Shari pulling up the blanket that was half slipping off.

"Hal, honey," she said. "Mr. Battle is here. About the plane."

"Uh-hum," he said, clearing his throat. He extended his hand and we shook.

"Well, I'll let you two boys talk," Shari said, excusing herself to fix us some iced tea.

Hal said, "Sit right down there, young fella," pointing to the leather couch with his one good arm.

Hal wasn't that much older than I was, if he was older at all, but I guess his condition gave him the right to address me so, which didn't bother me. He spoke out of the same good side of his mouth, with a whistley, spitty sound that was boyish and youthful. He asked what I did for a living and I told him it used to be landscaping, and he told me he was a private driver, or was until his stroke, the kind who drove around executives and VIPs in regular black sedans. He was a nice-looking fellow, with a neatly clipped salt-and-pepper mustache and beard. And I should probably not so parenthetically mention right now that Hal was black. This surprised me, first because Shari wasn't, being instead your typical Long Island white lady in tomato-red shorts and a stenciled designer T-shirt, and then because there aren't many minorities in this area, period, and even fewer who are hobbyist pilots, a fact since borne out in my three years of hanging out at scrubby airfields. Of course, my exceedingly literate, overeducated daughter

CHANG-RAE LEE

Theresa (Stanford Ph.D.) would say as she has in the past that I
have to mention all this because like most people in this country
I'm hopelessly obsessed with race and difference and can't help
but *privilege* the *normative* and *fetishize* what's not. And while I'm
never fully certain of her terminology, I'd like to think that if I am
indeed guilty of such things it's mostly because sometimes I worry
for her and Jack, who, I should mention, too, aren't wholly normative of race themselves, being "mixed" from my first and only
marriage to a woman named Daisy Han.

"What's your name again?"

"Jerry. Jerry Battle."

"So, Jerry Battle, you want to buy a plane."

"I believe so," I said. "There's nothing like the freedom of
flight."

"You bet. But listen, friend. Let me be up front with you. A lot
of guys have been by here who weren't really sure. Now, I'd love to
chat but you won't be insulting me if you decided right now this
wasn't right for you."

"I think it is."

"You sure?" he said, staring me straight in the eye. I nodded,
though in fact I was starting to wonder.

"Because sometimes guys realize at the last second they don't
want to buy a *used* plane. You know what I'm talking about, Jerry?"

He was looking at me queerly, and then suddenly I thought I
did know what he was talking about. I remembered a client with
a mansion in Old Westbury, beautiful place except they'd had a lot
of diseased trees, and we'd come in and replaced all of them and
did a lot of patio and pool work and redid the formal gardens. After that the place was mint. But the husband took a new job in California and they put it on the market, for whatever millions. They
had lots of lookers, but no offers, so they lowered the price, twice
in fact. But still nothing. So the listing agent suggested they con-

sider "depersonalizing" the house, by which she meant taking down the family pictures, and anything else like it, as the owners were black. They were thoroughly offended, but no one was biting and so finally the husband said they would, but then only if they listed the house at the original price. They ended up getting several overbids, and eventually sold to a party who'd looked the first time around.

So I told Hal, looking right at him, that I didn't mind a good used plane.

"Okay, good. Now. How long have you been flying?"

"A good while now," I said, thinking of course of my many hundred hours at the helm in coach, tray table ready. I don't know why I felt the need to lie to the man. Normally I wouldn't care if he knew I'd just touched down from my very first lesson and he thought I was crazy, but I guess seeing him like that, sitting invalid-style, made me think it might somehow push him over the edge to know a complete beginner would be manning his plane.

"I'm looking forward to pride of ownership," I said, hoping this might sound suitably virtuous, to us both. "Take my interest to the next level. As it were."

Hal nodded, though I couldn't tell from the expression on his half-frozen face if he was agreeing or was now on to me.

He said, "I bought the plane ten years ago. This just after my son Donnie was killed. Donnie was going to start medical school at BU. Six-year program. You know about that?"

"I think one of my customers' kids is in it. He got a perfect score on his SATs."

"Donnie did, too."

"No kidding."

"Some people don't believe me when I tell them, but you don't lie about something like that. You can't pretend yourself into perfection."

"I guess not."

"No way," Hal said, shifting in the hard wooden chair. You'd think he'd have a cushy, blobby-layered TV recliner (like I have at home), something upholstered in a pastel-colored leather with a built-in telephone and cup holder and magazine caddy that he could fall into to vegetate until the next meal or when nature called, but you could gather from the showroom setup of the house that Hal was the sort of fellow who preferred the rigor of the bench, who always had a dozen needle-sharp pencils ready on his desk, who believed in the chi of spit-shined shoes and a classic, cherry motor humming with fresh amber oil.

"Before he died I was in your situation," he said, glancing at me, "just getting up when I could, renting planes wherever we went on vacation, you know, to get the overview."

"Exactly."

"I would've gone on like that. Been happy with it. But then Donnie had the head-on with the drunk driver. Son of a bitch has been out of jail for a few years now. On the anniversary day of the accident I go over to his place in Melville and sit out front with a picture of my son. Shari doesn't like me to do it but it's not like I have a choice. That man is not going to forget Donnie. Nobody is."

Just then Shari came back in, bearing a tray of three tall plastic tumblers of iced tea, each bobbed with a straw. She seemed to know what Hal was talking about, because she left her drink on the tray and without a word went outside on the deck, sliding the glass door closed behind her, and began culling the plants for withered blooms. Our clingy hug in the foyer should have clued me in to where this visit was headed, how every other stranger you bump into these days (or try to buy something from) has the compulsion to unfurl the precious old remnant of his life for you, his own tatter of a war story, which would be bad enough but for the companion fact that those closest to you seem to clam up at every chance of genuine kinship, with undue prejudice. But I was here now and still interested in buying the plane and this was probably the last wholly appropriate occasion Hal would have to tell his story, which no decent citizen of this world, and certainly not Jerry Battle, could rightly refuse to hear.

Hal took a long sip through his straw, nearly finishing his drink in one take. "After things got settled down I realized I had all this money set aside for him, for tuition and the rest of it. It wasn't going to cover the whole shot but it was enough to get him going, you know, so he wouldn't be pinned with all the debts when he was done."

"That's great."

"It *was* great. But now what? All of a sudden I'm looking at this big pile of cash." Hal laughed tightly, in the way he could laugh, which was like a form of strained, intense breathing. "What do you do with something like that?"

"I'm not sure, Hal."

"Well, Shari felt we ought to give the money to charity. Maybe to the medical school, for a scholarship in Donnie's name. A scholarship was fine with me, Jerry, because it's not like I didn't have a decent war chest going for our retirement, which thank God we have now. I'm not too proud to say we've always been set up right, in regard to our family. But Donnie was a good kid, bright and talented, but most of all just plain good, and I got to thinking he didn't need to be memorialized by us, at least in those usual ways. He never flew with me, because his mother didn't trust the rental planes, but he always wanted to, and I got to feeling that maybe he would think it was kind of neat that I bought a plane with his medical school money."

"I'm sure he's tickled."

"Thank you for saying that, Jerry," he said. "When I was having the stroke up there, I was thinking just that. Actually I wasn't thinking anything for a little while, because I was seizing. Lucky for me I was at 9500 feet when it hit. I must have spiraled down in a wide circle, who knows how many minutes of blind flying, because when I looked out again I was only at about 300 feet, and crossing right over the Expressway. I could see some kids slap-fighting in the back of a minivan, and the first thing that came to mind was that this was my son Donnie's ship, dammit, and I ought to be more careful with her. There was no way I wasn't going to bring her in. I knew it was the last real thing I was supposed to do."

"It's amazing you were able to land, using just one arm and one leg."

"It's hard to know for sure," Hal said, rubbing his face, "but I'm almost certain I still had use of my entire body. The doctors told me it's unlikely, even impossible, but I know they're wrong. There are mysteries, Jerry, when it comes to the body and mind. Take Donnie, for instance. He didn't die at the scene. He was in a coma for five days in the ICU. On the fifth day he sat right up in his bed and told me that he was already dead. Shari wasn't there, she was down in the cafeteria getting us fresh coffee. I was shocked that he was awake but I said, 'What do you mean, son, listen to yourself, you're alive.' And Donnie said, 'No, Dad, it just looks like I am. I died on that road, and you know it.' I decided to play along, because I didn't want to upset him, and because I was so happy to be talking to him, and I asked him what it was like, to be dead. And do you know what he told me, Jerry?"

I shook my head, because I didn't want to know, actually, death not being a state I've found myself terribly interested in, then or now or come any day in the future.

"He said it was nice and bright and chilly, like a supermarket. And that there was no one else around."

"He was alone?"

"You got it. Like he had the place all to himself. But he said it was okay, really fine. Then he got tired and lay back down. By the time Shari was back, he'd dropped back in the coma again. And he never woke up."

Shari came in from the deck and she saw Hal's face all screwed up, and instantly I could see she was trying her best to hold it together. I made the mistake of going over and gripping Hal's shoulder, and both he and Shari lost it. Before I knew it we were all huddled together, and Hal was wheezing like his windpipe was cracked and Shari's face was buried in my neck, her muted sobs alternating with what felt like delicate, openmouthed kisses but were just her crying eyes. I glanced at Hal, who was covering his own face with his good arm, and as I stood up with Shari still draped on my shoulders, Hal mumbled, "If you two would please excuse me for a moment."

So I followed Shari into the kitchen, not unmoved by the display but also half-dreading an imminent Part II, HerStory, in which Jerry Battle would learn of the Turbulent Early Years, and the Cherub Donnie, and then of Waning Passions: A Late-Middle Passage, life chapters or what have you that I could certainly relate to and mourn and hallow with neighborly unction and sobriety, but that I would be wishing to decline, decline. But perhaps it was too late for all that, or simply that we were in her spotless kitchen, as Shari slipped into hausfrau mode and gave me a fresh glass of iced tea and a plate of oatmeal cookies and we were soon chatting about garbage pickup days and the recent spike in our property taxes, which would hurt retired folks and other people like them on fixed incomes. Apparently Hal had overstated their financial condition. They really had to sell the plane. Shari said they might even have to sell the house and move to a condo, though she said this almost matter-of-factly, without a hint of whine or anger, and for a moment she sounded just like my long-dead wife, Daisy, who, when not caught up in one of her hot blooms of madness, featured the casual and grave acceptance of someone who works outdoors and is once again caught in a lingering rain.

After a short while I told Shari I'd mail a check for the price they were asking, if that was all right.

"You're not going to bargain a little?"

"Should I?"

"I don't know," she said. "This seems too easy. We've been trying to sell it for half a year."

"I got that from Hal. Why it's been difficult."

"Oh that, that's poppycock," she said. "If anything, it's because they come and see him like he is, and they think the plane has bad luck."

"Does it?"

She paused, and then said, without looking at me, "No."

"Good," I said, though in fact for the first time since coming up with the whole headlong idea at the field I felt a little off-kilter, and scared. "Then it's settled, okay?"

"Okay, Jerry," she said, clasping my hand.

We went to tell Hal that the deal was done but he was fast asleep in his chair in the den, a wide slick of drool shimmying down his chin. Shari produced a hankie from her shorts pocket and wiped him with a deft stroke. He didn't budge. We tiptoed to the door and Shari thanked me for coming by and dealing with everything and helping them out, and I told her it was my privilege and honor to do so but that I certainly didn't believe I was helping them. And yet, all I could think of as we stepped out on the front stoop was that the rap sheet on me documented just this kind of thing, that I'm one to leap up from the mat to aid all manner of strangers and tourists and other wide-eyed foreigners but when it comes to loved ones and family I can hardly ungear myself from the La-Z-Boy, and want only succor and happy sufferance in return.

Shari and I hugged once more, but then she surprised me with a quick, dry peck on the mouth. On the mouth.

"I'm sorry," Shari said, stepping back. "I didn't mean that."

"Hey," I told her, my hands raised. "No harm done. See?"

Shari nodded, though I could tell she was feeling as if *something* was just done. She stood there on the stoop, self-horrified, trying to cover herself with her arms. Normally I would have begged off right then, made some lame excuse and neatly backslid to my car, but I couldn't bear to leave her hanging like that, so I wrapped my arms around her and closed my eyes and kissed her with whatever sweet force and tenderness I could muster, not even pretending she was my Rita, and not sorry about it either, except for the fact that I did enjoy it, too, at least macrocosmically, the notion of kissing a thoroughly decent and pretty woman who was another man's wife and not needing to push the moment a hair past its tolerances. And I think that it was in this spirit that Shari perhaps liked it, too, or appreciated the squareness of it, its gestural, third-person quality, whatever or whatever, for after we relented and let each other go she broke into this wide, wan, near-beatific smile, and then disappeared into the house. I waited a second, then got into my car and backed out of the driveway, when Shari came out again. She handed me two sets of keys to the plane.

"But I haven't paid you guys yet."

"I know you will," she said. "Just promise you'll look after it and keep it safe."

I told her I would. And then the awkwardness of the moment made me say that if she ever wanted to fly in the plane again, she could call me.

"I don't think so," she said. "But thank you. And don't forget what Hal always says."

"What's that?" I asked.

" 'There's no point in flying if you can't fly alone.' "

SOUND ADVICE, I believe, which I have tried to take to heart.

So here I am, afloat in the bright clear, surveying the open sky, measuring only what I fancy. I could go around again, which I sometimes do, swing back west past the spired city and over the leafy hillocks of northern Jersey, and if I desired make a quick landing at Teterboro and take a taxi to the taco stand in Little Ferry for an early dinner of chili verde and iced guava juice, then get up again and head south past the petro-industrial works of Elizabeth (not unbeautiful from up here), swing up the harbor and check the skyline for where the Twin Towers used to be, and then fly right along the pencil strip of Fire Island before I'd bank again, to head home for MacArthur. It's the grand tour of the metropolis I'd give if I ever did such things, or even fly with anyone else, which I rarely do anymore, and I doubt I will again. Indeed it turns out I'm a solo flyer, for a number of reasons I won't get into right now, but just say that it makes sense to me, and did right from the start.

Still, sometimes I wish I could bring Rita up here again, fly with her the way I used to on the clearest days to Maine or Nantucket, where we'd split a big lobster and bucket of steamer clams on the bleached sundeck of some harborside restaurant, browse the handicraft and junktique shops, maybe buy a bag of fudge or saltwater taffy, then fly back on buffets of just this kind of light, not talking much at all on our headsets save a name and then nod to whatever not-quite-wish-fulfilling town we happened to be passing over: *Providence. New Haven. Orient Point.* I'd land us as smooth as I could (touchdown the only part that scared her), then drive us back to the house with the top down in the old emerald Impala, our positions just the same, almost preternaturally so—man and woman in fast-moving conveyance—and we'd shower together and maybe make love and then nap like unweaned pups until the darkness fell, when we'd arise for a few hours to straighten up the house before the workweek began again the next day.

Now, I bring in my ship the usual way, making sure I fly over my house, which I can often spot without much trouble but is forever unmistakable now, ever since right after buying *Donnie* I had a roofing contractor lay in slightly darker-shaded shingles in the form of a wide, squat X. You can only see it clearly from up here, which is good because most of my neighbors would probably report me to the town if it were obvious from the street. I had it done for Rita, in fact, for she always asked me to point out our place from the air, which I did but to no use, as she could never quite find it anyway. I must say the sight still always warms me, not just for the raw-meat feeling that I've marked my spot, but for the idea that anyone flying or ballooning overhead might just wonder who was doing such a thing, this mystery man calling out from deep in the suburban wood.

Which would be somewhat ironic, because increasingly it seems I'm not a mystery to anyone, the very fact of which, as has been made more than clear to me on a number of occasions, is part of my so-called life problem. This from Theresa, mostly, though also from Jack (in Surround Sound silence), and from my once-loving Rita, each of whom holds to a private version of the notion, furious and true. The only one who seems unable to fathom my evidently patent, roughshod ways is my ailing father, who continues to misread my every motive and move, with the resulting accrual of enmity and suspicion steadily drowning out the few remaining vitalities of his mind (yet another mirthless progression to be considered and acted upon, and alarmingly soon). If anything, I'm afraid, he and I are long-steeped in a mystery without poetry, a father-son brew not just particular to us, of course, though ours is special recipe enough, and like the rest warrants further parsing, which I must try, try.

And as I aim my sweet ship in line with the field, I can just barely glimpse the X in the distance, faded enough from these brief seasons that it reads like a watermark on the broad, gently pitched roof of my ranch-style house, and the temptation is to interpret this muted-ness as muteness, my signage ever faint, and disappearing. This is probably true. I am disappearing. But let me reveal a secret. I have been disappearing for years.

two

FOR MOST OF MY LIFE I worked in the family business, Battle Brothers Brick & Mortar, a masonry company that my grandfather started in the Depression and that my father and uncles gradually turned into a landscaping company that I maintained and that Jack has plans for expanding into a publicly traded specialty home improvement enterprise to be renamed Battle Brothers Excalibur, L.L.C. (OTC ticker symbol: BBXS), replete with a glossy annual report and standby telephone operators and an Internet website.

The family name was originally Battaglia, but my father and uncles decided early on to change their name to Battle for the usual reasons immigrants and others like them will do, for the sake of familiarity and ease of use and to herald a new and optimistic beginning, which is anyone's God-given right, whether warranted or not.

Battle, too, is a nice name for a business, because it's simple and memorable, ethnically indistinct, and then squarely patriotic, though in a subtle sort of way. Customers—Jack says *clients*—

have the sense we're fighters, that we have an inner resolve, that we'll soldier through all obstacles to get the job done, and done right (this last line can actually be found in the latest company brochure). My father insists that the idea for the name originated with him, and for just the connotations I've mentioned, which I don't doubt, as he was always the savviest businessman of his brothers, and talked incessantly through my youth about the awesome power of words, from Shakespeare to Hitler, though these days he mostly just brings up his favorite blabbermouths on the Fox News Channel. But it's not just marketing—for the most part the tag has been true, though certainly more so in my father's generation than my own, probably more in mine than in Jack's; but this is world history and I'm not going to rail on about the degradation of standards or the work ethic. My father and uncles did their work in their time, and I did mine, and Jack will do his at this post-turn-of-the-millennium moment, and who can say who will have had the hardest go?

Sometimes I think Jack's is a tough slot, given the never-ending onslaught of instant information and the general wisdom these days that if you don't continually "grow" your business at a certain heady rate it will wither and die. Good for him that for the last four years he has seemed to be practically printing money, what with all the trucks out every day and him needing to hire extra help literally off the street each morning in Farmingville, where the Hispanic men hang out. Now with the economy in the doldrums he probably wishes he hadn't built his mega-mini-mansion but he doesn't seem concerned. In fact, we're all meeting at his new house this weekend, both to celebrate Theresa's recent engagement to her boyfriend Paul (they're flying in from Oregon), and my father's eighty-fifth birthday, which of course he has forgotten about but will enjoy immensely, as he does whenever he is celebrated, which Jack and Eunice will do in high and grand style.

I do sometimes worry about Jack, and wonder if he's grinding too hard for the dollars. Just sit down with him to lunch sometime and you'll see all the digital hardware come unclipped from his belt and onto the table, the pager and cell phone and electronic notepad and memo-to-self recorder. At least my father and uncles had the twin angels of innocence and ignorance to guide them and the devil of hard times to keep working against. I merely inherited what they had already made fairly prosperous, and did what I could not to ruin anything, though Rita often pointed out that I had the least enviable position, given that I really had no choice in the matter, expected as I was to sustain something I never had a genuine interest in. This is mostly true. I had no great love for brick and mortar. When I was still young I was sure I wanted to become a fighter pilot; I sent away for information on the Air Force Academy, did focusing exercises to make sure my vision stayed sharp, tried not to sleep too much (you grew in your sleep, and I was afraid of exceeding the height limit). But when the time came I watched the application date come and go, applying only to regular colleges, my inaction not due to lack of interest or fear but what I would say was my disbelief in the real, or more like it, the real as it had to do with me. I suppose therapist types and self-actualizers would say I have difficulty with *visualization*, how you must see yourself doing and being—say, at the controls in the cockpit, or making love to a beautiful woman, or living in a grand beach house—but even though I can summon the requisite image and can get a little fanciful and dreamy, too, I can't seem to settle on any one picture of myself without feeling a companion negativity whose caption at the bottom reads, *Yeah, right.*

And if it's no surprise to those out there who are thinking that was probably my father's favorite line I would say it certainly was (and still is), not just to me but to everyone in the family and the business, with the exception of my little brother, Bobby, who surely would have benefited from a healthy dose of skepticism had he ever returned from his first and last tour in Vietnam. In all fairness, however, I'm Hank (The Tank) Battle's son, with the main difference between him and me being that I was never able to summon his first-strike arrogance, nor develop the necessary armature for the inevitable fallout from oneself. And while there will be more on this to follow, I will not complain now, and add that choices are a boon only to those who can make good on them. I made a fine living from Battle Brothers, and was able to raise my children in a safe town of decent families and give them every opportunity for self-betterment, in which I believe I succeeded. I always worked hard, if not passionately. I never took what was given to me for granted, or thought anything or anyone was below me. I was not a quitter. In these regards, at least, I have no regrets.

And I had more than my fair share of good times. Through all the work, I still took the time to travel the whole world twice over, going pretty much everywhere, including the North and South Pole (well, almost) and even a few "rogue" states in Africa and the Middle East, and slipped into those countries I wasn't easily allowed to enter, like Cuba and North Korea (if you count that conference table in the DMZ). Of course this was after the kids were in college, and most of the time Rita came along with me, though often enough she didn't have the vacation days left and I went alone. The only typical places I haven't been, oddly enough, are Canada and Mexico, not even their side of Niagara, not even Cancún, but these glaring omissions never bothered me much, and I doubt ever will. I like to think I make up for any intracontinental bigotry by sending planeloads of tourists to popular spots across both borders, as I've worked for a couple years now as a part-time travel agent at the local branch office of a huge travel conglomerate (which I'll call Parade) that runs full-page ads in the Sunday *Times.*

When I sold out my shares in Battle Brothers four years ago I hadn't fully realized that there was no place left for me to go, and decided, on the suggestion of Theresa, citing my extensive résumé as a "passenger," that I ought to try my hand at being a travel professional, which, it turns out, despite her snide deconstructive terminology, was just my calling. For long before I donned my red Parade travel agent's blazer I could speak to most every notable sight in every notable town in this shrinking touristical world, I knew the better ranks of inns and hotels and tour and cruise operators, and I knew which all-inclusives and play-and-stay packages offered good value or were just plain sorry and cheap.

Likewise, I'm not the man to call if you are looking for some cloistered, indigenous roost in a cliffside sweat-lodge-cum-spa or a suite in a designer hotel where the bellboys wear gunmetal suits and headsets and the rooms are decorated in eight shades of white. I am suspicious of the special. I have always believed in staying in vacation trappings that are just slightly nicer than what I have at home, and certainly not any worse, where at least breakfast is included (even if it's just coffee and a gelid danish in the lobby), and the cultural tour, whether by coach or by foot, is led by a cheerleading guy or gal with an old-fashioned and gently ironic sense of humor and a thick local accent and a soulful character suffused with a grand and romantic self-aspiration. I have always preferred wayfaring with such a group, exchanging our white-man *arigatos* and *auf wiedersehens* with jolly inanity while hitting all the trodover sites and famous vistas, for the allure of traveling for me has never been in searching out the little-known *pieve* or backroad *auberge* but standing squint-eyed amidst the sunbaked rubble of some celebrated ruin like Taormina or Machu Picchu in the oblig-

ing company of just-minted acquaintances of strictly limited du-
ration and knowing that wherever I go I'll be able to commune
with fellow strangers over the glories of this world.

During her undergraduate years when she seemed angry about
almost everything I did, and pretty much saw me, she once even
said, as "the last living white man," my smart-as-heck daughter
often felt compelled to expose my many travels for the rapacious,
hegemonic colonialist "projects" that they were. At Thanksgiving
or Christmas she'd idly ask where I'd been lately and I'd mention
some island in the Caribbean or off the coast of Thailand and
she'd start in on how my snorkeling was undoubtedly negatively
impacting the coral reefs, and I'd swear I didn't touch anything
except maybe an already dead starfish (which I brought home and
had framed) and right there would be evidence of my integral
part in the collective strip-mining of an indigenous culture and
ecosystem. I'd answer that the locals seemed perfectly content to
strip it themselves, given the number of shell and sponge and
stuffed-bird shops lining the beachside streets, and then we'd get
into the usual back-and-forth about the false-bottomed tourist
economy (Theresa) and whether tourists should stay home so the
natives could still weave their clothes out of coconut threads (JB)
and the need for *indigenes* to control the mechanisms of capital
and production (TB) and the question of who really cared as long
as everyone was happy with the situation (JB) and the final retort
of who could possibly be happy in this unthinking, unjust world
(guess who)?

To which, when your once-sugar-sweet daughter, who used to
hang on your shoulders and neck like a gibbon monkey, now just
home from her impossibly liberal, impossibly expensive New
Hampshire college, is glaring at you desperately with bloodshot
all-nighter eyes from too much 3 A.M. espresso and clove cigarettes
and badly recited Rimbaud (and other activities too gamy to think

about), you're tempted to say, "I am," even knowing it would quite possibly put her over the edge. But then you don't, and hope you never do, just requesting instead that someone pass down the boiled brussels sprouts, which are as usual utterly miserable with neglect.

All this, it pleases me to report, has come full circle in our steady march toward maturation, as I'm now sitting at my desk at Parade Travel in Huntington comparing package prices for Theresa and her fiancé, the purportedly semi-famous (and only semi-successful) Asian-American writer Paul Pyun. I'm to say "Asian-American," partly because they always do, and not only because my usage of the old standby of "Oriental" offends them on many personal and theoretical levels, but also because I should begin to reenvision myself as a multicultural being, as my long-deceased wife, Daisy, was Asian herself and my children are of mixed blood, even though I have never thought of them that way. I must admit that I don't quite yet appreciate what all the fuss is about, but I've realized that words matter inordinately to Theresa and Paul, and far beyond any point I wish to take a stand on.

They're planning to get married sometime this coming fall or winter, right here on Long Island (Paul's parents, both medical doctors, live down the Expressway in Roslyn), and have asked me to look into a moderately priced one-week honeymoon in a tropical location. I assumed they wanted a -que holiday (*unique, boutique, exotique*), some far-flung stay with plenty of cultural sites and funky local flavor, but in fact Theresa told me herself that they were thinking something "spring breaky," maybe even a cruise. Apparently after endless backpacking forays into Third World sections of First World countries, they now desire the fun and the tacky, perhaps on the order of certain beachfront "huts" I can book them in Ixtapa, where they can roll out of bed and lie in the sand all day and get served strong, sweet drinks and only if they wish exert themselves with a paddleboat or parasail ride. No forced eco-hikes here. Theresa (and Paul, too, for that matter) can get her hair cornrowed and they'll have dinner at a "sumptuous international buffet" and then dance on a floating discotheque where they'll exchange tequila body shots and maybe even catch a wet T-shirt or naked belly-flop contest.

Here at Parade Travel we gladly enable much of this, as people would be surprised to find that it's not just college kids but young thirty-somethings like Theresa and Paul and then much older folks, too, getting into the act, more and more of our holidays geared to reflect what seems to be the wider cultural sentiment of the moment, which is basically that You and Everybody Else Can Kiss My Ass. No doubt you readily see this in play at your own office and while driving on the roads and almost every moment on sports and music television. I have to suppose this is the natural evolution of the general theme of self-permission featured in recent generations (mine foremost), but it's all become a little too hard and mean for me, which makes me wish to decline.

I wish to decline, even if I can't.

Still, I don't want to send my only daughter on such a trip, even if she thinks she wants to go. This is her honeymoon, for heaven's sake, and I won't let her spoil it with some folly of an ironic notion. For all her learning and smarts she has always had the ability from time to time to make the unfortunate life decision, plus the fact that she has much to learn about romance. Paul I don't know so well, but I suspect he can't be much different, or else totally cowed by her on this one. Luckily I've found them a tony plantation-style hotel in Mustique and have called the manager directly to request that he give them the best room whenever we know the exact dates (#8, according to knowledgeable colleagues). They'll get a champagne-and-tropical-fruit-basket welcome, and a special couples' massage, and though I know the antebellum trappings might initially speak to Theresa and Paul of subjugation and exploitation and death, I'm hoping they'll be spoiled and pampered into an amnesic state of bliss that they can hold on to for years (and if lucky, longer than that). This will be my secret wedding present to them, too, as their arts-and-humanities budget is barely a third of the final cost, even with my travel agent discounts.

Kelly Stearns, my coworker here at Parade, with whom I share a double desk, will tell me that I am a sweet and generous father any girl would be darn lucky to have. Each of us works three and a half days a week, overlapping for an hour on Fridays. Kelly is late again, however, as she has been quite often this summer. I'm worried about her, as it's not like her to take her responsibilities lightly.

Kelly is an attractive, big-boned blonde with a pixie, girlish face that makes her seem much younger than her mid-fortyish years, the only thing really giving away her age being her hands, which are strangely old-looking, the skin waxy and thin like my mother's once was. Kelly comes to us from the South, the Carolinas, which I mention only because it's obvious what an unlikelihood she is around the office, with her dug-deep accent and sprightly way of address and her can-do (and will-do) attitude, all reflected in the fact that her clients know exactly her days and hours. After the clock clicks 3, there's always a surge of call volume for "Miss Stearns," which I field as best as I can, though mostly they insist on working with her, even if it's just a simple matter of changing a flight time or booking a car. I suppose I come off like everybody else here on the Island, meaning that I'm useful to a point and then probably a waste of time. I completely understand this. Whenever I call a company or business and realize I've been routed to the Minneapolis or Chattanooga office, I feel a glow of assurance, as if I've been transported back to a calmer, simpler clime, and though I know it's surely all hogwash I can't help but fall in love just a little with the woman's voice on the other end, picturing us in an instant picnicking in the village square and holding hands and greeting passersby like any one of them might soon be a friend.

This is partly why I can talk to Kelly about almost everything, including the sticky subject of Rita, as she in fact has the stuff of kindness and generosity bundled right onto her gene strands, along with the other reason—namely, that she can summon the forgiveness of a freshly ordained priest. I should know, for she's forgiven me for certain transgressions, for which almost any other woman could only summon the blackest bile. You'd think she'd steer clear of me forever. This is not to suggest she's a pushover. I'll just say for now that we were intimate in the period after Rita decided to leave and did but then came back only to leave again, which Kelly always recognized as a difficult time, and she ultimately decided that whatever judgments were due me would be presided over not by her but by some more durable power, whose reckoning would be everlasting.

Another call comes in for Kelly but it's not a client. It's that tough guy again, the one sounding like Robert Mitchum, though even more diffident than that, and certainly charmless, and to whom I'm pretty much done showing patience. His sole name, as far as I know, is Jimbo (how he self-refers). I've had to field his calls the last few times she's been late, and was pleasant enough at first if only because I had the feeling he was her new boyfriend, which I don't think anymore, nor would I care about it if I did. Kelly introduced us once when he came to pick her up, Jimbo not even bothering to shake my hand, just offering a curt nod from behind his mirrored wraparounds. But the more I do think about it, I don't like the idea that Kelly has anything to do with him. There's a streak of the bully in his voice, a low whine that makes me think he's the sort of man who not so secretly fears and dislikes women.

"It's practically three-thirty," he complains. "She should be there."

"She's not."

"Did she call in?"

"No," I tell him. "Look, don't you have her number by now?"

"Hey, buddy, how about minding your own business, okay?"

"That's what I'm doing."

"Well, do yourself a big favor and shut your sassy mouth."

"Or what?"

"You'll know what," Jimbo says, all malice and mayhem.

"Why don't you come down here and show me, then."

He pauses, and I can almost hear his knuckle hair rising. "You're a real dumb fuck, you know that?" he says low and hard, and he hangs up.

I hang up, too, banging the handset back into the cradle. Where this will lead I don't know or care. These days every thick-necked monobrow in the tristate area likes to pretend he's a goodfella, some made guy, but having been in the brick-and-mortar and landscaping business I have plentiful experience with all varieties of blowhard, including the legitimate ones, who for the most part don't even hint at their affiliations.

I notice that the other people in the office have hardly looked away from their screens, except for Miles Quintana, our newest and youngest Parade travel professional, who *ack-acks* me a double machine gun thumbs-up, shouting, "Give 'em hell, Jerome!" He's young (and historically challenged) enough that he thinks I'm a member of the "Greatest Generation." He's seen *Saving Private Ryan* at least two dozen times and can describe every battle-scene amputation and beheading in digital frame-by-frame glory, and despite the fact that I've told him I was only born during that war he continues to see me as the reluctant hero, as if every graying American man has a Purple Heart (and Smith & Wesson .45 automatic) stashed away in a cigar box in his closet. Of course I'm sure he's playfully teasing, too, just slinging office shit with the old gringo, and if this is the way that a guy like me and a nineteen-year-old Dominican kid can get along, then it's fine by me.

Miles is the office's designated Spanish speaker (our office manager, Chuck, proudly taped up the *Se Habla Español* sign in the front window the day Miles joined up), and part of the company's efforts to attract more business from the large and growing Hispanic community in the immediate area. The interesting thing is that Miles, though a perfectly capable travel agent, is actually not so hot at *habla*-ing, at least judging by the conversations he has with clients in the office and on the phone, when he uses at least as many English words and phrases as he does Spanish, if not more. In fact I can confidently say that one need not know any Spanish to understand him when he's in his translation mode, which employs gesture and posture more than speech. Still, he continues to get referrals from the Colombians and Salvadorans and Peruvians and whoever else they are waiting their turn at his desk, proving that it's not always the linguistical intricacies that people find assuring, but broader, deeper forms of communication. This jibes with my own sharpening feeling that I can hardly understand anybody anymore, at least as far as pure language goes, and that among the only real things left to us in this life if we're lucky is a shared condition of bemusement and sorrowful wonder that can maybe turn into something like joy.

My phone rings again and I'm ready to communicate with Jimbo once more, in whatever manner he'd like to take up. But it's Kelly on the line. She's calling from her little maroon econobox, which I notice double-parked across the street. I wave.

"Please don't do that, Jerry," she says, sniffling miserably. I can see her dabbing at her nose with a peony-sized bloom of tissues. She's wearing big sunglasses and a print scarf over her hair, like it's raining, or 1964. "I don't want anyone there to see me."

"Are you all right? You sound terrible."

"I don't have a cold, if that's what you mean."

"Do you want me to come out there?"

"Definitely not, Jerry. I'm looking pretty much a fright right now."

"I'm worried about you, Kel."

"Are you, Jerry?"

"Of course I am." Her tone is alarmingly knowing, even grim. I press on, not because I want an impromptu lecture (which I'm pretty sure I'll get), but because my friend Kelly Stearns does not talk this way, ever. I say, "I don't want to butt in because it's none of my business. But that guy called for you again, and I don't need to ask what you're doing with him to know that it can't be too happy."

"It's not, Jerry. I've told Jimbo that we won't be seeing each other for a while. He hasn't accepted it yet. But that's not the problem."

"So what's the matter?" I say, being as even as I can, given our very brief if not-so-ancient history. "What's wrong?"

"Everything's plain rotten," Kelly answers, enough Scout Finch still leavening her mature woman's voice to make my insides churn with a crush. Her old-fashioned idiom strikes me to the core, too, and I realize once again that I am a person who is taken much more by what people say than by what they do. I tend to overrecognize signifiers, to quote my daughter; I'm easily awestruck by symbol and tone. Apparently this is neither good nor bad. And right now it's easy to gather that this isn't our usual belle Kelly.

She says, "I just want to crawl beneath a rock and die."

"Did something happen?"

"Nothing *happened*," she says. "This is me living my life."

"This is definitely not your life, Kel."

"Oh yes it is," she says. "Of all people, Jerry, I'd hoped you'd not try to give me a line."

"I'm not. You're in a rut, that's all. I've seen you worse, which is still a hundred times better than anyone else on a good day."

"You certainly saw me in one way," she counters, to which I can't really reply. She's double-parked but badly, her back end sticking out too far into the street, right near the yellow line. A minor jam is building in both directions. She says, oblivious to the pepper of horns, "I don't blame you, Jerry. You were gentleman enough. Even though you dumped me no less than three times."

"Not to defend myself, but I'm pretty sure you dumped me the last time."

"You know very well that it was preemptive. My final effort at retaining some dignity. When I still thought I had some."

"You've still got plenty," I tell her, noticing that she's unscrewing the top from an orange prescription bottle. It's a slim, small bottle, definitely not the kind they give you vitamins in. She shakes out some pills and pops them into her mouth, chasing them with a long straw-sip from a massive Big Gulp, her signature drink. Though it's silly to say, the only thing about Kelly that really bothered me was her use of the 7-Eleven and the like as grocery stores, the result being her drive-thru diet of chili dogs and Hot Pockets and Doritos and aspartame-sweetened anything; nothing in the least natural ever entering her body. Really the opposite of Rita, who even made her own corn tortillas. This shouldn't have been the reason Kelly Stearns and I couldn't be together forever, and I never brought it up to her even though I understood so from the beginning, but it was.

"What's that you're taking, Kel?"

"Jimbo gives them to me," she says, shaking the bottle. "Oxy-Contin. They say they're good for pain."

"I'm sure they are. Listen, why don't I come out there right now and sit with you. I'll tell Chuck you called in sick. It's real slow anyway, and I can take you back to my place and you can talk things out. We'll have an early dinner on the patio."

"I'm at my limit, Jerry. My outer limit. I know you don't feel that way because you've got it all together."

"You know that's not true."

"It is from where I'm sitting. You have your whole life accrued to you, and it's only getting better. You're a good-looking man who's going to be sixty but hardly looks a day over fifty. You have all your hair. You have your family nearby and enough money and you have Parade to pass the time with and you have your plane to go up in whenever you want to split. You can have all the girl-friends like me that you'd ever want."

"Kel . . ."

"I'm not criticizing. I'm a fairly nice girl but I'm not so special or unique and more times than not I get passed over. It's the truth and you know it. It turns out the only guy who wants to keep me forever is Jimbo."

"That's a load of bull."

"It's not. He makes love to me. Not very well, but he tries. He's not superbright or interesting or exceptionally kind. But he wants me. He needs me. It's as simple as that. Did you ever wonder about those women who get hitched to guys in jail? Why they would ever do that? Now I know. I'm forty-five years old today and . . ."

"Today?" I checked the desk blotter calendar, but I'd written nothing on it, today or any day.

"Yes, but I'm not giving you shit about that. I'm forty-five years old and never been married and I won't ever have children and I'm the only child of dead parents. I've got no pension fund to speak of. My furniture is rent-to-own. I color my own hair. I haven't done anything really terrible or wrong in my life but look, I've got next to nothing. All you have to worry about is keeping your health and not getting bored. I'm not criticizing. I'm happy for you. You're missing Rita, is all, but she's going to come back to you sometime, I'm sure of it. I talked to her yesterday. She asked how you were."

I'm not thinking much of anything for a moment, my heart clogging my throat. "You spoke to Rita?"

"I told her you were fine, but lonely, which is definitely the truth."

"How is she?" Kelly would know, as she and Rita have been friendly since the end of Kelly/Jerry II, meeting for Happy Hour at Chi-Chi's once a month or so, apparently jabbering about everything but me. I spied on them once, from the corner of the bar, tipping their waitress $20 to eavesdrop, which was not a good use of money, as the only thing she related was how they were joking about penis sizes.

"Same as you, Jerry, only not so lonely. She's still seeing Richard, on and off."

"Yeah." Richard as in Richie Coniglio, *coniglio* in Italian being the word for rabbit. Which he is—short, thin guy, kind who lives forever, fluffy in the hair, with prominent teeth, probably false. I've known him since middle school, when he followed me around the halls, as I was one of the few kids who didn't beat up on him daily. He was always smart, and he's become sort of a bigwig around here, with the charities and such. That's how he met Rita, at a hospital gala, where she was a volunteer hostess. He's divorced, exactly my age, though admittedly looks at least five years younger than me, Kelly's previous comment notwithstanding. He's a partner at a white-shoe New York law firm, collects Ferraris, and lives alone in a mansion in Muttontown. He takes Rita out east on the weekends, to his "cottage" in Southampton. I've actually spotted him out in public wearing jodhpurs, at the Bagel Bin with the Sunday *Times* tucked under his arm, his boots stuccoed with horse dung.

"I bet she's happy with him," I say.

"Don't beat yourself up, Romeo. Richard can be a peach but I think we all know where you and Rita are headed. I can hear it in your voices, and all around you. The tarantella has already started up."

"I wish."

"You better not just wish, Jerry Battle. You had better do. But why I'm bothering to tell you this right now astounds me."

"Because you're the sweetheart of Huntington Village," I tell her, already heartened immeasurably, though realizing that this has somehow become all about Me again, our chronic modality. So I say, "You should have told me it was your birthday. I'm going to hang up now and tell Chuck you called in sick and I'm going to take you out tonight. We'll go to the city. I'll get us a table at Smith & Wollensky. We'll get the double porterhouse."

"Don't you dare!" she shouts, the squawk almost hurting my ear. "Don't you even budge. I don't want to go to the city for dinner and I don't want you coming out here. I only stopped by to tell you I'm going away."

"What do you mean? Where?"

"I really don't know yet," she says, sounding high and tight like she's going to cry. "But I wouldn't tell you if I did. I'm not telling anyone. If you hear from me after today, it'll be from someplace far away."

"I don't like this word 'if,' Kel."

"Tough shit, Jerry!" she says, her emphasis more on my name than the expletive. But she gathers herself. "Listen. I don't want to yell at you. Just tell Chuck I'm taking a leave of absence. If he doesn't like it, tell him I quit. And don't you worry about me. I'm going to be fine. I'm going on a trip all by myself. I'm superhappy about it. Don't worry."

But I'm deeply worried, this spiky scare rappelling down my spine, especially with her mentioning how happy she'll be, the image of her splayed out on a motel bed with a hand mirror snowy with crushed pills, a plastic garbage bag, a straight razor.

"I'm coming out now," I tell her firmly, "whether you want me to or not."

But just as I put down the phone and stand up I see Kelly wave, wave, and not really to me, like she's on the top deck of the *Queen Mary*, embarking on an around-the-world. Her blond hair spilling out of the scarf. (Why there is a glamour in all departures, I don't know.) Before I can even get outside she's speeding away, her dusty little car clattering down the main street of the village, being nearly broadsided as she drifts through a red light. There's another clamor of protesting horns, and then, momentarily veiled by a white puff of oil-burning acceleration, she's gone. I try her cell over and over but all I get is her outgoing message, whose molasses lilt always manages to upend me: "Hi y'all, Kelly here. I ain't home right now. But do say something nice."

WHICH I HAVE tried to do, at the time and then throughout this evening, but all I've been able to muster is to say I am here if she needs me, whatever hour of the night. It's nearing midnight now. All this sounds pretty good, like I'm on call for her, braced by the nightstand, wracked and sleepless. Of course if I were a wholly better person (and not just a former-lover-turned-friend) I'd be out searching the avenues for her, having already called her friends and maybe even Jimbo (number from the office Caller ID), having already gone by her apartment, instead of half dreading the *blee-dee-deet* of my cordless as I sit here on the patio beneath a starless Long Island sky, steadily drawing down an iced bottle of cut-rate pinot grigio. I'm worried about Kelly, of course, not quite admitting that part of me is scared stiff she might try to hurt herself, but here I am taking up space in my usual way, as if waiting for the news to come on, some defining word filtering down from the heavens to let me know what ought to be done next.

This is what Rita found most chronically difficult about me, and what Theresa has begun openly referring to as my "preternatural lazy-heartedness." Jack has to this point professed no corresponding view, which I suspect is because he's finally realized that in this regard the apple hasn't fallen very far from the tree (or off at all), and is perhaps an even more fully realized version of its predecessor. Kelly Stearns, if I may take the liberty to suppose, would probably identify this quality of mine as how I'm most like "a real jerk," which is what she called me after the last time we slept together, not for anything that happened (or didn't) between the sheets (I've always tried to be at least eager and attentive in love's physical labors, understanding I'm no expert), but for the solidly marvelous days leading up to that last passionate if cramped union, when I took her on a fancy Caribbean cruise despite my unswervable intent of breaking up with her once again, and for all.

In her opinion, I should have dumped her before the trip, which by any standard of decency and decorum makes good sense, though in my behalf I should say that I did want to treat her and spoil her one last time, not as reward or consolation but because I genuinely cared for her and wanted to make her plain happy and frankly saw no other way to accomplish it save for going on a carefree junket heading nowhere in our immediate world. Kelly et al. (the entire office, except for Miles, who surprisingly falls to my side of the ledger in most worldly matters) naturally saw my aims as self-serving and usurious in spirit, a sneaky final lust-grab and cruel deception, made even worse by the fact that Kelly and I had reached that certain juncture in our relationship when a romantic luxury cruise might seem an odds-on prelude to proposing a union unto death. Indeed, in anticipation of something special Kelly had brought along some of her more wicked boudoir getups, including a melt-away fruit-roll teddy burnished in edible gold that the Parade gals had slipped in her carry-on, as well as a distinctly matrimonial gown, complete with lace train, just in case I had arranged for the captain of the ship to perform a surprise wedding-at-sea. The first hint of trouble was when I unpacked my garment bag and only had a Permapress travel blazer to hang up, the sight of which momentarily arrested all her functions, as if she'd looked up to see a complete solar eclipse. I asked her what was wrong and she tried to ignore me but then broke into a sweet smile and said brightly, "Whatever could be wrong, my ever casual man?"

Kelly, like all the Southern women I've known (three total—the other two being the identical Cohen twins from Decatur, Georgia, Terri and Traci, who were lifeguards at the Catskills camp where I landscaped several summers of my youth), features an inborn lode of a chin-up, good sport reserve that I can tell you positively jazzes a guy like me, though eventually invites some ill use and taking advantage of, too, if unwitting and unintended. The Cohen twins, I remember, besides being splendid swimmers, were deadly rifle shots and archers, their identical carriage buxomly and erectly Aryan, which the young Jewish-American campers beheld with a hushed adoration and trembling. That last summer I dated Terri (I'm pretty sure), my buddy Lorne seeing her sister, and by the middle of the camp session we'd convinced them that losing their virginity with a couple of Gentiles was probably an ideal way to go, there being no strings or expectations. Ever reasonable, they agreed. So one night we paddled our canoes to the little foot-shaped island in the middle of Lake Kennonah, outfitted with sleeping bags and candles and condoms and a fifth of Southern Comfort. The four of us drank together and then Terri and I hiked to the other side of the island and spread our bedding atop a broad flat rock right by the water. We could still hear Traci and Lorne talking and laughing and then getting very quiet, and without even kissing much we took off our clothes and started making love. I say this not because I loved her or am uncomfortable using cruder terms but because I thought then and still do that no matter who it is you're with or whether it's the first and/or last time, there's always at least one verifiable moment when you can believe you're doing exactly that, literally trying to *make* love, build it up, whether by alchemy or chemistry or force of will. With Terri Cohen it was no difficult task, for she was ardent and mostly unafraid and steadfast beneath me on that absolutely ungiving rock, which made me feel like I was going straight through to the igneous, like we were plunging another axis for the world. (This is but one of many a young man's egoistic virginal follies—sentimental and ridiculous, I know.) Afterward, not unhappy, and both quite sore from the vigorous but clearly unclimactic-able sex, we hiked back in silence to where we'd put ashore. We weren't thinking about Traci and Lorne, or at least I wasn't, and suddenly we came upon them in the candlelight, in mid-engagement, her slender heels tapping out time on his back, and perhaps it was because they were twins that Terri didn't pull us away or try to hide us. We watched as they crescendoed and decrescendoed and crescendoed again, until they finally came (Traci before Lorne, amazingly), when Terri grabbed my hand and hustled us back to our spot on the rock and astraddle of me swiftly finished us both.

Now there's the definition of a good sport.

I'm long accustomed to the umbraged, oversensitive, volcanically eruptive type, firstly my good mother, who could shame a false confession out of Saint Francis and who, during her last moments on her deathbed, scolded us arrayed there to go wash our hands before leaning on her Belgian lace bedspread. When I was young she and my father had horrific arguments over his handling of the business and the periodic dalliances he'd have with his young bookkeepers fresh out of night school, the nastiest of their fights ending with my mother wielding a rusty fish-filleting knife, swearing that she'd gut them both if she ever caught them, and my father (recklessly quoting Sartre and Camus and *Reader's Digest*) taunting her with the then recently announced death of God. Hank Battle has always liked a rousing fight, especially with family, whether fair or not, and if I were constituted more like him I'm certain I'd have ended up with a woman who would burn the bed before letting me tread too long over her.

And so it's never been strange to me that I've gravitated toward women like Kelly Stearns, and then my Rita, who hardly said a word until the end and then coolly informed me, sotto voce, as we were driving home from the multiplex after having watched *Jurassic Park II,* that she had rented back her old studio apartment in Hauppauge and would be gone by the end of the week. I didn't say anything, because it was no great surprise; I didn't protest, because I had no arguments for her, the previous long years providing evidence enough of what we might expect (past performance, in the recent stock-crazed parlance, being in this case a bankable guarantee of future results), and I drove home feeling as if I'd been bitten clean through right at the sternum, my heart pumping fast but pumping nothing, my lower half already marinating in the gullet of a beast named Rue. Rita was by then more sorrowful than angry, though still plenty bitter, as the next morning she gave me back the diamond-and-ruby ring I'd given her to celebrate twenty-one years of living together, but then carefully

packed for removal every last one of the expensive stockpots and
sauté and cake pans I'd bought her over the years (despite the fact
that she never cooked for just herself), understanding before I did
the full measure of how this would pain me.

As I step inside the kitchen, the wall clock (shaped like the nose
of a Sopwith Camel) mumbles "Contact" and fires up, the hands
whizzing around until they stop back at the present hour, midnight. Still no word from Kelly, so I call her again, at her apartment and cell phone, but to no avail. My next move, I think now,
is to call the police, to check if there has been any accident or report involving her, but then the phone in my hand rings and I
know this is she, and something aberrant in me lets it go a few
more bleats before I click it on.

I say, "Kelly . . ."

"Jerry?"

"Kelly, is that you?"

"No, Jerry. It's me. It's Rita."

I can't say anything, because of course I knew it was Rita, almost before she even spoke, which makes no sense at all. And I
have no sense now, the only feeling the clammy empty bottle in
my other hand.

"Listen. I'm at work. I just got on shift and I really can't talk.
Kelly is here. She came in about an hour ago. Actually she sort of
crashed her car by the emergency entrance."

"Is she hurt?"

"Not from that," Rita says, and not casually. "She must have
known she was in trouble and driven here, but couldn't quite make
it. She took a lot of pills."

"Oxy-somethings," I say.

"That's right. How did you know?"

"She told me she was taking them," I say, realizing how not
good this sounds, vis-à-vis me. "She's okay, though, right?"

"She'll be okay," Rita says grimly. "She didn't have enough to kill herself, but she could have really hurt herself. She's in a daze right now. She did ask me to call you. That's why I'm calling."

"I know."

"She said you might be looking for her."

"I was. I am."

There's an unsettling, sneaky long pause, the kind we got used to over the years, and then finally became sick of, though now I don't know that I'd refuse a great deal more of it, if this is all I'll ever have.

Rita says, nurselike, "She'll be okay, but she has to rest. She'll have been transferred to the main ward. You should go by there in the late morning."

"I'll come first thing," I say, knowing the night shift ends at 7 A.M., with a thirty-minute changeover, after which Rita will go back to Richie the Rabbit, snug in his baronial bedchamber.

"Let her sleep," Rita says, her tone riding somewhere between command and wish. "Listen, I've gotta go. Be kind to her."

"I'm always kind."

"Okay, Jerry. Okay. I'm hanging up now. Bye."

"Rita . . ."

But before I can say anything else she's clicked off. I punch *69 but it's the hospital operator, and by the time she connects me to the emergency room nursing station Rita's already unavailable, according to another nurse, as the paramedics are wheeling in a minivan's worth of teenagers from a nasty wreck on the Meadow-brook Parkway.

After this surprise brush with Rita, and then settling in with the increasingly sobering notion that Kelly may have really tried to hurt herself, I can't really sleep at all. I get up every other hour to satisfy my quick-trigger bladder and then poke around in the refrigerator and surf the late-night cable for anything remotely engaging (for me it's an infomercial for a rotisserie cooker, the chicken done to a perfect shade of polished cherry wood) and then sit in my old convertible out on the driveway, squinting in the scant moonlight at the just-getting-old guy in the parking mirrors. Not to worry, as this won't be that moment for a midstream self-appraisal heavy on deprecation and knowing charm, or a dark night of the soul's junket through the murk of a checkered, much remorsed-upon past. I won't suffer anyone bizarre fantasies or nightmares, as often happens in movies and books, because I'm not really capable of that sort of thing, being neither so weird nor smart enough. I'll simply relay what I can see, which is a man sitting alone at night in an open-air car, hands restless on the wheel, humming silently to himself, waiting for the sun to rise up so he can just get moving again.

Come morning, I'm already here, in the parking garage of the mid-county hospital. It's amazing how many cars are around at this hour, like it's the long-term lot at La Guardia during Thanksgiving week. You'd think that people (despite what they profess) in fact love hospitals, as they do everything they can (smoking, drug-taking, road-raging) to hurry themselves inside. Sometimes I used to pick Rita up from her shift (then the day shift) and they'd be practically lined up in the emergency waiting room in all manner of wreck and ruin, accidently poisoned, nearly drowned, stabbed and shot and burned, so that it seemed we were living nearer to Beirut than to Babylon, Long Island.

It's only just 7 A.M. and I'm determining exactly how I'm going to go about talking to Rita, or more to the point, have her talk to me. I've already visited Kelly Stearns in the adult ward, having told the nurses that I was her half-brother and had driven all night from Roanoke when I heard the news, leaving a couple of carnation-heavy bouquets of supermarket flowers (nothing else was open) and a surprisingly long and wholly loving note on her dresser, generally saying that I was sorry if I let her down and that I would never do so again. I was glad to leave the note, especially as she was asleep, and, strange to see but understandably, strapped down in restraints, and my one alarming thought was that she was going to wake up like that and might very well flip the hell out. So when the nurse left us alone I unfastened one of Kelly's hands, so that she could move a little bit, at least scratch an itch somewhere, if she needed to.

Concerning Rita, I know she'll exit the hospital from the ER entrance and come this way, past where I'm just idling, as her banana-yellow 1982 Mustang with the black racing stripes and fake chrome wheels is parked behind me, against the far wall. She bought the car used, already in a dinged-up, rusty condition, and oddly enough it looks no worse than it ever was. She liked to say it was her PR Mobile (as in Puerto Rican), which I'm surprised Richie Coniglio allows her to drive into his estate area in Mutton-town. Maybe he likes it, or maybe he has no choice. When she began living at the house with me I offered to buy her a new car, really anything she wanted, my heart breaking open with an un-characteristic (back then) generosity, with only the smallest cell of me doing it for unsavory reasons. I never gave a damn what the neighbors thought, never really knowing them anyway, but I must admit, during those first few months of domiciling, to a certain twinge in my gut whenever she'd jounce up the driveway. These past six months I have been waiting for Rita to return just like that, with me staring out the kitchen window in the afternoons, waiting for her to step out in her white shoes and pad up the walk. For her to use her key.

I first met Rita almost twenty-five years ago, on a boat. It was one of those Friday sunset booze cruises they used to run out for two-hour sprees in the Sound in the summertime. A few years back (actually, probably more like fifteen or twenty) a Commack woman fell overboard and presumably drowned (the body was never retrieved), and the company promptly got sued and had to close down operations. I went only twice, meeting Rita the second time. They crammed about sixty or so of us single people onto an oversized cabin cruiser, charging $20 a head ($10 for women) for a cash bar, baked brie and crudités, and a DJ spinning funk and disco and some oldies (this is 1977, when oldies seemed more like oldies than they do today, maybe because they were played on records, and literally *sounded* old). I was working a lot then, this after Daisy died, with mostly my mother looking after the kids and then some neighborhood women pitching in when they could, and finally a string of nannies who never quite worked out.

One night I ran into an old high school classmate, Rick Steinitz, at the then brand-new cineplex on Route 110, both of us just coming out of *Close Encounters of the Third Kind*. Rick called out my name and somehow I knew who he was and though he was with a date (leggy, pretty brunette) he seemed to want to linger and chat, perhaps more so for it. He was a podiatrist, with an office in Huntington. We hadn't been friends in high school and in fact hardly knew each other. As I recalled we were both shy loners, neither popular nor reviled, though Rick would heartily disagree about my memory of him. The final truth here is unimportant. It's enough to say that ours was one of those midlife friendships between men that happen not because of a shared interest like liquor or golf or even the pleasure of each other's company but from a mutual, pointed need for a fresh association. Rick was just divorcing for the second time, clearly in a rut, and when he heard I'd been widowed for over a year and was still unattached he seemed inspired, as though I'd presented him with a particularly challenging case. When his date excused herself to go to the ladies' room, he insisted I go with him on this booze cruise that launched out of Northport.

Rick was something of a regular on the boat, part of a core group of guys and gals who hadn't yet found their match and for the most part tried each other out but ultimately weren't interested, which was okay by them. They got bombed in the first half hour and always started the dancing, and the rest of the boat seemed appreciative of their shake and roar, which in another venue would have certainly been boorish, embarrassing behavior but was just about the right speed here. Belowdecks there were a couple of spartan staterooms, which Rick had informed me could be "toured" for a twenty-spot gratuity to the captain's assistant, Rem or Kem, a beanstalky Eurotrash dude with a bleached ponytail who wore mauve silk blazers and snuck peeks at Kerouac paperbacks in the quieter moments of the trip. But I think stateroom visits were pretty rare, as most people preferred public displays that seemed risqué and full of possibilities but in fact were fairly chaste and thus ceremonial. For example, the night I met Rita, Dr. Rick had set up shop on the foredeck and was "reading" the soles of women's feet, offering extra rub therapy to anyone who wanted it, which was nearly all of them.

Rita wasn't one of the women who lined up for a foot consultation, nor was she a reveler or a party girl. To be perfectly honest she initially stood out to me and probably everyone else because she was the only one who wasn't white. It's no big news that in most places people tend to congregate with their own, or at least who they think is their own, and in this middle of the middle part of Long Island we're no different, nearly all of us on that boat descended from the clamoring waves of Irish and Italians and Poles and whoever else washed ashore a hundred or so years ago, but you're never quite conscious of such until somebody shows up and through no intention of her own throws a filter over the scene, altering the familiar effects. When she and her girlfriend walked up the gangplank I heard some idiot behind me mutter, "Hey, somebody invited their maid," but no one else minded save one older lady who made a face. He was focused on Rita. Anyone could see she was pretty much a knockout, Puerto Rican or not. She was wearing a crisply tailored cream-colored blazer and matching skirt cut well above the knee, her legs just full and rounded enough that you thought if you were her husband or boyfriend you'd always grip them firmly, with a purposeful appreciation. I was the first person to talk to Rita, not for any honorable reason except that I was standing next to her when the boat cast off, and we bon-voyaged the landlubbers on the dock, as seafaring people will. Later on, the guy who made the remark was standing right behind me at the bar in his white polyester suit, and when I got the order of strawberry daiquiris for me and Rita and her friend Susie I turned and fell into him, square and true, leaving a wide pinkish Rorschach of what looked just like a woman's mouth, and though I bought his drinks and gave him extra for dry cleaning I have to say the rest of his evening was a certified flop.

When I returned, Rita noticed a couple of drops of red on my shirt collar and thoughtfully blotted them with a wet wipe from her handbag, leaning quite close to me, which I liked immediately and Rick winked at but which I had to step back from—figuratively, at least. For just as suddenly I was aware of how I myself was viewing us, and especially viewing her, this lovely darker-skinned woman attending to some average white dude she'd just met, which should be, of course, a completely silly, waste-of-time consideration but one that I was spooling about nonetheless, even as I was trying to breathe in every last molecule of her perfumed, green appley-smelling hair.

Rick then suggested we dance and the four of us pretty much took over the small square of hardwood they'd laid down on the fat part of the boat, Rick and Susie getting kind of wild with the synchronized pelvic movements, Rita and I more grooving than moving, early '70s style. Rick brought Susie over and started a kick line with us, boy-girl-boy-girl, arms and shoulders linked, something that can be genuinely fun for about ten seconds. But then I felt Rick's hand start to grab at my neck, and then claw, and I looked over at him and his face was the color of concrete. Susie screamed and let go of us. I caught Rick before he collapsed and Rita went right into trauma mode, ordering Susie to tell the captain to turn around for port. He was having a heart attack. Rick's eyes were open but they didn't seem to be focusing on anything. Then they brightened. He said, "I'm okay, I'm okay," as if he truly meant it, and I swear I was sure he would be, because that's what we all wanted. But his eyes went dumb again and he didn't say anything after that.

Rita attempted CPR continuously, though by the time we got back to the dock twenty minutes later he was pretty much gone. I can say she was downright heroic, and then immeasurably composed throughout the ordeal, and simply held his hand at the end. The EMS crew that was waiting took Rick away, and the three of us followed the ambulance to the hospital. After a short time in the trauma room the ER doctor came out and told us he had died. Susie began crying, mostly because of the trauma of it, for she hadn't met him before. I was the only one who really knew him, but when the nurse asked me whom they could call (his ex-wife or siblings or parents), I had no idea who they were or where they lived. This was the truly sorry part. They basically had to treat him like any other DOA who was wheeled in alone, needing the police to look up his records and locate next of kin.

Rita's friend Susie was getting more and more upset, and so Rita told her that she should go home, and that she would stay with me until someone from Rick's family showed up. She lived close by and could easily take a taxi. I told her I was fine and that she'd done enough but she insisted, and I agreed only if I could at least give her a lift home. Rick's sister and most recent ex-wife showed up and promptly nose-dived as anyone would, and when they righted themselves a little, Rita and I took our leave as gracefully as we could, hugging the aggrieved and leaving our phone numbers and generally feeling shell-shocked ourselves. I drove her to her apartment and before she got out of the car she must have seen something wrong in my face because she asked if she could make me a cup of coffee.

We went inside her tiny but very tidy apartment and talked for an hour or so. She was just starting as a nurse's aide, going to nursing school at night, and sometimes doing child care for extra money. When I told her I had been having trouble finding the right person to watch my kids after they came home from school, we both sort of lit up and I swear I had no visions of romance when I asked if she might want to give us a try. It was only after a couple of weeks that I began to think about leaving early from work and then get this I-dropped-my-ice-cream feeling when it was time for her to go. Why shouldn't I have? When I'd get home she'd already be feeding the kids some delicious meal and for once since Daisy died they'd be eating all of it, and though it wasn't part of her duties she'd make plenty of extra and then pop open a bottle of beer and I'd take it to the shower with me and when I came back out dig in like Crusoe to the *carne* and dirty rice or whatever else she'd made (the gourmet cuisine she developed later). After she'd clean up the kitchen we'd all sit around and watch a sitcom or two until bedtime for the kids. Those were good times, as good as the few Daisy and I had when she was alive, and maybe even better, full as they were with a quiet pleasure that wouldn't be sullied by sudden implosions of crying or madness.

These days, I'm feeling shorn clean by time and event and circumstance, so much so that I'm not even so hungry anymore. But now here's Rita, in her white shoes, walking out of the ER doors.

Her dark hair is straighter than before, a little shorter, devolumized of its natural kink. I have to believe this must be Counselor Coniglio's high-class influence, which I don't think in the least right, but none of it matters because she's a beautiful woman who's reached an age when her loveliness begins to haunt, in addition to the usual provoke and inspire.

Before I can wave she sees me. Halts for a beat. Finally comes forward, but not too close, staying near the front fender.

"I don't need a ride, you know."

"I know."

"Have you visited Kelly yet?" she says.

"She was asleep. I left her flowers. I'll come back later today."

"And where are you going now?"

"I was hoping to follow you somewhere. Maybe I can take you to breakfast?"

"I'm not eating breakfast anymore. Or lunch."

"What do you mean?"

"I'm on Slim-Fast."

"That shake stuff? You're kidding. You don't need to do that."

"I do. And don't be patronizing. You don't know, Jerry, what happens to a woman. How we age. You take everything for granted."

"You look great to me. Fantastic, even. Honest."

Rita just stares at me, I know rolling about that last word in her head. I am honest, certainly, and always am with her, but it's the doing more than professing that counts for the most, particularly in matters of love, especially when you've been long found out.

"I can sit with you, if you like. Just don't give me crap about my diet."

"I won't. Hop in."

"I'll follow you," she says, jangling her keys at me. "And don't try to take me anywhere near the house."

At a diner on Jericho Turnpike we take a window booth looking out onto the boulevard. It's backed up with the morning rush, as far as we can see, something that neither of us has ever had to deal with much, if at all, the sight of which makes our little square of space seem cozy and calm. Rita, looking better than great to me, her skin a summertime cocoa, orders just ice water and an extra glass. Out of sympathy I get a half grapefruit and toast and coffee, instead of my usual Mexican omelet. She takes a can of vanilla-flavored diet drink out of her bag and pours it, and it reminds me of those supplement formulas they give my father at the assisted living home, which he rails against but drinks anyway, mostly so he can complain how no one will ever again make the dishes for him that my mother did. Rita, as mentioned, is a gourmet cook, and it actually pleases me to think that she's having a shake for breakfast and for lunch and then a sensible (read boring) dinner with Richie, and not preparing him the scallop terrines and pepper-pork tenderloins and honey-glazed short ribs that made our years so thoroughly fine.

Or maybe she does, cooking just for him, serving it on fine china, in a sexy petite-sized uniform, nothing on underneath.

"Kelly told me you're still seeing Richie," I say, deciding that I probably don't have a lot of time (given our orders), or future chances. "How's it going?"

"I'm not sure it's any of your business. Especially since you know him."

"Only from a long time ago. Doesn't he ask about you and me? About all our history?"

"Actually he never has."

"Conceited little bastard. Even when he was a loudmouth runt who had nothing to be conceited about. That's why everyone picked on him. I was the only one who was nice to him, you know."

Rita doesn't defend him, or say anything else about it. She says, "How are the kids?"

"They're doing great," I say, for a second entertaining the fantasy that she is talking about ours, once little ones in jumpers with snot on their faces. "Theresa is engaged. To a writer. You never met Paul, did you?"

"Just once, briefly."

"You'll be there for the wedding, whenever it happens."

"I'm not sure yet."

"It would break Theresa's heart if you didn't show. You can bring Richie along, I don't mind. But I think you really can't miss it."

"I wouldn't bring Richie," she says, taking a sip from her drink. "What about Jack? How's his new house?"

"They've got space like you can't believe. It's about five times bigger than our place . . . I mean my place. They have refrigerated drawers in the kitchen, and a water tap right over the stove, for the pasta water. This is perfect for Eunice. She can only boil macaroni."

"She doesn't have time to cook. She's too busy with her decorating business."

"You mean too busy buying furniture and rugs. They're starting to buy art, and I don't mean poster reproductions. They went into the city last week for an auction at *Christie's*. I've got a feeling they brought back something grand."

"Sounds like Battle Brothers is doing well."

"Jack's expanding it like crazy. I never knew he could be such a mogul. He was always the shyest kid."

"He's like your father," Rita says. "Secret Mussolini."

"Oh God."

"Jack's not as confident as Hank. But he's a lot sweeter."

I say, "He cares too much what people think."

"Your opinion especially."

This is probably true, though I've never acknowledged it, for fear of making it forever stick. (Theresa has the opposite problem, by the way, which I have never minded, though often enough she can be a pain in the neck.) One thing I've learned as a parent is never to call a spade a spade when it comes to your offsprings' failings and defects, no matter their age. And now I remember, too, how well Rita knows my children, as she shepherded them through their adolescence when everything fell apart after Daisy died, and I was mostly absent to them and to much all else, save the business of shrubs and mulch.

"They love you, you know," I say, despite how completely low and unfair it is to bring up the kids like this. "They'll love you to death."

Rita of course instantly sees through all my stratagems but what I've said is undeniably true, and she can do little else but avert her gaze down into her foamy parfait glass and try not to relent. If I had the guts I'd follow with the coup de grace of how I feel about her, utter the words, or at least recite a few verses from the poet, to wonder if she might accept "The desire of the moth for the star/Of the night for the morrow, / The devotion to something afar/From the sphere of our sorrow"?

But Rita doesn't wait for me, the great never-poet, to even try, and takes one last sip of her breakfast. She wipes her mouth and loops a hand through her bag handles, leaving a dollar for the tip.

"I'm leaving," she says, rising. "Goodbye."

"Wait a second."

"No."

"I haven't even finished my breakfast yet."

"You eat fast. You'll be done before I'm in my car."

"Can't you humor me just a little?"

Rita sits back down, eyes afire, and says in a whisper, "You have a lot of fucking nerve."

"I do?"

"Yes, you do," she says, leaning forward. "Because you don't even care how obvious it is, what you're doing. You have no clue what you're saying or what it might mean."

"That Jack and Theresa think the world of you? I don't have to hide what that means. It means you can't just up and leave their lives. You're almost their stepmother."

"Oh please," she says, gathering up her things again. "Do you know how silly that sounds? *Almost stepmother?* Anyway, they're not concerned. They know they'll see me again plenty. It's you, Jerry, like always. You're the one never budging from the center of the show. You're forever the star."

"If that's the guy who's got to do all the worrying, then so be it."

"Right," she says, with an unappreciative smirk. "Why don't you just say what you want to say. I know it's not that you're so worried about Kelly."

"Hey, you said yourself she'll be fine. At least she's in good hands," I say, though now I'm regretting how I unpadlocked her. "It's you I'm not so sure about."

"Me? You've got to be kidding."

"How can that guy be right for you? How do you stand him? He has no idea how ridiculous he looks. Sir Richard of Chukkah. Does he imagine that they'll let his dago ass into Piping Rock or Creek Club?"

Rita says, "He's a member of both, actually. Not that I find that impressive. So what else?"

"Okay, then. What's he do all by himself over there at Tara? And why did his wife leave him? I bet he screwed around on her, for years. And then worked some legal hoodoo to boot her and the kids out."

"She cheated on him, and ran off and married the guy. She didn't want the place. And his kids and grandkids stay with him for most of the summers. And for what he does around the house, he likes to garden and read. He practices tai chi. He's also a very good Asian cook, Thai and Japanese."

"I always took you to Benihana's."

"Yes, you did."

So I say, full of it, "He sounds like the ideal man."

"He certainly isn't!" Rita says, like she's tired of the idea. "But at least he's interested in things. He's still curious. He never complains about being bored. He's always searching, but not in a stupid or desperate way."

"Sounds sort of pathetic to me."

"That's not a surprise."

"So why don't you marry him, then?"

"I'm thinking about it," she answers, with a little oomph.

"He's asked you?"

Rita nods. "The other night."

"Christ. You've barely been seeing him six months."

"We're not young people."

"He give you a ring?"

She pauses, then takes a jewelry box from her bag, cracks it open. Voilà. It's huge, a rock and a half, the size of something that you get from a gumball machine tucked inside a plastic bubble. It's frankly amazing, its sheer objecthood, this token-become-totem. Having nothing to counter with, I feel ushered aside already, obsolete, biologically diminished just in the way I'm supposed to be by another man's splendid offering.

"Of course Richard wants me to take my time, really think it through."

What I'm thinking is, Richard is a dope.

I say, "Only fair and right."

Rita says, "But I don't want to linger with this. No way. I'm not going to do that."

"Listen," I tell her, bearing down now, "you're not someone who makes quick decisions. It's not in your nature. You shouldn't do so, especially now. It's no good."

"You think I should do what I did for the last twenty-one years? You think that was good for me?"

This is the part where I usually answered that our legal union wouldn't have made things better than they were, and where Rita would say that she'd have something now, after all she put into our relationship and my family, and where I'd point out that it was her unilateral decision to leave, to which she'd respond that of course it wasn't about money or property but respect, meaning my respect for her and for myself. This is the part that is hardest to speak about, because all along I'd thought I was treating her like a queen. Maybe I didn't shop at Tiffany or Harry Winston, but I always bought her very nice jewelry from Fortunoff's, and we took plenty of trips to sexy all-inclusive resorts, and I never expected her to keep working as a nurse, if she wanted instead to just stay home and garden and cook and read (all the things she's clearly doing with Richie). The aforementioned seems, at least from my view, to be as good as it gets with a guy like me, or maybe with anyone who isn't an emotionally available millionaire or professional masseur (the two life profiles of men women desire most, according to a magazine at my doctor's office). But I guess I'm dead wrong again because the sum reality of my efforts is that I'm sitting here trying desperately to say something she'll believe, or that at least will gain me a temporary stay.

"You can't marry Richie" is what I muster. "You just can't. Can't."

Rita waits for the reason, the angle or argument, though soon enough she realizes there is none coming, just this obtuse plea from her just freshly aging former lover, who is limply waving a serrated grapefruit spoon. *Can't.* She wants to scold me, throttle me, certainly say hell all and scram, but she doesn't yet move, God bless her, she doesn't bolt.

"You make me so tired," she says, slumping back a little. "You should leave me alone."

"I was trying."

"You have to try harder. Otherwise, I can't see you. I won't." Her meaning: *Ever.*

"Don't marry Richie," I say, though sounding funny to myself, like I'm a lamentable young man in an old summer-love movie, flesh-and-blood wreckage. "Marry me."

Rita giggles, then laughs, out loud, with enough hilarity that the jelly roll gang hunched at the lunch counter turn around half smiling, to see what the joke is all about.

"I'm serious, Rita. Marry me."

Rita stops laughing. She glares, then picks up her handbag and walks out. I head outside after her, calling her, but she ignores me and quickly gets into her car, which she never locks. The windows are never rolled up either, and I stand right over her as she tries to get the old motor going, *karumph, karumph,* and if you didn't know any better you'd think I was a rapist or stalker or three-eyed space lizard, the way she's cranking that thing. I can tell she's flooding the engine, but I say nothing. Our waitress has followed me out, waving the check, but I'm not paying attention because this is a not-yet-depleted moment in what seems to be my increasingly depleted life, and I'm telling Rita to stop trying to leave as the waitress keeps saying, "Hey, buster," and tapping my arm, and finally Rita steps out of the car and whacks me hard on the chest, not quite open-handed.

"She's talking to you, Jerry! Listen!" Rita digs a ten-spot from her bag and gives it to the waitress, who shoots me a kick-in-the-shins smirk if there ever was one. Rita shouts, "What's the matter with you?"

"I'm serious," I say, feeling the stamp of her hand bloom hot on my skin. "I really am."

"Doesn't matter," she answers, now getting back in the driver's seat. She tries to roll up the window, but it only goes three-quarters of the way. "You think our not getting married is still the issue, don't you?"

"It's not not, is it?" I say, the idiot in me inappropriately focused on the unexpected palindrome. This is an excellent way to get into trouble. Though I rally. "I realize that it's not the whole problem."

"And what, in your mind, is that?"

"*C'est moi,*" I say, though maybe a bit too eagerly. "It's me. It's all about me."

Of course this is accurate enough, though rather than illuminate or chart a new course, this mostly deflates the moment, which seems to be a growing skill of mine.

Rita says, as if she's been holding her breath forever, "Fine, then."

"Can you come out of there now?"

Rita shakes her head. She looks down into her lap, slips her sunglasses on, and starts turning the engine over again, now going *badank ba-dank.* I'm sure it will soon quit entirely, but then somehow the damn thing rumbles to life, all muscle and smoke, spirit ghost of Dearborn. She clicks the car into reverse and tells me to watch my feet.

"Don't do anything yet," I say, "at least not until after the weekend. Theresa's flying in, and we're having a get-together at Jack's. Why don't you come? Everyone would love to see you."

"I'm sorry, Jerry."

"I'll pick you up on Saturday afternoon."

"Please don't," she says, backing it out.

"I'll call you!"

She mouths a big *No* and gives a tiny wave, like she's peering out the window from two thousand feet. Then she squeals rubber to accelerate out onto the jet flows of the Jericho Turnpike, and is gone.

three

THE HOUSE THAT Jack built is in a gated development called Haymarket Estates, a brand-new luxury "enclave" that sits on what was a patch of scrubby land a few exits east of where I live. From the Expressway you can actually catch a glimpse of the rooftops peeking out over the barrier wall, the covenant-defined cedar shake or slate tile shingles trimmed out with polished copper ice dams and gutters, the stone-faced chimneys and hand-crafted lintel work fresh and gleaming, with the sole unglamorous detail being all the mini–satellite dishes looking up toward the southern sky with a strange kind of succor. When Jack bought the dusty .47-acre lot a few years ago for what seemed an inexcusable amount of money, he assured me that it'd be worth at least twice as much now, which has proven true despite the flagging economy, given what the last remaining parcels sold for in recent months. The heady rise in land values prompted him and Eunice to go ahead with plans for a much bigger house than they had originally wanted, not minding that the structure would take up most of their property, rendering it useless for any large-scale kids' play or a decent-sized pool. The proportion is really the opposite of my place, where my modest ranch house sits right smack in the middle of the property (just over an acre), so that I have plenty of trees and shrubs and lawn to buffer me from my good neighbors.

The side of Jack's house, on the other hand, is only about ten of my paces from the side wall of his neighbor's, which would be normal-looking in an old suburban neighborhood of row-type houses but feels as narrow as an olde London alleyway given the immensity of the houses. But as Jack has pointed out, who wants to be outside where it's buggy and noisy with the Expressway and in the summertime the rumble of the AC compressors (four for his house alone). Jack's house is around 6500 square feet, not including the full-length basement or three-car garage, which is pretty typical of the development, or more than three times bigger than the house he grew up in. Eunice decorated the place herself, which continues to be a full-time job. You walk in to a vaulted two-and-a-half-story circular entryway with green marble floors inlaid with a multicolored sunburst, a double-landed soapstone stairwell rising up to the second floor. On the main level there's a media room with a widescreen television and every kind of audio component, including ones that seem not to do anything but monitor the sound, for frequency response and digital dropouts and some such. There's a separate rolling caddy for the army of remotes, which Jack has actually just replaced with a console-sized touch-screen unit that supposedly controls everything in the house, including the lights and HVAC and security system. There's of course the French country manor living room that no one ever uses and then the "library," which is in fact pretty gorgeous, lined as it is with panels of glass-smooth walnut and custom cabinetry and furnished with leather club chairs and sofas and antique Persian rugs. Jack even installed a special ventilation system in there, so he can smoke cigars with his golf buddies when they come back to play poker. The funny thing is that the bookshelves are mostly taken up by rows and rows of home and design magazines that Eunice gets each month, and then the big coffee-table art and design books, though Eunice says that they'll be getting some "shipments" of real books soon enough, as she's joined several book-of-the-month clubs, where you get twelve tomes for a penny. And there's a television, too, as there is in every room, though this one is regular-sized and discreetly tucked behind cabinet doors, maybe in deference to the dying world of letters.

The stainless-steel-and-granite kitchen is enormous, certainly, as it has to house two of everything, from refrigerators to dishwashers to trash compactors. Eunice and Jack like to entertain, as they are doing today, but on a wedding caterer's scale, which you can tell by the size of their baking sheets and stockpots, the latter being the kind you see in cartoons in which the natives are making soup of the hapless explorer. Off the kitchen is the plain two-room suite where the nanny/cook/housekeeper, Rosario, stays six nights a week, only leaving on Sunday morning to spend a day and night with her husband and two children and mother, who live somewhere deep in Queens. Eunice, in the parlance, doesn't work "outside the house," but as far as I can tell Rosario is doing all the heavy lifting inside, plus the light duty, too. I don't blame Eunice, as it's her prerogative and privilege to spend her days poring over her decorating books and taking yoga and not toasting a slice of bread unless it's a full-blown event (when she transforms into Lady Sub-Zero, her tools and prep lists and chopped and measured ingredients c/o Rosario laid out on her island counter in military formation), but I wish sometimes she'd spend more casual, horsing-around time with the kids, just lollygagging, rather than scheduling the endless "enrichment" exercises and activities for them that are undoubtedly brain-expanding but must be as fun as memorizing pi to twenty-five places. At bedtime she or Jack will read them only library-recommended books and then retreat to their 1500-square-foot master bedroom suite featuring his and her tumbled-stone bathrooms fitted with steam shower/sauna and then the *lounge-in* closets that could make perfectly nice studio condos in Manhattan, Jack checking the company website and e-mail and Eunice surfing the six hundred channels for a movie she hasn't seen yet. (Once, in the downstairs media room, I browsed all the channels one by one, pausing long enough to get a good glimpse of each, and it took about thirty minutes to get back to where I started, which I realized was like watching a TV show in itself, and not in fact a half-bad one, relatively speaking.)

And as I drive past the gate (where the surly goateed guard still calls up the house to check if they're expecting me, this after about thirty visits), and turn onto the single long circular street of the development past the other not-so-mini mansions, I have to tell myself again that my son is doing more than all right, that I should be so lucky to have to worry that these bulwarks of his prosperity (not just the house but his German sedan, the luxury SUVs, the country club membership, the seasonal five-star vacations) are maybe too much for anyone to handle, and especially Jack, who's always been a bit impressionable and unsure of himself and sometimes too eager to please. Why he's like this I don't like to muse upon too much, as it more than likely has to do with what happened to Daisy when he was nine, though maybe this is not the whole story; Theresa (only a year younger) went through the same shitstorm of unhappiness and is totally different. Though again this may be her particular psychic response to misery and sadness, which made her become more like herself than she would have been had she been raised under neutrally pleasant laboratory conditions.

I suppose the Grandeur of Life does this to all of us, forging us into figures more like ourselves than we'd otherwise be, for better and/or worse, and so you wonder what ramifications in substance and detail there'd be, say, what kind of house Jack would be living in, had his mother never died, whether he would have married an altogether together woman like Eunice, whether he would have taken up the business of Battle Brothers at all. Naturally I think too of what might have become of me in that time line with Daisy still alive, if I'd be with her still, or else have gotten divorced and married Rita forthwith and had children with her. With the exception of the first six months and a few assorted days early on (the birth of the kids, a couple of anniversaries, that one Thanksgiving when Daisy practically carbonized the bird and we ended up in the city at Tavern on the Green, jaunting afterward down Fifty-ninth Street giddy with the Christmas lights and a bottle of Chablis, the kids riding high on our shoulders), there was rarely if ever joyousness or glee, with Daisy scuttled and sunk down in the troughs of her gray day moods. Probably I dug everything a bit deeper with my attitude, which back then was one of constant irritation and stress, as the economy was in the dumper and my father hadn't yet fully retired from Battle Brothers and the kids seemed only to speak the language of lament and whine, being generally neglected and cast aside, and then that episode of the $7000 Bloomingdale's charge. Still, I was a jerk, seriously unhappy as jerks often are, though this is no excuse for anything, and certainly not for what would become my chronic habit of abstaining from the familial activities of the house, in the evenings sitting alone in my study poring over the travel guides to places I wanted to go, highlighting the sights and restaurants like I was already on the tour charter, the little bottles of wine lined up on my tray.

Jack would sometimes come in and tell me Daisy wasn't in the house, and after a few times I'd stop asking where she'd gone to and just put him back to bed. Daisy would then come home at two or three in the morning wearing a fuck-me outfit smelling of cigarettes and Lancer's wine, and if we argued at all it was about her making too much noise when she came in. Jack would run out of his room crying for us to stop yelling, sometimes getting upset enough that he'd pee in his pants. It thus makes sense to me that Jack would end up being the one to feature this grand house (Theresa perfectly content with whatever post-doc-style housing she and Paul can flop in each academic autumn with their fold-up Ikea furniture), and then always gathering us for dinners and parties and taking "candid" black-and-white pictures, as if he and Eunice were trying to recast our family into one that might appear in a fashion magazine spread titled something like "The Spoils of Battle."

We'd probably be just right, too, for such a shoot, not only because we have a nice generational mix going (white-haired patriarch, sportive young parents, peach-cheeked toddlers) but also because we're an ethnically jumbled bunch, a grab bag miscegenation of Korean (Daisy) and Italian (us Battles) and English-German (Eunice) expressing itself in my and Jack's offspring with particularly handsome and even stunning results. As a group you can't really tell what the hell we are, though more and more these days the very question is apparently dubious, if not downright crass, at least to folks like Theresa and Paul, whose race-consciousness is clearly quite different from mine. I suppose what's critical to them is who's asking the question, for if it's an average white guy like me there's only awkwardness and embarrassment ahead, the assumption being I'm going to blindly buy into a whole raft of historical "typologies" and "antecedents" and turn around and plonk somebody with the label of Other. This, by the way, is and isn't a terrible thing. They inordinately fear and respect the power of the word, having steadily drawn down the distinctions between Life and Text. Let me say that when I was growing up the issues could be a lot heavier than that, a switchblade or Louisville Slugger being the *text* of choice, and one not so easily parsed or critiqued.

Jack, on the other hand, seems totally unconcerned about such matters, and always has been, but I can't say for certain, because we've never discussed the subject. He's never been what anybody would call a brainy kid, and not just in the test-taking academic sense (which was how smarts used to be measured), but I suppose none of that mattered much because he's done more than fine and seems happy enough and doesn't seem to wrestle with questions too big or medium or small. Maybe he has strong feelings and painful memories of awkward and searing experiences as to his identity and character but it's just as likely not. I've often thought it's because he's very fair and Anglo-looking, tall and long-legged and with barely a lilt to the angle of his eyes. Such as it is, I believe he's always *passed*, any lingering questions quickly squashed by his model-good looks and good-guy demeanor, which have always attracted plenty of the popular crowd to the house, to my eye at least. I can't remember his once dating a girl who wasn't your classic American blonde (from the bottle or not), Eunice (you-*NEECE*) Linzer Robeson being the most impressive of the bunch, and easily the sharpest. I see her now, outside on the massive slate-stone front landing of her house, cordless phone ever in hand. She waves, and I pull into the semicircular part of the driveway already packed with cars. This surprises, as I thought the party was to be an intimate family affair, but then I should know that the Battles of Haymarket Estates can't do anything too downscale/downmarket, as if they'd ever really have a cookout of burgers and dogs.

"Where have you been, Jerry?" she says brightly, covering the mouth holes. "Jack's out getting more ice and juice boxes."

Eunice kisses me and sends me inside, signaling Rosario's teenage daughter, Nidia, as she's now getting into issues with the caterer about the flatware and wineglasses, which as usual aren't exactly what she requested. In these situations Eunice never yells or raises her voice, but rather speaks at the downward angle of a third-grade teacher, with a patient, if often chilly, enunciation. In the clickety marble rotunda Nidia, in a crisp white shirt and black skirt, greets me with a flute of Champagne, and I note that she's looking exceptionally womanly, particularly in the important parts, and I contrive to make her linger a little as I down the first glass and then take another. I've seen her perhaps once a year for the last four, each time appreciating more deeply the march of youth's time. She smiles (not unwickedly?), and trots off. In the rotunda I notice the walls have been stripped of the "old" wallpaper and freshly painted, and the windows newly shaded with a single panel of muted silken fabric, clearly redone to complement the quartet of abstract paintings that recently arrived from the auction house, which, at least to my Art History 101 eye, look like real Kandinskys (and I very much hope are not).

In the great room/media room, Jack's kids, Tyler (girl) and Pierce (boy), are watching a Britney Spears concert DVD on the widescreen with a handful of other slack-jawed toddlers and young children who I'm sure are also named for minor presidents, and when I kneel down to kiss them they do manage a faint grunt and smile. This is true love, given the circumstance, which I appreciate and don't question. Along my sight line from here through the kitchen I can see the score or so of grownups mingling outside on the back deck, friends of Jack's and Eunice's and old buddies of Theresa's, some of whom I recognize and could speak to of specific times way back when but whose names I could hardly remember then and have no clue to now. Theresa used to get furious at me whenever she'd bring friends home and I'd dance around having to address them and afterward I'd plead early Alzheimer's but she knew it was because I never quite paid full attention. Unfortunately she thought it was only her but really it was a much more global problem than that and something I'm not sure she's over yet, or will ever be. It's funny how my grandkids (and their playmates) are now the ones calling the shots, as they're endlessly fussed over by Rosario and their preschool teachers and by Eunice and Jack and then even by me. The only one not readily kowtowing is my father, whose firm and sometimes gruff stance with them is not so much about teaching deference or respect but reminding one and all of his own status as family patriarch/ biggest boy.

He's nowhere to be found, though, and I head out onto the massive multilevel redwood deck, where Theresa and Paul are holding court by the buffet table. Paul sees me first and waves the big wave. Theresa glances over and nods, still talking to her friends, while Paul approaches. As mentioned, Paul grew up only a short distance from here, but after having spent a number of years on the West Coast he's no longer outwardly pushy and irritable like a lot of people on the Island. He talks softly, with an almost Western, cowboyish loll to his speech, which frankly is strange to hear from an Asian face. He wears his straight black hair quite long and somewhat ratty, though today he's gathered it in a ponytail, which is neater but still gives me the willies. From the back you'd swear he was a girl, with his short, slightish frame and periodic horsey tosses of the head, but from what I gather these days long tresses on a man usually indicate a hetero-supreme, a type, surprisingly, to which Theresa has always been drawn, and then to older ones, which Paul is (by eight years). I like him very much, despite his hemp-cloth-and-bead exterior, as deep down he's a thoroughly decent and affable fellow without a lot of that self-important artistic gaseousness that has to fill whatever room its owner finds himsel in.

His parents, Dr. and Dr. Pyun, who aren't here today because this party was only recently planned and they had long booked (through me) an eighteen-day Bella Extravanganza tour to all the famous spots in Italy, are a sweet and always smiling couple, at least on the surface, though I can tell, too, like the few other Asians I've come into contact with over the years, that they are not so quietly tenacious about what they want. When they came into the office to set up their trip I got the distinct feeling that they were sure I was going to sell them the most expensive package, and were intent upon starting from the bargain-bin tours I'd normally only recommend for pensioners and Catholic school teachers. I'd heard from Paul that they were interested in going to Italy (for the first time), and I called them directly and urged them to come in to see me. Maybe my zeal was suspicious, plus the fact that they weren't sold on the idea that I was a travel agent for reasons other than the sorry pay and needling customers (they'd certainly never imagine passing their retirement that way). Mrs. Dr. Pyun even asked a few times what the trip would cost "not counting commissions." Undeterred, I took them through the whole range of offerings, noting what I thought were the best values and itineraries, and they decided to go with a great mid-priced tour called "Savors of the Past," which mixes art and ruins with food-and-wine-oriented excursions. When I informed them that I'd of course not only credit them my commission but also try to sneak them in at a special industry rate, they positively burst with happy refusals, saying there was absolutely no need, and Dr. Pyun said something to his wife in Korean and she said something back that somehow sounded to me like *Why not?* Soon enough they were insisting on taking the ultraluxe package I had only briefly mentioned, and only if they paid the regular price. Afterward we had a gyro lunch at the Greek place next door, where they basically told me that they believed Paul (much unlike their two other sons, who were Ivy League grads and established attorneys) had no real prospects and they would not be surprised if I was very upset, being Theresa's father. I told them I wasn't, and that I was confident Paul's career would soon take off, and that his talents would be fully appreciated, if not in financial terms. They both sort of laughed, which I took to be their way of throwing up their hands, and Dr. Pyun said with finality, "Ahh—he's never going to be famous."

But apparently Paul is somewhat famous, at least in certain rarefied academic/literary circles, which is great if true but also means that no one I've met on a train or plane or in a waiting room has ever heard of him, much less read his books. And I do always ask. *I've* read his books (three novels and a chapbook of poetry), and I can say with great confidence that he's the sort of writer who can put together a nice-sounding sentence or two and does it with feeling but never quite gets to the point. Not that I've figured out what his point might be, though I get the sense that the very fact I'm missing it means I'm sort of in on it, too. I guess if you put a gun to my head I'd say he writes about The Problem with Being Sort of Himself—namely, the terribly conflicted and complicated state of being Asian and American and thoughtful and male, which would be just dandy in a slightly different culture or society but in this one isn't the hottest ticket. I know, for example, that his big New York publisher just recently parted company with him, deciding not to publish his latest manuscript, which was also passed on by the other major houses and will be issued instead by a small outfit called Seven Tentacle Press near where they live in Florence, Oregon, in a softcover format.

"Hey there, Jerry," Paul says, giving me his usual lovechild hug, wiry and sneaky strong. "What's shaking?"

"Nothing much. Congratulations, by the way."

"Thank you," Paul says, his eyes checking me. "You truly okay with this?"

"Are you kidding? I'm thrilled. Theresa is lucky to have you."

"That's what you think. She's the one with regular employ-
ment."

"Of course she is," I say. "But you're the one everyone should
support. You're the artist."

"The Artist Formerly Known as Publishable."

"Come on, now, you'll get this new one out and those editors in
the city will come begging, checkbooks ready. There'll be piles of
the book at Costco, right next to Crichton and Grisham."

"Sure," he says. "I bet there are remaindered copies at the All
for $1 store, between bins of cheap nail polish and Spanish-labeled
cat food."

"Well, you're wrong." But this makes me pause for a half second, as last year in fact I did find his second novel, *Drastic Alter-
ations*, at such a place in the Walt Whitman Mall. I ended up
buying all seventeen copies and giving them as Christmas gifts to
the employees of Battle Brothers, only one of whom, my longtime
foreman, Boots, e-mailed me with comments ("Kinda tough read
for me, skip, but English wasn't my best subject. Also, I didn't get
the small print at the bottom. Thanks, anyway"). I began to reply
that the "small print" was *footnotes*, as in a research term paper,
except that this was a story with *avant-garde features*, but then I
realized Boots might not have finished high school, or even middle school for that matter, and I just commended him for trying.
Of course I would never tell Paul about any of this, as I'm sure it
would plainly depress the crap out of him, and further ratify his
recent thinking about how his career was going, as he's put it, from
"mid-list" to "no-list." In our last few conversations he's joked a
bit too pointedly about self-publishing and getting into teaching
or editing or even Hollywood screenwriting, perhaps trying to
warn me that my daughter was marrying a fellow with ever-
diminishing prospects. But that's the case with almost everyone in
the broadening swath of middle age, isn't it, that we're all fatigu-

ing in some critical way (sex, job, family), some prior area of happy vitality and self-definition that is now instead a source of anxiety and dread.

"Hey," I say, glancing over to Theresa, who's likewise been glancing over to me while talking to her friends, "I think it's high time you introduced me to your fiancée."

"Of course, of course," Paul says, and we slide over into the group, and Theresa steps forward and gives me a light hug.

"Hello, Jerry," she says, pecking me on the cheek. Theresa has called me Jerry pretty much since her mother died. I didn't correct her then, out of fear she'd be further traumatized or something like that, letting her do whatever she wanted, and we both grew accustomed to it. Right now I'm happy she's clearly not unhappy to see me, which is a welcomed happenstance, as more often than not she'd have been simmering about something I said or did since the last time we got together, gathering up this prickly potential energy to let loose on me when I was thinking all was perfectly fine. And she looks great to me, a little fuller everywhere, her skin warm with a summer glow.

"You remember Alice Woo and Jadie Srinivasan, don't you?"

"I certainly do," I say, shaking their smooth, petite hands. They address me as Mr. Battle, which fortunately jogs my memory of them, but not as being half as attractive and self-assured as they are now, more like gangly and foreign and shy. When they were young the three of them would sometimes play Charlie's Angels when they had slumber parties at our house, and they'd set up Jack's walkie-talkie, with me in the kitchen and them in the living room, and I'd say, "Hello, angels," which would delight them no end, and they'd act out whatever crazy story line they could come up with, and then vamp around a little bit, too, in sleazy makeup and clothes. But whenever I picked them up at the middle school after band practice or drama they slunk, as if trying to stay under the radar as they walked to the car, other girls running in from the fields in their team uniforms, ruddy-faced, hollering all, hair jouncing in shimmers of chestnut and strawberry and blond. I never drove them to the kinds of parties Jack was always invited to, mostly dropping them off for the train heading for New York or the art house cinema in Huntington Village. Of course I never said anything but wondered to myself what my daughter and her friends really thought of things, and of themselves, whether given a choice they'd remain just as they were or instead trade their black Edgar Allan Poe capes for field hockey skirts and Ray-Bans and the attentions of boys from Jack's crowd, the type who could swim (and soon enough drink) like fish and instinctively lace a pure backhand down the line. It turns out that Theresa and Alice and Jadie are exactly the sort of midnight-eyed young women you see increasingly in magazines and on billboards, which to me is a generally welcome development (being the father of such Diversity), though I'll not lie and say I'm at ease with most of the other attendant signs of our cultural march, one example being how youths from every quarter openly desire to dress as though they're either drug-addled whores or runaways or gangstas or just plain convicts, as though the whole society has embraced dereliction and criminality as its defining functions, with Theresa of course once pointing out to me that decades of governmental neglect and corporate corruption and pilfering have resulted in this hard-edged nihilistic street-level expression. At the risk of sounding like my father, I'll say that her reading of this doesn't really wash with me, though I have recently begun to accept her notions about the ineluctable creep in the realm, that the very ground beneath my feet is shifting with hardly my notice, to travel invisibly, with or without me. Though I did actually utter "My bad" the other day to Miles Quintana, after messing up a cruise reservation. So maybe I'm moving along, too.

"Do you remember," Theresa says to me, "how the three of us melted the top of the bathroom vanity with a curling iron, and you came home to all those fire engines in the driveway?"

"I don't. Did I get upset?"

"I thought you were going to have a coronary," Alice Woo says. "I'll admit right now that it was all my fault. I desperately wanted curls, just like these guys."

Jadie cries, "We practically fried your hair. But it wouldn't take."

"You needed Jeri-Curl," I say, trying my best. The girls chuckle, Paul laughing loud in his special way, a nasally yuck-yuck.

"You know, Mr. Battle, I was totally afraid of you," Jadie now says. She's very dark-complected, with immense brown eyes and a tiny silver stud piercing in her nose. Later on I'll learn that at merely thirty-one she's chief corporate counsel for a software company, where I suppose piercings and tattoos are a-okay, and maybe recommended issue, like French cuffs used to be. "Theresa can tell you. I'd always ask if you were going to be home. I thought you didn't like us coming over."

"That's not true," I say. "I was always happy for you guys to hang out."

Theresa says, matter-of-factly, "Jerry just didn't like it when people were having fun and he wasn't."

Alice offers, "That's understandable, isn't it?"

"You got that," I say.

"Sure," Theresa says, "but for a *parent*?"

This momentarily quells the moment, not to mention cutting me deep, because of course she's right in both principle and practice. I've never sat by well when others were at play, not when I was five, or fifteen, or fifty. I'd like to believe this was a question of my desiring involvement and connection, rather than of envy or selfishness. I'd like to blame my ever-indulging, spoiling, obliging mother (God bless her), or my wonderful brother Bobby for guilt-lessly using up the years of his brief life; I'd like to blame my father for giving me almost everything I required but really nothing I wanted, but that's the story of us all, isn't it, or of my particular American generation, or maybe just me, and nothing one really needs to hear about again.

"Though to be honest," my daughter now says, actually looping her arm into the crook of mine, "at least Jack and I were instructed by the master. Paul can tell you what an ornery bitch I can be, if I see he's doing a crossword when I'm washing the dishes."

"She once squirted me with the Palmolive," he says. "Right on my pajamas."

Jadie nods. "But our Theresa was like that from the beginning. When we played Barbies, Alice and I always had to keep our dolls in the camper, cleaning and making the beds, while Theresa's Barbie was outside tending the campfire, roasting hot dogs and marshmallows."

"My Barbie was chef de cuisine. You were my *femmes de chambre*. There had to be a clear order to things."

"This is sounding very sexy," Eunice says, flanked by Rosario, who is bearing a tray of canapés. Eunice explains they are "polenta blinis" topped with Sevruga caviar and lobster meat and chived crème fraîche. I'm sure Eunice did put together at least one or two model canapés, as I witnessed once at another party, with Rosario making the rest. Everybody takes one, Rosario nudging me with the tray edge to grab a couple more. I comply.

"Incredible. Did you really make these?" Alice asks, to which Eunice smiles modestly but distinctly. Rosario drifts across the massive deck, to offer them to the others.

"It wasn't so difficult. The key is good components."

"We would have been happy with carrot sticks and onion dip," Theresa says, "but I'm glad you went all out."

"Oh please, it's nothing special."

This is true. Ever since she and Jack got married I've never had so much Muscovy duck and Dungeness crab and Belon oysters coursing through the old iron pipes. Rita cooked fancy but always with modest ingredients, being loath to use anything that cost over $3 a pound. With Eunice it's only the rare and *cher*, artisanal meats and breads and cheeses, exotic flown-in fishes and fruits, wines from exclusive "garage" vintners, coffee from secret hillsides in Kenya and Nepal and Vermont. As she says, it's all about the components, which indeed are often wondrously tasty, reminding one of the fundamental goodness of the plain and natural; but there's still, I think, an even more satisfying gut-strum in what someone can magically do with a little herb and spice and heat, Rita's pulled-pork casserole being exquisite proof of that. Eunice can surely wow almost anybody with her deft arrangements, but I will swear there's a *love* to be found in your basic Crock-Pot alchemy, which even the sweetest lobster tail or dollop of sturgeon eggs cannot easily provide.

"I still cook the way Jerry taught me," Theresa says. "Remove pork chops from package, generously salt and pepper, bake at 375 degrees until there are no signs of moisture."

"Amazingly, it works with any meat or fish," Paul says. "Fowl, too."

"Now, I wasn't that bad," I say, mostly for the benefit of Eunice, for Alice and Jadie were sometimes actually there, watching me along with Theresa as I fumbled through the cabinets for the Shake 'n Bake and Hamburger Helper before Rita showed up. I couldn't afford a full-time nanny, and Battle Brothers was sinking fast, and I'd get home at six to cranky, hungry kids and burrow through the freezer for something that wasn't too brown-gray at the edges. "You have to realize I never had to cook until Theresa's mother died. Then it was every night I had to come up with something."

"At least until I took over," Theresa says.

"You were very advanced."

Eunice asks, "Why didn't you have Jack cook? He's older."

"I don't know. I guess Jack just didn't seem up to it."

"Jerry was afraid of feminizing him," Theresa says, right on cue. And here comes the rest. But she looks up at me and appears to wink—which is the tiniest thing but wholly a salve. What she says isn't quite right, though, which I can say with some surety because I wasn't completely unaware of what I was doing back then. The fact of the matter was I didn't want Jack to have to think of his dead mother every night, at least in a ritualized way, which in my thinking was sure to happen if he had to don an apron and fry up hamburgers. For a year or so after she died he hardly said a word, he was just a kid with eyes, and as Theresa seemed the sturdier of the two in almost all respects, I made an executive decision to have him do other chores like repainting the back fence and raking leaves and hosing out the garbage cans, which he never once complained about, and I like to think it was the bracing physical activity that eventually snapped him out of it, though I'm probably mistaken on that one.

Some of Theresa's college friends (retro eyeglasses, thrift-store chic clothes, goatees galore) come around, and the talk gets a bit too pop-cultural and swervy and superallusive for me, and so I wander about the deck, briefly mingling with couples who are obviously friends of the hosts. They're decent enough people, well-heeled youngish parents with stiff drinks padding about in upturned collars and Belgian driving loafers, crooning incessantly about the cost of beach houses and Jag convertibles and nannies, the basic tune being why all this good living should be so dear (though of course if it weren't, what would they take such fascination in, or not-so-sly pride?). One magnificently bronzed, lean-armed woman named Kit sits me down and practically goes stone by stone through the immense landscaping project she is having done on her North Fork property, the massive excavation and Teletubbies berming, the football-field-length retaining walls of Vermont slate, the 2000-square-foot limestone patio and the blue-stone-decked and -bottomed pool, and the literally hundreds of mature shrubs and trees, the job (which Battle Brothers Excalibur is fortunately doing) to ring up at nearly three hundred grand alone. The recession is not of her world. Kit isn't complaining or angling for special treatment, but rather simply telling me her story, as if she is some Old Testament figure chosen to endure an epochal test from which she might someday emerge righteous and whole.

By the time Kit is all but strapping me into her Mercedes SUV to drive me out east to her place in Southold and show me the work-in-progress, Jack pats me on the shoulder, having returned from the store. Kit practically leaps into his arms, hugging him a bit too firmly for even a pleased and grateful customer, and I'm sure it's nothing even though you still hear stories these days of people offering more than loads of money to get good contractors to sign up for a job. In my day you had to dress nice and chat for as long as the customer wanted when you showed up to give an estimate, parking yourself for a long spell at a lady's kitchen table trying not to stare at the widening gap in her robe and listen to whatever she needed to tell you about her never-home husband or sick mother or super-rotten kids, knowing that nine times out of ten you wouldn't get the job. Jack chastely pecks her on the cheek and excuses us, saying that the Battle men are being requested inside, and Kit tugs at his hand, reflexively unwilling to let him go.

I trail Jack into the house. He's just a shade shorter than I am,

6'1" or so, and built a bit differently, being lower-slung than I am, his torso longer and thicker and his gait just like Daisy's was, meaning he moves in a slightly bowlegged fashion, knees pointing outward, a little bit like a pet iguana we once had, their similarities something I used to tease him about. He's got a hockey player's body, though he never played that, sticking to football and lacrosse, sports in which he excelled. As already mentioned, he's very good-looking, probably professionally so, and I can say with some pride that he's got my best features, which are a strong chin and a thick tousle of naturally wavy hair and those sparkly eyes that some people have, speckled (and in our case, hazel-colored) irises that certain folks not-so-brightly wonder aloud about— namely, whether they're bad for your vision. But it's flattering, anyway, and as Jack knows well enough is almost unfairly attractive to the opposite sex, for really all you need to do is just meet someone's gaze and hold for a moment, like the first time I met his mother, or when I met Rita, take a long, slow-shuttered picture, and watch the thing steadily develop. I go into all this mostly because I find myself admiring Jack and Theresa more and more, not so much for the people they are (they are fine people) but for their physical qualities, and I know you'll think I do so because ultimately it's all about me, my legacy and what I've bestowed upon them and so on, but it's just the opposite. Perhaps it's seeing them both here today, in full-blown adulthood, but the notion occurs that whatever I have given them is in fact very little, and diminishes with each day, and that it's already happened that they define me probably more now than I do them, which of course is just as well.

In the kitchen Nidia points us toward the powder room saying it's Pop, my father, who I didn't realize was already here but of course had to be the whole time. Eunice is talking to him through the locked door, Rosario standing by. When she sees us she steps back and says he's been moaning as though he's in pain but won't let anyone in. Just then Pop yells, "I don't need anybody. You people go away." He says *people* like we're a crowd on a subway platform, nobody he cares to know.

Jack tries the knob and says, "Come on, Pop. Let's open the door now."

"Everything stinks!" is his answer. For some reason this is my cue to make a try.

"We just want to know that you're not hurt, Pop. Are you hurt?"

"Is that you, Jerome?"

"Yeah."

"Where the hell have you been?"

"Outside on the deck."

"Well, then, everybody clear out. I only want Jerome to help me. I want my son."

"You still have to open the door for me."

"I can't," he says, weakly now. "I can't."

Jack pulls out his fat Swiss Army knife (which I taught him from early on to carry always) and plucks out its embedded plastic toothpick for me, so I can push in the lock.

"Okay, everybody scram," I say loudly. "I'll take it from here." Jack opens his hands and I wave him and Eunice and Rosario away, as well as the few kids—none from our clan—who've gathered in the hallway to rubberneck. When they've all gone back to the party I tell my father I'm coming in. He grunts, and I click out the tumbler.

My father's on the floor, his pants around his ankles. He tells me to lock the door again. I do. And then I realize that everything *does* stink, something fierce, like surly death itself, or maybe worse.

"All those damn goat cheese toasts gave me the runs," he says. Then more sheepishly, "I ran out of paper." The cabinet door to the vanity is ajar, a couple rolls of tissue spilled out onto the floor.

He's made a mess of himself, soiling the edge of the seat and basin. His nose is bleeding. I try to sit him up but he groans hard when I lift him. I'm afraid it's his leg, or worse, his hip. He shrugs me off. "Goddammit, Jerome, just help clean me up first."

The stuff is all over his undershorts and slacks, riding up on his lower back and side. It's no great leap for me to think of the days when Jack and Theresa were swaddled babes, to remember carefully pinning tight their cloth diapers, holding the ends of the dirty ones and flushing them in the toilet, but this job is on another scale entirely, like in middle school when the science teacher brought out models of the Earth and Jupiter. Who could have imagined the actual difference? I know Pop has been having some control difficulty recently, enough so that the case nurse at Ivy Acres has recommended that he wear incontinence pants all the time, to prevent accidents and "needless embarrassment." I didn't bring it up with him, because I know where he'd tell me to stick it, though I note to myself that I'll soon try.

After taking off his soiled clothes I'm lucky to find a washcloth in the vanity, but it's awkward to use the bar of soap to clean him properly, and instantly understanding this Pop points to the spray bottle of Fantastik beneath the sink basin. I tell him it might burn his skin and would undoubtedly be unhealthy in any case but he says, annoyed, "You think I care about genetic damage or something? Go ahead."

The act of which is very strange, spraying him down like he's some mildewed vinyl couch brought up from the cellar. I can tell that the foam isn't sitting too well with him, his tough olive skin beginning to glimmer pink, but he doesn't wince or say a word. He just lies with his big squared head down on the tiled floor, like a sick horse or mule, not looking at me, which is a great mercy for us both. The sharp industrial scent of the solvent is an unlikely balm, too, and I clean him as quickly and thoroughly as I can.

When I sit him up there's a huge grapey bruise on his upper thigh just below his hip. His wrist and elbow still sting from the short fall off the toilet but he says he can get up. I tuck my shoulder beneath his armpit and we rise. I feel the dense weight of his limbs, more of him now than there ever was, the last few years of sedentary living accruing to him like unpicked fruit, this useless bounty, and I think it's not only his body but his mind, ever cramming with unrequited notions and thoughts. As his clothes are ruined and I'm no doubt the closest in size, I take off my pants and give them to him, so he can get upstairs and shower off.

As I open the powder room door he says, "What the hell are you gonna do, walk around in your skivvies?"

"I'll get some sweatpants from Jack."

"Sounds like that's all that boy's going to be wearing, if things don't get better."

"What are you talking about?"

"What do you think? Some of us still call over there every day, you know, even though we retired a thousand years ago."

"And?"

"Sal said they've been having cash flow problems. They barely made payroll the last two weeks."

Sal is the bookkeeper for Battle Brothers, and has been since I was a kid. "Jack hasn't said anything to me."

"You ever talk shop with him?"

I don't offer an answer, and my father snorts knowingly. I still care about the business, though certainly not the way he does, and then never enough to shadow Jack all the time, nosing over his shoulder to armchair quarterback. In fact I'd say from the very beginning I tried not to mention Battle Brothers if I could help it, for just those reasons, and then partly in the hope that he would eventually pursue his own career. But I suppose such strategies are flawed and hubristic in the realm of family life and relations, that no matter what you do or don't do in the service of good intentions your aims will get turned about and around and furiously boomerang homeward. I don't doubt that one of the reasons Jack stayed on with Battle Brothers was that I exerted so little pressure on him, probably causing him to wonder why I wasn't bothering, and as a result eliciting in recent years his ever-redoubling efforts in expanding the enterprises of our family concern.

But what my father purports—and it is just that until proven true, given his mental state—deeply troubles me, as I've pondered how densely luxurious this house of Jack's has become, a veritable thicket of money-spending; I know for a fact that while there are still a handful of Eighth Wonder of the World jobs like Kit's, there aren't the ready scores of smaller, more modest projects that normally keep our manpower and machinery humming at near capacity. Jack is clearly a natural at broadening Battle Brothers' reach—unlike me, he's always been pretty fearless in exploring the unknown and untried, like the time when he was six or seven and without pause scrambled down a drainage pipe to retrieve a baseball I'd overthrown—but it's uncertain how or even if he'll understand that he needs to pull back in slow times, quickly beat a retreat, and if I've bestowed anything on him I hope it's my quick trigger for cutting one's losses, in business always and maybe also in life.

With my help Pop limps through the kitchen to go up the back stairwell, Eunice and Jack and Rosario standing by, just in case. Tyler, my sharp granddaughter of four, asks no one in particular why I'm wearing only my "panties," and why it stinks like poop.

"Your grandpa Jerome had an accident," Pop whispers to her, winking and paddling her behind. "But don't spread it around."

"Skanky," Tyler sneers, regarding me with what is already a distinctly teenage disdain. I note to myself that I must speak to Eunice about what the kids are watching all day and night.

"Help us upstairs," I say to Jack. He leans under Pop's other side and the three of us trudge upward trying to get our steps in sync. After we finally get Pop in the shower, Jack lends me a pair of Gore-Tex running pants, and we sit in the living area of the master bedroom, the double bathroom doors (of Jack's *toilette*) swept wide so we can keep an eye on Pop in the shower, who is the picture of old manhood as he lathers up behind the unfrosted safety glass: a hairy, saggy pear on legs. We offered to help but he growled, "You'll get plenty of me before I'm done," meaning not now but in the course of his remaining days. This is true, on many levels, though none I can really pause and think deeply about now. All I know is that today's episode is merely the beginning of the beginning, like the first intemperate days of winter, which always seem like mildest tonic later on.

While we wait, Jack's grabbed a couple beers for us from the under-counter refrigerator in the kitchenette section of the bedroom. There's a short run of cabinets and a microwave and an electric stovetop and even a mini-dishwasher, the effect being of a studio apartment, or grad student housing, though of course a lot nicer than that. Basically, he and Eunice wanted to be able to have a snack or make a cup of coffee without having to trek downstairs and to the other end of the house where the kitchen is, which seems reasonable enough until you realize that this is the kind of lifestyle detail that brought down the railroad barons and junk bond kings and dot-commers and whoever else will next rocket up and flame out in miserable infamy.

"You're good to throw Theresa and Paul this party." I say. "She seems pretty happy, don't you think?"

"For once in her life," Jack says.

"I suppose so," I reply, acknowledging the truth of his statement, but also caught off guard by its unexpected edge. "How's everything with you?"

"Couldn't be better."

"The house looks great."

"It's all good. It's all working."

"I guess business must have slowed down a bit."

Jack takes a long pull from his beer bottle. "Some."

"If you ever want me to come in it's no problem. I have all the time in the world."

"Okay."

"I'll ride along with the guys, if you want. Or I can even help Sal with the books."

Jack sits up. "You think Sal needs your help?"

"Why not? He's practically Pop's age. He's got to be making mistakes with that abacus of his. He's still using it, I bet."

"He does," Jack says. "But I check everything over, and everything's fine."

"I'm just saying, that's all."

"Sure you are."

"I am."

"Good, Dad. It's done. Really. It's all good."

There's nothing to counter with, mostly because Jack is a Battle and as a Battle is not unlike me, and thus endowed with a wide range of people-shedding skills, the foremost of which is how to curtail further talk when the talk gets most awkward, and so potentially perilous. Ask Rita, Kelly, maybe you could ask Daisy if she were here, ask Eunice about Jack, ask them all how difficult the footing becomes, how suddenly sheer the incline. Theresa, to be fair, manifests much of the same impassability, though her terrain features the periodic (and unaccidental) rock slide, an avalanche of obstructing analysis and critique and pure reason.

Pop curses from the shower, and we both nearly jump, though it's just him turning the handle the wrong way for a long second and getting all hot water instead of none. He's okay, if a bit scalded, and Jack gingerly helps him towel off, a splash of pink on one of his shoulders and upper chest. Pop tells us he's tired and wants to take a nap. Jack gives him a T-shirt and we walk him to the bed, tuck him in. Is this what growing old is about: another small though dangerous moment, somehow survived?

Downstairs the kitchen is crowded with people, as it appears everyone has come in from the deck, and Eunice, now seeing me and Jack, gently rings her Champagne glass with a spoon. The murmur and chatter subside. Rosario and Nidia are quickly going about offering fresh flutes and refilling others.

"We're so thrilled to welcome Theresa and Paul back home. And we are especially happy on this, the wonderful occasion of their wedding engagement." Eunice beams at Theresa and Paul, who seem tickled enough but also a shade uneasy, as academes and other intellectualized types sometimes are in real-life situations not squarely cast to be ironic.

"I'd like to propose a toast on the recent announcement of their nuptials, as well as offer our home as the place where Theresa and Paul and their guests can rendezvous whenever next year they'd like to celebrate the wedding. As all of us old married folks know, the time up through the wedding and honeymoon is the sweetest of all. Sad but true! So may you savor it! Cheers!"

A call of "Cheers!" goes around, and while everyone bottoms-up I notice that Theresa and Paul are more conferencing than celebrating, Paul shaking his head to whatever Theresa is insisting upon, which is what I imagine anyone dealing regularly and intimately with my daughter must learn to do. Theresa tries to get everyone's attention and Eunice, now seeing that she wants to speak, tinkles her glass again. Theresa nods.

"Paul and I want to thank my sister-in-law for the always luxurious party," Theresa says, her voice low, almost somber. "We thank Rosario and Nidia for their time and patience. And of course we thank Jack, too, for giving all three complete and total control." This elicits a laugh, and Jack, who's next to me, glumly raises his beer bottle.

"Paul and I wanted to let all of you know, too, that we're not going to get married next year. Don't worry. We're getting married this fall, probably in October."

"That's too soon!" Eunice cries. She's obviously been counting on producing the whole affair, as she does with everything having to do with our clan. (I should quickly note that Eunice is the only child of two very successful and prickly Bostonian parents, which for me is explanation enough for why she's such a zealous and tyrannical arranger.)

Theresa says, "On the plane we decided we didn't want to wait, and while we were never going to have a big wedding it'll be a very small ceremony now. But if I can take up Eunice's generous offer right here on the spot, I hope she'll have all of us back in a few months, for a little celebration."

"Certainly you can," Eunice says, doing her best not to sound curt. "We'd be thrilled."

Now Alice and Jadie and the rest of Theresa's friends pinch in on her and Paul for a new round of congratulatory hugs, and when I murmur to Jack about Theresa maybe being pregnant he responds with a blithe "Who knows?," which wouldn't normally bother me but does now with an unexpected sharpness. I shoot him a look but he's already drifted off, to help Nidia gather some used glasses and plates. Jack is considerate and generous like this and always has been, but if I have to tell the truth about him I would have to say he's never demonstrated the same feeling for me or Theresa that he does for his club buddies and employees or even strangers at the mall. And while I can try to accept our relationship as less than ideal (because of the usual father-son issues of superdefended masculinity and cycles of expectation/resentment and then the one of his mother suddenly dying when he was young, for which he squarely and silently blames yours truly), it pains me to the core to see how meager his expressions are for his younger sister, how bloodless and standard, as if she's merely a person jammed next to him in the middle seat on a plane, a reality and mild inconvenience to be affably addressed and elbow-jockeyed from time to time. Of course I'd always hoped and maybe too quickly assumed that they would cling for dear life to each other after what happened to their mother, but really just the opposite occurred, even as young as they were, both always heading to their rooms before and after supper, both always shutting the doors.

After the lifting hubbub of the news and the subsequent enervation, people start to leave. I walk by and see Paul sitting alone in the empty-shelved library, swirling a glass of white wine. I've already hugged and kissed Theresa, who hugged me quite vigorously back, whispering that we'd all talk later on, tomorrow maybe. Before I could ask what about, she begged off for a quick ride to the 7-Eleven with Jadie and Alice to buy bridal magazines, for what reason she wasn't sure, though citing her interest in cultural fodder and ritual. Yeah, yeah. She said she'd be back after dinner, as they were going to hang out for a while, and it struck me how pleased I was to see her acting so plainly girlish and silly.

Paul says, "Pull up a chair, Jerry. You want some?"

He pours me a glass of Eunice's "house" chardonnay, which it literally is, as a winery out on the North Fork sticks her own handmade labels on her annual ten-case order. We clink and sip and sit without talking, which is unusual for us. Paul is one of the few people who can always draw me out, and not just in a social, good-guy kind of way. I don't know why exactly, though perhaps it has something to do with the fact that he's not like me at all, that we come from dissimilar peoples and times and traditions and hold

nearly opposite views on politics and the world, and so have neither the subtle pressure nor the dulling effect of instant concord,
an ease and comfort I've enjoyed all my life but find increasingly
wanting now. Maybe I'm a racialist (or racist?) and simply like the
fact that he's different, that he's short and yellow and brainy (his
words, originally), and that he makes *me* somehow different,
whether I really wish to be or not.

"You're probably wondering what's going on with us," Paul says.

"Not really," I say. "You kids can get married whenever the hell
you want, in my book. And I was going to tell Theresa but I might
as well tell you. I'm going to give you twenty-five thousand for the
wedding, which I set aside a while ago."

"You know we'll probably just go to a justice of the peace."

"Doesn't matter to me. The money's yours, to use as you
please."

"Well, thanks. But it's not necessary."

"Listen. Maybe you want to use it for a down payment on a real
house—you know, one that'll be big enough for all of you."

"We've never needed much room."

"Little ones take up a lot more space than you think," I say.

"I suppose that's so," he replies, though not in a way that in-
spires a load of confidence, and I'm reminded that these two have
very narrow expertise, like probably only knowing how to prepare
milk for cappuccinos.

"I'm just suggesting that you keep in mind where you two will
be three or four years from now. What you might want. I'll always
help you out, you know. Jack's doing better than fine, and so I figure I can give you and Theresa whatever you need, funds included.
Kids are expensive, too."

Paul has a funny look on his face, a sort of smile if a smile
weren't necessarily a wonderful thing, as though I've definitely
said something awkward, and suddenly he's got his head in his

hands, and barely shuddering with what must be joy, still holding his glass just now sloshing over with wine. I half expect this, given the combination of bardic and new age male sensitivity, and I reach over and pat him on the back, saying how eager I am to be a grandfather again, how happy, though wishing now that they weren't living clear on the other side of the country.

"Is it that obvious?" Paul says, looking up at me now, his eyes red.

"No, but this shotgun wedding announcement is a clue."

He chuckles, and we tip our glasses. I say, "You're welcome to stay with me until the wedding, if you like. Unless you have to go right back to Oregon."

"No, we're not doing that," Paul says, a bit uncomfortably. "We were hoping to hang around for a while, actually. Theresa has the fall term off, and she misses being back East."

"I'm happy to hear that."

"Eunice wants us to stay here but I know Theresa would prefer being back at your house."

"Really?"

"Sure," Paul says, "as long as it's all right with you."

"I said you're welcome, didn't I?"

"Just want to make sure."

"It'll be great, like summer vacation again," I say, warmed instantly by the idea that Theresa might ever choose to stay with me at 1 Cold Creek Lane. "Hey, the three of us can take an old-fashioned car trip somewhere."

"Okay," Paul says. "But can't we all fit in your plane?"

"It'd be a little tight. And I'm not sure I like the pressure, of piloting the next generations."

"I thought going by car was the most dangerous way to travel."

"Private planes are probably a close second."

"If there's anybody I'd trust, Jerry, it would be you."

"Oh yeah?" I say, steeling myself for the inevitable warm and fuzzy stage of our conversations, which I in fact have begun to half look forward to, and probably now nudge along, unconsciously and not.

"Certainly. You're the sort of fellow who's totally reliable, in the mechanical arts. I think you're an engineer in your soul. You have that beautiful machine expertise, that beautiful machine faith."

"I've just been a dirt-mover, Paul. But thank you."

He raises his glass, and we clink. Suddenly I realize that Paul may be a little drunk, or a lot drunk, I don't know, because he normally doesn't partake of more than a glass, for the reason that many of his brethren seem not to, as they turn beet red in the face after a couple of sips, looking as if they've played three sets of tennis in the tropics, teetering on some sweaty brink.

"Well, we don't have to fly," Paul says, brightly. "How about let's drive to D.C. You can give us the Jerry Battle special tour of the Air and Space."

Now he's talking, and I'm reminded yet again of one of the many reasons that I always enjoy his company: Paul is sensitive to what invigorates a guy like me, the kind of acknowledgment that really makes me levitate with a foursquare satisfaction, which is what you feel when you believe you've been thoroughly understood.

I say, "You know it's going to be great having you guys around for a little while. Just the idea makes me wish you didn't live so damn far away. Maybe you can move back. There are plenty of nice colleges around here. Stonybrook's just a short drive."

"Theresa just started her tenure track at Cascadia State. But we're not against coming back East, if there's an opening for her. It certainly doesn't matter where *I* live. I can write myself into obscurity just about anywhere."

"Hey, you have to stop talking like that, Paul," I say. "I know the literature-making business isn't the sort of thing where you have to be all rah-rah and gung-ho, but it can't help to run yourself down like that."

"You'd be surprised."

"But you're not the miserable angst-ridden writer type. At least not from where I'm sitting. You like the sunlight and kidding around and you genuinely like people. Everybody who knows you knows that. I'm not trying to give you advice, but it seems to me that you could put your easygoing nature to work for you."

"You mean write fluffy coffee-table books?"

"Don't ask me. But hey, come to think of it, Costco is full of them, and people snap them up like they do the twenty-four-count muffin packs. I know you're not in it for the money, but I have to assume the publishers are."

"You got that right. The one exception is my new publisher. The patron of my new press does it solely for vanity, so she can lord it over the rest of her Aspen circle that she cultivates boutique international writers."

"See, you're doing it again."

"I'm sorry, Jerry," Paul says, sliding deeper and deeper into the club chair. His face and neck are mottled several shades of lobster red-pink, a pretty clear sign that his genetically challenged liver has begun bucking this unusual overtime shift. I could gently chide him, but what the heck, for it's one of those seriously fortunate pleasures, is it not, to sit down with your (soon-to-be) son-in-law and a bottle of smooth, buttery vino and breezily tie one on and not have to swoop and dodge the baggage-strewn recriminations of a shared past (as you'd have with your own son), but rather wishfully opine on what joys the coming years might bring with unflinching sentimentality that says nothing is beyond our grasp, that the ceiling's limitless.

And in this spirit, I say, unqualified, "Hey, Theresa looks great, really great."

Paul takes a big quaffing gulp. Lets the medicine go down. He answers, "She does, doesn't she?"

"Her mother got just like that when she was pregnant. I think just before a woman is showing is when she's most beautiful. Like she's just stepped out of a hot shower. Lucky for me, Daisy showed very late. How far along is she? It can't be too much."

"She's not well, Jerry," Paul says. "I hate to tell you this. Theresa didn't really want to just yet. But I told her we had to tell you."

"Hold on. There's something wrong with the baby?"

"The baby is fine." Paul tries to smile, or not to, I can't tell. He says, "It's Theresa."

"Oh yeah? You better tell me."

"She has something."

I don't say anything. I don't want to say anything, but I say, as if I'm out on a job with the crew, "What the fuck are you talking about?"

Paul stares down into his wineglass. "It's a cancer, Jerry."

"Jesus, Paul. You're fucking kidding me. Where is it?"

"It's sort of not that kind. Besides, right now, she wouldn't want me to say."

"I don't care what she wants. You tell me now."

Paul takes another big gulp. He says, hardly saying it, "It's non-Hodgkin's lymphoma."

"What the hell is that?"

"It's cancer in the lymph nodes."

"But she'll get treatment, she's getting treatment."

He shakes his head. "We've been to every doctor in Oregon and Washington. We're seeing someone at Yale Medical School tomorrow. But I think it's going to be the same story. It's not something they can operate on, and the chemo and radiation would hurt the baby."

"So what the hell are you two doing? What the hell is this?"

"She doesn't want to hurt the baby, Jerry," he says. "We've fought over this and fought over this and I haven't been able to change her mind. She's going to try to wait until after the baby's born. It's due in December."

"She can have another baby!" I say. "She's only *thirty*, for heaven's sake! Am I missing something here? You can have a half dozen more, if you wanted."

"There's the problem of the chemo causing infertility. That's not certain, though. But really, it's that she's decided she wants this one. You talk to her tomorrow. Please talk to her. I can't anymore. Right now I just have to support her, Jerry, because there's no other way."

"Dammit, Paul, this is all fucking crazy. You're both fucking crazy!"

"Don't you think I know that?"

"Oh fuck it!"

We're suddenly shouting at one another, standing toe to toe, and I realize that I've gripped my wineglass so tight that it's snapped at the stem. One of the points is digging into my palm. I'm stuck and bleeding. I drop the two pieces onto the chair cushion. Paul reaches for a box of tissues and gathers me up a wad, and when I press it I get a sharp, ugly surge of that old feeling again, when Daisy was so lovely and so fragile, the feeling like I want to break or ruin something. Something I'll always need.

four

THE DAY THAT DAISY DIED was a lot like this one, early July, with the sun seeming stuck right at the top of the sky, casting the kind of light and heat that make all the neighborhood kids vault over themselves with pant and glee and then cows everyone else, moms and dads and us older folks and teenagers and the family pets. Daisy liked the heat, and though she didn't know how to swim she'd spend plenty of time in our backyard pool, tanning in her plaid one-piece in the floating lounger or else dog-paddling with an old-fashioned life ring looped under her arms. I tried to teach her how to swim a couple of times, but I'd end up cat-scratched about the neck and shoulders, and then half-drowned besides, Daisy lurching and pulling up on me whenever I let her go, yelling out if her face or scalp got wet. She wasn't so much dainty or persnickety but for some reason hated being submerged or drenched. She always showered with a cap and on alternate days shampooed her hair in the sink, the drain of which I'd have to unclog every couple weeks of the thick black strands, using a pair of chopsticks.

And I swear—I swear, I swear—that I never imagined for a second that the pool was dangerous, at least for her. Sure I jumped in a half-dozen times to pluck out one of my kids or their mangy, booger-streaked friends thrashing fitfully in the deep end, but Daisy was always careful and tentative, even after she started to change and began seeing our family doctor for meds. She always entered the water as if it were as hot as soup, then pushed off from the steps with her float tube and kicked, her taut chin just barely hovering above the surface.

Hey, honey, she'd say to me, the ends of her hair slicked to pencil points, I'm a mermaid.

Sexier than that, I'd say, through the Sunday paper, through the summer haze.

It was nice like that, a lot of the time. I remember how Theresa and Jack would spend pretty much every second between breakfast and dinner in our backyard pool, or else run about on the concrete surround and the lawn spraying each other and whatever friends were around with water pistols filled with Hi-C punch or sometimes even pee (I caught them once in the rickety little cabana I'd built, giggling and pissing all over their hands trying to fill-er-up). If it was the weekend I'd be out there for a good while, too, chuck the kids around in the water and play the monster or buffoon and do a belly flop or two for a finale, then dry off and wrap a towel around my waist and drag a chaise and a beer beneath the maples and snooze until one of the kids got hurt or fell or puked because they drank too much pool water, all of which in the heat and brightness and clamor made for a mighty decent time. This, of course, was dependent, too, on what mood Daisy was in, but in those early days she was pretty solid, she was pretty much herself, she was just like the girl I fell in love with.

In those days she would set up the patio table with all kinds of vittles, she'd have the soppressata and the sugar ham and the crock of port wine cheese and the Ritz and Triscuits and she'd have plenty of carrot and celery sticks and pimiento olives and then she'd have the electric fryer on the extension cords snaking back through the kitchen window, to fry up chicken wings or butterfly shrimp and french fries right there on the table, so it was hot and fresh. If my folks or other people were going to be over she made sure to put out her homemade egg rolls and some colorful seaweed and rice thing that we didn't yet know back then was sushi, which people couldn't *believe* she had made, and maybe some other Oriental-style dishes like spicy sweet ribs and a cold noodle dish she always told us the name of but that we could never remember but which everyone loved and always finished first. She had this way of arranging the food on the platters that made you think of formal gardens, with everything garnished by fans of sliced oranges or shrubs of kale or waterfowl she'd carve out of apples, giving them shiny red wings.

I was working a lot then, having just been made second-in-command at Battle Brothers by my father and uncles, and Daisy was like a lot of the young mothers around the neighborhood, meaning she took care of the house and the kids and the cooking and the bills and whatever else came up that I could have dealt with but somehow didn't, for the usual semi-acceptable reasons of men; but I will tell you Daisy didn't mind, that was never a problem between us, because when you got right down to it she was an old-fashioned girl in matters of family, not only because she wasn't so long removed from the old country, but also because her nature (if you can speak of someone's nature, before she changed and went a little crazy and ended up another person entirely) preferred order over almost all else, and certainly didn't want any lame hand Jerry Battle could provide.

In fact the first real signs of her troubles were the kinds of things you see whenever you go into most people's houses, stuff like piles of folded laundry to be put away, some dishes in the sink, toys loose underfoot, everything finding its own strewn place, but for Daisy, when it began to happen, it meant there was maybe a quiet disaster occurring, a cave-in somewhere deep in the core. One time, a day just like this, kids frolicking about, our guests arrayed as usual around the backyard and the spread of piquant goodies on the patio table, Daisy sort of lost it. I don't know what happened exactly but maybe one of the kids bumped the other table where she was working the deep fryer, and the hot oil lipped over the edge and splashed the table and then spilled down onto her sandaled foot. I knew it happened because I saw her jump a little and leap back, and it occurred to me only later that she didn't shout or scream or make any sound at all. I went over to see if she was burned but before I could get there Daisy did the oddest thing: she picked up the fryer by the handles and turned it over and sort of body-slammed it on the table, the oil and chicken wings gushing out sideways, luckily in nobody's direction. I ran up and quickly yanked the extension cords apart and asked her if she was all right and she had this sickened look on her face and she said it was an accident and that she was sorry. By this time our guests had descended and I'm sure no one saw what had really happened, as everyone was appropriately concerned, but I knew and I got angry (if only because I was confused and a little scared) and yelled at her about being more careful. She started crying and that pretty much brought an end to the afternoon, most of our guests deciding to leave, among them some neighbors who never called us again.

Of course somewhere not so deep down none of what happened with the fryer was a surprise to me. From the moment I met her on the main floor at Gimbel's in the city, where she was offering sample sprays of men's cologne (I think it was Pierre Cardin, a huge phallic bottle of which I bought that day and may still have in the bottom of the bathroom vanity), I knew Daisy was volatile, like the crazy girl who haunts every neighborhood, the one always climbing fences and trees and eating flower petals and terrorizing the boys with sudden kisses and crotch-grabs. At Gimbel's Daisy sprayed me before I consented and then sprayed me again, and I would have been really pissed except she was amazingly bright-eyed and pretty and she had these perfect little hands with which she smoothed down my coat collar. She had a heavy accent to her English but she wasn't a tentative talker like some who come to this country and seem just to linger in the scenery and either peep-peep or else have to bark to get your attention. Daisy just let it all spill out in her messy exuberant froth of semi-language, clueless and charming and quite sexy, at least in that *me Tarzan you Jane* mode I welcome, with its promise of most basic romance.

For I had no idea what real craziness meant. I thought people like my father and my mother and my brother Bobby were off-kilter and in need of professional help. I didn't know what it was to be DSM-certified, described in the literature, perhaps totally nuts. And it was a month or so after the deep fryer incident that the first genuine trouble reared itself, when Daisy went off to Bloomingdale's and charged $7000 for a leather living room set and a full-length chinchilla coat. We had a terrific fight, me rabid with disbelief and Daisy defiant and bitter, talking about how she "knew class people" and mocking me for "working in dirt" like some peasant or field hand. Her eyes were wild and she was prac-tically spitting with hatred and I swear had she been wielding a knife I would be long in the grave.

I didn't know that the previous days in which she bought her-self and the kids several new outfits and served us filet mignon and lobsters and repainted our bedroom a deep Persian crimson trimmed in gold leaf were indicative of a grandiose run-up to a truly alarming finale; in fact, I was pretty pleased, for Daisy seemed happy and even ecstatic for the first time in a long time. She was lively with the kids and once again we were making love nightly, and though she worried me a little with her insomnia and solo drinking and 2 A.M. neighborhood walks in her nightgown I figured I was still way ahead of a lot of other guys with young families I knew, who were already playing the field and spending most of their free time away from the house. I tell you if Daisy hadn't blitzkrieged our net worth at Bloomingdale's nothing much would have changed; probably I wouldn't have cared if she was only steadily depleting our bank account, a time-honored way in our civilized world. But this was 1975, when the economy was basically shitting the bed, and Jack and Theresa were seven and six and I was making $20,000 a year at Battle Brothers, which was a hell of a lot of money, actually, and much more than I deserved. But $7000 for anything was of course ruinous, so I had to beg the store manager to take everything back (with a 10 percent restocking fee, plus delivery), and then cut up her charge cards and take away her bank passbook and start giving her the minimum cash allowance for the week's groceries and sundries and gas.

As you can imagine, Daisy wasn't exactly pleased with the arrangement. It was a suggestion/directive from Pop, whom I hadn't consulted directly but who had overheard my mother telling Aunt Vicky what her daughter-in-law had done. The next day Pop barreled into the messy double office we shared at the shop and plunked his backside onto my desk blotter and asked me what the hell I was doing. I had no clue what he was talking about, and as usual in those days I just stared up at him with my mouth half-crooked, indolently probing my upper molars with my tongue.

"I'm talking about *Daisy*," he growled, as if he were the one who had married her, as if he were the one having the troubles. I should mention that Pop always adored Daisy. From the second he met her it was clear, he could never stop talking about how gorgeous she was and how sexy and whenever they met he'd corral her with a big hug and kiss and then twirl her in a little cha-cha move, all of which Daisy welcomed and totally played into like she was Audrey Hepburn in *Roman Holiday*, just the kind of humoring and ass-kissing that my father has always lived for and measured everyone by.

"I hear she went on a spree at the department store and damn near bankrupted you."

"Not near," I said. "It was seven grand."

"Holy Jesus."

"But it's fixed now. I'm making it go away."

"Damn it, Jerome, it's just going to happen again! Don't you know how to handle your wife yet?"

"I think I've learned something in these last eight years, yes."

"Bullshit. Listen to me. Are you listening, Jerome? This is what I'm telling you. You have to squash her every once in while, I mean completely flatten her. Otherwise a beautiful woman like Daisy gets big ideas, and those ideas get bigger every year. If she were a plain sedan like your mother you wouldn't have to worry, you'd only have to deal with a certain displacement, you know what I mean? But with a sleek machine, you've got to tool a governer onto the sucker, do something to cut her fuel."

"I have no idea what you're talking about, Pop."

"What I'm saying is you've got to be a little brutal. Not always, just every once in a while. Now is a good time. All this women's-libbing and bra burning is confusing everybody. Treat her badly, don't give her any money or attention or even a chance to bitch or argue. Don't let her leave the house for a week. Then when she's really down in the dumps bring her some diamond earrings or a string of pearls and take her out to a lobster dinner. After, screw her brains out, or whatever you can manage. Then everything will go back to normal, you'll see."

"And how do you know any of this works, if Ma isn't that kind of woman?"

"Trust your Pop, Jerome. I have wide experience. And if that doesn't do it, call Dr. Derricone."

Yeah, yeah, yeah, I must have said, to get him off my desk and case. But that very night when I got home Daisy was undertaking a complete overhaul of our house décor; she was going through a couple of hundred fabric swatches piled on the kitchen table, she had four or five different dining room chairs, some Persian rugs, several china and silver patterns, she had odd squares of linoleum and porcelain floor tile; she had even begun painting the dining and living room with sample swaths of paint, quart cans of which lay out still opened, used brushes left on the rims, dripping. For dinner she was heating up some leftover pasta on the stovetop. In the den the kids were watching TV, rolling popcorn in baloney slices for their predinner snack, and then spitting streams of Dr Pepper at each other through the gaps in their front teeth. When I asked her what the heck was going on Daisy simply looked up from her work and answered that she couldn't decide between a shiny or not-so-shiny silk for the living room curtains and what did I think?

She was grinning, though sort of painfully, like part of her could see and hear the miserable scene and understood that another part was taking over, and probably winning. I couldn't holler right then the way I wanted to, and instead just grumbled my usual "Whatever, dear" and went to the bedroom and stripped out of my dusty workclothes and turned on the water in the shower as hot as I could bear, because there's nothing like a good near-scald to set you right again, take you out of a time line, set you momentarily free. And suddenly I was even feeling a little chubby down there with the hot trickles in my crack and so gave myself a couple exploratory tugs but maybe I was still too pissed (which is usually plenty good reason), when Daisy opened the shower door and stepped inside, paint-splattered clothes and all.

"Jerry," she said, crying, I think, through the billowing steam, "Jerry, I'm sorry."

I didn't answer and she said it again, said my name again, with her rolling, singsong, messed up Rs, and I hugged her, clutching her beneath the spray.

"So hot!" she gasped, recoiling, and I let go, but she grabbed back on and held me tight, tighter and tighter until she got used to the temperature. Then she kissed me, and kissed me again, and when I kissed her back I thought I was tasting something mineral, like thinner or paint, but when we broke for air I could see the faded wash of pink on her chin, on her mouth, as she'd bitten her tongue trying to stand the hot water.

I pointed the shower head away from us and she took off her wet clothes and she said "Make love to me" and we started to screw on the built-in bench of the shower stall, something we hadn't done since we first bought the house, before Jack was even born. I remember Daisy being five months pregnant and showing in a way I didn't expect to be so attractive (both our kids, by the way, were tiny when they born, barely six pounds full-term), the smooth, sheened bulge of her belly and her popped out bellybutton and the changed size and color of her nipples, long like on baby bottles and the color of dark caramels. Daisy was not voluptuous, which I liked, her long, lean torso and shortish Asian legs (perfectly hairless) and her breasts that weren't so full and rounded but shaped rather in the form of gently pitched dunes, those delicate pale hillocks. I realize I may be waxing pathetic here, your basic sorry white dude afflicted with what Theresa refers to as "Saigon syndrome" (*Me so hor-ny, G.I. Joe!*) and fetishizing once again, but I'm not sorry because the fact is I found her desirable precisely because she was put together differently from what I was used to, as it were, totally unlike the wide-hipped Italian or leggy Irish girls or the broad-bottomed Polish chicks from Our Lady of Wherever I was raised on since youth, who compared to Daisy seemed pretty dreadful contraptions.

Unfair, I know, unfair.

Though that evening in the shower eight years into our marriage I wasn't so enamored of Daisy as I was hopeful for any break in her strange mood and behaviors. I thought (or so I thought later) that some good coarse sex might disturb the disturbance, shunt aside the offending system, and it might have worked had our little Theresa not opened the shower door and stood watching for God knows how long as I was engaging her mother in the doggie-style stance we tended to employ when things between us weren't perfectly fine. (Note: I've always suspected that it was this very scene that set Theresa on her lifelong disinclination for whatever I might say or do, and though she's never mentioned it and would reject the notion out of hand for being too reductionist/ Freudian, I'm plain sorry for it and hate to think that knocking about somewhere in her memory is a grainy washed-out Polaroid of me starring as The Beast or The Rapist.) Daisy must have peered around and seen Theresa standing there sucking on her thumb and shoved me off so hard I slipped and fell onto my back, providing a second primal sighting of me in my engorgement that made Theresa actually step back. I covered myself and asked her what she wanted and she couldn't answer and then Daisy yelled at her to tell us.

Theresa said, "The macaroni is on fire, and Jack can't put it out."

"Take care of her!" I said to Daisy, and then I grabbed a towel to wrap myself with and ran down the long bedroom hall and then the next hall down to the kitchen, where Jack was tossing handfuls of water at the frying pan roaring up in flames. The steam and smoke were pooling at the ceiling, and I quickly pulled

Jack away into the dining room; he impressively fought me a little, trying to go back, to fight the good fight. He was always a com-
mendable kid, earnest and vigorous, and for a long time (right up
through high school) I really thought he might become a cop or a
fireman as most young boys say they want to be at one point or another; I could always see him donning a uniform, strapping on
that studly *stuff,* charging hard with his mind unfettered into the
maw of peril, "just doing his job." Sometimes it still surprises me
how damn entrepreneurial he is now, what a *multitasking* guy he's
become, as the term goes, though I wonder if being a CEO really
suits him, even if it is heading a fundamentally working-class outfit like ours.

"Dad, it's burning the metal," he said, pointing to the steel
hood above the stove, its painted surface blackening.

"Stay right here," I told him, tamping down on his shoulders,
"okay?"

"Okay."

I rushed in and knelt below the range top and opened the bottom drawer of the stove, where Daisy kept the pot lids, searching
for one large enough to cover the big skillet. I found one and tossed
it on but it was about an inch shy all around and the flames only
flickered low for a second, then vengefully leaped up again. Daisy
always used a lot of butter or oil, and so I took off my bath towel
and folded it and tried to smother the whole thing, the fire licking
up where I wasn't pressing hard enough, singeing my forearm and
chest hairs and making me instantly consider all things from the
narrow, terrified view of my fast shrinking privates. Then Jack ran
forward and tried to help by tugging down the edge of the towel.
I picked him up and carried him to the living room and practically
hurled him into one of the as-yet-unreturned sofas, shouting "Stay
put!" and also warning him not to soil the upholstery, if he valued
his life. But by then the towel had caught fire and instinctively I

did exactly what Jack had already tried, splashing on water with my hands and then a coffee mug, which did no good at all. So I finally took the skillet by the handle and opened the sliding door to the deck and stepped out. The deck was cedar and I didn't know what else to do but maybe toss it over the edge onto the back lawn. The firelight caught the attention of our back neighbors, the Lipschers, who were throwing a small dinner party on their patio. I'd spoken to the husband maybe once or twice, the wife three or four times; we'd invited them over a couple of times for barbecues but they never actually made it over. They were into tony, Manhattan-type gatherings, with candles and French wine and testy, clever conversations (you could hear every word from our deck) about Broadway plays or Israel or their favorite Caribbean islands, everyone constantly interrupting everyone else in their bid to impress, all in tones that said they weren't. Though the sight of me clearly got their attention. Someone at their table said, "Look at that!," and with the skillet in one hand I kind of waved with the other, the Lipschers and their guests limply waving back, and for some reason it didn't seem neighborly to chuck the frying pan and so I just held it out in full flambé, Daisy now stepping out in her towel with the kids in tow, all of us waiting for the fire to die out. It took a while. When it finally did Barry Lipscher said, "Hey there, Battle, you want to end the show now? We're still eating here, if you don't mind."

To this Daisy unhooked her bath sheet and wrapped it around my waist, then turned to the Lipschers and guests in all her foxy loveliness and gave them the finger. If I remember right, Theresa did the same, Jack and I grinning idiotically as we trailed our women inside the house.

But in truth, I'm afraid, it didn't quite end up as nicely as all that, young family Battle triumphant in solidarity, chuckling over the charred cabinetry and the toasty scent of burnt pasta.

"Clean this up," I said to Daisy, my voice nothing but a cold instrument. "We'll talk tomorrow."

The next day I instituted what Pop had suggested, basically placing Daisy under house arrest for the week (no car keys, no credit cards, $20 cash), and promising her that I'd never speak to her again unless she sent back all the samples and swatches and kept the house in an acceptable state and made proper meals for the kids and checked with me from that point on before she bought anything—I mean *anything*—other than staples like milk and bread or underwear or school supplies. Back in those days I could actually utter such a thing, threaten someone like that, even a loved one, and I have to say that I regularly did. I naturally got into the habit at Battle Brothers, hollering at the fellas all day and lecturing my subcontractors and sometimes even talking tough to my customers, if they became too clingy or whiny or just plain pains in the ass, which at some point in every job they all did. But maybe it wasn't so much the habit itself as it was its effectiveness that I kept returning to, how reliably I could get all sorts of people to move it or jump or shut the hell up. People say that I'm like Pop that way, that I'll get this expression on my face, this certain horrific look, like whatever you're saying or doing is the most sickening turn, this instant disease, and that for you not to desist seems purely contemptible, a veritable crime against humanity. And then I'll say what I want to have happen, what I want done, as I did that day to Daisy. She could hardly look at me as she sat on the edge of the tub as I shaved, her straight hair screening her face like those beaded curtains we all used to have, her palms pressed down against the porcelain, her elbows locked. I repeated myself and left for work and didn't call all day and when I got back (a little early, for I had the horrible thought that the house might be burning down) the whole place was peerlessly clean and quiet and the kids were in the den playing (Jack) and reading (Theresa) and there was a tuna casserole bubbling away in the oven, four place settings sparkling and ready on the kitchen table. The only thing missing was Daisy. I asked the kids where she was and they didn't know. I looked out back and in the street. Then I went into our bedroom to change, which was empty but trimmed out and neat, and when I walked into the bathroom, there Daisy was, still dressed in her pink robe with the baby blue piping, sitting on the edge of the tub exactly as she had been eight hours earlier, as if she'd been cast right into the cool porcelain.

"I fixed the house," she said, her voice husky, dried-out.

"Yeah," I said, just like I might to the guys, as though it was simply what I expected. It's always best, when you're trying to get things done, to utter the absolute minimum. You made it rain? Okay. You moved Heaven and Earth? Fine. This, too, was part of my general studies education à la Pop; he's the one who showed me how effective it can be to say grindingly little at the very moments you ought to say a lot, when you could easily be sappy and effusive and overgenerous with praise or forgiveness, when you could tender all you had and no one would ask for anything extra in return.

I know. I know about this. I do.

So when Daisy went on to say, "The other stuff, too. I got rid of it all. I did what you want, Jerry," what did I say back but simply, "Right," with a slight tip of the noggin, with a tough-guy grunt, which you'd think would be just what Daisy had had to deal with all her inscrutable Oriental/Asian life, and probably had, and was part of the reason she'd ended up with someone like me, some average American Guido she'd figure would have more than plenty to say, entreating every second with his hands and his hips and with his heart blithering on his sleeve.

Daisy didn't say anything and neither did I and for a moment our normally cramped en suite bath got very large in feeling, the only sound coming from the running toilet tank, this wasteful ever-wash I've always meant to fix but never actually have, even to this day. Daisy got up then and brushed past me and I could hear her walk out of our bedroom and down the hallway to the kitchen. I showered and changed and when I got to the table the kids were already eating their dinner, as usual furiously wolfing their food like a pair of street urchins who'd stolen into a cake shop. Daisy was making up my plate. As little kids, Jack and Theresa were forever hungry, a trait only parents must know to be peerlessly endearing, and the only time I can remember them not eating was after Daisy was buried and we had a gathering at the house, the two of them sitting glumly on the sofa, a plate of cold shrimp and capicola balanced between them on their legs.

Daisy set down my dinner and she sat, too, but wasn't eating. After serving all of us seconds she took our plates and began cleaning up. The kids chattered back and forth but Daisy and I didn't say a word to each other. In the morning, breakfast was the same, and it was like that for the rest of that week and the next. Finally I got tired of the whole thing and when he asked I told Pop his method was fine save for the rageful misery and silences. He told me to keep it in my pants a bit longer, that I'd break her and also break myself of "the need to please her all the time," and that he and Nonna would stop by on Saturday to run interference. I asked him to just come over and play with the kids, so I could patch things up with Daisy, maybe take a drive to Robert Moses and sit on the grassy dunes and tell/beg her that I wished for our life to be normal again, though in truth their visit would mean that Nonna would take the kids out to the playground or to a matinee and then somehow cobble together a gut-busting dinner of meatballs and sausages and pasta and a roast, with Pop haranguing me about the state of our business and then inevitably bringing up Bobby, which he did anytime we spent more than an hour together.

When my folks arrived Daisy was still in the bedroom getting dressed. No matter her state of mind or what was going on she always pulled herself together for them, and particularly for Pop. She'd wear her newest outfits and full evening makeup and jewelry and maybe she'd tie a little rolled silk scarf around her neck, which gave her a fetchingly game barmaid look. Pop of course lapped it up. He loved how she made silly mistakes with her English and always laughed at his jokes and patiently listened to all his stories and theories and opinions about the brutality of man and falsity of religion and the conspiring forces of a New World Order that would enslave all good men in a randy socialist vise-grip of eco-feminism and bisexuality and miscegenation (not withstanding my and Daisy's lovely offspring). Daisy, I really have to say, always kissed his ass, and I don't really know why, as there was never anyone else but Pop who could elicit that kind of humoring and attention from her, no one I'm sure except for Bobby Battle, M.I.A. (the best degree, for Immortality), whom she met a couple of times only but I know would have loved.

Daisy floated out in a new hot-pink-with-white-polka-dot silk mini-dress and matching scarf tied around her throat as mentioned, with a white hair band holding up her black-as-black tresses. As annoyed as you might be with her you couldn't help but think she looked good enough to eat. She kissed my mother, who was already unloading the fridge of everything that we might possibly eat for dinner, culling as she went for mold and wilt and freezer burn. My mother, God bless her soul, was nothing if not dependable. It's a terrible thing to admit, but I used to think she wasn't the swiftest doe in the forest, because she rarely did anything else but keep house and feed everybody and try to make Pop's life run smoothly and comfortably, even as he was often a jerk to her and had several love affairs and was universally acknowledged to be a Hall of Fame jerk. She rarely read the newspaper and never read a book and wasn't even interested in movies or television, her main personal activity being shopping for clothes, not haute couture but sort of Queens Boulevard country club, bright bold colors and white patent leather bags and shoes and bugeye sunglasses. Every once in a while on no special occasion Pop would spring for a marble-sized diamond ring or a string of fat pearls, and I suspect it was my mother exacting tribute for his latest exposed dalliance. Lately I've been thinking that her lack was more emotional than intellectual; it wasn't because the gray matter didn't work well enough but that she preferred to keep her life as uncomplicated as possible, more thought and rumination leading only to misery and remorse and the realization that she could never leave him, that she could never really start over again.

Daisy twirled for my father and said, "What you think, Pop?"

"Gorgeous, doll, gorgeous." Pop used *doll* whenever they were together, *Your old lady* or *Your wife* when speaking about her to me.

"I got it at Macy's," she said, hardly glancing over. "It wasn't on sale price, but I couldn't wait."

"On you, it's a bargain at twice the price."

"You super guy, Pop."

"But I'm speechless at this moment," he said, smiling his Here's-how-to-handle-a-woman smile. "As Santayana once said, 'Beauty as we feel it is something indescribable; what it is or what it means can never be said.'"

"You too much, Pop!"

"Is this a liver or a beefsteak?" Nonna said, holding up a frozen brown slab.

No one answered, as no one knew.

Nonna, accustomed to the nonreply, said, "I hope it's a beef-steak."

"The dress looks real good," I said to Daisy, feeling I should utter something, bring at least some bread to the table, if not wine. And then I was all set to offer even more, maybe I was going to suggest running her right out to the department store and buying a bauble to go with the pretty dress, some earrings maybe, when Pop pulled a long dark blue velveteen jewelry case from his pocket and presented it to Daisy.

"For me?"

"Of course it's for you, doll. Open it."

She cracked the lid. It was a string of freshwater pearls, the beads small but delicate and dazzling in their iridescence. It was amazingly tasteful, even for Pop, who always surprised you with his eye for finish and detail, which somehow was more Park Avenue than Arthur Avenue.

"Look, Jerry, look what Pop got!" Daisy said.

"A customer of mine imports these from Japan, and he gave me a nice rate on them. They're just as good as Mikimotos."

"It's not my birthday even," Daisy said, hushed by the glitter in her hands. "This is so nice. This is so pretty."

"Call it a reward, for all the hardship of the last couple of weeks. Ask Nonna over there. It's no picnic, putting up with us Battle men. We're stubborn and prideful and we ask no less than the world of our women. The world. Your husband Jerome here is no different. We all know he can be sullen, but that's because he's always been too serious. Not like Bobby, who knew what real fun was. He was just like you. So you better learn patience, with this one."

Pop tousled my hair, and I let him, because incredulity freezes you, because I was like that back then, because Pop was Pop and I wasn't. Daisy was the one who stopped him, if only because she was hugging him, kissing him on the forehead and cheek, hooting a little, practically vibrating with glee and gratitude. Nonna had already ceased paying further attention to the scene, gone back to the daily calculus of how to make a meal from what was at hand. The kids ran in from outside and Pop had a handful of hard candies for them, as usual, toffees and sours and butterscotches. This was the minor parade my father always finessed for himself, wherever he went: my wife and kids, joyous with the old man. I drifted around the gleeful huddle and asked Nonna if she needed anything.

"I don't think so, honey," she said, never, ever ironical. She was scraping the freezer burn from the ice-hard meat, a little pile of root-beer-colored shavings collecting at the edge of her knife blade. "I think I have everything I need."

IN THE WEEKS AFTER Pop came bearing gifts, everything pretty much went to shit. It did, it really did, though not in the manner I thought it would. I figured I'd be the one generating the enmity, the one beaming out the negative vibes, the go-to-hell shine first thing in the morning and stay-on-your-side rays before clicking off the bedside lamp at night. I thought Pop's stunt (which I should have been ready for) and Daisy's giddy celebrations would lend me the pissy high ground, at least for a few days, long enough to keep Daisy on the defensive and not out there spending our future, long enough so I could figure out how to fix the problem without forever placing her under house arrest. But the fact was, Daisy was the one who took further umbrage. She wouldn't speak to me, not a word, her silence made that much more unpleasant by the fact that she seemed livelier and brighter in her dealings with everyone else.

Did the time mark a strange kind of renaissance for her? Was it, in language Theresa might employ, an epochal turn? I really don't know about that. What's clear to me is that Daisy pretty much exploded with life, and our life, as it went, exploded right along with her. Up to then, my basic conception of crazy was still the one I'd held since youth, the picture of a raven-haired Irish girl named Clara who climbed the trees in her pleated Catholic-school skirt not wearing underwear and lobbed Emily Dickinson down to me in a wraithlike voice (*I cannot be with You/It would be Life/and Life is over there/Behind the Shelf*), my trousers clingy with fear and arousal.

With Daisy, I didn't know, nor did anyone else, for that matter, including Dr. Derricone, the extent of her troubles, the ornate reach and complication. Those initial shopping sprees would in the end seem like the smallest indiscretions, filched candy from the drugstore, a lingering ass pat at a neighborhood cocktail party, nothing you couldn't slough off with a laugh, nothing you couldn't later recall with some fondness even, with wistful rue.

The first thing was, she would hardly sleep. If at all. After Pop *venit* and *vidit* and *vincit* that weekend and she stopped talking to me, Daisy's metabolism went into overdrive. We usually went to bed at 11 or so, after the news for me and maybe a bath for her, but she started getting up at 5 in the morning, and then 4 and 3 and 2, until it got to the point when she didn't even get *ready* for bed, not bothering to change into a nightgown or brush her teeth or even take a soak. A couple times in the middle of the night I awoke to the *plash-plash* of water, and I peered through the curtains to see, in lovely silhouette, Daisy paddling around in the pool with the inner tube hooped beneath her arms. She was naked, just going back and forth, back and forth, and I had the thought that I should go out there and keep her company. But I desperately needed my sleep back then (these days it's a different story, as I lie in wait for the muted *thwap* of the morning paper on the driveway) and rather than get up I know exactly what I did, which was to just fall back into the pillow and scratch at myself half-mast and maybe dream in sentimental hues of gorgeous black swans, who must always swim alone.

After a couple weeks I didn't even notice that Daisy was never in bed. She probably slept a couple of hours while the kids were watching TV, but I can't be sure of that. As for sex, it wasn't happening, and not just because of the fact that she decided not to talk to me. Pure talk was never that important to us anyway, even at the beginning, when it was mostly joking and flirting, for though her English was more than passable it was just rudimentary enough for us to stay clear of in-depth and nuanced discussions, which suited me fine. The truth was that while I was hungering for her I had an equally keen desire to hold out as long as I could stand, because if she had any power over me it was certainly sexual power, which, most other things being equal, is what all women should easily have over all men. Daisy could always, please forgive me, float my boat, top my prop, she could always crank up the generators at any moment and make me feel that every last cell in my body was overjuiced and soon-to-be-derelict if not immediately *launched* toward something warm and soft. In her own way she was a performer, as they say actors can be when they enter a room; something in them switches on and suddenly everybody is pointed right at them, abject with confused misery and love.

And this really happened, mostly while I was slumbering. I don't know how many times she did it, but one night the doorbell rang and roused me from a deep sleep and I trudged tingling in the limbs to the door to find my wife wrapped in a big blue poly tarp with a burly young officer of the local law standing behind her waving a long flashlight.

"Are you the head of this household, sir?" he asked, momentarily blinding me with the beam, and fully waking me up.

"You wanna kill the light, chief?"

"Sorry, sir," he said, slipping the flashlight into his belt. "Are you the head of household?"

"If you mean am I the owner, then yes."

"Is this your wife?"

I looked at Daisy, who just looked glum and down in the mouth, as if this whole thing was yet another chore of her unglamorous life.

"Yes. She's my wife."

"She was at the elementary school, in the playground there. There was a complaint."

"What? Is it illegal, to be over there?"

"I believe there's a school grounds curfew, sir, but that wasn't the whole problem."

"Oh yeah?"

Daisy then said, "Just cut it out, Jerry. Good night, officer. Thanks for the ride home." She tippy-toed and pecked him on the cheek, and then stepped inside. "Oh, this is yours."

She peeled the tarp from herself, and handed it to him. She was wearing only sneakers, white Keds with the blue pencil stripe on the rubber. The young cop thanked her and said good night, like it was a goddamned date or something. Daisy disappeared inside.

The cop said, "Sir, if you could please tell your wife I'll have to cite her the next time."

"There's not going to be a goddamn next time!"

"I'm just saying . . ."

"Good night," I said, and I slammed the door.

I found Daisy in the kitchen, making tuna-and-egg salad for a sandwich. She had the eggs going at furious boil in the stockpot, the bread in the toaster, she had the jars of mayonnaise and mustard and sweet pickle relish out on the counter, she had the celery and carrot and onion on the cutting board, and she had the ice blue German chef's knife in her hand, the one Pop had given her at Christmas. But the strange thing was that she did it all so casually, as if a nude woman in sneakers chopping vegetables at three in the morning after a neighborhood police sweep was *de rigueur* around here, our customary midsummer night's dream.

"What the hell are you doing?"

"I'm hungry. You want to eat, too?"

"No, I don't."

"You have trouble sleeping?"

"What do you think, Daisy?"

She didn't answer, engrossed as she was in the julienned stalks of carrot and celery. She was working carefully but fast, making perfect dices as she went, the crisp *chock-chock-chock* of the blade on the cutting board undoubtedly keeping time with her ever-quickening synaptic pulses. I didn't want to disturb her, I was going to wait until she was done, but maybe it was my state of angry half-sleep or the searingly bright fluorescent kitchen lights or the notion of my supple-bodied immigrant wife tooling around in a squad car with a wide-eyed cop, that I had to holler, "This is total shit!"

She looked around with unfeigned gravity and said, "Go back to sleep, Jerry."

"This is going to stop," I said. "You're going to see Dr. Derricone tomorrow. I'll go with you."

"Go to sleep, Jerry."

"You're going to see him about this, and I mean it this time. No more ranting at him. No more threats. No more scenes with his receptionist."

"He's a *complete fool*," she said, with a perfect, and faintly English, accent, as though she'd heard some actress say the phrase in a TV movie or soap. Daisy was a talented mimic, when she got the feeling. *"They are all complete and utter fools."*

"I don't care if you think he's the King of Siam. Dr. Derricone has been around a long time and you'll show him respect. He's seen it all and he's going to help you. I made him promise, and though you treat him like dirt he's not giving up."

"I don't want help from him, or nobody!" she cried, confusingly, though of course I knew what she meant.

"That's it, now, Daisy! I mean it. I've had enough!"

"Me too!" she shouted, in fact really screamed, and I thought about the kids for a second, how they'd wake up to their mother's distressed cry and probably think I was doing something horrible to her, like flicking a backhand at her or grabbing at her throat, which I never, ever did. But the whole truth be told, in those days I let myself think about such things every now and then, I too easily imagined picking her petite body up and flinging her onto the bed like you might a cat, mostly because you thought she could handle it, and that the ugly pleasurable surge would somehow satisfy the moment and make everything good and right. Spoken like a veritable wife beater, I realize, and I really can't defend myself, except to say that Daisy was never a completely passive or feckless party in our troubles, she being ever ready to say or do whatever it took to make me feel the afflictions settled so insolvently within her.

"Quiet down," I told her. "You'll wake up the kids."

"I don't care!" she cried, and then that's when it happened. She lunged at me, in her splendid nakedness, knife and all, her eyes dull with dark no-method, with the chill of empty space. And I will tell you that I froze, not so much with fear (of which there was plenty) as with a kind of abstention, for the horror of what was happening was too realistic to even begin to consider; it was actually enough to make me say, *I must depart, I must depart* (perhaps this the seed of my eventual interest in flight), and not mind whatever the rest. And the significant detail (of the rest) is not that Daisy missed my throat with the chef's knife by a mere thumb's-width, jabbing the point into the door of the refrigerator a good two inches beneath the vinyl skin (the perfect slit is still there, rusty around the pushed-in edges), but that when we both fully returned to the moment, our faces almost touching, we each saw in the other the same amazing wish that she'd not flinched and hit her mark.

Not that I didn't want to live.

I did want to live, just not that way.

Daisy, suddenly scared out of her craziness, broke down and collapsed in a naked heap on the linoleum floor, crying her eyes out.

So with the first light good Dr. Derricone appeared with his scuffed black visiting bag, and before the kids were even awake he gave Daisy a sample bottle of Valium with instructions to keep taking them as long as she felt, as he put it, "Too frisky." I don't know what a trained specialist would have said, what a psychiatrist or psychologist would diagnose as her particular state or behavior and duly prescribe; I wasn't even thinking of "the right thing to do," but was instead just needing to jam hard on the brakes, do whatever it took to stop the train, indeed, do just what Theresa would no doubt say was my only modality and like most lazy modern men compel the desired result with the most available and efficient measure on hand, which often, not surprisingly, takes the form of another lazy modern man but with better credentials. Frank Derricone was Ma and Pop's doctor; he'd delivered me and Bobby and dozens of my cousins and nephews and then Jack and Theresa, and he was indeed a general practitioner of the grand old school, in that he believed in his skills across the disciplines, that good doctoring, as in most professions, was a matter of common sense, empirically applied. This salty view had no doubt served him well for the thirty years up to that point, and for the twenty or so more years afterward, and I don't doubt that Daisy was but among a handful of his patients who didn't end up healthy and long-lived. And while I don't blame Frank Derricone in the least— I'm not the one who can, not in any scenario or space/time continuum or alternate universe I can come up with—I do naturally wonder what might have been, and can't ignore what the good doctor said to me at a party in honor of his retirement, that it probably wasn't the best thing to have kept Daisy on sedatives after she'd come down from her manic heights, in that period of trough. For who really imagined that there could be a state grayer than that for our mad, happy Daisy, lower than low, beneath the bottom, when suddenly it was all she could do to lift herself out of the bed in the morning and drag a brush through her tangled, unwashed hair? Who knew that while I was at work and the kids were at day camp she'd steadily medicate herself on the back patio with Valiums and a case of beer, and on one stifling summer afternoon in August go so far as to induce herself into a dream of buoyancy, such that she, unclothed as preferred, drifted floatless into the pool, perhaps paddling a calm yard or two, before flying, like a seabird, straight down to the bottom.

five

A STORY IN THE NEWS has caught my eye in recent days. It concerns a guy about my age who is trying to balloon around the world, solo. No surprise that he's a billionaire, some slightly daft and extra fit British entrepreneur with knighthood, Sir Harold Clarkson-Ickes, who's making his third attempt at spanning the globe. Of course he's not up there in his silvery high-altitude upside-down dewdrop float *absolutely* alone; he's got several laptops and a satellite linkup and digital cameras set up such that the whole world can check up on him via the Internet. You can track his flight path and the coming weather patterns and browse still pictures of him working his instruments and making himself hot cocoa in his mini-microwave and looking terribly brave, if cold. You can even send Sir Harold an e-mail, which the website says he promises to answer, if not in flight then afterward, *When the mission is complete.*

I wasn't planning to e-mail him, as I figured he had plenty to do and probably had thousands of e-mails jamming his in-box, but last night, driving back from Jack and Eunice's party, and not having talked to Theresa about *that* (she called Paul to say she was staying out late to go to the city with Jadie and Alice), I heard on the radio that Sir Harold had entered a massive storm somewhere over the Indian Ocean. After getting into bed and tossing restlessly for a couple hours I went to the study and turned on the computer. There was no new information on the website, only that his last verified position was some six hours old, the point at which he was likely to have entered the eye of the system and his GPS signal flickered out. I didn't know exactly what I was feeling about the situation, but I found myself typing out this message:

Sir Harold! We go with you into the vortex! Stay the lofty course! Godspeed!

—an American friend

I intentionally used the exclamation points, as I imagined the winds wickedly whipping and tossing him around, and wanted to convey the sense that our hearts and minds were truly with him, up there in his high-tech basket. As for the crusty tone, I figured what else comes naturally to such moments for explorers and their fans, and hoped, too, that he'd appreciate my lame attempt at speaking his language, as Kelly Stearns or Miles Quintana will do for me in their respective ways, and see as a note of goodwill. And all in all it was probably better than "Keep your head down, chief," which is the advice I generally dispense for most situations, no matter the weather, if I even bother to give it anymore.

My interest in Sir Harold is somewhat unusual, as there was never a time in my life when I was known to be a *fan*, of anyone or anything, even when I was still a bachelor and living on my own and not yet fully involved with Battle Brothers. You'd think a fairly sportive, not unconventional guy like me wouldn't mind hooking on to the fortunes of, say, a hometown team, to lend a little modulation to his days, a little virtual drama, and thereby connect with the necessary direness and commonality of this life. That and having a socially acceptable mode of publicly acting out, which is a form of pleasure that your sometimes overintellectualized types (perhaps like Theresa and Paul) and those others long cosseted by a tad too much safety and comfort (perhaps like yours truly) don't or can't quite appreciate anymore.

Sure, I tagged along a couple times with some guys on the crews to a Giants game at the Stadium, but I couldn't quite muster the flushed-neck hoorahs of my spittle-laced compadres, and I'd only rise halfway to the occasion, getting up on my toes for a big play and groaning in concert with the thousands and drinking maybe one jumbo brew too many. Afterward I'd just trudge down the banked exit ramp with only a syncopated tic in my gut, a half-lurch like nothing really got started, never quite feeling the pure sheer liberty that comes from stomping your feet and hollering out your lungs because some burly throwback with a digit sewn onto his shirt has just dived for and reached a certain chalk mark on the field.

I waited for another fifteen minutes, sifting through the cluttered nil of the Web, which to me feels like a flaky neighbor's junky attic, then checked my e-mail, but of course there was no answer, and I woke up this morning actually thinking first about Sir Harold rather than Theresa, wondering whether he had come out of the storm and was still floating, or else scuttled at the bottom of the seas. I then felt a grave jolt of guilt, though one I'm accustomed to, and I tried to think it was simply what Rita would deem my deeply lazy emotional response, but even I couldn't bear the thought that I could be that anemic, and so I called over to Jack's house when the hour at last seemed appropriate, meaning a couple ticks past 8 A.M.

Theresa answered the phone, catching me totally off-guard.

"What's up, Jerry?" she said, sounding fresh and snappy.

"You're up. You went out last night?"

"Yup. Alice and Jadie and I had dinner at a bistro in Tribeca, and then danced at a club. It was a blast. We got back at three in the morning."

"Should you be doing that?"

"Why not? I feel great."

"Come on, Theresa," I said, trying my best to be calm. "I had a conversation with Paul."

"Oh yeah. I heard."

"You heard."

"I was going to talk to you, but I'm kind of glad he went ahead."

"You mean about you being pregnant, or the fact that you're seriously ill?"

"Hey, Jerry," she said, that old unleavened tone instantly rising. "Take it easy."

"Are you serious? Those are two pretty damn big things. I wonder when the hell you were going to tell me what was going on."

"You're the first."

"Thanks, honey."

She paused. "Of course I was going to, about the pregnancy, but it was too early. And then when it wasn't, we found out about the other thing. It got complicated, and I thought we should wait."

"Wait for what, the 'other thing' to kill you?"

"I'm sorry you're so mad."

"How can I be mad?" I said, thinking that there were probably a thousand ways I could be, though none of them very useful. And all of a sudden I had the feeling that I was talking to a much younger version of myself, she being perhaps even more like me than her brother, whom I'd always considered the one who took after me.

I said, taking a breath, "I assume Jack doesn't know yet."

"I'm going to try to talk to him today. When we get back from the doctor."

"Who is this doctor?"

"She's the wife of a grad school friend, at Yale–New Haven. Don't worry, she's an expert."

"Look, I'm sorry I have to say this, but can you tell me what the hell you think you're doing?"

"I'm doing what I can."

"But what's the point of experts if you won't let them do anything?"

"You have to trust me, all right?" she said, quiet and serious. "Okay, Dad?"

I couldn't answer, as the *Dad* part unexpectedly knocked around inside my chest and throat for an extended beat.

"Paul's already outside. We were just leaving."

"Come pick me up. I'll go with you. I'll keep Paul company in the waiting room."

"I don't think so," she said, firmly, the way I do when I believe the conversation is over. "I promise, we'll come back with a full report."

"When will that be?"

"Dinnertime. Or maybe not. We'll call. Paul and I want to shop a little in the city. But we're going to stay with you from now on, right?"

"What do you think? Of course you are. I'll get your room ready."

"Thanks. Gotta go."

"We're going to talk about this, Theresa. Really talk. I mean it."

"I know. See you later. Bye."

After we clicked off, though, I began to wonder what I'd really say to her and Paul, when they came back with nothing different, to thus continue with their Christian Scientist–style plan of waiting out the "other thing," which of course is pure unalloyed madness, and exactly *not* what I, or anyone else in my family line, would do, or so I'd hope; besides this, you'd think such a thoroughly hip and progressive postmodern/postcolonial type woman like Theresa, who marched on our nation's capital at least a half dozen times in her youth for a woman's right to choose and unionism and the environment and affirmative action et cetera, would do as any other liberal overeducated professional-class person would do in her situation, which is hand-wring and wallow in self-pitying angst and consult countless other liberal overeducated professionals before "finally" coming to the "difficult decision" to cut one's losses (you know what I'm talking about) and move on, which is what most other people (like me) would decide to do in about a half minute, underscoring the notion that most of us (at least in this centrist Western world) are pretty much of the same mind, though we believe in and require vastly different processes in the getting there.

Of course I spent several hours online doing all sorts of searches on the disease, there being an astounding amount of material and hot links and hospital and pharma company sponsored sites on Hodgkin's and non-Hodgkin's lymphoma, and soon enough realized that I could search within these for pregnancy issues. This second stage of Googling/Yahooing, however, yielded surprisingly few "results," and what there was only outlined predictably general recommendations for what a woman in Theresa's situation might do, the basic wisdom (no surprise) being that you treated the cancer as soon as the baby was born (or prematurely induced if the condition of the mother was serious), or the pregnancy was "terminated," either way trying to ensure the best "outcome" for both but then certainly favoring the health of the mother over that of the fetus, though of course this was never actually expressed. What seemed clear, though, was that the *time* of diagnosis would determine whether (if early) you would end things right away and move on and hope you could get pregnant after you were cured, or (if late) you would make the best of it, as long as that seemed prudent. Nowhere did I read any mention about an early diagnosis *and* riding it out, as if that scenario weren't the purview of medical professionals but some other more philosophically capable group.

So the question is, How, then, does our own Theresa Battle resolve to take the path of essentially a person of faith (or epochal stubbornness)? I don't know. Perhaps it's that I never introduced her to the ready comforts of institutionalized religion, even after her mother died, or that her intellectual studies were in good measure predicated upon the Impossibility of Meaning, or that our tidy post-Daisy troika has really been the loose association of three very separate, unconnected beings, who share only the minimum genetic material and the securely grounded belief that a full belly makes for a carefree, loafing soul (zealous eaters that we are). Maybe it shouldn't surprise me at all, then, that Theresa should take a whopping leap right here and choose for the moment her fetus's life over her own (despite the chances that neither might make it), and commit to something so wholly unreasonable that it would seem no other act in her days spent or to come would ever be as pure.

But I don't know. This is the sort of thinking often proffered in deadly serious novels full of nourishing grace and humanity, but which seems, served up in our famished real life, to be about as satisfying as a radish. Maybe this in turn explains my undue interest in and empathy for imperiled billionaire balloonists, whose public trials are patent and palpable and, as in the worst of our own ordeals, ultimately self-inflicted. And maybe Sir Harold, and Theresa, and the rest of us presumedly wracked agonistes, are in fact making very simple choices, dull to ramification, as we are unable to do much of anything else.

After eating a breakfast of plain live-culture yogurt and honey maple granola and bananas and black coffee, which I mention only because it's the exact breakfast Rita always had, every day, without fail, even when we were in Paris and the baguettes and café au lait were magnificent, and which she probably still eats with Marquis Richie in his wrought-iron-and-glass conservatory breakfast room, I tried to see what new news there was about Sir Harold. There was nothing in the paper and after futilely trying for thirty minutes to log on and sign in to my often balky Internet service, the popular one that every person I know under thirty-five tells me is for dodos and suckers, I gave up and drove over to the Battle Brothers "office" near Commack to use their computer. I sometimes do this when I can't connect, as Jack has of course installed a special connection line that is 10 or 100 or whatever times faster than what I have at home, and which is always on, and which I don't understand. At Parade our computers are solely travel reservation terminals, though that will soon change, I hear, and besides I don't like to go in when it's not my workday, as there's often a backup and I'm pressed into duty. I'm still not quite sure why Jack needs the fast line at Battle Brothers, unless he thinks keeping the guys on the crews hyped up and happy with the constant streams of electronic smut is a necessary and important company perk. Before the trucks get sent out at 7 A.M., you'll see a bunch of guys huddled around a computer in the back office checking out some website featuring Nasty Teens or Horny Housewives and making the age-old locker room comments about the gynecological wonders of this world. I've perused these sites myself, of course, as at least 90 percent of the e-mail I get each day is linking advertisements to sites for every sexual practice, taste, and persuasion imaginable and unimaginable (the computer guy voice should really say, "You've Got Porn!"), the rest being get-rich-quick schemes and second-mortgage offers and then every once in a while an e-mail from someone I actually know, usually not a personal message but a forwarded joke or humorous news item or, alas, some doctored nude picture of a celebrity.

When I drive in through the gate it's already past nine and so the yard has pretty much cleared out of trucks and equipment trailers. Jack's SUV isn't here, either, which dumb thing of dumb things gives me a welling of idiot pride, all because I imagine he's out directing his men, which he probably isn't, as he's probably doing estimates and yakking with suppliers or meeting with his bankers to discuss the possible IPO, which seems less likely every day. I must say the place looks pretty decent, despite the fact that the whole property is paved and fenced and should be nothing special to look at, if not a typical industrial zone eyesore. The three acres Pop and his brothers paid diddly-squat for after the war is probably worth at least a million now as long as there's not some huge environmental problem with it because of all the motor oils and fuels we keep around here, not to mention the fertilizers and lawn chemicals.

Down the road is a cluster of smallish houses from the 1950s where a girl I dated one summer named Rose lived with her mother and aunt and sad drunk of a stepfather who she said touched her once but never again because she practically bit the tip of his ear off and he got spooked and cried like a baby, and I mention her mostly because since then I've somehow always associated Battle Brothers with her, if in the smallest way; in fact there's not been a time I've come here that my thoughts haven't ranged to the Cahills' cramped, dusty house that always smelled of frying bacon and stale beer, and to Rose, who would tug down my undershorts back in the far bay of our garage with a wry sneaky smile and handle me so roughly with her short fingers I sometimes had to ask her to stop. We got along fine enough, but the funny thing was that Rose saw me as a rich kid and I suppose compared to her, with her big toe poking through her thirdhand Mary Janes, I definitely was; after necking we'd walk back to her house and sit on the front stoop, and more than once she said I had it made in the shade for the rest of my life. I knew even then that she was probably right, which made me feel equal parts pride and resentment for Pop and the family and a kind of unfair dominion over her that I've admittedly also felt with Daisy and Rita (and Kelly), who all came from pretty hardscrabble backgrounds and though generally not into money weren't exactly naïve about it either. And maybe they all partly fell for me because of the very inevitability of my future, which is the happy, lucky curse of much of my generation and the next but I'm not sure will be for Jack or his kids, despite these flush times. Sometimes I think Jack and Eunice subconsciously know this, too, and maybe that's why they tend to go overboard with the spending, as if they're not just suburban American well-to-do but jet-set wealthy, to get theirs while they still can.

As for the Battle Brothers building, Jack has changed quite a few things since I early-retired, including the old hand-painted script signage of "Battle Brothers," which he switched out for hefty three-foot-high stainless steel letters that were drilled into the building. Jack likes to refer to the place as "the firm," but to me it'll always be just a shop. A few months ago construction was finally finished on a new suite of offices that were built on the street side of the double-height eight-bay garage, a funny-looking free-form mass of an addition (based loosely after the style of some world-famous architect), which itself has three different kinds of façade claddings and colors and oddly placed windows cut into it like a badly done Halloween pumpkin. I guess it's interesting enough to somebody knowledgeable, for Eunice got a fancy design magazine to come out and take pictures of it outside and in, but to me it looks like the leavings of some giant robot dog, a freakish metallic pile of you-know-what. The new reception area is all Eunice's doing, outfitted with custom-hewn panels of Norwegian birch wood and a long two-inch-thick glass coffee table suspended by tungsten wires coming down from the ceiling, a banquette upholstered in graphite-hued crushed silk running along the walls, which are adorned with contemporary paintings, these changed out monthly to feature another avant-garde local artist (no impressionistic seascapes or boardwalk scenes here). If you didn't know any better you'd think you were in the lounge area of some trendy Asian-fusion restaurant in SoHo, as the receptionist behind the shoji-style console, a hot little multicultural number (like a young Rita but with some West Indian or Thai mixed in) always sporting a walkabout headset, with a tough set to her mouth and given to wearing clingy black T-shirts embroidered with sequins spelling out things like QUEEN BEE and PRECIOUS, will serve you with unexpected earnestness a freshly made espresso or cappuccino from the push-button automatic Italian coffee machine Eunice insisted upon, or else offer you a selection of juices and mineral waters or even steep you a personal pot of green or herbal tea.

"Hey, Mr. Battle," the girl says a little too brightly, as if it's a shock I'm really here. Her shirt today reads SWEET THANG. "Your son is out. We don't expect him back until the afternoon."

"I'm just here to use the computer," I say, liking the white-shoe sound of "we" but wondering who exactly that is, or might be.

"Sure thing," she says, and gets up to walk me back to where the "public" computer is. Eunice designed the main office space back here as well, continuing the theme of Chic Eastern Calm, though here there are additional touches of what Eunice informed me during renovations is Comfy Bauhaus, meaning lots of clean surfaces and lines, to inspire efficiency and high creative function. She even instituted a set of office rules about paper and knickknack clutter so that her design scheme wouldn't be sullied. She needn't have worried, though, because there aren't enough employees as yet to fill the space, just Sweet Thang there out front and Jack's assistant, Cheryl, a forty-something looker who normally sits outside Jack's private office but is out sick today, and then the bookkeeper Sal Mondello, who has been with Battle Brothers since pretty much the beginning and refuses to move out of his original office in the old part of the garage. Upstairs in this new wing is a showroom of the work Battle Brothers will soon be doing, mock-up designer kitchens and bathrooms and media rooms with real working appliances and big-screen TVs and furnished (or *appointed*) as luxuriously as Jack's own house, with antique rugs and heirloom cabinets and framed oil paintings and mirrors. The master plan as indicated by the empty desks is that the administrative and professional design staff will soon expand with the company's gradual shift to work in high-end home renovations, which seems to me to be a bit too gradual, as I haven't yet heard of any confirmed jobs or commissions. Right now Jack and Cheryl and the receptionist and Sal can handle the steady flow of the usual landscaping work and I'm glad to see that Jack hasn't gone ahead and already hired two or three more girls to sit around stripping off their nail polish.

I can't remember her name and so I'm hesitant to start any small talk, though with her clingy top and even clingier matching micro-skirt with no panty lines discernible and heel-to-toe catwalk lope, a springy internal automata makes me want to utter some-*thing*, some-*thang*, some-*thong*.

But nothing acceptable comes, and I give up.

"I'm really sorry, but would you please tell me your name again?"

"Maya."

"Of course. Hiya, Maya."

She giggles. "Hiya, Mr. Battle."

"*Jerry.*"

"Okay, Jerry," Maya says, sitting down at the computer. She palms the mouse, and the screensaver (a group shot of the whole Battle Brothers gang, leaping in unison) instantly disappears, revealing the last image viewed, which is an overly exposed picture of a pasty-looking white couple doing it doggie-style on the polished deck of a powerboat. They're ordinary right-down-the-middle Heartland-type people you'd see at any shopping mall, both looking straight at the camera with an expression of the same prideful glee that fishermen have in photos when they've just hauled in a prize sailfish.

"Oops," she says, quickly clicking on the boxed X in the corner to get rid of it. But another nested picture of the same twosome takes its place; this time they're waving (the woman leaning on her elbows), like they're saying, *Look, no hands.*

"Sorry," I hear myself offering in an avuncular, sensitive-to-harassment-of-any-kind mode. "I'll have Jack talk to the fellas. They shouldn't be looking at this stuff here."

"It doesn't bother me," Maya says. "It's a free country. Anyway, I'd rather have to look at porn than some dumb chart of the stock market."

"Really?"

"Why not? As long as no one's forced into anything, I don't see why I have to freak about it. I'm a big girl. Most of the guys know that just because they look at this stuff here doesn't mean I'm available to them."

"Most? Who doesn't? I'll set them straight."

"It's actually just one, but it's all right. He's harmless."

"You can say. Who?"

Maya points to the door on the garage end of the room.

"Old Sal?"

"He leaves dirty notes on my desk. He thinks I don't know it's him but he handwrites them and I know his script."

"Really?"

"Wait a sec." She goes up front to her desk and returns with a full card hand of square yellow Post-it notes, indeed marked in thick lead pencil with Sal's distinct left-hand scribble, fat and squat and bent the wrong way: *Rock hard for you. Will lick you clean. Prime my love pump.*

"See? He sometimes leaves them for the temps, too."

I nod, certainly embarrassed for her, and for myself and Jack, and for the near-venerable institution of Battle Brothers, and although I'm ashamed of Sal and feel pity for him, I can't help but also admire the sweaty, slick-palmed adolescent tone, the undiminished gall and balls of an old dude whom I always thought of as randy from the waist-high stacks of skin magazines he openly kept in the wide, low washbasin of his grim, dank bookkeeper's office that Pop had converted from a janitor's closet, this when Pop didn't think Battle Brothers needed a full-time ledger man. When I was in high school I once caught him lying down on his desk with the secretary (named Roz) squatting on his face so you could just see his bushy head of hair poking out from her skirt as if she were sitting on a fuzzy pillow. Sal has to be pushing seventy-five now and I don't think he ever married, though he did have a long secretive affair with Pop's baby sister Georgette until she was killed in a car accident in 1965. After Pop handed over the reins to me everyone figured Sal might quit, given that I obviously didn't know or care too much about the business; when Sal came in my first day as head honcho he asked for a "meeting" after work, and I was expecting he'd demand a slice of the company and was all ready after consulting with Pop to offer him 12.5 percent and not a half point more. But all he asked me for was a $50-a-week raise and when I said I'd give him $45 he took it without another word.

"Sal is harmless," I say. "But I'll have a talk with him anyway."

"What talk do you want, there, Jer?"

"Hey, Sally."

It's Salvatore Mondello, just arriving to work. He's dressed as usual in his low-rent white-collar style: short-sleeve dress shirt, too-short stubby tie, trim-fit gabardine slacks, worn cordovan wing tips. He's one of those handsome lanky Northern Italian types who age magnificently. His skin has a clean-scrubbed light olive glow, his hair still thick and full and streaked with enough dark strands that it appears spun straight from silver. If he had been a slightly different man he could have enjoyed a long career as one of those duty-free international playboys jetting from the Côte d'Azur to Palm Beach with a wealthy mistress waiting desperately in each hotel suite for him to blindfold her with his silk ascot, fragrant of musk and Dunhill 100s, and do things to her with his tongue and lubed pinky finger that her inattentive jerk husband long gave up doing.

But fortunately or unfortunately Sal is not a slightly different man, and while he is plenty smart and has let his dick lead him through life like a lot of the rest of us, I would say he did so without a companion ambition for fame or money, and so is who he is, which is basically an old local stud who worked just hard enough to pay the rent and take out fresh pussy every Friday and Saturday night. This until maybe eight or ten years ago, when I think the high mileage on his purportedly horse-sized rig (this from one of the mechanics, who early on in Battle Brothers history caught him jerking off in the john and described Sal's action "like he was buffin' a toy baseball bat") finally caught up to him and broke down, relegating him to a retirement of titty bars and dirty Web chats and twice-a-year Caribbean cruises on a popular line on which he travels free for serving as a nightly dance partner for singles and widows, though with this new hard-on wonder drug they've invented, Sal might soon fly the flag high once again.

"What, Jer, they fire you over there at the agency?"

"Not yet. I'm just saying hello today."

"Hey there, Maya."

"Morning, Sal," she answers him, without a hint of umbrage. Though not with great warmth, either. "I gotta get to work."

"You do that, honey," Sal says. When she's back out front he says, "If I could just be sixty again."

"Yeah? What would you do?" I say, remembering as I do almost daily now that I'll be that very age in a matter of nothing, just when the world tips on its axis and our propitiously temperate part of it starts to die out again, wreathe itself in the dusty colors of mortality.

"Are you kidding? Me and that amazing piece of ass would be balling all day like those horny monkeys on the nature program. What do they call them, bonobos? Those monkeys just screw each other all day, and they'll even get into some dyke and fag action when nobody's looking."

"No kidding?"

"Saw it just last night. The girl monkeys, you know, with the bright red catcher's mitt twats, will squat back to back, rubbing themselves on each other. The boys will hang upside down and play swords with their skinny units. These monkeys are different than other ones who would rather fight viciously than fuck. I guess we're supposed to be more like the fighting monkeys."

"I guess you're a bonobo, huh, Sally?"

"You got that right. What about you?"

"Probably neither," I say, thinking that there must be a third kind of monkey, only slightly more advanced, who sits high up in the trees and collects his fruit pits, indolently noting how much he's eaten.

"How's Rita treating you?"

"You don't know?"

"Oh, Christ, Jer, don't tell me something's happened to her."

"No, no, nothing like that. She just left me. Almost a year ago, I guess."

"Oh. That's even worse. It means she's with someone else."

"Yeah."

"Do I know the guy?"

"Richie Coniglio. From the neighborhood. Hairy little guy."

"That pipsqueak? What's he do now?"

"He's a fancy-pants lawyer. Richer than God. He lives over in Muttontown."

"I guess we all knew that little wiseass was headed for loads of dough. But he has to end up with your girl, too?"

"I know. It's not good."

"And when that girl is somebody like Rita. Christ. I've always liked Puerto Rican chicks because they're like black chicks who aren't black, if you know what I mean. But when you started up with Rita I was especially jealous. She's a sweet lady and a great cook and then she's got those big chocolate eyes and the nice skin and that gorgeous shapely round . . ."

"Hey, hey, Sally. It's still pretty fresh, okay?"

"Sorry, Jer. I'm just telling you how good you had it with her. Did you fuck things up or did she just get sick of you?"

"Both, I think."

"Probably you weren't giving her enough head. These days women expect it."

"You're probably right," I tell him, reminded now why over all these years Sal and I never got to be closer, despite the fact that

I've always liked him well enough and even looked up to him like the older brother I sometimes wished I'd had. Sal has a way of making you agree with him not because he's a bully but because you don't really want to get into the full squalid array of details necessary to complete a typical conversation with him. I'd like to add here, too, that Rita didn't expect anything in the labial way, and while she clearly liked it plenty whenever I did do my oral duties, she was generally of the mind that men shouldn't get so right up close to a woman's petaled delicates, if they were to remain in the least secret and alluring and mysterious.

Or so she told me.

Sal adds, too: "Seems like these young ones like Maya up there don't even care for old-fashioned penetration anymore. They'd all just rather be lesbians, if they had it their way. If you don't believe me it's on the Internet."

"Whatever. But if you can do me a favor, Sally, just keep it in your pants here at the office."

"What," he says, looking up front. "Has there been a complaint?"

"No, no, nobody's said nothing. But you hear about what's going on these days with sexual harassment. Jack doesn't need anybody suing the company because the work environment is, you know, whatever they call it, 'predatory.'"

"Hey, I'm not the one wearing suggestive T-shirts."

"I'm just saying, Sal, let's keep it professional around here, okay? Keep the shop going like it is."

"No problem with me, Jer," he says. "It's Jack you should worry about."

"What? He's fucking around?"

"I wouldn't know about that," Sal says. "I just think he's running Battle Brothers into the ground."

"What are you talking about? It seems like we've got more work than we can handle. Seems like the trucks are always all out."

"Sure they are. We're doing nice business, just like we have the last five years. But that's the *old* work. The dirt work. We get decent margins there, but nothing fantastic. You know that."

"Sure."

"The new stuff is what's the problem. See all those new workstations and plotters?" he says, pointing to the six custom maplewood desks with large flat-panel computer monitors and a huge plotter for making large-format prints. "That's Jack's design operation. He and Eunice spent top dollar on that equipment and software, almost seventy grand. We could probably design fighter jets on those things. But we've only been using one of the terminals, and half-time at that. The high-end construction and renovation work is out there, but we're not getting it. People know us as landscapers and stonemasons, not kitchen and bathroom designers. Jack's idea that he could become this supercontractor for the whole tristate region is an interesting idea, but he's spending all his hours driving to Cheesedick, Connecticut, to do an estimate and getting squat. I think he's finally landed a couple jobs, but I think he had to lowball to get them, and after looking at the bids I won't be surprised if we lose twenty-five or fifty grand on each. And do you know how much this new office and showroom wing is costing us? Five hundred grand, and counting."

"Jesus. I had no idea."

"But that's not the worst of it, Jer. I hate to tell you this, but I'm pretty sure Jack's been borrowing against the business. I think he's been trying to hide it from me but I got some statements by accident about interest payments on a big note against the property, and then another on the business itself."

"How big are they?"

"They add up to a million and a half."

"Anything else you want to tell me?"

"That's it. Though I can't promise that these aren't just the ones I've gotten wind of. I don't know what he's doing, Jer, but I think you better talk to him."

"Yeah. I will."

"Jer?"

"Yeah?"

"What's your line on me and Miss Curry Pot?"

"Way long. I'd keep it platonic for now. Okay, Sally?"

Sal smirks, and heads to his office through the frosted-glass door that is the partition between this expensive sleek new world and the grubby oil-streaked one of old. On the computer I type in the address of Sir Harold's site and actually have to pause before tapping the Enter key.

The news is good. He emerged from the storm shortly after I'd last looked, and is flying high again, his path only slightly altered, and just a few hours shy of schedule. The electronic message board for him is lit up with hundreds of emphatic postings, such as "Fly, Harold, Fly!" and "Tally Ho!" and "You Can't Keep A Good Man Down," and though I'd like to add my two cents to the feel-good kitty (mostly if not exclusively for the psychic benefit of us onlookers), I can't quell this steady pulsing dread that trouble still lies ahead for him. Because when you think of it, the truly depressing thing is that the trouble will probably not be a limitation of Sir Harold himself or his wondrous technology but just the fact of something as guileless as the winds, and the weather, these chance clouds that should determine a person's ultimate success or failure. This is why I fly my *Donnie* only when the sky is completely clear, with no threat of weather for at least another day, as I want no obstacle or impedance to a good afternoon's soar. Of course this also means I've never ranged too far from here, never hopped from small airfield to airfield the way most guys have on weeklong junkets to Florida or California, never flown after dusk in the watery blue light or through the scantest rains; I have to wonder what will happen if I ever do find myself in an unforecasted fog, how well if at all I'll work the controls and fly solely by instruments, if I'll be able to forge through the muck and break back into daylight.

And as I pad into Jack's plush office and sit in his broad leather desk chair that seems to promise only good fortune and prosperity, I feel somewhat bereft (and not because of any monies he's maybe lost or losing), for I don't quite know what I'll say to him, or more specifically, what I'll say that won't deeply cut or insult him or make him talk to me even less than he already does. If, as I've noted, the main problem with Jack is that he too much needs to impress, the very close second problem at this point is that he knows that's exactly what I'm thinking whenever I step into his cavernous home or visit one of his jobs or come calling around here. And perhaps over time it's this already anticipated turbulence that brings a family most harm, the knowledge unacknowledged, which at some point you can try and try but can't glide above.

s i x

NOW AND THEN, clear out of the blue, just as he did when I first arrived at Ivy Acres this afternoon for an early dinner visit, Pop will tell me, "Bobby was the one who should have married Daisy."

At the moment, he's dozing hard, his mouth laid open, unhinged, his eyes pinched up like something really, really hurts.

I shouldn't rouse him.

To be honest, I used to burn inside whenever Pop said that. Mostly because I know how dead wrong he'd be, if that had ever come to pass. Bobby met Daisy maybe twice before he left for basic training in the fall of 1968. That summer he was playing in the instructional league in Puerto Rico but got sick of the heat and the bugs and the food, and like a dope signed up for the Marines instead of seeing what might have come of his raw talent for the game. Bobby and Daisy got along instantly, Bobby taking her for a ride in the gleaming emerald green '67 Impala convertible that Pop had bought brand new for himself. I remember them coming back with ice cream cones, with both of them, ego-typically, sporting triple dips. After a brief stint at Camp Pendleton he was shipped to Vietnam, stationed who knows where, serving six months of duty until the night he was separated from his Marine platoon during a chaotic firefight and never heard from again. They searched for his body over the next few days and found his helmet and a bloody boot, but then the whole division had to quickly pull back under an intense VC counterattack and naturally the next thing that happened was a carpet bombing of the area, which obliterated everything living or dead. After the war he was on the long roster of MIAs submitted to the Vietnamese government during prisoner and bodily-remains exchanges, but even Pop knew that that was pretty much the end of the story for Robert Henry Battle of Whitestone, New York, and never fought the reality or was one of those people who made pilgrimage to Vietnam or agitated for more efforts from the government.

I think Pop made the best of the situation, at least for himself, for while he didn't have Bobby's body he could entertain the notion of Bobby Ongoing, which was unassailable and ever-evolving. Not that Pop was under any delusions that he was still alive somewhere, but he could imagine Bobby growing older, Bobby maturing and marrying, Bobby as a father and the scion of the family business, all this without interference from any Bobby Actual, whose presence, like all our presences, would have been an inglorious mitigation. Ma, of course, was inconsolable for a long time; she wouldn't talk much when she and Pop came over and just trudged about the kitchen wiping surfaces or occupied herself with pressing my shirts down in the basement or sweeping the patio. In her own house she wouldn't let anybody into Bobby's room, not even Pop, until a leak in his dormer after a bad storm eventually led to a smell that couldn't be ignored, and when Pop and I finally went in there, it was like a lab lesson in the varieties of fungi and molds, green-gray splotches on the walls, grayish shadings on the window panes, and then a cottony white fur growing in and out of his old sneakers and shoes. The room was so sharply musty that Pop had a contractor come in and tear it down to the studs and floor joists before building it back again.

Almost nothing of Bobby's was salvageable, none of his clothes or pennants or books. The only items Ma could keep were his many baseball trophies, which she soaked in a tub of bleach and then displayed on the mantel in their living room, where they remained until I moved Pop into Ivy Acres. They now sit atop the microwave in his quasi-efficiency suite, pedestaled brass Mickey Mantle–modeled figures, posed in their home run swings; these, by the way, are the only objects from the old house that Pop has kept for himself. It'd be squarely sad-sweet, for sure, except that Pop sometimes confuses whose trophies they are and will brandish one and compliment me on my glovework at the hot corner, or worse yet, talk about his own power to right center field, the bolting line drives that even Willie Mays couldn't have run down.

Bobby was by any account a memorable baseball player, and I won't go into it except to say that he was a speed demon on the bases and definitely the one with the flashy glove and power to the alleys and perhaps could have gone all the way, given the physique and skills he had. He was built like Jack but was more lithe than Jack could ever be, big and strong and flexible the way most of these extremely tuned and pumped up professional athletes are today but that back then was quite rare, especially as expressed (if you'll excuse my saying) in some neighborhood white kid. After the instructional league ball in Puerto Rico, he signed up at a Marine kiosk, leaving behind both a minor league contract and a full college scholarship, which would have put off his being drafted, and maybe changed his luck entirely. I'd already been a Coast Guard reservist, and during those years I spent every other weekend on a boat sailing mostly nowhere, which was perfect for me.

And like I've said—although I never said it to anyone—I thought Bobby was a fucking idiot, and on several important levels (and not because it was Vietnam, because Vietnam wasn't Vietnam yet, at least to us back here), but to my amazement nobody considered what he was doing to be a terrible idea, not even Ma, who seemed to think going into the service was like an extended sleepaway camp, and not even Pop, who thought Bobby should spend a year or two and take in the sights of Southeast Asia and just come back and lace up his old spikes for St. John's or the Columbus Clippers, no problem whatsoever. Like everybody in our neighborhood Bobby was patriotic enough but it wasn't love of country or sense of duty or anything else so fudgeably grand and romantic that made him do such a thing. For no matter how excellent he was at something (and there were many somethings besides baseball, like acting and singing and then drawing, which I remember all the girls adoring, because he'd sketch them to look as lovely as they'd ever be, accentuating their eyes or lips), Bobby had a habit of cutting short his involvement before anything really great could develop. He was what people these days would term a grazer, a browser, a gifted Renaissance kid who never quite wholly commits (one could maybe think ADD). But really, if I have to say it, Bobby was Bobby because he didn't ultimately care. It wasn't a nihilistic streak, nothing dark like that, but rather a long-ingrained insoluble indifference, which sprang from how easily he could do things, like pick up any instrument, or a new sport, or have a beautiful girl fall in love with him, with what was always this effortless sparkling performance of Himself, which he was mostly unconscious of, and thus why most people instantly championed and loved him. And so you could think his predraft enlistment was just another circumstance to be easily sailed through, but I have thought that what it really was was Bobby pushing the venue, pushing the parameters to include, finally, the chance of testing his mortality.

Which turns out is what many of us otherwise self-tucked in chronic safety will do, and with surprising regularity, whether we're aware of it or not.

If Bobby were still alive it is almost certain that he would have ended up running Battle Brothers; although we were seven years apart (Ma had two miscarriages between us), I would have simply put in a few years until Bobby was old enough and then gone off on my own and probably pursued something to do with flying. Although I always dreamed of being an ace of a P-47 Thunderbolt (long ago manufactured by Republic down the road in Farmingdale) or an F-86 Sabre like in *The Bridges at Toko-Ri*, I didn't end up applying to the service academies and thus had no genuine shot at being a fighter jock and having a subsequent career as a big-jet commercial captain. I do believe I would have been like a few guys you hear about around the hangar lounge who try to climb the ladder themselves, average Andys who just love flying so much that they wait for their chance to pilot commuter puddle-jumpers or regional mail runners or even just drag those message banners above the South Shore beaches that say MARRY ME ROSALIE or MAKE IT ABSOLUT. Or if I didn't quite do that maybe I'd have my own little travel business, by handle of My Way Tours, offering eight- and fifteen-day guided re-creations of all of Jerry Battle's favorite trips ("Serengeti Supreme," say, or "Blue Danube"), because anyone knows that the best way to make a living is to spend the workaday hours submitting to your obsessions and that everything else is just plain grubby labor. But that's the life of the charming and the lucky and the talented (i.e., people like Bobby), and for the rest of us perfectly acceptables and okays and competents it's a matter of persistence and numbness to actual if minor serial failure and a wholly unsubstantiated belief in the majesty of individual destiny, all of which is democracy's spell of The Possible on us.

Still, and though Pop would never agree, Bobby would have probably run Battle Brothers into the ground. I can say this because he was always too generous, and would have undoubtedly bid too low for jobs and been a soft touch with the crews and not cut enough corners when he could with the customers or the vendors and who/whatever else there was holding down our margins. I'm no natural business whiz and the worries never once kept me up at night but Battle Brothers was the whole of Pop's life and in the sum of it pretty much mine. I think my career-long effectiveness came from the fact that I could funnel all of my frustrations and exasperations and notions of self-misprision into just the right kind of fierce mercenary pressure, which I could reserve until called for and then unvalve on some poor sucker caught in the wrong place at the wrong time.

Christ I could holler. Mostly, though, I was just in a pissy mood. Some of the guys, I know, would kid around and refer to me as Jerry Not So Merry or Jerry Sour Berry (their other, nonpublic names for me I'm sure much more rank and vile). At the annual landscapers' association banquet (last year emceed by the dashing Jack Battle at the Brookville Country Club), I never particularly associated too well, always choosing to sit with the newer contractors on the periphery and pretend I didn't know anybody. The Pavones and Richters and Keenans and Ianuzzis would hold their royal blowhards court and roast each other and get fresh with the hired girls and undoubtedly scuff up the putting green with their drunken fisticuffs, these overtanned, blunt-fingered guys upon whom I would wish a horrid pox or blood plague but who in fact weren't unlike us Battles at all.

Bobby was the one who would have fit right in; he was ever

willing to tolerate those he considered to be any kind of comrade in arms, and not at all for business reasons. I don't know where he got this need to be part of the crowd, part of the gang, as neither Pop nor I is so constituted, but then again he was universally adored, and after we had his memorial service there came together what amounted to a big block party for him in our old neighborhood, which wasn't thrown by us, as Ma for once in her life didn't much feel like putting out a spread for company and went right up to her bedroom to change into her nightgown and take a few pills for sleep. Pop trudged down into our finished basement and clicked on the talk radio extra loud, and though I don't like to think about it probably just played with his 1/175-scale USS *Arizona*, which took him at least three years to make, painting included. Daisy refused to come, as she despised funerals and cemeteries and was back in Long Island with the kids, and so I moped around the kitchen for a bit until I heard music coming from the street.

When I went out there I was amazed to see how large and festive the gathering was—it was more a celebration than a wake, some kind of commencement, like a demigod had been approved to ascend Mt. Olympus. Everybody was hauling out their extra card tables and chairs and setting out the Pyrex casseroles of baked ziti and lasagna and sausages and stuffed clams and bean salad that was probably just their family dinners. They had a keg of beer for the men and jugs of blush wine for the ladies, and the kids were playing Red Rover and Kick the Can at the end of our coned-off street, and even a couple of cops had stopped by for a cold one. Basically it was like one of those Saturday night city street fairs except there weren't any flashing string lights or cotton candy machines or necking couples, though I do remember seeing a kid puking on the Radoscias' garage door, probably having filched too much leftover Lambrusco.

Everybody was hugging me and friendly in a way I had never known them to be friendly, which, if I have to be honest, was clearly not so much about condolence or sympathy but rather whatever they might have sensed of Bobby as residually expressed in me (he had those sparkly eyes, too, and the same wavy dark hair). But none of it was unpleasant or even sad, and I can tell you that I felt more comfortable and at ease that evening on 149th Street than in all the years growing up there as a not unhappy youth, because when you're among others and don't have to be exactly in your own skin it can be the strangest blessing, not to mention the added effect of feeling an afterglow as warm-hued as Bobby Battle's. (Perhaps this explains my love of travel, because when you're walking along some quay or piazza or *allée* there's an openness and possibility and that certain intimacy with strangers which is near impossible on an American street or food court, the scale still hunched and human.) Guys were toasting me and making sentimental speeches about Bobby's honey singing voice and stunning bat speed, and the ladies were the ones who seemed to be putting on a serious buzz, as I'd be passed from one to another in a rope line of tangos, and then later that evening when almost everybody had folded up camp and gone inside for the night, a woman named Patricia Murphy came up to me and told me she had gone out with Bobby for a little while during middle school and asked if I would walk her to her car.

I actually remembered her, or thought I did, as she was one of those fourteen-year-old girls who are physically developed beyond anybody's capacity to handle too well (much less craven adolescents). She had a grown woman's hips and thighs and she had a bigger, fuller chest than any senior girl in the high school. She was certainly okay-looking but it probably wouldn't have mattered if she looked like Ernest Borgnine she was so built, and like too many girls in her position she probably ended up giving away a bit too much for popularity's or some other sake to those very boys in the school keen on taking as much as they could.

Bobby wasn't one of those, certainly, and I remember they were in a school production together, something called *A Medley of Shakespeare*, featuring bits from three or four of his plays, and maybe their romance lasted a couple weeks at most afterward, I'm sure ending with the requisite study hall dramatics and tears. That night after the funeral Patricia was in a funny kind of mood, which is odd for me to say given that I didn't know her at all. She was sort of laughing to herself and gently poking at my ribs and arms like my sexy cousin Wendy Battaglia used to do at those big Sunday family dinners that nobody ever throws anymore, and when we got to her car, which was parked right in front of our house, she announced she was too drunk to drive and could we maybe sit inside for a little while? I figured that made good sense and by that point I was feeling pretty valorous with all the back slaps and glad hands accrued to me during the evening. I figured my folks would be sound asleep, which they were, as I could hear Ma's high snoring titters, *wee-ha, wee-ha.*

So I went into the kitchen and put on a pot of coffee for her, but when I turned Patricia Murphy was right there, practically pressing up against me, her chest maybe not any bigger or fuller ten years later but still plenty magnanimous, with a kind of space-age uprightness and pomp that makes you think this is why you live in this confused post-Newtonian world. She asked if I could show her Bobby's room. I didn't think anything of her request, really, or her proximity, and we went up the tight stairs to the second door on the left with the old Polo Grounds poster tacked on it.

Bobby Battle's bedroom, pre-fungus, was as advertised, the picture of American Golden Boy-hood, festooned with pennants and posters of starlets and books on log cabin construction and model rocketry. I thought she'd maybe poke her head in the closet or sit on the bed or try his still supple third baseman's glove on for size, but she stood apart from me at an awkward distance and then said in a coquettish thespian whisper, "You are merry, my lord." I replied, confused, "Who me?" and before I knew it she fell upon me, down to her knees, swiftly unlatching my belt. And as she took me barely chubby in her dryish small mouth I finally for once that evening thought of my brother, lost somewhere back in Vietnam, his soul wandering the death fields, who would go on forever and ever, like any true titan, through all of our flawed enactments, whether he would wish to or not. And that's when I first really felt what must have been a pang of brotherly lacking, which for me wasn't so much an emptiness as this mysterious prosthetic groan, from down deep. And I was thinking of Daisy, too, of course, and how I'd ever begin to explain myself if she found out, and was just in fact planning a delicate extrication when Pop walked in and caught me and Patricia Murphy, duly arrayed. He could have been angry, certainly, or at least repelled, but he simply looked at her, and then at me, and said like it was quarter to four in the afternoon on a job already running a day behind, "Let's pick it up here, Jerome."

Pop has never mentioned that night, not even in these recent months when it's just that kind of best-forgotten off-color item exclusively crowding his memory, and which he'll tell you all about, over and over again: the time he was playing golf on the Costa del Sol and caught the future King of Spain hocking a loogey in the water cooler on the fourteenth tee, or when he got the clap from a hooker in Kansas City and was afraid to touch Ma for three months, or the time he was out on a big job in North Hills and saw the lady of the house naked in the kitchen, brushing her nipples with salad oil, for no reason he could fathom. He'll tell you his awkward stories of all of us, of his cousins and employees and people on television and especially the politicians he reads about

in the stacks of ultraright and left-wing newsletters he subscribes
to, the power plays and conspiracies to cover up what he believes
runs through everything and everyone, which is corruption, total
utter corruption, of heart and mind and of the soul. Only Bobby,
no surprise, is not subject, which is fine by me, and maybe even appreciated, because if Pop were exposing him, too, I'd wonder what
light or verity was left to him.

For Pop, unlike Bobby, isn't so unconcerned about dying. Sure
he talks about having me dive-bomb *Donnie* into this place, or
bribing the nurse's aide to sneak him a couple bottles of Sominex,
or dropping the next-door-suite lady friend's curling iron into his
bathwater, but in fact he's as death-averse as any striving red-
blooded man of his generation (or mine, for that matter), and
would always prefer to cling to life forever, even if it meant constant physical misery and a near-vegetative mental state, not to
mention the utter depletion of the Battle family reserves. The
thing to remember about Pop is that despite the denuded superego
and messy accidents there is nothing really too wrong with him;
his blood pumps at more pacific pressures than mine and his bad
cholesterol is lower and he still eats (and normally shits, he assures
me) like a draft horse, and as long as he has someone helping him
up and down steps and out of loungers and beds so he doesn't fall
and break a hip, he might well preside at my funeral, part of me
suspecting how it would give him a peculiarly twisted tingle of accomplishment, this last, last patriarchal mumble over his sole sur-
viving issue, finally succumbed.

A soft triple tone goes off in a minor key, like you'll hear over
the public address in many Asian airports, which immediately
wakes Pop out of his slumber; it's the call for chow in the dining
room for those who aren't otherwise being served a tray in bed.
Pop points to his robe and I help him with it as he tucks his
pontoon-like feet into his slippers. He's unshaven as usual and his

oily silvery hair smells like warm beeswax, and though we're the same height he's seeming ever-shorter to me now, the hunch in his shoulders growing more and more vulturesque with each visit.

"How do I look?" Pop says to me, the one thing he'll always ask in earnest.

"Like a man with a plan."

"I'm seeing a woman, you know."

"You mentioned that last time. Who is she again?"

"A looker named Bea. But don't ask me anything else, because I don't know the first thing about her. It's just a lot of hot sex."

"That's great, Pop."

"Don't be such a wiseass, Jerome. At least your old man is getting his share in here. It's the only thing that makes this place bearable. That reminds me. Next time you come bring a bottle of that Astro Glide, and not a dinky-sized one, either. Get the one with the pump."

"Got it."

"That stuff is a miracle. They ought to make it taste better, you know."

"I said I got it, Pop."

"You'll see, when it's your turn. You'll want your whole life lubed up."

"I'm sure I will," I say, thinking how maybe I don't want to wait. "Listen, don't you want to throw on a shirt for dinner?"

"Bea's no uppity broad."

"All right. How about some real pants?"

"Forget it. Let's go, I'm starved."

Down the hallway we go, Pop holding tight on to my arm, and it shocks me to see how unsteady he is. Maybe it's that he's still somewhat sleepy, or it's just part of his well-honed act of late (Decrepitude on Ice), but it is frankly alarming to feel the dire vise-grip of his fingers on my elbow joint, the tremolos of each heaving step, and then to hear the wheezy cardiacal mouth breathing that is all too typical around here at Ivy Acres, these once exuberant smokers and whiskey drinkers and steak eaters now sitting down to three mostly color-free meals a day, easily eaten with a spoon.

The dining room is actually pretty nice, if you like pastelly framed harborside prints and bleached oak tables and chairs and piped in Lite FM (a Grateful Dead song actually came on once, freezing me and the staff, though only momentarily), the décor done right along the lines of Kissimmee Timeshare, which I'm sure is no accident. The ambience around here is meant to evoke the active vacationing life, which for most of these folks is exactly what they remember best and most fondly, not sweet youth so much as those first dizzying years of their retirements, twenty-five or thirty years ago, when all their spouses were still living or vital and they still could walk every side street of San Gimignano and dance all night in the cruise ship disco and didn't mind in the least a three-city routing on the way to the Marquesas Islands, so they could live (just a little) like Gauguin. (This is what Rita and I should be doing, rather than painting ourselves into recriminatory corners with love's labors lost, the fact of which depresses me all the more, knowing that I might not have such memories when it's my turn to be thoughtfully assisted into oblivion.)

It seems a good quarter of the folks here in the dining room are wheelchair-bound, maybe half of those requiring help from the nursing aides to put spoon to mouth, and Pop leads us to the back of the room, far from the entrance, where the more able-bodied (if not -minded) types take their accustomed chairs.

Bea, Pop's object of affection, if that's what she is, is already eating her dinner of cut green beans and roasted turkey and mashed potatoes, and says, "Good evening, Hank," to him as we sit down, sounding uncannily like my mother. He says hello back with no great passion, and introduces me to her again, for perhaps the fifth or sixth time. Bea has a little trouble with her short-term recall, which I don't mind because there's not much to talk about and so it's good to get acquainted over and over again. She is usually pulled together and face-painted for dinner or the evening movie, and then decked out in a strictly nautical/maritime style, with the sign of the anchor featured on every last piece of her clothing, even her little white socks, appliquéd and stitched in and printed on, repeated enough that it has begun to read like some ominous Occidental ideogram, this admonitory vision of the two-sided hook. I could go further into this imagery à la Theresa, how it suggests my own guilt about "placing" Pop here and my attendant anxiety about being dragged along with him (now in mind, later in body), but I won't, because despite the fact that this is the most socially acceptable means of getting back at him for all those years of his being a pigheaded domineering irascible bull in the china shop of life, your typical world-historical jerk, I still 110 percent respect the man, even if I can't love him, which I probably do anyway, though I would never ever say.

What Bea sees in him I'm not exactly sure, but maybe at this stage and locale it's enough for a man to have any bit of spirit left, any whiff of piss and vinegar, to make the ladies swoon. There is, as Pop purports, more action going on around here than anyone cares to imagine, and it's not what we'd like to think is just some smoochy doe-eyed cuddling in the dayroom. Bea isn't looking terribly right this evening (or afternoon, as 4:45 is the first dinner seating), for she's also wearing her bathrobe and slippers, and her shoulder-length hair, which I recall being thoroughly warmly blond, is now white for an inch at the roots (has it been that long since I last visited?), and not brushed. With no makeup on her face I can hardly recognize her, her eyes seeming that much sleepier, sunken, the unrouged skin of her cheeks so sheer as to seem trans-

ANG-RAE LEE

parent, her faintly purplish lips dried and cracked. Maybe I'm old-fashioned and don't mind being duped by a deft hand with the Maybelline, but I don't think I'm overstating things when I say that if she weren't otherwise eating with some gusto and sitting upright I might say poor Bea was about to kick the bucket.

"Jerry, are you Hank's brother or son?" Bea asks me, like she's asking for the very first time.

"He's my son, sweetheart," Pop tells her. "He's the one who put me in here."

"Then I should thank you," she says, "for sending me my sexy companion."

"Please don't use that word," Pop says.

"Sexy?"

"*Companion.*"

"Why not?"

"It sounds fruity."

"So? You are fruity. Fruity with me."

"Yeah, but I don't want my son to know."

Bea grins at me, with her perfect set of porcelain choppers, a speck of green bean clinging to her incisor.

The nursing-aide-posing-as-waiter approaches and tells us what's on the dinner menu, which is just what Bea is working through, save the option of fish instead of the turkey. Pop asks what kind of fish it is and the fellow says a *whitish fish,* of course meaning he doesn't know or care. Pop says we'll both have that, and I don't fight it. He's always ordered for everyone, even the guys on the crews when the lunch truck came by (he made a point of buying lunch whenever he was around), because he's proud and he's a bully, and he'll be buying dinner for as long as his triple-tax-free munis hold out. The other folks at the table, two men and a woman, appropriately clad, all order the turkey, and while we wait for our plates to be delivered I check out the rest of the room, now nearly filled up with most of the residents of Ivy Acres, whose mission is to serve those, according to its glossy brochure, "moving between self-sufficiency and a more needs-intensive lifestyle," meaning of course the heading-downhill-fast crowd. What strikes me is that there's never as much conversation as I think there will be, there's just this sedate bass-line murmur to accompany the piped-in easy-listening format, because as much as I'd like to believe that these old-timers can hardly contain their accrued store of tales and opinions and observations, the truth of the matter is they would rather talk to anybody else but their Ivy Acres brethren, wishing to be a part of the chance daily flow again, the messy unknown arrays of people and situations that you and I might consider bothersome or peculiar or annoying but to the institutionally captive are serendipitous events, like finding a ten-dollar bill in the street. So I feel it's part of my duty whenever I visit to eat with Pop and listen to whatever his tablemates have to say about their neglectful families or their lumbago, and nod agreeably to their shock at the price of a gallon of gasoline or a three-bedroom house in Centerport, and patiently discuss their views on abortion and the right to bear arms. Bea usually tells me about her divorced eldest daughter, the one who has a son who is a junkie and a daughter who is already a lesbian ("at the age of thirteen!") and who asks her for monthly counseling money for all three, which Bea knows she uses instead toward a lease on a new Infiniti sedan.

Across from us sit Daniel and his fraternal twin Dennis, who ran a family bakery in Deer Park, and are decent enough fellows, though one of them is hard of hearing and so they both talk way too loudly, and both spit a bit doing it. They like to argue with each other about the Middle East crisis, one of them approvingly Zionist in the conservative American Gentile tradition and the other something of an anti-Semite, inevitably bringing up the idea of Jewish conspiratorial influence in Washington and Hollywood and on Wall Street. They can sometimes get quite angry at each other—one of them might even slap the table with a big loafy hand and leave red-faced—but Pop assures me that they hardly speak when visitors aren't around, and just get up together at 3 A.M. out of lifelong habit and play Hearts to kill time until coffee is served in the Sunrise Room.

There are, of course, a number of residents that you never see, who are housed in a special wing of the complex called "Transitions" (though informally known as "The Morgue," as it is situated, in a somewhat unfortunate attempt at an expensive contemporary look, behind a massive pair of polished stainless steel sliding doors). This is the unit where the living isn't so much *assisted* as it is *sustained,* and while I've been invited multiple times of late by the executive administrator to take a tour of its specialized facilities and meet its staff I've not yet done so, the reason, I think, being not exactly denial of the coming reality but my feeling that I'd rather be cathartically jolted by shock and dismay and surprise by what Pop requires than have to ruminate too much now on all the grim complications and possibilities. Maybe that's a sneaky form of denial, too, but it's what I can do.

Our dinners are brought to us and it's no stretch to say that Pop gravely misordered. The fish on our plates is an unnaturally rectangular fillet of meat, grayish and bluish and not nearly whitish enough, with veiny streaks of brown running through the engineered block. A glum slice of lemon is steam-adhered on top. The fish has been poached in its own past-due juices, which are now infiltrating the green beans and mashed potatoes and the overfancy garnishes of carrot flowers and parsley. I can hardly stick my face over the plate, but Pop is digging right in, and nobody else at the table seems to notice, or cares if they do. I'll remind you that Ivy Acres is an upscale nursing facility, and it's amazing to think what they might be serving at some of the other homes I looked at, which were but half the price. What would it take to slap a decent piece of sirloin on the griddle and let it sear to medium-rare, and serve it the way Rita does with a pat of sweet herbed butter and maybe even a half glass of dry red wine? I've always thought that Ivy Acres spent too much dough on the glossy brochures and advertisements and then on landscaping the grounds, which I can say from my former professional point of view is clearly top-shelf, with the pea-stone pathways and English garden perennials and a high-end playground set for the visiting grandkids (who don't go outside but just sit in the dayroom watching whatever the residents are watching). In fact I've never seen any of the residents hanging out outside except when their families insist on "getting some air." Like everything else here the money is spent by management for the sake of us visitors, the same way pet food is designed to please the owners, to assure us in our wishful thinking that our folks are already, as it were, in a better place.

I used to joke to Rita about the idea of having assisted living centers for the perfectly able and independent, places where busy families and lazy empty-nesters and even single professionals could live in residence hotel–style accommodations and enjoy valet services and a modified American meal plan (no weekday lunch) and organized Club Med–type activities on the weekends. The notion isn't so far-fetched, if not already being developed, for it seems a lot of people of even historically modest means now demand a host of services simply to maintain a decent middle-class standard of living. They have their dry cleaning picked up and delivered and have bottled water contracts and lawn and pool service and the week's meals prepared and apportioned by a local caterer and delivered frozen in a tidy Styrofoam cooler every Friday night. The only real difference is that they still live in their own homes, but as any owner will tell you, the constant upkeep and maintenance (whether you're doing it yourself or paying someone else) can be a steady soul-wearying grind. I think a hell of a lot of our nation's people would give up some privacy and separateness (as they happily do on their vacations) in exchange for the ultimate luxuries of Ease and Convenience, which these days are everyone's favorites. I'd site my place in a semi-rural area with lots of covered parking and call it something like Concierge Farms, the hook being "Just bring your clothes."

Not that I would sign up myself, even if Rita were to agree to come back to me and were willing to live in such a place, which she never ever would. My hope for my years of degradation and demise is no different from any other guy's—namely, that I drop instantly dead at the Walt Whitman food court with Cinnabon in hand or in my (please, please, still conjugal) bed, and thus endure none of the despoiled lingering of contemporary death. And in this sense I very much feel for Pop, whose complaints about being here at Ivy Acres are fundamentally just surrogate grousings for what is addressable by only the greatest poets: the much bigger, hairier Here, which nobody but nobody can easily escape. I'll never admit it, but whenever Pop talks about offing himself I'll dismiss him with a sigh or impatient guffaw but also silently whisper *Go ahead*, not with any righteous ease or malice but with what would be humble grace and mercy if I were in any position to bestow such lovely things. But I know, too, that my inward bleatings carry as much resolve as I might twenty or thirty years from now, when Jerry Battle's the one dangling the hair dryer above the surface of the bath water, which is to say none whatsoever, as I'd cry up the water level another inch before ever letting go.

I'm still prodding at my rigid tile of fish when I see that everyone else is mostly done. Pop is a world-class stuffer and always has been and it is actually a semi-pleasing sight now, to watch him pack in the gizzard. It's like every bite is a necessary breath, an angry little war against extinguishment. Daniel and Dennis are already onto the dessert of cling peach crumble, which from here looks like dirt-topped soup, with the other woman at the table, Sarah May, trying to fish out a slippery peach slice with her fingers. Daniel jabs it for her with a fork and hands it to her, like she's his baby sister. I see Bea, on the other hand, sort of scratching at her throat, and I immediately think of how peaches and pineapples have some chemical that makes me sound hoarse. I ask if she'd like a fresh glass of water, but she doesn't answer, still idly scratching away with a faraway look on her face, the face of maybe five hundred peaches ago, that time coming home from the Jersey shore when her father stopped the car at a farm stand and bought a half bushel and they ate them all the way up to New York, a pile of wet peach stones collecting on the floorboards. But of course that's my memory, with Pop insisting that he stop again for another half bushel so my mother could put up some preserves, but when we got home most of the new ones turned out to be mushy and wormy and Ma put them out for the neighborhood raccoons. I'm sure Bea is having a similar recollection, because she's sort of grinning now and looking girlish and reaching out for Pop's hand, which he sweetly automatically takes, and I am noting to myself that I'll remind him of this the next time he starts in on a complaint about the grimness of this place when Bea stands up and without so much as a warning splash-retches her dinner on the table.

Pop lets go as he pushes back and cries, "What's the big idea, Bea?"

The others hardly move and I am looking for one of the staffers to clean up the mess that doesn't smell at all like vomit when I see that Bea has now fallen onto the floor. She's shaking, and her eyes have rolled up, and I realize she's been choking this whole time. Pop is already kneeling down beside her and he orders me to do something. I prop her up and try Heimliching her a couple of times, to no use. A few staff people descend and practically throw me off and they try the same. But Bea is still down and now purple-faced, and though there's instantly a shouting crowd of medical people and staffers and curious residents pinching in upon poor Bea at the bottom, it's my father that I can hardly bear to see, for he is crying as I've never seen him cry before, not for Ma or Daisy or even for Bobby, with great shuddering gasps rippling the almost operatic costume of his billowy stained robe and polka-dot pajamas, and though I want to do something utterly basic like put a hand on his shoulder or nudge him or do anything else to bridge the widening gap, I really can't, not from any of the usual intimacy issues but because for once in my life, really for the very first time, I am scared for him.

seven

JACK CALLED ME EARLY this morning and said to turn on
CNN. I asked him what for and he said, "It's your Englishman."

I thanked him and hung up, and after some tense moments of
searching for the remote I was looking at a low-quality video of a
helicopter surveying rough water somewhere in the South Pacific,
with the caption at the bottom of the screen reading, Around-the-
World Balloonist Feared Downed. The voice of the reporter spoke
about Sir Harold Clarkson-Ickes's control team having made last
contact with him some twelve hours before, but said that yet another intense weather system had developed directly in his path
and engulfed him. It was hoped that Sir Harold would have
emerged from the storm a couple of hours earlier, perhaps blown
significantly off course but with his pod intact and communica-
tions still functioning. At the moment, though, they had no word
and were considering him to be downed some 500 kilometers east
of New Zealand. A desperate search-and-rescue mission was in
progress, but as yet there had not been any sign of the floatable
high-tech carriage or the silvery-skinned balloon.

I watched for another hour or so through a couple news cycles but the story wasn't changing and I decided to take a drive in the Impala. In fact I started to head out to MacArthur so I could get up in the nice weather and feel as though I was doing something for Sir Harold instead of just sitting there like snuff-show sleaze waiting for the gruesome signs of his death. But after I got to the field and took the tonneau cover off *Donnie*, and removed the cowl plug and pitot tube and wheel chocks, and climbed inside to check the electronics and test the play of the ailerons and rudder, I suddenly felt completely ridiculous, like I was some dopey kid pretending to be a salty air ace, dreamily preparing to set out and look for the poor bedraggled explorer himself (which I'm not sure I would do had Sir Harold splashed down right smack in the middle of the Sound, out of dread of actually spotting the deflated balloon floating forlornly in the water like a tossed condom, but also because I can't bear too much traffic anywhere, and especially up there), all of which seemed too utterly safe and symbolic even for yours truly. And I realized perhaps, perhaps, while taking off my headset, that the crucial difference between me and Sir Harold was not only a few extra zeroes in the bank account or that he possessed a genuine thrill-seeking Type-T personality (whereas mine, as Rita once snidely suggested, was really more Type-D—i.e., Down-filled-Seeking), but rather that one of us would always be peeking about while venturing forth, checking and rechecking for the field, no matter how fair the air. So for the first time ever I buttoned *Donnie* back up without flying her, and went about idly cruising around the county under the dusky-throated power of 327 cubic inches of prime American displacement, the sound of which can almost make you think you might actually be *accomplishing something*, if unfortunately these days in a selfish world-ruinous sort of way.

At one point I passed near enough to Ivy Acres to consider (and

ALOFT

feel the obligation of) stopping in to check on Pop, but I knew he'd be in the same unsettled mood he's been in since what happened to Bea, and I decided to keep on rolling. Bea, I should report, has made it, but not in a good way. In fact I can say without hesitancy that it couldn't be worse. After I and the staff and then the actual licensed medical personnel took our turns not getting out what was lodged in Bea's throat, she was rushed to the hospital, where the ER doctors finally removed the foreign object from her airway (a diamond-shaped patch of renegade turkey sternum that had somehow slipped through the boneless-breast-roll machines) and got her heart pumping again. Soon thereafter they put her on a ventilator and apparently it was touch and go that night. But she is now, a week later, finally breathing on her own, though it seems that she is no longer saying or thinking or feeling very much, or at least showing any signs of doing so, now or in the near future.

The near future being all Bea—and a lot of the rest of us— has left.

What's a bit shocking is how thoroughly fine Pop seems to be with the whole thing, or how far he's already moved past it. I drove him over to the hospital and we had a decent enough visit with Bea but the next day before I was to pick him up again he called to tell me he didn't want to go. I said no problem, that I could take him whenever.

"Don't bother yourself," he said, his voice uncharacteristically hoarse, like a smoker's. "I don't want to see her anymore."

"You don't mean that," I said.

"Yeah, I do."

"You're just exhausted by all this. Sounds like you're coming down with something."

"Probably. I don't feel good."

"I'll come over and have someone take a look at you."

"Forget it."

"Let's talk tomorrow," I said. "You'll feel different I bet."

"I don't want to see her anymore, Jerome. I'm not kidding you. It's over between us."

I didn't quite know what to say to that last bit, which made it sound as though he and poor Bea had a falling out, a lovers' quarrel, rather than the atmosphere-obliterating airburst that it was, and is.

"Okay. Maybe in a few days."

"No way. She's not for me."

"She's not herself right now, Pop. You know?"

"Not herself? Did you take a good look at her, Jerome, with her arms and legs as stiff as pipes? Who else do you think she might be? Esther fucking Williams?"

"I'm sure she'll get physical therapy soon. Maybe when she gets out of the hospital and they bring her back here, to the Transitions ward."

"Hey, buddy boy, I know the whole story. The nurses' aides will have to cut her toenails and fingernails and sponge-bathe her, too, but probably won't do a good job of it, so she'll start to smell bad and they'll resent having to deal with her even more than they do now. So they'll treat her worse and worse until the last dignified remnants of the old Bea get so fed up that she won't open her mouth to eat or drink."

"You have to stop thinking like this, Pop."

"I'm not thinking!" he says, loudly enough that his voice distorts through the handset. "I don't have to *think*. I've got eyes. And I've seen enough of what happens to the dried-out hides around here to know none of it is pretty. So don't expect me to put on a brave face and make the best of it, because that's all horseshit. I'm not a pretender, Jerome, I think you know that. I've never run my life that way and I'm not going to do it now. So listen to me. Bea is

gone, gone forever. You can do me a big favor and not mention her anymore. Because if she ever does come back here from the hospital I'm not going to talk to her or visit her or go hold her hand or do anything else like that. She's kaput, okay? Dead and buried. I'm done with it, I'm finished."

"So what are you going to do now?"

"Whatdya mean, what am I going to do? I'm busy as hell. I'm gonna sit here and grow my nose hair. I'm gonna grind down my corns. If I'm lucky I won't slip in the tub and break my ass. What's this I hear about Theresa maybe being pregnant?"

"Who told you that?"

"Jack. He visits me every week, you know."

"I didn't know that."

"He's no emotional deadbeat."

"She told him?"

"He thought she looked like she was showing at the party. And now they're getting hitched sooner, right?"

"I guess."

"So what else is there?"

"Not much," I said, though at that moment I surprised myself by nearly asking for his advice, which wouldn't be advice so much as an opinion on what he would do and the blanket idiocy of any other course, probably to the tune of me putting my foot down and telling her that if she didn't jettison the baby and start treatments asap, she and Paul would have to pack up and leave and expect no support from me because I wasn't the kind of guy who would stand by tapping out the inexorable countdown of life while his daughter was ensuring her own doom, or something like that. So I said, "It's early. She's not due for a while."

"Well, I decided if it's a boy I'd like him to be named Henry. Or Hank. Tell her that. I don't care if he's got hardly any Battle in him. Jesus. How did our family get so damn Oriental? I guess you started it. Even Jack's kids—you'd think with that Nazi wife of his they wouldn't look like such little coolies."

As usual I didn't say anything to this, because there's no point, no point at all, though in truth I've thought the same basic thing countless times, if in somewhat more palatable terms, merely to muse upon the fact and not at all to judge, though whether that makes it generally acceptable or not I'll never be sure.

"I'll swing by later."

"Don't do anything on my account."

"Come on, Pop. Cut me a break, okay?"

"Yeah, yeah, whatever."

"Tell me you're going to be okay."

"Tell yourself," he growled, and he clicked off before I could say anything else—our customary truncation, which is necessarily fine with me.

But I am bothered, and worried. I'd like to think that part of Pop's swift turn of sentiment is just a self-defense stratagem, or that it's because he doesn't have a long history with Bea, but to be honest I know of course Pop is right, that he has already dug right down to the core of the matter, as he does, alarmingly, most all of the time, for Bea *as is*—her limbs wooden and immobile, her pupils coal blue and unfixed, completely speechless and soundless save for the feeble high-pitched wheeze she'll make when the nurse shifts her in the bed—is really nothing but precisely un-equivocally herself, the same "ain't nobody else" that Pop and I and you and yours will turn into (if even by a senseless accident) and instantly, wholly, embody.

Naturally, by any standard, Bea deserves better from him (and certainly from her daughter and grandchildren, who just departed on a monthlong Maui vacation, according to the Ivy Acres scuttle-butt), not to mention the fact that none of us really knows the full extent of her sentience, what she might be taking in. But at the same time I can't blame Pop for moving on, if that's what he's really doing. What concerns me is that as distraught as he was when it happened he's definitely being a bit too dispassionate now. Right now, whether it was for Bea's sake or not, he would normally be railing against our society's urgent program to isolate its old folks in air-conditioned corporate concentration camps, to expunge all signs of disease and disability from public view, to sanitize not only death but the conspiracy to deny its existence, all his archly negative highfalutin notions that remind me where in fact Theresa comes from. Instead, he is sitting alone in his room with a dismal slump to his shoulders, his toenails hoof-like with neglect, not even bothering to watch the logorrheaists on the Fox News Channel.

In fact, I'd trade this lingering quietude for an angry jag or two of paranoid bombast, just to know he's still there. I'm worried about him as I've never worried about him. Not to mention that he's sounding slightly short of air, emphysemey, which is not like Pop at all, who has always been the free-breathing type, having spent most of his life outdoors in the superfertile waft of suburban gravel and loam. This last little detail had a sneaky effect on me, and when a little while later I called him and he answered again in the same existence-weary tone, I actually hung up on him. I couldn't quite bear to hear it, though I wanted to confirm, too, that he wasn't just doing it for me, the broken-down geezer act.

I almost called him again, given my habit/condition of disbelieving the Real. The fact is, I don't think I've ever seen him seriously sick or injured. Maybe once or twice, when I was a kid, he had a bad enough headache after work that my mother had to prepare a bowl of ice-cold compresses to place over his eyes as he lay down on the living room sofa, and another time at an extended-family picnic when his cousin Gus accused Pop of screwing his second wife (smoldering Aunt Frannie, of the perky sky-searching tits) and attacked him with a bat during the traditional softball game, knocking him out cold for ten scary minutes. Other than that, Pop has been as physically solid as the masonry work he and his brothers used to do at the big North Shore mansions, artisan-perfect brick walls and slate patios and Carrara marble pillars and stairs that will probably last five hundred years as long as there's no asteroid strike or polar ice cap melt or some other civilization-ending event. So perhaps it's also my disbelief in the Real that leads me to think and hope—and ultimately, truly, believe—that all this cruddy rime will soon slough off and that Bea will rise up from her broccoli dreams to once again give Pop tender dentureless head in the moonlit corners of the dayroom after everyone's been medicated for another passage through this world's turn. And that he himself will remain exactly as is, in his costume armor of crazy old titan, while the universe trembles through and beyond him in its darkly incessant expansion. And yet, voilà, *non* mirabile dictu (as Paul or Theresa will sometimes sigh, I think unironically), the Real insists, it heeds no time or other cosmic dimensionalities, brooks no terrestrial dissent, it ignores even the poignant majesty of our noblest human wishes, which are like ground mists to the hot morning sun, lingering as long as they can before being almost instantly transmogrified, dispatched, forgotten.

Ask Sir Harold how quickly things can fall apart.

Which is why, with no one to call, Theresa and Paul gone out on an errand somewhere, and Jack on the road to present another bid, and feeling distinctly outside of things, I have given in to what is my most accessible trouble and driven over to Muttontown, where I am now, parked outside of Richie Coniglio's brick Georgian-revival mansion. The house is from the 1920s or so, the last time in our history when they really did build it right, with its glossy black shutters and white window trim and tendrils of ivy curling up over the patinaed copper gutters, the muted, multihued slate roof a stolid, stately cap over it all, bespeaking (or bellowing, more like) a hushed rampart of the Establishment. The rest of the neighborhood is of similar scale and order, the houses and properties primped and manicured enough but not so much as to seem nouveau, and some aspects of me must look the part, as the private security guard drove past and slowed and then gave me a toadying salute. The gleaming car, no doubt, helped do the trick—it's just the kind of nostalgic set of wheels the salt-and-pepper neighborhood fellows (or a visiting friend) would tool around in on a fine summer Sunday.

I've guessed right, because Rita's yellow Mustang is parked in back by the five-bay carriage house (going back two cars deep), along with another dusty not-so-late-model coupe, which is probably the housekeeper's car, and one of Richie's Ferraris, the other six or seven new and vintage no doubt tucked neatly inside. Richie is somewhat famous in the area as an avid collector (being featured in full-color spreads in local periodicals like *Island Lifestyle* and *Nassau Monthly*), and even races a couple of specially tuned models at rich-guy rallies in California and Italy. Out front, on the semicircular drive, are two BMW sedans and a Range Rover, and it's not hard to figure that the Rabbit is entertaining guests, which in another circumstance and time might have dissuaded me from inviting myself in, but today feels like no big thing at all.

At the door, a portly older black woman dressed not in a uniform but in a dark, severe housedress that might as well be one asks if she can help me.

"I'm a colleague of Rita's," I say, hoping that she'll assume I'm some kind of doctor or hospital administrator. "She asked me to drop by."

The woman nods, tight-lipped, impressive with her high-domestic manner, an utterly neutral bearing that still leaves every-thing about you in doubt. Her accent is faintly Caribbean. "Just a moment, sir. Your name, please?"

"Jerome Battle," I say, suddenly liking the way that sounds.

"You will wait in the foyer, please."

"No problem."

She regards me for an extra beat, as if she's telling me with her eyes that every wall hanging and knickknack in the room is now accounted for and catalogued, as are my height and hair and eye color. I fix/flash the ol' sparkle eyes, but no dice. The lady has a ro-bot heart. She pads down the long hall in black orthopedic shoes and slides open a pair of pocket doors, glances at me once more, then disappears, closing the doors behind her. I'm listening for voices, but I can't hear a thing, not a single thing, as if all the rooms are hermetically sealed off from one another. This is not quite the case in my drafty ranch house, where (when I wasn't liv-ing alone) you could hear every footfall on the creaky floorboards, every middle-of-the-night toilet flush and throat-clearing. Luxury means privacy, to people like Richie, even inside your own home. To a somewhat lesser degree it's the same deal at Jack's house, though there the new construction is in fact shamefully light-duty, so that you'd hear everything, too, if the place weren't so huge and many-winged.

Here in the Rabbit's lair, after I glimpse into the parlor on one side of the foyer, and the library on the other, it's instantly obvious that we're talking all custom material, even beyond the ultra-high-end stuff Jack wants to peddle, the kind of prime antique furnishing and ornamentation that you would never be able to put together if you weren't bred in the life, or didn't handsomely pay someone who purported that he or she did, which was clearly Richie's route. I know where he grew up, the Coniglios living in the same nice but not great Atomic Age Italian neighborhood of

Queens as we did, in a brick shoebox house on a ⅛-acre lot, where the single garage door below the living room was barely wide enough to squeeze a fat-ass Buick inside. Mr. Coniglio, like a lot of the dads, was some kind of mechanic or driver or municipal employee, a policeman or fireman or garbage man, a something-man with his name stitched on his workshirt or number stamped on a badge, a guy who didn't mind hitting you fungoes in the street after his shift in his tank undershirt, and afterward maybe letting the bunch of you split one of his fresh cold beers. Where he grew up, the smells drifting out from the houses weren't of sandalwood and myrrh, you were careful not to scuff the then-new Formica and Congoleum, and high art was a deep-shag wall rug of sailboats or wild horses your mother and aunts had hand-knotted, or else posters of hilly seaside villages in Italy and Sicily, every one of them brittle in the corners and fading too fast. And yet knowing all of the above makes me feel a little more generously inclined toward Richie than I otherwise would, given his station and current intimacy with Rita (which is another detail that speaks well for him, not caring that she's a brown person), because no matter what, you have to hand it to a guy who never peeked or looked down on his way up to the top, who never paused or wondered or else settled too readily into any of life's intermittent drafts of friction-free gliding.

After what seems like barely a ten-count (as if she sprinted here on hearing my name), Rita appears in the doorway of the library, where I'm poking through dusty, moldering leather-bound volumes of late-nineteenth-century English maritime law, just the sort of deductible decorative element white-shoe attorneys love to impress visitors (and interlopers) with, having bought out some law library annex. Rita, on the other hand, looks absolutely fresh, *phhht!*, right out of the can, as she's dressed in tennis whites, a tiny little skirt and sleeveless top, pom-pom peds, and brand-new

Reeboks, and my first thought-picture is how the skirt must flip up to reveal the frilly white underbrief against her smooth mocha thighs, and suddenly I'm more than a bit piqued.

"You don't play tennis," I say, sounding maybe too much like Pop, that aggrieved, aggressive combo of knowing nothing and knowing-it-all.

"What are you doing here, Jerry?" she says, not moving any closer. "I swear, you're losing it. You have to leave, right now. Please leave now, Jerry."

"But you don't play tennis."

"Will you stop that? Anyway, I've started. I'm taking lessons."

"From Richie?"

"No. The pro at his club. Though Richard is a pretty good teacher. Listen, why do you care?"

"You never told me you were interested in tennis."

"I didn't know I was. I didn't know about a lot of things I might have enjoyed."

"You say that like it was my fault."

Rita shakes her head, her pinned-up hair making her look like a schoolgirl. I swear I would have fallen in love with her, at any age. Think of Jeanne Moreau, who looked good at every age, but with a darker complexion, a sweeter manner. She says, "Let's leave it alone. And anyway, that's not the issue. The issue is, What are you doing here? I asked you not to come around here, remember?"

"I wanted to talk."

"You could have called me at home. He's having guests today."

"Champagne brunch and tennis."

"That's right."

"You know I'm thrilled that you're not saying 'we.'"

"This is Richard's house, not mine."

"And when you're married?"

"That's none of your business."

"He has you signing a prenuptial, right?"

"I'm not talking to you."

"I knew it. He's got it all spelled out, I bet. If you divorce or he dies, you don't get the house, or the cars, or the bearer bonds, or the Aspen ski lodge, or the bungalow in Boca. You just get whatever clothes or furs or jewelry he bought you, plus some parting gift, a check to cover six months' expenses."

"That would be a lot more than I got from you."

"Hey, you never asked. And I would have given you anything you wanted. Anything. I would have given you my house. My plane."

"What would I do with your plane, Jerry?"

"I'm just saying. Come on, Rita. Come back home with me. I'll build you a tennis court in the backyard. There's plenty of room, where the pool was. I'll make it whatever surface you like, concrete, clay. I'll even do grass. It's a bitch to maintain but I can get the special mowers. . . ."

"Will you please stop, Jerry? I just want you to leave, before Richard comes in and you embarrass me. I'm asking you nicely now but I swear if you don't listen to me I'll never talk to you again. Never, never, I swear. Are you hearing me?"

I am hearing her, hearing her good 'n' plenty, as my mother liked to be silly and sometimes say, but that doesn't seem to matter because I'm not moving in the direction she wants—namely, out the door—and instead I'm still just standing here in this mahogany-paneled purgatory and jabbering what is clear pure reason to me but obviously sheer bankrupt babble to this woman I have loved perhaps wisely but not too well (or maybe not even that). Rita is glaring at me and crossing her arms in the way she does and I've long known, which might appear like plain pissed-offness but is really, if you could touch her, a steady boa-like self-constriction, the kind of anal-retentive stress response that you'd think would never afflict a beautiful fiery Latina; but in fact Rita is neither too fiery nor too much of a Latina, and never was, which is in no small measure why she and yours truly could have any history at all. The last gasp end of said history, I can finally see, has long commenced.

And that is when I tell her, out of body, and amazed with every word, "Theresa's in trouble."

"What trouble?" she says, stepping toward me now. "What are you talking about?"

"She and Paul have seen a doctor."

"They're pregnant? Something's wrong?"

"Yeah."

"What's wrong? Is something wrong with their baby?"

"It's complicated."

"If you're pulling something here, Jerry. . . ."

But right then who pops in but Solicitor Coniglio, in his own shock-white tennis togs, looking tan and trim and not even that gray up top, an upmarket Jack La Lanne.

"I had a suspicion it was you, Jerry," Richie says, shaking my hand, all bluster and smile, like he's the fucking chair of the membership committee. "Have you eaten lunch yet?"

"Nope."

"Come outside, then, Alva's got her special buffet going. She's an amazing cook, you know. Rita can vouch for her. Her curried lobster salad is stupendous."

I glance at Rita; she's been thrown enough off balance, I can see, not to call me out on the kilim. And now I'm sorry that I brought up Theresa at all, because Rita has always loved both the kids, though naturally in different ways, tending to mother Jack and be girlfriendy with Theresa, which was just right for who they were.

But then she says weakly, "He was just going."

"Oh come on, Jerry, that's silly," he says to me, like I'm the one protesting. "You're already here. Besides, my doubles partner just pulled up lame, with a tight hammy. We'll all have a quick bite, and then you can fill in."

He says to Rita, "You know, Jerry used to play a lot."

"Not really," I say. This is mostly true, save for the summer before senior year in high school, when I decided to try something different from the Catskills camp and took care of a three-court tennis club up on the coast of Maine. I played with anyone needing a partner, and I found the game came naturally to me. By the end of the summer I was giving this small college-team player a run for his money, and when the school year started I lettered on the tennis team, at #2 singles, somehow making all-league honorable mention.

Rita's eyes plead no contest, and I plead the Fifth, so Richie ushers us through the kitchen and dining room to the back patio, where his colleagues are sitting around a large wrought-iron table with their drinks, a huge market umbrella shading them from the hot sun. The women are out on the court, playing Canadian doubles. I'm introduced by name only, and everyone tells me theirs, though I forget them instantly, as I'm sure they do mine. The men are attorneys in the firm, one of them younger than Richie and me by at least ten years, the other two quite a bit younger still, this clearly being the senior-partner-hosting-the-underlings sort of gathering, probably so that he can remind them again why they're billing 3000 hours this year and next year and every year after that.

But it's not an altogether typical crew (though probably I'm dead wrong), as the two young lawyers are minorities, black and Asian (their wives or girlfriends are both white, I should note), only the older one being more or less what you'd think, this vaguely Teddy Kennedy–looking fellow with a florid, Irishy face and a gut and obviously pushing fifty and a first bypass. He's the one who's strained a muscle, no doubt trying to hold up his end competing with Richie against the young-uns, who I'm certain feature assured, classy games groomed at Hotchkiss-Choate-Trinity-Williams. They're of completely different races, of course, but they look to me like they're very much the same, oddly identical in their cool, semi-affable carriage, that self-satisfied apprentice master of the universe demeanor with which they encounter everyone but red-phone Richie, who rates the alpha-wolf treatment of flattened ears and tucked tail and gleeful yelps of respect and gratitude, and not so metaphorically speaking. The Asian associate is a bit more brownnosing than the black one, in that he laughs too heartily at Richie's jokes and observations and talks just like him, too, in tenor and rhythm. The black kid is somewhat careful, superpolite, his tentativeness masking what is probably a world-shaking ambition. Lame Teddy K. over there comports himself with plenty of self-possession, but probably exactly as much as Richie will allow. You can't blame any of them, certainly, because it is, if you'll excuse me, pretty fucking incredible around here, even in my long experience working for the Island gentry. Richie's property stretches magnificently beyond us in this run of lawned space long enough that I could probably land *Donnie* on it in a pinch, the Har-Tru tennis court tastefully sited to one side and screened by a low boxwood hedge "fence," so as not to spoil any vista, trees and shrubs and paths like something you'd find in the Tuileries, the stonework weathered to just that seemly state of honorable decline. And then there is icy Alva's kitchen handiwork, an all-white tulip centerpiece accenting a buffet spread that would put any cruise ship's to shame, not just with its curried lobster and other pricey salads but also littlenecks on the half shell and gargantuan deep-fried prawns and fan-sliced tropical fruits and breads and a colorfully arrayed homemade dessert cart that includes my personal favorite, fresh coconut cream pie.

Richie flashes a china plate and asks what I'd like, apparently ready to serve, which I can't help but notice instantly warms his guests toward my surprise presence. It seems, though, to have an opposite effect on Rita, who suddenly excuses herself and heads inside. Richie, meanwhile, piles on the grub, and as I eat (Why not? It's here, and I like the idea of making my own minuscule ding in the ocean liner of his bank account) Richie, most surprising to me, tells his guests the story of how I once saved him from a certain beating by a greaser known as The Stank (from Stankiewicz). He's doing this to show his softer side, I have to guess, though the tale is conveniently set more than forty years in the past and thus is effectively about somebody else.

The Stank was a hulking kid, in that he'd been left back two or three times early on and by eighth grade was pretty much a manchild, with muscled forearms and full mustache and the armor-piercing b.o. of a plumbing contractor. They didn't know it then, but he had one of those rogue bacterial problems that no amount of washing can cure, which it was rumored he did at least two or three times a day, slipping off to the locker room to shower between classes. He wasn't so much mean or a bully as he was volatile—say, grabbing an earth science teacher's throat if he thought a question was meant to embarrass, which may or may not have happened but became part of school lore. I never had any problem with him, even though I was one of the bigger kids in the school, which can often mean in the eyes of the school that we'd have to square off, almost by default, like they do with top prizefighters.

Richie, as he tells it now, made some wiseass comment about the barnyard odor of the lunch selections; The Stank stood a couple kids ahead on the cafeteria line, and being extra-sensitive about his aroma, glared with rage.

"I saw The Stank's face," Richie says, "and to be perfectly honest I hadn't meant to insult him. I wasn't a complete fucking idiot."

His guests chuckle uneasily, throttling back in case this is just underling bait.

"But you guys know how I like to work."

"Balls on the block," the Asian associate croons, tipping his glass toward Richie. "Ass in the fire."

"You got it, Kim-ster," Richie replies, animated. "But I couldn't help myself, something came over me, and I kept talking shit, louder and louder. The Stank is about to explode, but he gets his food and walks off, and I think I'm home free. But when the bell rings he's waiting for me and drags me outside. I'm saying the Lord's Prayer, because I'm about eighty-five pounds, and The Stank's easily one seventy-five. He's got me literally pinned up against the school building, in a choke hold, my feet kicking. I was just about to black out when Jerry here happens by."

"You kicked The Stank's butt, Mr. Battle?" the other associate asks. I think his name is Kenton.

"No way," I try to reply, through a mouthful of smoked-trout frittata.

"My old friend Jerry here talked some sense to him. I don't remember now. What did you say, Jerry?"

"I think I told him he should probably reconsider, because he really might kill you, and then where would he be? He'd spend the rest of his life at Sing Sing, where they'd let him shower just once a week."

"In fact the same insult," Richie points out.

"I guess he let you go soon after that."

"I guess he did," Richie says, gazing off into his pastures. "After that, Jerry was my hero. I think I bought you sodas for a week."

"I would say about that."

There's a bit of a lull then, just the soft pocks of the women's ground strokes, and it's clear that the story didn't quite entertain in the way Richie perhaps thought it might, though I can't see how it would, at least from the perspective of impressing his colleagues. But then among a certain class of people, tales of woe and near-ruin have a sneaky kind of honor, these badges of pathos that lend some necessary muck to otherwise wholly splendid, smashing lives. Although Richie and I both left out a few details of the conclusion of that incident—namely, that The Stank (who was not as dumb as people thought) insisted on exacting his own price for Richie's wising-off, such that Richie had to do all his homework for the rest of the year, and also submit to one small physical punishment, both of which, I guess, I brokered. And if you look real close at Richie now you can spot it, how he has the scantest hitch to his gait, this infinitesimal hop to the left foot, where all 175 pounds of The Stank jumped up and landed with his steel shank shitkicker boot, breaking the bones of Richie's foot into an extra dozen little pieces.

"Rat and I'll stomp your fucking head," The Stank said, and Richie, to his credit, just nodded through clenched teeth. I helped him to the nurse's office, where he told her a big rock had fallen on him. She was incredulous, but didn't care enough to pursue it.

The women come back from the tennis court, saying it's getting too hot and humid to play, which it is. We meet and greet. They're all elite professional types, two lawyers and a portfolio manager, as well as very attractive, though not in the way I prefer, meaning they're a bit too thin and sharply featured, like you might jab yourself if you hugged and kissed them with any real verve. Daisy was slim, but she had a round moon face and was unusually supple of body, and Rita, of course, is a lovely plenteous armful, legful, everything else, which I'm sure makes a man like me not really yearn to conquer or destroy or run my part of the world, but rather just dwell and loll and hope to float a little, relinquish the burdens.

And I'm wondering how long she'll remain inside, when Richie suggests the men play doubles; but the younger guys balk, saying they're too full with brunch, obviously just wanting to drink more beer, the older fellow still leaning on the table, trying to stretch out his leg, and Richie takes a racquet and hands it to me, practically supplanting my luncheon fork, and tells me I'm up.

"No way. I haven't played in more than twenty years," I tell him, not an untruth, the last time being at a divorced/widowed singles holiday mixer at an indoor tennis bubble, and only because I was bored to death.

"We'll just hit."

"I'm not dressed. Look at my shoes." I show him (and everybody else) my knockoff Top-Siders from Target. I'm wearing long shorts and an old polo shirt with a Battle Brothers logo on the breast, the head of a rake.

"What's your sneaker size?"

"Twelves. There's no way I'd fit into one of yours, what, you're an eight, nine?"

"We've got lots of extra pairs around here. Alva, if you can take a look, please."

"Yes, sir."

"Forget it. Anyway, I just ate."

"So did I."

"I haven't finished."

"Listen, Jerry," Richie says, irked, in his sharp conference table alto, "when are you going to figure out that there's no free lunch around here?"

Suddenly everyone's calling on me to play, except of course for Alva, who has just disappeared inside the house on her errand.

"Okay," I say, looking back to the house for Rita, my only ally, though thinking that perhaps she's been instructed to stay inside by Richie, so that she won't be a good health professional and dissuade this fifty-nine-year-old idiot from killing himself on the court.

We start hitting, or at least Richie does, as I blast his first three balls to me over the fence; after the third, Richie tells me to cut the bullshit. But I'm not playing games; it's my first time with these new titanium racquets, my last weapon being a lacquered wood model (Jerry Kramer Special) strung with natural gut that you could nicely spin the ball with but had to whip to get any decent pace. This feather-light shiny thing feels like a Ping-Pong paddle in my hand, its head seeming twice as big as it should be— yet another game-improvement technology that makes anyone instantly competent in a sport he should probably never pursue but will anyway, leading to a lifetime of further time/financial investment. But after a couple more moonshots and a few overspins that dive and hit the court on *my* side of the net, I start to get the old stroke back, my arm feeling like the twenty-year scaffolding around it has been dismantled, and soon enough I'm solidly striking my ground strokes, at least those I don't have to range too far for, as my footwork is shot and probably gone forever. And *Ah yes,* comes the revelation, *I have legs, I have knees.* Richie, on the other hand, appears to be playing a narrower court than mine. He's always hitting from the correct body position, knees flexed, shoulder to the target, weight moving forward, and though he doesn't hit for power he consistently places his balls deep, right inside the baseline, and periodically shaves a nasty cut backhand that skids low on the Har-Tru, making me bend that much more than I really can. He's good, for sure, obviously not self-taught, nothing natural about it, but thanks to hundreds of hours with his pro and a home ball machine and traveling tourneys with his club, he's got game.

"Not too shabby, Jerry," Richie calls out. "Not too shabby at all."

I can't really answer because it's taking all my energy to keep the rally going, and although I'm enjoying the action and its rhythms, the breezeless air suddenly seems unbearably humid, like I'm playing inside a dryer vent, and I just stop, letting his approach skip past me unharmed.

"What's the matter?" Richie says, poised at the net.

"I think I'm done."

"Not possible, Jerry," he says, chopping at the top of the white tape with his racquet. He's excited, though hardly breathing. "You gotta keep going. You're just getting into a groove. I think we're nicely matched. I usually play against guys who hit it pretty flat, but you have a lot of topspin on your shots, even your backhand."

"I'm done, Richie. Plus my feet are killing me."

I slip my sockless foot out of the deck shoe, half afraid to look. But it's not horrible, gone the color of watermelon, just that shade (white) skin turns just before the blisters puff out.

"Come on, it's nothing," he tells me, like his play date is being cut short. "Anyway, look, here comes Alva. Rita, too."

I turn around, and indeed the two of them are approaching the court, Alva holding an orange shoebox, Rita sporting an expression of extreme confusion and alarm, as if the sight of me holding a racquet near Richie were tantamount to wielding a machete, as in what is that lunatic Jerry doing now?

Alva flips the box top and hands me a pair of brand-new Nikes. "Twelve on the dot, Mr. Jerry," she says, it seems to me a bit gleefully. "I already laced them up for you. With fresh socks inside."

I say to Richie, "Where did you get these?"

"I told you," Richie says, coming on to my side of the court, "we keep tennis shoes around, for guests. You can keep them."

"He doesn't need them," Rita breaks in. "Jerry, I'll talk to you later, all right?"

"Hey, now, Rita," Richie says. "He's a big boy."

"Jerry!" she says, her voice firm and sharp enough that I reflexively begin handing the sneakers back to Alva.

Richie pushes the pair into my chest and says to Rita, "Hey, sweetheart, be a nice girl and sit down, okay?"

"Jerry was just going . . ."

"We're having *fun* here, Ri-ta," he says, more pronouncing her name than speaking it. "We'd like to focus on the business at hand. Please sit down and watch, or else join my friends and have something more to eat. Can I ask you to do that? Is that too much for me to ask? Because if it is, I'm confused. Maybe I'm dumb. But hey, if you insist, I'll do what you want."

Rita doesn't answer, because it's really not too much to ask but of course it is, especially when you ask that way, and I understand now why I never really liked Richie Coniglio too much, why I never really regretted standing by while the The Stank made a tortilla out of his foot, and why, too, maybe the worst kind of bullies are the ones who exert brain power rather than muscle power (as they can badly mistreat anyone they like, women and children, too, and still remain upstanding, for they leave no marks). Guys like Richie get pretty much 98 percent of whatever they want, that's their core talent, what they actually do for a living, the only thing slipping their grasp being that tiny sliver of unalloyed good feeling from friends and acolytes and lovers and other parties who should be celebrating but definitely are not. And maybe in a somewhat related manner, the people near and dear to me have perhaps decided that I'm not altogether different, that if I'm no rainmaker extraordinaire like Richie I'm a fellow who has enjoyed a bit too much calm flying for my (or anybody's) own good, and thus should suffer regular baleful storms of ill will to dash so unbuffeted a route. There's sense in this, for sure, but I'd say, too, that there's no other mode in this life of ours as sanctified as the one in which you glide to the finish, supine, reclined, as sleepy-eyed as a satyr.

"Let's play, Richie," I say, without pleasure or merriment. "One set."

"You got it. But what's the stake?"

"Whatever you like."

"Oh God," Rita says, starting back for the house.

"How about our wheels?" Richie says, straightening the strings of his racquet head. "What are you driving these days?"

"Impala convertible, '67."

"Yeah, I'll put up my '92 Testarossa. It's the one there by the garage. Four hundred original miles. It's worth at least eighty."

"Fine with me."

"Sure, but you'll have to do better. The Chevy's worth what, twenty at most? Don't you own a little plane?"

"You don't fly, Richie."

"You watch. I'll learn."

Rita has stopped, her posture and expression disbelieving that this has pretty much come to a pissing contest (though that would be a lot quicker and easier). She's waiting for my answer.

"Okay," I say, the sound of it harmless, not quite believing that this is for real, which is no doubt how chronic gamblers blithely invite utter ruin. Rita turns and immediately heads for the house. I tell everybody to wait a second, and follow her, at a respectful, cool distance, but once inside she goes right into a powder room next to the kitchen.

"Come on, now," I say through the walnut door. "We're just playing a game."

"You two are jerks."

"I still think he's worse than me."

"Just leave me alone, Jerry. Leave me alone."

I keep talking, but she doesn't answer, and soon just keeps flushing the can to drown out my words.

On the way back out I notice on the kitchen desk a laptop computer that's on, and hooked to the Web (the bastard has this same incredible fast line in his house that Jack does back at the shop), so I quickly tap in Sir Harold's address, and there it is, right on the big full-color flat screen, a grainy shot of Sir Harold's deflated silver balloon afloat in the water, signage of the party definitely being over, a skinny brown fisherman corralling it with a long-staffed hook. Another shot is of the damaged pod, its hatch missing, one side of it crushed in like a half-eaten whorl. The text is brief, and is addressed to Our Friends and Supporters:

The Magellan III pod has been located. Sir Harold Clarkson-Ickes has not yet been found. Our search will continue.

One of the women knocks at the French doors and waves at me to come out. I click off the site and follow her to Richie's Centre Court, where the others are buzzing with talk of the wager.

But as I tie on my new sneakers I picture Sir Harold stiff-limbed and suspended in the dark water of the ocean, his hair streaming out in wildness, his gray-tipped beard fixed forever with its tragic explorer's-length growth, the shoes and socks knocked off his now bare feet, and his eyes, his eyes, gazing out at the terrible immensity of the deep. He surely loved to be alone, but not down there, submerged, caught in the wrong element. I feel suddenly sick to my stomach, and I step over behind the beautifully clipped boxwood and retch all of Alva's fine cold lobster curry. The shrub is tinseled in reds and greens. My eyes tear with the gagging, of course, but for a few seconds I really let go; I can't remember the last time I bawled like this (not even after Daisy), and it's only when I feel a hand on my shoulder do I suck it up.

"Maybe you ought to take a pass, Mr. Battle." It's Kenton, offering a napkin. "You look real sick."

"Oh, he'll be all right," Richie calls over. "Just game-day nerves. Come on, Jerry, let's get this show on the road."

Richie, being the lawyer, goes over the whole deal: one six-game set, 12-point tie breaker at 6–all, honor system for calls, and (this clause for me) any play-ending injury or other inability to continue resulting in the forfeiture of the match and the keys to his car and my plane, which we've placed in a wineglass on the courtside table, where everyone but Rita is sitting.

Not surprisingly, I start out slow, serving first and promptly losing the game love, dumping three of the points on double faults. Richie easily wins his serve, and in the next game I do better, though still lose, chunking one game-winning volley into the net, and then completely whiffing an easy overhead on an out, for an instant 3–0. No one is saying anything at the side change, least of all Richie, who simply micro-adjusts his wristbands and smiles the tidy smile of a man who knows the future. The fourth game looks bad for me, as Richie is working his big-kicking serves into my body, which I can't do much with save return harmlessly to him at the net, starting a predictable chain reaction of his crisp deep volley and my lame lob and his controlled smash and my desperate, futile get. But after those I sneak a couple skidding line jobs, and at 30–all he double-faults, I don't know how or why, but this squarely irritates him, I can see, because his whole game is not to commit any unforced errors, and on his ensuing serve (a bit flatter and wider) I go for broke and bust a forehand winner down the line. Game, Mr. Battle. I even pump a fist in the air, not just for me but also for Sir Harold, and while I'm mentally feting myself (because it sure feels to me as if I've already won), Richie breaks my serve again in a love game to go up 4–1; and as we change sides it dawns on me with a big fat *duh* that he's maybe eight lousy points away from taking my *Donnie*. But rather than inspire me, the circumstance paralyzes, I'm choked with dread, the picture of Richie soaring on high at the controls surveying the contour and line of his own earthly garden and then the rest of us gravity-stricken bipeds literally taking my breath away, and I have to clutch the net post to keep from falling down.

"Somebody give Mr. Battle there a drink," Richie says, already waiting at his baseline. "Nobody's going to croak here today."

Kenton comes and gives me a bottle of spring water, and says, with a hand on my shoulder, "You okay?"

I nod, finishing the bottle in one quick pull. He gives me another, this time advising me to drink it slow. When I look into his eyes I can see how he's seeing me, as a bedraggled pathetic heap, a veritable *old man*, which maybe I am but I'm not (but maybe I am?), and though *Donnie* is in jeopardy and I'm losing my ability to perspire, it's this that really shakes me, halts my breath.

Richie says, "What the fuck, Kenton, you nursing him now?"

"Jes bein a good water boy, boss," he says in a thick pickaninny accent, which gives them all a good laugh, including Richie.

"Well let's move it along, son."

Kenton yessuhs, and I mutter "Thanks, buddy" to him, and as he hands me my racquet in exchange for the empty bottle he says in a voice so low I can hardly hear him, "Play low to the forehand."

I don't acknowledge him, of course, because I can hardly manage anything more than the basics, but when play resumes I think about what he said and begin doing it, hitting short cut shots to Richie's forehand whenever he's well back, which normally wouldn't be recommended against a solid net player like Richie but is strangely effective, as he seems to have some trouble handling a shortish ball on that side, resulting in flabby groundstrokes that are long and out, or, if in, I can hit back hard. Maybe Kenton has played enough with Richie to have learned this tendency, but after yet another short ball that Richie has to scuttle forward for I realize perhaps the reason why: it's his left foot that leads that particular shot, his left foot broken in youth by The Stank. Maybe it plain hurts when he lunges on it, or maybe it's a phantom hurt (which can be just as disturbing, if not more), but the fact of the matter is, it's working for me, not just for cheap and easy points but also because he's at last clearly tiring, no longer trying to run down every ball. So I keep cutting and then pouncing, and somehow winning, and although I'm feeling a little wooden in the legs I'm really zipping my strokes with this newfangled racquet, hitting the ball with a ferocious pace Richie is obviously unaccustomed to, and not at all liking. With my mounting success his colleagues and their s.o.'s have begun to cheer each of his points, even Kenton barking for Richie with feeling (we can all act in a pinch), but it's no matter; eventually the score is 6–5, Richie still in the lead, but I've got him at triple break point and I step forward practically to the service line and Richie implodes, jerking both serves into the bottom half of the net.

"Fuck!" he shouts, tossing down and kicking his racquet, and then turns to his hushed gallery. "You can clap for him, for chrissake. He's goddamn playing well enough."

So they do, and with what I detect is an extra measure of appreciation for my helping to make this something other than your standard boss's brunch, not to mention the fact that they would always gladly pay good money to see Richie suffer a substantial hit to his ego, if not bottom line. But none of it matters, because in my game focus I just now notice that Rita has been watching at courtside, maybe for a whole game or two, her face still sour for this endless intrusion, for my once again (I can anticipate her now) thrusting myself in the center ring of everyone else's business and pleasure.

"Why don't you two call it quits now," Rita says. "You're tied and we've had our fun."

"The fun's not over," Richie says, testing his racquet strings against his heels. I'm sitting on the ground, trying to stretch my legs, which are feeling suddenly hollowed out but calcified, these toppled, petrified trunks. "Come on, Jerry, get up, let's do it."

"Why do you want to do this?" Rita says, to us both. Maybe only I can tell, for she's not yelling or gesticulating and her expression hasn't changed, but she's really very angry now, practically livid. I know because her chin is noticeably quivering, something that happens to most other people when they're on the brink of crying. But she's far from that.

"Don't you see how disgusting this is? You really have to take away each other's toys, don't you? It's vulgar, Richard. And Jerry, let's be honest, you can't afford to lose your plane."

"Hey now . . ."

"I'm not talking about just *money*. What would you do without it? What, Jerry? Come on, tell me. What are you going to do?"

It's an excellent question, exactly the kind of query I get all the time from my loved ones, thoroughly rhetorical but also half holding out for some shard of the substantive from yours truly, some blood-tinged nugget of circumspection and probity. But maybe just not right now, as I'm wondering myself how I'm going to un-sticky this wicket I'm in, despite the 6—all tally I've worked, for my legs (are they mine?) feel absolutely inanimate, dumb, these knobby flesh logs that might as well be delicatessen fodder, glass-encased in the chill.

"I can't get up," I say to Rita. "I can't move."

"Cut the horseshit, Jerry," Richie says. "You've had enough rest. Come on. Your serve starts the tiebreak. Then we serve in twos. First one to seven."

"I really can't, Rita," I say. "I'm not kidding."

Rita quickly approaches, kneels down beside me.

"Are you serious?"

"Everything just froze up."

"Both legs?"

"Yeah. But in different parts."

Rita turns to Richie, who's now coming to inspect. She tells him, "Okay, that's it, Richard. He's all cramped up. He's probably totally dehydrated. Game's over."

"Hey, if that's what he wants."

"That's what's going to happen," Rita says, firm and nurse-like.

"I guess I'll start taking flying lessons," Richie says.

"You can't do that," she says. "You can't take his plane because of this."

"I'd rather not, but I will. You were inside when we agreed to the rules."

Rita looks at me as though I've descended to yet another circle of stupid-hell, and I can only, lowly, nod.

She says to him, "Richard. Don't be a jerk. Just call it a tie and Jerry can go home and everybody will be happy."

"Listen, Rita, you're completely missing your own point about toys. That's exactly right. There's no purer pleasure. So would you butt out right now, okay? Jerry and I made an honest wager with clear guidelines, and Jerry himself will tell you that if I were in his shoes, or in my own, to be exact, he would be doing the same thing. Ain't it so, Jerry?"

Of course I don't want to, but I have to nod, because he's absolutely right, even Rita knows it, I'd be righteously slipping that fat Ferrari fob on my mini–Swiss Army knife keychain before even helping his skinny ass up off the deck.

"I can't stand this," Rita says, using my thighs as a support to stand. It hurts, but sort of helps, too. The cool touch of her hands. She doesn't say anything, but just picks up her straw handbag (the one I brought back for her from the Canary Islands, with a heart cross-sewn into the weave) and just walks away, traversing the lawn straight to the carriage house, where she rumbles her banana mobile to life. For the whole time we watch her, neither Richie nor I saying a word, though I wonder if what he wants to say to her is just what I want to say, which isn't at all original, or earth-shaking, or even romantic; it's the most basic request, what a guy like me who always has plenty to say but never quite when it counts, wants to say most often: *Don't go*. And as I mouth it, she whirs her car backward on the driveway and into the street, and then, with a bad transmission jerk, rattles off.

Richie says, "Okay, Jerry, now that *that's* done, what the fuck are you going to do?"

I can't answer, angry as I am with his *that.*

"Come on, Battle, get up now. Or quit."

And I will tell you that Jerry Battle gets up on his feet then. And I make my legs work. And I make Richie pay for what we both should have done.

At least in that, I am magnificent.

eight

HERE AT MY SHARED DESK at Parade Travel, the foe is always inertia.

No one mentions it by name, certainly not me, but every trip or vacation I book for my customers is one more small victory for those of us who believe in the causes of motion and transit. This morning, for instance, I set up a December holiday for Nancy and Neil Plotkin, sending them first on a ten-day cruise of Southeast Asia, ports of call to include Bali, Singapore, and Phuket, where they will disembark and switch to overland on the Eastern Oriental Express for an escorted railway tour of the famous Silk Road, snaking up through Bangkok and to Chiang Mai, after which they'll fly back to Hong Kong for a two-night stay at the venerable Mandarin Oriental, to shop for trinkets and hike Victoria's Peak and take a junk ride across the harbor to the outdoor markets of Kowloon.

Pretty damn nice. The Plotkins, like me, are semi-retired, Nancy now periodically substituting at the middle school where she taught for thirty years, Neil actively managing their own retirement portfolio instead of the institutional mutual fund he ran since Johnson was president. They're pleasant enough people, which is to say typical New Yorkers, charming when they have to be and surprisingly generous and warm when they don't, though instantly skeptical and pit-bullish if in the least pushed or prodded. And they're easy customers to work with (this is the fourth big trip I've arranged for them), not just because they have plenty of time and disposable income and have varied touristical interests, but more that they seem to understand that a primary aspect of traveling is not just the destination and its native delights, but the actual process of *getting there*, the literal *travail*, which is innately difficult and laborious but also absolutely essential to create any true sense of journey. Unlike most customers, who naturally demand the shortest, most direct, pain-free routings, the Plotkins are willing to endure (and so savor, too) the periods of conveyance and transit, even when it's not a fancy ocean liner or antique train. For they don't dread the cramped quarters of capacity-filled coach, they don't mind arranging their own taxi transfers in unfamiliar ports, they don't balk at climbing aboard a rickety locals-only bus in some subtropical shanty-opolis, or an eight-hour layover at always grim Narita. Of course they needn't suffer any of the aforementioned, but rather, as I gather they have in the past, they could buy a package deal and take whatever direct charter to any number of esteemed beaches and deposit themselves on cushy towel-wrapped chaise longues and enjoy plenty enough seven no-brainer days of wincingly sweet piña coladas and a satchel of sexy paperbacks bought by the pound, choosing their own spiny lobsters for dinner and maybe on the last full day taking a back country four-wheeler ride to a secluded freshwater falls, where they might sneak a quick skinny dip beneath the lush canopy of jacaranda and apple palm, all of which I must say is perfectly laudable stuff, and nothing to be ashamed of.

And yet I feel especially eager to get Nancy and Neil's itinerary just right, not for the purpose of "challenging" them and making the trip strenuous for its own sake, but to remind them of what it is they're really doing as they jet and taxi about the world, let them feel that special speed and ennui and lag in the bones. In the future there will be no doubt some kind of Star Trek transporter device by which travelers will be beamed to their destinations, so that some Plotkin in the year 3035 might step into a light box in his own living room and appear a few seconds later in a hotel lobby in Osaka or Rome or the Sea of Tranquility, but I think that will be a shame for most save perhaps businesspeople and families with small children, as this instantaneous not-travel will effectively reduce the uncommon *out there* to the always *here,* to become like just another room in the house, nothing special at all, so that said Plotkin might not even bother going anywhere after a while.

Nancy and Neil, in the meantime, will indeed bother, arm themselves to the teeth with guidebooks and maps and travelogues of those who forged the paths before them, critiquing each other constantly (as they do whenever they show up at my desk) about what routing and accommodations and dining will prove most compelling, take them furthest and farthest, these two Dix Hills stratospheronauts by way of Delancey Street. They're plucky and sharp and understand at this most bemusing time in their lives that above all else they crave action, they need the chase as the thing, and when Neil handed me his credit card to pay for the trip he sighed presciently and moaned sweetly to his wife, "Ah, the miseries ahead."

Lucky you, I wanted to say.

Because in fact I don't know if I myself could manage any of these big trips anymore, as I used to do with (though mostly without) Rita tagging along, this when business at Battle Brothers was humming on autopilot and the kids were both in college and my wanderlust was at its brimming meniscal peak. Back then (not so many years, frighteningly), I would actually plan my next trip during the flights home, carrying along an extra folio of unrelated guidebooks and maps so that I could chart my next possible movements as if I'd already gone, play out scenarios of visited sites and cities, all the traversed topographies, basically string myself along, as it were, on my neon Highlighter felt-tip, to track, say, the Volga or the Yangtze or the Nile. Such planning quickened my heart, it offered the picture-to-be, and I can say with confidence that it was not because I dreaded being home or back in my life. This was not about dread, or regret, or some sickness of loathing. This was not about escape even, or some sentimentalist suppression. I simply wanted the continued promise of lift, this hope that I could in my own way challenge gravity's pull, and feel for whatever moments while touring the world's glories the mystery and majesty of our brief living.

A lot to ask, I admit, from a rough ferryboat ride from Dover to Calais.

And yet, even now, when I don't much travel anymore, and just get up top every so often in my not-so-fleet *Donnie* (who, I can try to believe now, was never in danger of being manned by Richie Coniglio, whose V-12 Ferrari sits with quiet menace in my garage, like a big cat in the zoo), I will still peer down on this my Island and the shimmering waters that surround and the plotted dots of houses and cars and the millions of people I can't see and marvel how genuinely intimate it all feels, a part of me like it never is on the ground.

And perhaps that's the awful, secret trouble of staying too well put, at least for those of us who live in too-well-put places like this, why we need to keep taking off and touch landing and then taking off again, that over the years the daily proximities (of your longtime girlfriend, or your kids, or your fellow suckers on the job) can grind down the connections to deadened nubs, when by any right and justice they ought only enhance and vitalize the bonds.

It's why the recurring fantasy of my life (and maybe yours, and yours) is one of perfect continuous travel, this unending hop from one point to another, the pleasures found not in the singular marvels of any destination but in the constancy of serial arrivals and departures, and the comforting companion knowledge that you'll never quite get intimate enough for any trouble to start brewing, which makes you overflow with a beatific acceptance and love for all manner of humanity. On the other hand, the problem is you end up having all this gushing good feeling 10,000 feet from the nearest warm soul, the only person to talk to being the matter-of-fact guy or gal in the field tower, who might not mean to but whose tight-shorn tones of efficiency and control literally bring you back down.

Theresa, I wish to and should mention now, is in no imminent danger, at least as she characterizes the situation. Although of course I'm relieved, even thrilled, I'm not sure I 100 percent believe her, as she isn't at all willing to go into the same ornate levels of jargony detail that typically mark much of her and Paul's talk, their specialized language whose multihorned relativistic meanings I feel I should but don't much understand. Thus it worries me that all she'll say to me now, in referring to the neoplasms perhaps growing right along beside her developing child, is that "the whole thing" is "totally manageable," exactly the sort of linguistically lame and conversation-ending phrasing I myself instinctively revert to whenever I'm in a pinch.

Even more unsettling than this is that she has already named the baby (*Barthes,* after a famous literary critic), a step that clearly signifies her rather strict intention to push through, and to whatever end. Naturally I've tried to extract more detailed information out of Paul, but he, too, has been frustratingly vague and blocking. But I know *something* is askew. For instance: for the past month now that Theresa and Paul have been back at home I've found their company, though always a pleasure, oddly unstimulating (a modifier I never imagined applying to them), as they've been unusually antic and adolescent when together. When I got home from Parade Travel the other day they were actually wrestling in the family room (fully clothed and nonsexually, thank goodness), and when I wondered aloud whether such activity was advisable they paused for a second and then burst out laughing, as if they'd been smoking weed all afternoon.

But there's a deep seam of mopiness there, too, which becomes apparent whenever one of them is out, the other just heading for their bedroom and the stacks of novels and texts of literary criticism they've brought along and also buy almost daily, this play-fort made of other people's words. I've tried to remain on the periphery, not forcing any issues or criticizing, consciously conducting myself like any other happy soon-to-be-grandfather sporting a solicitous and mild demeanor, though I'm beginning to wonder if I'm doing us any good service, while we all let the time pass, and pass some more, everything swelling unseen. If nothing else I assumed that I would always be *included*, in the big matters at least, and not simply contracted to wait for my bit part to come up, a small supporting role that I've depended upon over the years for easy entrances and exits but seems awfully skimpy to me now.

Another odd happening is that Paul is cooking up a storm. Though I'm not complaining here. I never knew him to be a cook, at least not a fancy one. He could always throw together a decent pasta dish or some baked stuffed trout when I once visited them out in their ever-misty coastal Oregon town, but his tastes and skills have evolved impressively in these past few years he's been in the academic world with Theresa (lots of free time, enough money, discerning, always ravenous colleagues). Theresa, I should mention, has been eating like a grizzly bear during a salmon spawn, being absolutely insatiable whenever she's awake, though lately her hunger seems to have subsided. This is the one clue that makes me think she's all right, and so okay to be doing what they're doing. Each morning after a huge breakfast of oatmeal and eggs and fruit and pastries, she and Paul will roll out the Ferrari (why the hell not, as I don't like to drive it anyway; the sitting position is a bit too squat for my longish legs and it revs too hotly such that I can't make it do anything but jerk forward in ten-yard bursts) and lay down that fourteen-inch-wide rubber around the county in search of organic meats and vegetables and craft cheeses and breads, foodstuffs Eunice of course has FedExed in daily but that I had no idea could be had out here in Super Shopper land, where there are always nine brands of hot dogs available but only one kind of lettuce (guess which). They only buy what we'll be eating that evening, which works out because the Testarossa doesn't have any trunk space to speak of, only a tiny nook behind the two seats (which, by the way, is just enough room for a couple of tennis racquets). My sole complaint is the might-as-well-eat-at-a-restaurant cost of the supplies, not to mention the premium gasoline they're burning at the rate of a gallon every seven miles, but once you've had seared foie gras with caramelized-shallot-and-Calvados-glacé, or wild salmon tartare on homemade wasabi Ry-Krisps, and eaten it right at your own dreary suburban kitchen table where you've probably opened more bottles of ketchup than imported beer, you happily fan out the fresh twenties each morning and utter nary a word, counting yourself lucky that you can tag along, and in an odd way I feel as if we three are moving quite fast through the world, consuming whatever we can.

And yet the trouble pools on our plates. The other morning, while sitting at the kitchen table, with Theresa sleeping in, Paul at the counter mixing a whole-grain batter for pancakes with raspberries, I let down my mug with enough oomph to make the coffee splash up and over onto my *Newsday*, to which Paul said, "Just another minute, Jerry."

"It's not about the chow," I said.

Paul pretended not to hear me, decanting the oil into the skillet and lighting the burner beneath it.

Since they've moved in and Paul's been cooking with high heat like a pro, the house gets heavy with a savory smoke that makes me think Rita's been around, a redolence all the more dear and confusing and depressing at present, as she's not returned any of my phone messages since the brunch at Richie's two weeks ago. Maybe a guy like me has to figure he's got just a couple chances in this life for full-on love with a woman he's respected every bit as much as physically desired, and if I've really squandered my allotment I probably ought to be hauled off to the woods in back and shot in the name of every woman who was surely meant to enjoy more loving than she got but didn't, mostly because of some yea-saying bobblehead, who semi-tried as hard as he could but always came up short.

"Look, Paul," I said, "it's time to start clueing me in."

"I agree," he answered, carefully ladling in three pancakes. He put a ramekin of maple syrup in the above-range microwave to warm. "But you know, Jerry, I really don't know anything either."

"Gimme a break, huh?"

"I'm not kidding you," he said.

"Now you're pissing me off."

"Well that's *goddamn tough*," he said, bang-banging his ladle against the edge of the mixing bowl. The microwave stopped beeping and he popped the door button too hard and it flung open, hitting him in the face. He plucked out the syrup and slammed the door, which popped back out, and so he slammed it again. For a second I thought he might come over and jump me, as I could see him gripping and regripping the spatula; and to tell you the truth I would have been fine with it, not because I wanted a fight but simply to initiate something. I thought maybe his plonking me might loosen the clamps of all this goddamn Eastern restraint ratcheting in on us, which is no doubt an easy lazy pleasure to abide most of the time but is, of late, becoming a kind of torture to me.

But he didn't jump me, and I said, "You must have talked to the doctor, at least."

"Of course I have. A dozen times. But she's only telling me what Theresa allows her to."

"But you're her fiancé! It's *your* baby. This definitely can't be ethical, or Hippocratical, or whatever."

"It's Theresa's call, Jerry, whether I like it or not."

"Well, you can't just sit by. Don't you have *rights*?"

"What would you have me do, take her to court?"

"Maybe. You could sue her, over her treatment decisions. Or maybe I should do that. You could just threaten to leave her."

"She'd know I was just bluffing," he said. He flipped the pancakes, one by one by one. "Or else she might turn around and leave me."

I didn't answer, because it occurred to me that Theresa could very well do that, if only temporarily. When she was a teenager she only had one boyfriend (that I can remember), a lanky, melancholic, semi-creepy kid who wore a black scarf no matter the weather and wrote science-fictional love poems to her, a few of which I found in the pockets of my old letterman's jacket (which she liked to wear with the sleeves pushed up); for whatever inexplicable reason she was madly in love with the kid, as she'd spontaneously burst into tears at the mere mention of him, regularly enough that before I could even say anything she herself began refusing his phone calls, and because of nothing he did, which made her even more miserable for a while (and him as well, the poor goth neuralgic), but soon enough she'd cured herself of the crying jags and they went steady until she dropped him, she told me later, because she was really tiring of "his work."

"You know what the doctor finally said to me when I talked to her on Friday?" Paul said, handing me my plate of flapjacks, syrup on the side. "Theresa and I had a bad little fight, so after she went to take a nap, I called. They wouldn't put me through but I pretty much freaked out and the doctor came on. So I gave her a whole speech about responsibility and the benefits of shared knowledge but it was like she didn't hear a word."

"Some lady doctors, you know . . ."

"Well, whatever it was. She didn't have time to talk, so she just said that perhaps I ought to consider getting us to couples therapy, if our 'communication levels' weren't where they should be."

"What a superbitch! I hope you told her off."

"Unfortunately, I did. I told her she could go fuck herself."

"Really?"

"I shouldn't have."

"Good for you!"

"It was *stupid*. She's our *doctor*. But you know what, Jerry? She might be right, about our communication."

"What the hell are you talking about? All you two *do* is talk."

"Yeah," he said wearily, slumping down in the chair. He wasn't eating yet. "But maybe not in any way that counts."

"Let's not get ridiculous here. It's not a great situation, by any stretch. That, and you're someone who's definitely got a reserve of patience and faith in people that's larger than the next guy's."

"You don't have to sugarcoat it, Jerry. I know I'm a pushover."

"You're not!" I told him, firmly holding on to his arm, not letting go until I'd made my point. "You love her, and love her dearly. As her father, I couldn't be happier about how obvious that is. It's all I'd ever worried about for her, if you know what I mean. Theresa isn't the easiest gig around. Okay, okay, so maybe you could push back a little more, because people like Theresa respond to shoves more than nudges. But if you really can't it's only because you think the world of her. And maybe I'm not the guy who deserves to say it, but there's nothing else of any worth."

Paul then said, "I'm scared to death here, Jerry. You know, I'd give her up now if someone promised me that nothing would happen to her."

"Nothing will. And you're never going to give her up. Just keep busy, like you're doing."

"Me? I can't do anything."

"Is the writing still on pause?"

"It's full stop. I haven't even *thought* about one line of poetry since the diagnosis, much less written one. I've officially quit the novel I was already not writing. You'd think I'd have all this determination and energy left over to focus on this thing, but I seem to have less and less every minute."

"You're sure cooking a helluva lot."

"Theresa seems like she wants to eat, so it's easy."

He smiled, but then he looked stricken again. He got up. "You want more?"

"Maybe just one, if you're making some anyway."

"It's no problem."

Paul clicked on the burner, and just then Theresa came padding into the kitchen in her bare feet, wearing summer-weight men's pajamas, short-sleeve Black Watch plaid.

She crooned, "Morning, Jerry."

"Morning, dear."

She kissed Paul on the mouth, goosing him slightly in the butt. The tired pinch of his eyes seemed to soften. "Those for me?"

"Yeah," I said.

Paul asked, "How many you want?"

"Just two, today. I'm not feeling so hungry."

"I'll make you an extra, just in case."

"Okay."

And soon enough we were back to our customary places at the kitchen table, Paul and I sitting on either side of Theresa, who's generally been settling down in yours truly's place at the head since they've moved in, the new array of which doesn't feel in the least awkward or wrong. Maybe it's even right, as Paul and I seem ever balanced in our need to glance over constantly at her, to keep a tab on how it's all going down, whether she's eating a little less today than yesterday, which in fact appears the case, though the gleaned quantities must be minuscule, in our inexact but somehow confident science.

I'm definitely on the warpath, eating everything that comes my way. Unbidden, Paul packs me a lunch on the days I come into the office here at Parade. Yesterday it was some vegetarian maki rolls, today a panini with prosciutto and mozzarella di bufala and a tub of roasted sweet peppers sprinkled with extra-virgin olive oil and fresh basil.

Miles Quintana now enters, carrying his own lunch of two bulging fast-food bags, and shoots me a "S' up, bro?"

I S'-up-bro him back. He's a little early for his 3 P.M. to 9 P.M. shift (I work until 5), and as is customary he'll eat one of his meals now before getting into the routine of checking fares for his clients and greeting the walk-in browsers and booking impulse vacations for the fed-up after-work crowd, then heat up the other bag later in the office microwave, for a quick break/snack. Being technically still a teenager Miles requires the triple-meat cheeseburger with ultrasized fries and chocolate milkshake value meal, 4000 calories of pure pleasure and doom, though of course none of it appears to be slowing him now, as he's maybe 150 pounds fully optioned in his slick Friday night dancing slacks and wine-red silk shirt and black-and-white bowling-style shoes. At the close of the evening his ever-silent baby-faced buddy Hector will pick him up in his low-riding hi-rev tuner Honda waxed to a mirror finish, and then they'll streak up and down the Northern Parkway dusting bored family men in their factory Audis and Saabs and afterward hit some under-twenty-one club, where they'll pick up unruly rich girls from Roslyn and Manhasset and ferry them to Manhattan for a couple of hours of real drinking and dancing before each taking (if the girls are willing, which they always are) a half-night room at a truckers' motel on the Jersey side of the Lincoln Tunnel. They'll stay until dawn and then eat steak and eggs at a diner before cruising back through the conquered city, to drop the girls off at their parked car before heading back for their mothers' row houses in Spanish Huntington Station. Not a bad life, if you ask me, and once Miles even suggested I tag along sometime, just for the hell of it, but I knew better than to take him up on it, as my presence would certainly obliterate his evening and probably our good working friendship, which depends in part on our mutual view that the other is somehow exotic and thus a little bit glorious.

There's no one here but us (it's slow in the summer, especially in the afternoons, and Chuck the manager is at a travel seminar in Mineola), and so Miles pulls up a chair to my desk and we eat together. I naturally filch a few sticks from his mountain of fries.

"So what's up with our gal Kelly?" Miles says, already halfway through his burger. "Is she ever coming back to work?"

"Maybe today. The plan is today."

"No shit. You talked to her? How is she?"

"She's doing all right," I say, though more wishful than sure. I had indeed talked to her, at the hospital and then at her place after I brought her back home, but I can't say we conversed, as Kelly was pretty much mum about everything, and after I fetched her some basic groceries she ushered me out with a weak embrace and promised that she would definitely be in touch, which she has not been. So a few days ago I went over to her apartment and spoke with her through her door, which she wouldn't open because she wasn't, as she said, her "pulled-together self," and when I reminded her that I'd seen her plenty of times in all her preablutionary glory she emphatically shouted, "Well, you're not going to see any more of that, Jerry Battle!" The sharp response unnerved me, and I literally stepped back from the door, for a second imagining Kelly with her hair on fire, carving knives in her hands, waiting for me to try something heroic.

Miles says, "I don't see why she tried to off herself."

"She didn't. She's just confused. It's a tough time in her life."

"Doesn't seem so tough to me," Miles says. "She's got a decent job and a nice place to live and she's still pretty good-looking, for an old lady."

"Forty-five isn't old, Miles."

"Sounds old to me."

"It isn't. She's a baby."

"Yeah, sure."

"She is," I say again, insistently enough that Miles actually stops chewing for a second. I tell him, "You have to understand something here, buddy. You've got another twenty-five years before you're that age, so it's hard for you to fathom. But it's going to go quick. Before you even know it, you'll look up and suddenly your buddies will have beer guts and will be getting gray all over and they'll be talking about sex but not in great anticipation, but with dread."

"Now that's some crazy-ass shit, Jerry. You're creeping me out, man."

"I'm not trying to scare you. That'll only be the surface. But what I'm really saying to you, Miles, is that, mostly, you won't change. At least not in the way you think of yourself. You'll stay in a dream, the Miles-dream."

"The what?"

"The Miles-dream. Maybe you'll have more than one. It's like this. You'll have an idea of yourself being a certain age, and for years and years when people ask you'll still think you're twenty-five, or thirty-five, or whatever age that seems right to you because of certain important reasons, because that will be the truth of your feeling inside."

"Oh yeah? So what's the Jerry-dream?"

"I don't know. Maybe I'm thirty-two, thirty-three, something like that."

"What, were you getting a lot of pussy back then?"

"I wouldn't put it that way, exactly."

"Yo, I was just kidding! I'm just fucking with you, man. But hey, you were happy, right?"

"Actually not really too happy, either."

Miles looks somewhat confused, as he should be, because I haven't explained myself very well. To do so I'd have to back up, tell him the whole messy story of Jerry Battle, for all he knows of me is that I work here a few days a week, and that I live in the area, and that I was dating our coworker Kelly for a couple of months before things fell apart; I'd have to tell him all about Rita, and about Theresa and Jack, and then of my marriage to Daisy, the time of which, at least in the beginning, was how I thought of myself for a long, long time, even after she died.

Miles revisits his burger, maybe thinking that the Ol' Gringo is finally losing it, and that he ought to just humor me while I'm on the loose out here in the world. Though often enough he hears this kind of midbrow poetic phooey from me, which he never appears to mind. Miles is in fact seriously bright and sensitive beneath his resplendent El Cojones exterior, always telling me about his classes at the community college where he's forever taking a part-time load and working toward no particular degree. He'll take whatever odd course or two strikes his fancy, from Topics in the Internal Combustion Engine to Feminist Archaeology to his current favorite, Greatest Hits of the Romantic Poets (I note that I should definitely hook him up with Theresa and Paul, as I'm sure they'd intrigue and delight one another with their varied approaches to all manner of Material and Text), where he says his professor gets downright weepy over "all that natural beauty and shit" in Keats and Byron and Wordsworth.

O there is blessing in this gentle breeze, I even overheard Miles say recently to a visiting client, in sealing the deal on a large corporate group trip to the Bahamas.

Miles asks, "So how 'bout now, man? Did the Jerry-dream ever change?"

"I guess not. I just felt that way when I was in my early thirties," I say. "That was it for me."

But of course that's not true. For I am sure, absolutely, that in twenty years (if I'm still around) I'll think of myself as being in this very time, the last Jerry-dream I'll probably ever have. The strange thing is that maybe I'm having the Jerry-dream right now, too, this prescient sense of the present, this unsettling prenostalgia whose primary effect is to lay down a waxen rime of both glimmer and murk upon everything that is happening with Theresa and Rita and probably very soon with Pop; this is why I'm suddenly hesitant to say anything more to my young friend Miles, because you can reach a point in your life when The Possible promises not so much heady change and opportunity but too frequent rounds of unlucky misery. We want action and intensity, we want the bracing scent of the acrid, but only if it's "totally manageable," which most times it's not.

Then it's just plain woe and trouble, which is apropos of the present moment, as who drives up and parks and now stands outside the office entrance but Kelly Stearns, with no less a personage in tow than the stout little guy and our mutual friend Jimbo, wearing a big gold necklace in the shape of his name and a shiny emerald-colored track suit and thus looking all in all very much like a steroidal leprechaun.

They appear to talk with happy animation, his hands bracing her shoulders, coachlike, though he only comes up to Kelly's chin, and Kelly is no towering Amazon. She nods meekly to his instructions, like they're going over a play at the time-out and she's his ungainly backup center. To my surprise she is all gussied up, in a toffee-colored skirt and blazer and white cotton blouse, and quite possibly looking more glamorous than I've ever seen her before, though not in an entirely fetching way, with her goldenrod locks glazed-tipped and pinned up and off her pale neck, her face powdered and painted more colorfully than usual, and today set off by glittery pendant earrings and a necklace that must surely be costume, given the sizes of the stones. There's also a fat, multiclustered ring, also not in the least keeping with her style, and I realize that this may prove yet one more instance in which I'll have to partake in a testy social challenge/display with a rival du jour.

I should be perfectly happy for Kelly, as I desperately want to be, but there's something about this new guy that irks me, nothing innately to do with him but whatever he is/does that makes Kelly not quite herself. Maybe our brief love affair wasn't exactly ideal but I know that she never had to change her spots for me, inside or out, I never once asked her to be anything else but who she was, a decorously sweet, affable Southern lady with honey eyes and a broad firm bottom and just enough pluck to soldier through the big messes. She is not someone, I still think, who would take too much OxyContin and try to crash her car into an ER entrance. She is not, I think, someone who would shout and holler through closed doors. She is not, I still hope, a woman who would relinquish her strength and will to anyone, me included, but especially to some Micro-Mafioso (with both a neck and trouser inseam size of 21) who will probably just get harder and meaner the longer they're together. But what do I really know, because the two of them are now kissing in the parking lot like it's VE Day on the Place Charles-de-Gaulle, Jimbo practically dipping her to the ground and laying one on her so long and wet that even Miles has to say, "The little dude's going deep."

When they finally come up for air Jimbo walks her to the entrance and opens the door for her, casting me a scathing look, as if I'm the one who gave her the "pain" pills, and as ridiculous as it is I can't help but glare back at him like we're on WWF Smackdown or some such, both of us madly flexing the small muscles of the face, The Little Green Giant versus Jerome "The Bulge" Battle. But it stops there, as he heads back toward his car and makes a call on his cell phone while Kelly walks in, bearing along her usual tutti-frutti scent of hard candies but then, too, more than a hint of his musky aftershave, which sours me. She plunks down her handbag on her side of our double desk.

"Okay, Jerry, I'm here. You can go home now. Please just wait a minute for Jimbo to leave."

"I still have another two hours."

"I'll cover for you."

Miles gives me the bug eyes and mutters, "Got to get to work," and ferries the remains of his lunch back to his desk. His phone rings and he picks it up but he keeps an eye on us as he talks.

"Listen, Kel," I say. "Just hold on. Why don't you sit down and let's talk."

"Let's not bother, please?"

"I know I should have come by your place more, after you left the hospital. I was feeling that way, but then the other day, I guess, you pretty much suggested you wanted privacy."

"That's a real funny way to look at it."

"Maybe it is. Anyway, I'm sorry. I really am."

"Oh, Jerry!" she says. "You don't even know what you're sorry about!"

"Sure I am. I'm sorry about all that's happened."

"And what do you think has happened?"

"Well, for starters, how about the pills, or crashing into the ER, or that ham hock standing out there by the car . . ."

"Don't you say a word about him, Jerry. You of all people don't deserve to."

"Okay, fair enough," I say. "But just because you're deciding again that I didn't do right by you last year, doesn't mean we can't talk like we always have, does it? You can despise me a little, but you don't have to hate me forever."

Kelly groans. "You just think everything's your fault, don't you? Well, let me tell you buster, I'm sick of it. Sick of it." She leans over the desk and starts to push at my shoulder and chest. "I didn't try to hurt myself because of you. I wouldn't do that. Never ever."

"Fine. Then for God sakes, why?"

"I did it for *me*, you big dope. Me and me alone."

"That makes no sense at all! Attempting suicide isn't exactly *therapy*, Kel."

"Maybe it is, when Jerry Battle's involved."

This one stings, and certainly more deeply than she intended, one of those special heavy metal–tipped rounds that penetrate the armor and wickedly bounce around inside, for maximal flesh damage.

"I'm sorry, Jerry. See? You better just lay off."

"I'm not going to lay off, because you're my friend," I say, adding, "Maybe my only friend."

"An ex-girlfriend who can hardly stand the sight of you is your only friend?"

"I know it's pathetic."

"Oh, Jerry," she sighs, heavily, terribly. "I love you sort of and I hope I will always love you sort of but I definitely can't stand you anymore."

This almost soothes, but really it's no great news, for yours truly, and after a brief moment I take gentle hold of her arm and say, "Come on. What do you think things would be like for all of us if you really went through with it?"

"Not so different. And I'm not being sorry for myself. Everyone would be suitably upset. Maybe Chuck would have to find another agent and Jimbo another girlfriend and you'd be down in the dumps for a few days. But like all the bad weather in your life, Jerry, it would quickly pass. Or if it didn't, you'd take up that plane of yours and just fly right above it."

"It's not like that."

"Yes it is."

She looks away from me but I see her eyes are shimmery and as she gasps a little I bring her close, and she hugs me, with Miles flashing a "go for it" hand signal as he jabbers Spanglish into the handset; and although I have to admit that it feels squarely, preternaturally good to hold Kelly once again in all her big-framed honey biscuit-smelling glory, I remind myself not to cling too long or too tightly, lest one (or both) of us gets what would certainly end up being the wrong idea of trying to do something right, which would be emotionally lethal for us, or worse. But Kelly apparently has the same notion, as she pinches me very hard where she was holding me on the love handles, holding and pinching before pushing away. This hurts, and not so good. But just then the metal-framed glass door bangs open and it's Jimbo, still clutching his cell, his pixie face all pinched up and flushed, like he's been holding his breath out there this whole time, and now heading toward me like I was the one clamping off his airway, this mad, mad little missile. A funny sound comes out of Kelly, an airy bleat, and for a nanosecond I can't help but think of a night in

Phuket when I was almost killed on a side street by one of those crazy-looking pickup-truck taxis called *tuk-tuks,* the thing screaming to a stop about three inches from me, and then innocently honking: *bleat-bleat.* And perhaps that is why I don't, or can't, now move, this false sense of déjà vu, for when Jimbo's pointed shoulder hits me in the gut I am practically giddy with astonishment and wonder for this unusual world, and I am ready to decline.

I decline, Mini-Jim. I really do.

But the next thing I know, Miles and Kelly are pulling the homunculus off me, though not quite in time to spare me a serious new-fashioned "bitch slapping," at least according to Miles. Apparently Jimbo stunned me with the tackle to the solar plexus, knocking the breath out of me, and as he wailed away with his cub paws while straddling my chest, all yours truly was able to manage was to cover up his overrated mug and plead a misunderstanding. After what seemed to me a lethal fifteen rounds but was probably a quarter minute at most, Miles finally got him to desist and drive off (with Kelly) by wielding a Parade Travel paperweight, an etched, solid-glass globe the size of a grapefruit that we sometimes present to our best customers (the Plotkins have one), and yelling in a puffed-up, profanity-laced Spanish. It was as good a language display as I ever heard from him, though probably it was all in the delivery, the ornate hormonal tone, and I must say I felt a warm rush of what was almost parental pride and gratitude from down in my sorry horizontal position, hearing his flashy street defense of me. And while I'm sure Jack would have pummeled my assailant silly, I'm pretty certain he would have done so with little of Miles's relish or animation.

WHICH IS NOW PART of what I'm noodling about, as I drive slowly home from Parade, my face tingling and raw, my gut muscles tightly balled and sore, acridity abounding, because when anything squarely intense happens these days I get to thinking about *la famiglia*, as most people might, though in my case it's not just to count heads and commune in absentia but to wonder in a blood-historical mode about how we got to be the way we are, whether okay or messed-up or deluded or, as usual, just gently gliding by. In this sense maybe I should thank Jimbo for providing some contour to the day, though of course I should ultimately thank myself for being an utterly serviceable, companionable boyfriend to a more-fragile-than-it-appears woman like Kelly caught in an eddy of middle life, a combination that meant I was mostly useless and lame. And as I cross over the ceaselessly roaring Expressway and turn into my aging postwar development just now beginning to look and feel like a genuine neighborhood, the trees finally grown up in a vaulted loom over the weathered ranches and colonials, I wish I could have certain countless moments back again, not for the purpose of doing or fixing or righting anything but instead to be simply there once more, present again, like watching a favorite movie for a third or fourth time, when you focus on different though important things, like that stirring, electric moment in *To Kill a Mockingbird* when the upstairs gallery of black folk stand up to honor Atticus Finch after the verdict goes against Tom Robinson, their expressions of epic suffering and dignity laying me low and then more generally instructing me that there are few things in this life as heartbreaking as unexpected solidarity.

A chance for which I'll maybe have once more today, for as I coast down the driveway I see Jack's Death Star–style luxury Blackwood pickup parked to one side of the turnaround, which is a surprise in itself, and boosts my spirits. He rarely comes by like this during the workweek, if ever, and when the garage door curls open I see the Ferrari parked inside, Theresa's and Paul's driving caps tossed on the seats. I tuck the broad-fendered old Chevy snugly in the other bay, the family gas guzzlers at rest, the clan all here except for Rita Reyes, who should have long been Rita Battle, and may yet be Rita Coniglio if yours truly doesn't conjure up some serious voodoo very soon.

The sound of familiar voices echoes from the backyard. I pause for a long moment before stepping around the corner of the house, to listen, I suppose, though I'm not sure for what or why, and I hear Jack explaining something about the prime rate and the state of the economy in the dry unmodulated way he talks about everything having to do with business. Paul asks about home mortgages, whether the rates will be lower in the fall; this is good to hear—they're still planning ahead. While Jack responds I don't hear a peep from Theresa, though, which deflates me a little, for maybe what I was hoping for was to happen upon some easeful sibling exchange, some cheery, smart-alecky shorthand that they'd pepper each other with, to no harm. And I even hoped she wasn't present, but when I step into the back I see that the three of them are there, sitting out beneath the umbrellaed patio table with soft drinks and salsa and chips.

"Hey, what happened to you?" Theresa says, in mid-dip.

"Nothing," I say, all of them examining me. "Why?"

"Looks like you just had an all-day facial," she says, patting her cheeks. "I think maybe I should try that."

"You don't need a thing, sweetheart," Paul tells her. "You're perfect."

"I just never had one, you know."

Jack is the only one drinking a beer, and I murmur that I could use a cold one, to which he dutifully rises and steps inside to the kitchen.

"You do look a little puffy, Jerry," Paul now says, looking at me

ALOFT

with concern. Paul can feature the unruffled manner of a sea-
soned doctor sometimes, a mien he clearly gets from his parents.
"You may be allergic to something."

"Dad's allergic to workplaces," Jack says as he returns, with un-
characteristic sharpness, I might add, sounding like his sister in
her youth. He hands me an icy bottle, holding two others that
must be for him.

"Here you go, old fella. The swelling should go down soon
enough."

I look into Jack's eyes and they seem to laugh a little, and suddenly I realize he may in fact be inebriated. This is not at all the
usual. I glance at Theresa and she gives the slightest shrug.

I say, "Jack's half right. It's probably all the dust kicked up by
the power blowers. I guess after all these years I've finally developed a sensitivity. In our day, we used to rake and then sweep up
with gym brooms."

"You mean you had me and the guys raking," Jack says.

"I guess that's true, too. But I did my fair share."

"The noise of those blowers is incredible," Theresa says. "I
never realized how loud it is in the suburbs. Paul and I are the only
ones here all day, and it seems like the landscapers never quit. Not
to mention all the renovation and construction crews. You're practically the only one on the block not doing work to the house, Jerry."

"Cheers to all the work," Jack says, finishing up his bottle and
opening a fresh one. "Every one of those remodels needs new
lighting and plumbing fixtures and tiles and cabinetry. And it's all
high-end stuff, exactly our Battle Brothers Excalibur products.
How do you think I keep Eunice living in the style to which she's
accustomed?"

"I thought it was your style, too."

"It's fine," he answers her, "but I don't need it to be that way."

"I've never seen a house like yours," Paul says. "The kitchen is amazing. I love that folding faucet over the stove, so you can fill the pots right there."

"Eunice got the idea from a show on HGTV. That particular fixture is triple-nickel-plated, from a maker in Northern England. It retails for eighteen hundred. We just won the bid to be the exclusive dealer in the metro area. They supply all the European royalty, including Monaco."

"And now the whole North Shore of the Island," Theresa adds. "Just perfect."

"Hey, if people can afford it, they have a right to whatever they like."

"Well, I don't quite know about that," Theresa autoresponds, but then she somehow thinks better of it, and quickly recasts. "But hey, Jack, it's no big deal."

"Yeah it is," he says, with an edge. There's a tenor to his voice I don't like, like he's not speaking to his baby sister, like he's never even had one. "I thought everything's a big deal with you. Isn't that what you do for a living? You criticize—excuse me, *critique*. Every little thing is so critiqued, so critical and important, life or death or purgatory. Everything can mean everything."

Theresa says, "That's in fact a good way of looking at it, though context is also everything. . . ."

"Whatever. I believe someone can pay his hard-earned money and buy a faucet he likes and it's perfectly okay if he doesn't think about all the possible injustices and implications of doing so. He doesn't have to think about anything."

"You must really believe that."

"Yeah, I do."

"Okay, then."

Jack says, "Okay what?"

"I said *okay*," she says, sounding suddenly weary, and not just of the conversation. She has sunglasses on, so I can't see her eyes, but there's a hunch to her shoulders that seems more pronounced than it should in anyone so young.

Jack says, "It's not like you to agree. Why are you agreeing?"

"Hey, hey, guys," Paul says, "we were enjoying the early evening sun here."

"That's right," I say, "let's cut it out now."

Jack says, "I'm in 'the sun' all day, okay, so I don't exactly need to enjoy it like all you people who are retired or might as well be. I came over to talk. But suddenly all the talkers don't want to talk."

Silence, except for the sound of the neighbor's electric waterfall, this blocked old-pisser trickle none of us noticed before.

"I think I need to lie down," Theresa says, getting up. Paul gets up, too, and holds her arm as they step into the house.

"See you later, Jack," Paul says. "We'll be by."

Jack mutters *Yeah, Paul,* like it's a Scandinavian language, and then downs the rest of his beer in one clean, long gulp.

He rises to leave, too, but I tell him to sit and stay awhile. He does, which is good, but this is again indicative of what sometimes irks me about him, his too-quick compliance, at least to me, no matter the situation. He's definitely been drinking before he got here, being a bit flushed about the cheek and ears and neck, a reaction he doesn't derive from me (I tend to get paler with every glass of jug-decanted Soave), and I wonder if he's doing this every afternoon at 4 o'clock, in some skanky out-of-the-way lounge or the polished wood-paneled men's grill room of his country club. Though this in itself would be neither surprising nor worrisome. In our business you can have a lot of empty time on your hands no matter how numerous and busy the jobs are, especially toward the end of the day when the guys are slowing down and just about to gather the tools and roll everything up into the backs of the trucks, and the clients are no longer so anxious and clingy, when there's just enough of a reason not to go straight home because after a long day of ordering and hollering and assuring and brown-nosing you want to talk to someone (including your wife) without having to convince or sell them on anything. Sometimes this means you mostly choose to just sink deeper in the captain's chair of your smoked-glass truck, with not even the radio on. In my prime years with Battle Brothers I'd tell the guys I was going to do an estimate but instead I'd park my work truck in some random neighborhood off Jericho Turnpike and spread a Michelin map on the passenger seat, mentally tracing a slow route from Nice to Turin, every switchback like a sip of a cold one.

But Jack Battle really isn't Jerry Battle, which I should be glad for but am not, at least right now, because if he were perhaps it would be easier to say something to him that I could be sure was tidy and effective, an impartial communication, like a patriarchal Post-it note with simple, useful information (how to make a noose, how to pile up charcoal briquettes), or else something slightly chewier, some charming Taoist-accented aphorism bespeaking the endlessly curious circumstance and befuddlement of our lives.

But like everybody else around here (save maybe Paul) I can't quite help myself, and I say, without any delight, "What the hell is going on with you? I don't get it. With what your sister is going through right now?"

Jack twists the cap off another beer.

"Are you hearing me, Jack?"

He says, "To tell you the truth, Dad, I really shouldn't know. I should know nothing. Because no one told me."

"Theresa didn't tell you?"

"No, she didn't," he says, roughly setting down the bottle, hard enough that it splashes and foams and spills through the metal mesh of the table. He stands up and shakes his workboots. "Do you know how I know? I had to hear it from Rosario, who I suppose heard it from Paul. Come on, Dad, what the fuck is that?"

"It's not like them . . ."

"You mean it's not like Paul. Your daughter is another story. Eunice, if you care to know the truth, is furious. The worst part is she really feels like dirt, and I don't blame her. She went all out and threw a big party and offered to throw the wedding reception and now she feels like we're goddamn nobodies in this family."

"I thought they told you, or I would have, right away."

"Well, they didn't. You should have, automatically. Automatically. Paul is one thing, but you."

"I'm sorry," I say. "This won't make you feel any better but I found out mostly by accident, too. And I don't really know what's going on now, because she refuses to go into details. But I think we should give your sister some room here. She's no dummy, and we have to trust her to make the right calls."

"Would you be saying that if I were in her place?"

The question surprises me, both in its sharpness and implied self-criticism, and in the face of it I say (too automatically, perhaps), "Of course I would."

Jack mutters, "Yeah," and drinks some more of his beer.

"You don't think so?"

"Forget it," he says. He gazes out over the backyard, and though I feel like telling him he's being childish, I don't, not just because I only ever get dangerously close to doing such a thing but also because nothing he's saying is off the mark. And for the first time in a very long time I can see he might be genuinely hurt, this indicated by the pursed curl in his lower lip, the slight underbite that he would often feature when he was a boy, when his mother wasn't doing well, and then after she was gone.

"You should let me send the guys over and redo this place," Jack suddenly says. "It's getting to be a real dump, you know."

"I wouldn't say that."

"I would," he says, but not harshly, and he's already up out of his chair and out on the lawn. He's standing on the spot where the pool used to be, now just another unruly patch of grass, splotchy and scrubby, the erstwhile beds bordering the pool now unrecognizable as such, with the sod grown over so that they look like ski moguls in the middle of the lawn. All the surrounding trees and shrubs are in need of serious pruning, the brick patio having sunk in several spots and gone weedy in the seams, the yard appearing not at all like a former professional landscaper's property but rather what a realtor might charitably appraise as "tired" or "in need of updating" or, in fact, if you were really looking hard at the place, a plain old dump.

"Listen," Jack says, gesturing with his long-necked beer, his tone unconsciously clicking into just the right register for what he does, what I call contractor matter-of-fact, assured and fraternal and with just enough of a promise of prickly umbrage to keep most customers at bay. "It wouldn't be a big deal. I'd shave these mounds flat and scrape away the whole surface and lay down fresh sod. Then we'd get into the trees and cull the undergrowth and prune up top as well. I'd want to replace all the shrubs by the patio and maybe put in a few ornamental fruit trees over by the driveway, to create a little glade. The patio we'll do in bluestone, finished out with an antique brick apron, to match the siding of the house."

"Sounds pretty nice. But I wouldn't want to tie up a whole crew," I tell him, as I know Battle Brothers would never charge me a dime. "Especially when it seems there's so much work out there."

"It's actually slowed down a bit," he says, sipping his beer. "Don't worry, we're at a good level now. We can spare a couple guys."

"Maybe I will have you do some work. I've been kicking around the idea of moving to a condo the last couple years, but I don't seem to be doing anything about it."

"Why should you?" Jack says. "The house is paid for, isn't it? Pop is tucked away and taken care of. You're on Easy Street, Dad. I'd just enjoy the air, if I were you, and make this place nice for yourself. Nothing's in your way."

"Nothing's in your way, either," I tell him.

Jack says, "Nothing but a jumbo mortgage and two kids to send to private day school and a wife with exceptional taste."

"Eunice does like nice things," I say. "But you do, too."

"I go along."

By now I've joined him, and we walk around the inside perimeter of the property, bordered by those overgrown trees, Jack making suggestions to me and jotting notes on the screen of his electronic organizer. He doesn't seem even mildly drunk anymore; it pleases me to think that maybe the work mode enlivens him.

"What about there," I say, referring to the expansive swath in the center of the property. "Just leave it as lawn?"

"I don't know. Maybe you ought to put a pool back in."

"A pool? I don't need to swim anymore."

"Sure, but the kids would love it. Lately I've been wanting to put one in, but there's not enough room at my house for a nice-sized one. If you had a pool back here again, you'd see the kids all the time."

I nod and say, "That'd be good," even though I've already worried that I might not *like* his kids if I spent a lot of time with them (even if I'll always love them).

"Plus," he says, "maybe Theresa and Paul will move back to Long Island someday, with their kid, or kids."

"I was thinking of that, too."

"Sure. If you wanted, my pool guy could drop in an integrated hot tub for you, right alongside the regular pool. I'd have him install a slide instead of a diving board, though."

"Kids like slides."

"Definitely," Jack says. "I always wanted one."

"Really?" I say. "I never knew that. You should have asked me. I would have gotten you one, no problem."

"I know. I don't know why, but it never occurred to me to ask you. But then, I suppose, it was too late."

"I guess it was," I say, not quite understanding that we're all of a sudden talking about *this*, about which there's never been any great family prohibition or denial, any great family taboo, but still.

"I bet Mom would have had a blast with a slide," Jack says.

"Maybe," I answer, "but she'd have had to go down with her ring float on."

Jack looks at me like I'm crazy.

"You think?" he says.

"I guess not," I answer, realizing how stupid I must sound, talking about her *float*. So I say, "Your mother would have done whatever she liked."

"That's why we loved her, right?" Jack says brightly, with just the scantest tinge of edge and irony.

I can only nod, and just stand there with him in the middle of the big patch of messy lawn, and I don't have to try hard to recall how he and Theresa spent most of their time right here (at least up to a certain age), especially in the summer, turning as brown as coconuts as they hopped and raced and climbed atop everything in sight. Every parent says it, but they really were like those tiny tree monkeys you see at the zoo, their faces all eyes and their fingers and limbs impossibly narrow and lithe. They'd be crawling onto and off you and tugging at your shoulders, your ears, then (unlike most primates) leaping with abandon into the pool, even before they learned how to swim, thrashing about half-drowning before I'd pull them out.

And I'll say right now it really was a very decent pool, just what you'd imagine for a solidly middle-class postwar family house, a

20-by-40 inground with a meter-high diving board and nice porcelain tile work around the lip, though after what happened to Daisy and with no one around during the work hours to supervise I decided to have the guys fill it in, which in fact none of us seemed to regret, not even Jack, who was a natural swimmer and the star of the neighborhood club swim team. In fact it amazed me how quickly he got past it all, how intensely he threw himself into his other sports, and to astounding success, in turn becoming socially confident and popular, the tight busy orbits of which allowed him, I suppose, to recover fully, even if these days everyone even half-witted thinks that to be a spurious notion or concept. But I'm not so sure. Maybe the key to returning to normalcy was my quick response, my instant renewal of our little landscape, that I filled in and bulldozed over the offending site and rolled out perfect new sod that they could at least play upon without a care or thought, if never really frolic in the same way again.

"Tell Theresa I'm sorry," Jack finally says, gathering his things on the patio table, to head out. "I'll call her later, too."

"That would be good," I say, as I walk him to the driveway.

"So what about it?" he says, nodding back to the yard. "I'll send the guys around. But what about the pool?"

We'll see, I say to him, or I think I do anyway, and before he steps up into the saddle of his impossibly high-riding vehicle I give him a healthy pat or two on the back, to which my son grunts something satisfyingly low and approving, a clipped rumbling *yyup*, and I think of how good it is to have both of them here again, regardless of the terms, because (and you know who you are) you can reach a point in your life when it almost doesn't matter whether people love you in the way you'd want, but are simply here, nearby enough, that they just bother at all.

nine

JERRY BATTLE hereby declines the Real.

I really do.

Or maybe, on the contrary, I'm inviting it in. An example is how I now find myself here in my dimly lighted two-car garage, the grimy windows never once cleaned, sitting in the firm leather driver's seat of the Ferrari, its twelve cylinders warbling like an orchestra of imprisoned Sirens, and only when the scent becomes a bit too cloying do I reach up and press the remote controller hooked on the visor to crank up the door, the fresh air rushing in just like when you open a coffee can.

"What the hell are you doing?" Theresa shouts from the wheel of the Impala. She's idling on the driveway, staring out at me from behind Daisy's old Jackie O sunglasses, which she found in a night table I'd put down in the basement probably twenty years ago.

I back out the machine, in two awkward, revvy lurches. I sidle up to her. "I sometimes forget to open the door first."

"You big dummy. Are you sure you want to do this?"

"I'm sure. I'll buy you guys another car."

"Forget it. We don't really need one. We'll use this one, when you're not working. Hey, I want to stop at the Dairy Queen on the way out."

"Didn't we just have breakfast?"

"I need a milkshake and fries, Jerry. Right now."

"Okay, okay, that's good."

It's amazing how quickly she'll get her back up these days, not for the conventional reasons of my political and cultural illiteracy/idiocy, but for any kind of roadblock to calories sweet and fatty and salty. I'm glad that she's ornery, still feeling hungry, for with this thing looming she seems extra vulnerable, like an antelope calf with a hitch in its stride. We thumbs-up each other, like pilots and comrades will do, and I lead us out, remembering there's a Dairy Queen just off Richie's exit.

I've continued to be respectful and am hanging back, willing in my lazy-love (as opposed to tough-love) manner to leave the navigation to her, but something about the status of the status quo has set off a sharp alarm in my viscera, this clang from the lower instruments that we're pitched all wrong here. And so a good part of the reason I've decided to return Richie's car to him, no gloating, no strings, is not just that I'm a wonderful guy, or that it's an inherently hazardous machine for Theresa and Paul to be tooling around in among all the sport-utes riding high and mighty, or that I will never be able to make the car really feel like mine (even though I know Richie would have had *Donnie* already repainted and the seats reupholstered, if he didn't immediately sell her for a month's share of an executive jet), but to try to simplify, simplify, what seems to be our increasingly worrisome matters of family. I should probably be effecting this by gathering all my loved ones and doing something like passing out index cards and having everyone write down for candid discussion three "challenges" that face us (as I saw suggested in a women's magazine at the supermarket checkout the other day), but it's easier to begin by clearing out whatever collateral stuff is crowding what appears to be our increasingly mutual near future, a category in which the Rabbit-mobile neatly fits. As much as Theresa and Paul like using the car, I've been feeling that it's literally a foreign object, plus the fact that it reminds me too much of Rita's disdainful regard.

So here we are, Theresa and I, in our convertible caravan of two. I glance back in the rearview every ten seconds, and wave. She waves back, glamorous in the gleaming chariot. It gives me plea-sure to see her at the wheel, reminding me of the days when she and Jack used to sit up front with me and take turns sitting in my lap and driving. Of course you'd probably get arrested these days for doing such a thing, charged with child endangerment, but back then Jack would even press the horn when a patrol car passed, the officer answering Jack with a little *whirrup* from his siren.

We have a decent ways to go before we get to Richie's town, which I'm not minding, as it's midafternoon, everyone still at the beach, with the Expressway moving along at a fine smooth clip that feels even headier from the open cockpit of this High Wop machine supreme. As I pass the cars on my left and right, their drivers, I notice, can't help but take a good long look at me, men and women both, but especially the men, younger guys and middle-aged guys and guys who shouldn't still be driving, and I know exactly how they're thinking what a detestable lucky-ass piece of shit I am, the respect begrudged but running deep as they unconsciously bank to the far edge of their lanes, to give me room. The younger chicks are the ones who drift closer, closer, maybe to see if the hair is a rug or weave, if I've got a flappy gobble to my neck, this one saucer-eyed blondie jouncing alongside in a Jeep Wrangler even raising her sunglasses up on her head to wink at me and mouth what I'm sure is a smoky *Follow me home.* Maybe Jerry Battle should reconsider. The wider shot here is pretty okay, too, the broad roadway not seeming half as awful as I think I know it to be, and I have to wonder what else—for our kind, at least— really makes a place a place, save for the path or road running straight through it, ultimately built for neither travel nor speed?

At the Dairy Queen we're pretty much alone, given that they haven't officially opened. Theresa got the two teenage employees to open early for us by telling the somewhat older assistant manager that she'd let them try out the Ferrari after they filled her order. They're both husky and greasy-faced, your basic big-pore, semi-washed, blank-eyed youth who in fact run almost everything in our world-dominating culture, but you've never seen soda jerks in this day and age move as fast as these two do now; they've got the fries bubbling in the hopper and the ice cream in the blenders and they're even filling a squeeze bottle with fresh catsup. I've joined Theresa in the front seat of my antique wheels. Like carhops they bring out our snack on a clean tray and I throw the assistant manager the keys and ask him not to maim or kill anyone, and before Theresa can even pop her straw into her shake he is smoking the fat rear rubber, wildly fishtailing down the avenue.

"Have some fries, Jerry."

I help myself, though I'm completely not hungry, something I've been a lot lately, no doubt inspired in some latent biological way by the sight of pregnant kin. Or maybe I shouldn't be eating at all, to leave more of the kill for her. In any case Paul, who is enabling this behavior, is back at the house dry-rubbing Moroccan spices on a hormone-free leg of lamb he'll grill for dinner and serve with herbed couscous and butter-braised *spargel*, German white asparagus he found on special at Fresh Fields for a mere $5.99 a pound. He's been cooking even more furiously than ever, preparing at least four or five meals for every three we eat, so that we're building up enough surplus inventory to last us a couple of weeks, in case there's some threat of a late-summer hurricane and a run on the supermarkets. Last week I made Paul quite happy by cleaning out an old freezer in the basement and plugging it in and then buying him one of those vacuum sealer machines so his lovely dishes wouldn't get freezer-burned. Every day since it seems he's vacuum-packing not just hot food and leftovers but dry goods like roasted cashews and Asian party mix and banana chips and Peanut M&M's, apportioning and shrink-wrapping whatever he finds bulk-packaged at Costco that catches his eye. No one's said it, for of course these are meals that would certainly come in handy after the baby is born, but that's many months off and then maybe not quite appropriate, as it doesn't seem quite right that you'd be heating up a maple pinot noir glazed loin of veal or halibut medallions in aioli-lemongrass sauce between breast feedings or diaper changes. Or maybe you would.

While I'm pleased that Paul is thusly keeping busy with what one hopes are therapeutic activities, I'm growing increasingly worried that he's maybe starting to sink in his soup, that he's getting too engrossed in work that seems worthwhile and positive but is in fact the culinary equivalent of obsessively washing one's hands. Yesterday as he was coming up from one of his nearly hourly descents to the basement freezer I asked him again (casually, gently, as if accidently) if any writing was going on. He weakly chuckled and muttered, "What?" and then in the next breath asked me in a serious tone if I thought he had what it took to sell Saturns at the new dealership just opened up on Jericho. When I realized he wasn't kidding I told him yes, he'd probably be great at it, for Paul with his gentle, trustworthy, liberal carriage is no doubt just right for those haggling-averse academic-type customers (though he still probably ought to lose the ponytail and hemp huaraches), and after leaving him to roll up some pounded chicken breasts with a spinach chevre pignoli-nut stuffing I wandered off thinking how utterly disturbing this whole mess must be for him, despite what has been since his first disclosure to me an otherwise thoroughly affable Paul Pyun performance. People say that Asians don't show as much feeling as whites or blacks or Hispanics, and maybe on average that's not completely untrue, but I'll say, too, from my long if narrow experience (and I'm sure zero expertise), that the ones I've known and raised and loved have been each completely a surprise in their emotive characters, confounding me no end. This is not my way of proclaiming "We're all individuals" or "We're all the same" or any other smarmy notion about our species' solidarity, just that if a guy like me is always having to think twice when he'd rather not do so at all, what must that say about this existence of ours but that it restlessly defies our attempts at its capture, time and time again.

Richie's car streaks by in a red candy flash, the shearing whine of the motor indicating that the assistant manager is driving in too low a gear. He leaps back and forth between the two lanes, weaving in and out of the slow-moving traffic with surprising skill, and turns down a side road, to disappear again. His coworker, shaking his fist in the air, is shouting at the top of his lungs expletives of high praise.

"I forget, how old is Pop again?" Theresa asks out of the blue, between slurps of her vanilla shake. I'd wanted to bring up the Big Issue, but Theresa is now tolerating no talk whatsoever of her pregnancy or the non-Hodgkin's (the *non* always throwing me off, like it's nonlethal, nonimportant, nonreal), and then practicing deft avoidance maneuvers whenever I try to pry.

"He was eighty-five, around the time of the party."

"And you're fifty-nine."

"Yup," I say, thinking how that number sounds better than it ever has before. "Sixty, on Labor Day. You're probably thinking, 'How ironic.'"

"Gee, Jerry, you must think I'm the most horrible person."

"No way. But you can be honest."

"Okay, so maybe I had a flash of a thought. But nobody would say you haven't worked hard all your life. Not even Pop."

"Only because he's not saying much." Though this is not quite true. Pop's actually been in a decent mood since the immediate aftermath of the incident with Bea, generally behaving well during my visits, being soft-spoken and circumspect and displaying what for him is an astoundingly modest demeanor, even pleasant, the unvolubility of which should be frightening me to death but that I'm simply glad for whenever I'm there, the two of us slouched in his mauve-and-beige-accented room for a couple uneventful hours (with him propped up in the power bed, and me in the recliner, likewise angled) staring up at the Learning Channel or the Food Network. This might sound dismally defeatist, but when you can't pretend anything else but that your pop is in the home for life and his former main lady is now permanently featuring a bib and diaper, you tend not to want to examine the issues too rigorously, you tend to want to keep it *Un*-real, keep the thinking *small* because the issues in fact aren't issues anymore but have suddenly become the all-enveloping condition.

Theresa says, "Would you like a party for the big one?"

"Definitely not."

"Why not?" she says. "It'll be great fun. We'll have a birthday roast. We'll invite all of your friends."

"I don't have any friends."

"That can't be true. What about all the Battle Brothers guys?"

"We're still friendly, but we're not friends. Never were."

"Then some other group, neighbors, people from the neighborhood. School chums. Don't you have buddies from your Coast Guard days?"

"I told you, I don't have friends. I never really have. I just have friendlies."

"Then we'll invite all your friendlies. It doesn't have to be a huge thing. I'm sure Paul will be happy to cater it."

"It seems like he's already started."

"Isn't he great? Actually, Paul's the one who mentioned doing something special for your birthday. I didn't know, of course, because I'm so damn assimilated, but in Korea the sixtieth is a real milestone. I guess numerologically it's significant, plus the fact that in the old days it was quite a feat to live that long."

"It still is," I say. "It's just that these days nobody really wants you to."

"Oh, stop whining. In my mind it's settled. We'll throw you a sixtieth birthday party. That will be our present, as we have no money. I'm sure Jack and Eunice will get you something huge, like a new plane."

"That's just what I'm afraid of." I'm trying to tune in an oldies station on the radio, as the ones that I've always liked to listen to (in this car especially) have somewhere along the line fiddled with their programming, shifting from '50s and '60s songs to mostly '70s and '80s pop, which are of course now oldies to Theresa and often completely new to me. Finally I have to switch to cruddy lo-fidelity AM to find the mix I want, which is no mix at all, just Platters and Spinners and Chuck Berry and James Brown, though it comes out scratchy and tinny like from the other end of a can-and-string telephone. This, of course, is part of the ever-rolling parade of life, slow-moving enough that you never think you'll miss something glittery and nice, but then not stopping, either, for much anyone or anything. And by extension you can see how folks can begin to feel left behind or ushered out, how maybe you yourself come in a format like an LP or Super 8mm that would play perfectly fine if ever cued up, if the right machines were still around.

But they're gone, gone forever.

And I say, unavoidably, hoping not desperately, "I've got some time."

"Sure you do. But you never know, do you, Jerry?"

Theresa, bless her soul, can always bring it on.

I say, "You never do. I could have a bad stroke right now, not be able to brush my teeth, and you'd have to put me in Ivy Acres."

"You could be roommates with Pop," she says, almost brightly. "I wonder how often that happens."

"I'm sure it's rare."

This is a prospect I haven't yet considered, but one I probably need to; not that it will actually happen or that I would let it, but I should realize that this is how people my daughter's age might naturally see me, and not even because they wish to.

"But you wouldn't really want that, would you?"

"To live with Pop in the home?"

"No," she says. "Just the home part."

"Is there an alternative?"

"Sure there is."

"Like what?"

"You know."

"I do?"

"Sure you do."

Or I *think* I do, but I'm afraid to say it first, the idea instantly replenishing the abandoned gravel pit of my heart. I think she's talking about what all of us not-for-a-while-middle-aged folks would love to hear whenever we get together with our grown kids, which I'll unofficially call The Invitation. Since they moved into their big house I've been secretly waiting for Jack and Eunice to float the idea that I eventually sell my house and move in with them, maybe agreeing to give them half the equity for my future maintenance by an attractive home nurse, the other half going to the kids' education or an inground pool or whatever else they deem to be worth the misery and trouble. I've hoped this even despite the fact that Jack and I aren't close in any demonstrable way, or that I'm undeniably only so-so with the kids, being willing to take them to a carnival or the zoo but otherwise unable to sit with them for more than a few minutes in their great room amid the ten thousand plastic toys and gadgets. I admit even to murmuring admiration over recent years for Jack's half-Asian blood, periodically extolling the virtues of filial piety (which Daisy once accused me of knowing nothing about, after forbidding her to call long-distance anymore to Korea, as she was running up bills of $200 a month), hoping that he'd someday put aside our thoroughly unspectacular relations and decide to honor some vague natal charge I'd slyly beckoned, some old-time Confucian burden that wouldn't depend (lucky for me) on anything private and personal. On this score I think us old white people (and black people, and any others too long in our strident self-making civilization) are way down in the game, and it wouldn't surprise me at all if the legions of my brethren about to overwhelm the ranks of assisted buttressed life prove to be among history's most disappointed generations.

As for Theresa, I never imagined she would ask me to join her crew, even if she were in a position to do so. But perhaps the current circumstance has initiated in her what is proving a sentimental bloom of hope and generosity, and in the sweet light of this I can't say much now, except to burble, genuinely and gratefully, "You've got plenty to think about with yourself and Paul."

"I know, I know. But so it's even more important to talk about it."

"Absolutely right," I say.

The Dairy Queen boys switch, the second one a bit more tentative than the first, as he seems to have little experience driving a stick, a video game probably the extent of it. The first customer presently turns in to the parking lot, and the kid at the wheel nearly hits him as he pulls out onto the road. We watch him as he bolts down to the next light, stalls, U-turns at the signal, stalls, and then hustles back.

Theresa finishes the milkshake, drilling about with the straw to draw up every last drop. Over the past couple weeks she's gained weight from Paul's four-star training table, as have I, with her cheeks and neck and shoulders looking fleshy and sturdy in her crème-colored cotton tank top. As she sits coolly at the wheel of my Impala wearing the Jackie O sunglasses, I can't help but wonder how close the two of them might be, she and Daisy, how they'd be plotting the family milestones, how, if I were a very lucky man, they'd be endlessly teasing me and causing me troubles and generally giving me a constant run of heartbreak.

"I'm glad to hear that from you, Jerry," Theresa says. "I was discussing it with Paul last night. About me."

"You?"

"Of course me. We decided that if things got horrific and the baby was already out and there was nothing left but blind faith, that he would help me take the necessary measures."

"Necessary measures? What the hell are you talking about?"

"What we're talking about."

"I thought we were talking about our *future*."

"Exactly," she says. "I don't want Paul and you and maybe Jack, if he even cares, to carry me beyond what's reasonable. I'm not going to go for anything heroic here. I'm not interested in lingering. Besides, I think it's appalling, the level of resources our society puts toward sustaining life, no matter the costs or quality."

"I don't care," I say, doing my best to switch gears unnoticed. "I think it's noble."

"Noble? It's craven and egotistical. This when thousands of children are born each day into miserable conditions, when our public schools are crumbling, when the environment is threatened at every turn. Really, it's ridiculous, how antideath our society is."

"Look, honey, I don't know what you want me to say, but I'm definitely antideath. Especially yours."

"You may think that now. But if I were down to eighty pounds and I couldn't hear or see, and the pain were so great I couldn't stop moaning, all of it costing you and everyone else two thousand dollars a day, would you want me to endure every last breath?"

"I don't like talking about this."

"You're a big boy, Jerry."

"Okay. All right, then. I think you deserve your turn."

"My *turn*? You think Pop is enjoying his turn?"

"You're missing my point," I tell her. "Pop is where he is because there's no better choice. I put him there for his own good but he's not locked up. He doesn't like Ivy Acres, but in fact he doesn't want to live with me or Jack or anybody else. He can walk out anytime. What he really wants is his old life back, which he can't have. So he's doing what everybody does, which is just to ride it out for the sake of his family, so Jack and his kids can go over there and sit with him for an hour and fiddle with the bed controls and watch *The Simpsons*."

"It doesn't matter that nobody's really enjoying themselves?"

"Nope. It's just part of what we have to do, and Pop's job now is to be Pop-as-is. I'm not talking about heroics here, because there's no way that I would want you to suffer. But if things don't go so well I hope you don't do something sudden. There's a certain natural run to these things and I think we'll all know if it's really time. But I don't think it truly ever is."

"Don't you think Mom did something *sudden*?" Theresa says, the scantest edge in her tone.

"Of course not. She didn't commit suicide."

"But it wasn't purely an accident either, right? If she hadn't been so miserably unhappy, maybe she'd have been more careful."

"Could be," I say, focusing on the *miserably unhappy*, not so much the truth of it but the fact of Theresa, as a young girl, knowing her mother in such unequivocal terms. This not even getting into all her possible views on my contributions to that unhappiness, the broad intense feelings probably swamping her back then and the thousands of chilly extrapolations she's made since, all of which, coming from her, are liable to scare me straight unto death.

"I've been thinking, Jerry," she says, looking serious now. "I want to ask you to promise something."

"Whatever you say."

"I want you to promise you'll take care of Paul and the baby."

"Theresa . . ."

"And when I say Paul, I mean even if the baby isn't around."

"Jesus, I don't like you talking like this."

"I mean it. I want you to look after him. Maybe he can stay at the house with you a little while. My life insurance from the college is lame and would only hold him for six months, tops. He won't ask his parents for a dime."

"Would he ask me?"

"No, but if you offered he might accept your help. He's too messed up by what his parents think of his career choice to ask them for anything."

"Good thing he doesn't care what I think."

"It is," Theresa says. "Paul's an excellent person and a fine writer but he's sometimes too much of a good boy. He has this need to please them and by extension most everybody else, which is okay day to day but in the long run is going to get him into trouble. I haven't yet said anything to him but I think it's become a problem as he's gotten older, especially with his work. He hasn't really sloughed them off yet. I don't need to get into this with you,

ALOFT

but he's sometimes too fair in his treatment of things, too just—like he's afraid or unwilling to disappoint or offend. An artist can't be averse to being disagreeable, even tyrannical."

"Hey, I like that Paul is nice to me."

"And he always will be. But you don't quite make the father-mentor-master pantheon for him, if you don't mind my saying. Paul can just hang out with you, exemplify nothing extraordinary or special, which is why I think you're good for him. He can be one of the guys with you, Jerry, a part of the wider male world."

"Why am I not feeling so complimented?"

"Oh, relax. All I'm saying is that he'd be most comfortable with you, in a way he certainly couldn't be comfortable with his father or mother or even, for that matter, a lot of our friends and colleagues back at the college. Sometimes I think that if I weren't around they'd all prove too strong for him, overwhelm him, and he'd end up just sitting there at his desk doodling in the margins."

"It's a good thing Jerry Battle is just filler."

"But you're fine filler, Jerry. You're always just there, taking it in. Like tofu in soup."

"Wonderful."

"It is. I always thought you were just right, especially as a dad. Maybe not for Jack but for me. You were never in the least pushy or overbearing, even when I was getting totally out of hand."

"When was that?"

"You know, that one summer, my biker-slut period. When I basically ran away and you and Jack had to drive out to Sturgis and bring me back. You didn't even yell at me. You were pissed, but only because you'd just lost your Chevron card. Jack was the one who was genuinely angry, about having to miss a few lacrosse matches."

"We stopped at the Corn Palace, didn't we? You and I taste-tested BLTs and chocolate milkshakes, state by state."

"See? You were enjoying yourself."

"I guess so," I say, though I'm not as tickled by the memory as I'm making it sound. For despite the obvious satisfaction I might have from hearing that my ever-skeptical daughter has generally approved of my parenting style, the notion of being Daddy Tofu seriously mitigates any lasting appeal. And the now insistent implication—something Theresa always seems to evoke for me—is not that Rita might view my years of boyfriending in a similar metaphorical light (which she no doubt does), or that there might be anything I can do to reform her perspective (save the usual dumb and desperate measures, like asking her, now, after all these years, and when she's no longer mine, to marry me), but rather that I should be addressing right now, posthaste, chop-chop, what I should not have let slide for hours much less weeks, which is to demand to know what the hell we're (not) talking about, to be part of what's going on with her, and how we are to proceed.

To not, yet again, profess my desire to decline, which I so wish to.

So I say, with as much resoluteness as I can muster, "Listen. The question isn't about me and it's not about Paul. You can be certain I'll keep an eye on him. I'll do whatever it takes. He can live with me as long as he can bear. But what I'm having great difficulty with is that you're not including me."

"I'm saving you the trouble. Remember, Jerry, you don't like trouble?"

"Dammit, Theresa! This isn't *trouble*. Trouble is what I have with Rita. At this point, trouble is still what I have with Pop, which I suppose I should be grateful for. But this is way past that. Let me tell you, I appreciate that you're trying to make this a nice extended summer visit to your dad, where we eat like gourmands and go to the movies at night and plan a modest little wedding for you. But I can't just allow myself to just sit by any longer, if that's what you're hoping for."

"I'm not hoping for anything," she answers, without tenor. "But fine. What do you want to be included in?"

"I don't know yet! You have to tell me!"

"Okay," she says, staring me right in the eye. "Do you want to be included in the fact that my red blood cell count is falling like crazy right now? Or that my doctor is warning me that my placenta might be seriously weakened? Or do you want to be included in my morning sickness ritual, which is to vomit right before and after breakfast, this morning's being bloody for the first time?"

"Bloody? What does that mean?"

"I don't really know, Jerry."

"Shouldn't you call your doctor?"

"I don't want to. We're seeing her next week anyway."

"Call her now," I say, handing her my cell phone. "I'll drive you tomorrow."

"No."

"What do you mean, no?"

"It'll just give her more reason to bring up termination, which I don't want to hear about anymore."

"Maybe you should hear it."

"Hey, Jerry, just because you're included doesn't mean you have a say."

"I think I do."

"I don't see why."

"I'm your *father*, Theresa. That still means something."

"Doesn't matter. Paul is mad all the time now, but he's heeding me, so you should, too."

"We don't have to be quiet about it."

"Sure. And *we* don't have to stay with you any longer, either."

We both shut up for a second, not a little surprised at how quickly things can reach an uncomfortable limit, which often happens when you start playing chicken with a loved one. My first (obtuse) impulse is to just say hell with this and drive over to the field and crank up ol' *Donnie*, fly her as high as I can get her. But I can't help but marvel at my daughter's hissy don't-tread-on-me attitude, courtesy of Daisy, and then wonder, too, in a flash that scares and deflates me, how bad the situation might really be, for her to be so darn immovable. She's hands down—along with Jack—the very best thing I've brought about in my life, the true-to-life sentiment of which I trust and hope is what every half-decent person thinks when he or she becomes a parent. But the slight twist here is that I am pretty sure Theresa has always known this to be the case as well, not because she's particularly high on herself, but from what has been, I suppose, my lifelong demonstration of readily accepting whatever's on offer, which I'm sure hasn't escaped her notice. From her angle, I could see, I haven't been much of a producer or founder, nothing at all like Pop, or millions of other guys in and between our generations, rather just caretaking what I've been left and/or given, and consuming my fair share of the bright and new, and shirking almost all civic duties save paying the property taxes and sorting the recycling, basically steering clear of *trouble*, the mode of which undoubtedly places me right in the vast dawdling heart of our unturbulent plurality but does me little good now, when I need to be exerting a little tough love back.

But then Theresa says first, "I'm sorry, Jerry. I can be such an ornery fucking bitch."

"Don't you say that," I tell her, as firm as I've ever been. "You're Theresa Battle, and you should be like nobody else, and you're perfectly great as you are."

"You think so?"

"I've never not."

She leans over and gives me a quick kiss on the cheek, stamp-like and tiny the way it felt when she was a kid, before Daisy died, and she would kiss me all the time.

"You know you're a pretty silly Mr. Empowerment."

"I don't care. If you don't."

"Of course not. Hey, are you going to finish your milkshake?"

"Go ahead."

More customers have pulled in, enough so that the assistant manager steps out near the road and waves his hands, to get his partner to come back. The kid finally does, swerving in neatly right next to us. He gives me the keys, trying to thank me but unable to say anything but an awestruck *fuckin' hot!*, over and over again, and the thought occurs to me that I should just give the damn car to these two soft-serve-for-brains, fodder for a nice feature on the local news, *Old dude just gave us the keys!*, they'd be saying, but they'd probably kill themselves in it or worse hurt somebody else like a pregnant sick young woman out for a cone. But they're decent enough, because as we're pulling out the younger one sprints to Theresa's car and hands her another large shake for the road.

As we near Richie's place there's a discernible hush, a lurking prosperity, the oaks and maples ascendant. The only sounds are the throaty low-gear gurgles of the Ferrari, and I still can't help but make the back tires squeal as I sling and lurch around these generous mansion-scale streets. Theresa, trailing half a block behind, gently rudders the old boat down the lanes. I've called Richie's house but only the machine answered and I didn't leave a message, and anyway I'm thinking it's best if I just park the car out on the semicircular driveway and drop the keys through the mail slot, with not even a note. Let Richie figure it out.

And that's exactly what I do, though giving his machine a last few screaming redline revs in neutral before shutting it down right at the front entrance. But after I shove the keys through the slot (cut into the brick façade rather than the door), and turn around to leave, the front door opens and who's there but Richie, in a dingy off-white bathrobe, Saturday afternoon unshaven, his half-height reading specs perched on the end of his narrow nose. Really, he looks sort of terrible, not in the least Waspy and up-market, suddenly bent over and darkish like any other of us newly aging New York Guidos, and for the first time since he was a kid I feel as though someone (if not Jerry Battle) ought to cut him a break.

"What's the big idea?" he says, holding out the keys to me. "I don't welch on my bets."

"Relax, Richie," I say, standing on his pea-stone driveway. "I just don't want it anymore."

"That car was the bet. You can't have a different one."

"I don't want a different one. I'm not trying to trade it in here. I'm giving it back to you."

"Why don't you sell it, then? Sell it and pocket the cash. It won't bother me. Who's that in your car?"

"My daughter."

"Your daughter?" Richie waves, and Theresa waves back. "She's a beautiful woman."

"She's pregnant, and engaged."

"Well good for her. Congratulations, Jerry."

"Look, I'm giving back the car. I'm not going to sell it."

"Well, I can't take it back," he answers, suddenly sounding not in the least like he's from the old neighborhood.

"Why the hell not?"

"My colleagues all witnessed the match. They verified the terms. I entertain them and others in the firm here regularly. If they saw the car around I couldn't possibly explain to them why you'd ever give it back."

"You can hide it in the garage."

"I'm not hiding anything."

"Tell them I'm a nice guy."

"Nobody's a nice guy."

"Tell them I was trying to trade it back to you for Rita."

This stops Richie for a second, as he absently jiggles the keys. "That they might believe. Anyway, it doesn't matter. Rita's not mine to trade."

"I know that."

"No, you don't," Richie says. "We broke up last week. She was here earlier this morning, to pick up the last of her things."

"You're kidding."

"I'm not."

"I don't believe you."

"Well, what the fuck do you think this is?" He reaches into his robe pocket and shows the diamond ring, the one with the stone as big as a hazelnut.

"What happened?"

"I don't know. After you came by that day it all went to shit. But I'm not blaming you. Maybe she got sick of me. Maybe she didn't like my friends. Maybe she still loves you."

Something Jerry Battle can always hear. And I can't help but ask, "Did she say that?"

Richie's smarting, which I've never quite seen from him, and before I can mercifully retract the question he says, "Not exactly. I'll say one thing. It's amazing what certain guys can get away with. I don't see why she'd even speak to you, with how you strung her along and wasted her youth. But maybe the long-term dodge is the most effective kind."

"She never said one word about wanting to get married."

"Well, even I know that doesn't mean a damn thing," he says, shaking his head. "You have no idea how lucky you are, do you, Jerry? You've always had steady attention from the girls, and I'll be honest and say you're also not a terrible guy, and so it's no surprise you got plenty of ass. With me, I always knew I'd have to make a shit load of dough to get a pretty woman to share my bed."

"Hey, Rich . . ."

"That's okay, I know what I look like. It got me focused early. I've taken nothing for granted, women or money or anything else. I'm not bragging here, I'm just saying how these things don't come easily to guys like me, and maybe people assume I wouldn't want to be anyone else but a partner at a top law firm with a big house in Muttontown and five Ferraris."

"Six, now."

"Okay, six. I'm not saying I want to trade places, but I'm not early-retired like you, I'll still be working seventy hours a week five years from now. I'll croak in the saddle, looking right over Park Avenue. And I'll grant you there's always some hot ambitious broad wanting to have a wealthy guy for a boyfriend but it's no guarantee of having the love of a beautiful, good woman like Rita."

"Which I don't have either," I remind him, "plus no big bank account."

"You got Rita still thinking about you, you big dumb fuck. That counts for a lot right there. Don't try to say anything or pretend you're insulted. You're going over there now, I already can see it in your eyes. So when you see her tell her I'm not about to keep this with me. I don't need something around to pull out and depress me."

Richie takes my hand and slaps the engagement ring into it. I try to give it back to him, because I can already see Rita's face when she sees me with it, here's Jerry up to something low-down and dirty, some sly scheme whereby she'll be finessed into opening up a half inch too much and he'll instantly squinch himself in and inhabit the gap, but Richie steps back inside and closes the door on me, and when I tell him to open up he says, with heartache and defeat, "You already bought the ring with the car, Jerry. Now go away. She's all yours."

ALL YOURS, Jerome, all yours. I keep thinking this as Theresa drives away, to do some last-minute ingredient errands for Paul, leaving me on the sidewalk in front of the deep, narrow row house Rita rents the back half of so she can have her summer vegetable garden. This is a risky strategy, I know, to have yourself left seven miles from home at the doorstep of your ex-girlfriend's without a way to get back under your own power, but at the last second before begging Theresa to stand at the door with me I decide to play this one as straight as I can, for reasons not altogether clear. Perhaps I'm realizing that I've been too willing to share my life's loads with loved ones, never having the stomach to endure anything alone, how after Daisy died even given the tough circumstance I leaned way too hard on my mother and her sisters for help with the kids, and on Pop, too (at least as far as my livelihood went), and then soon thereafter on Rita, especially Rita, who never said a word and soldiered on raising Jack and Theresa through the hairy messes of adolescence, despite their lukewarm attitudes and provisionally stanced love and amazing chronic underappreciation of her cooking (at least until they returned home, respectively, after a couple months of college dining). But none of this was as bad as my daily, hourly, by-the-minute want of her total participation in all things me, her Jerry Husbandry, finding expression in even the most insignificant details I somehow got her to take care of, literally right down to the level spoon of sugar she'd stir into my morning coffee, the pat of butter she'd leave melting on my toast. Certainly I'd do any heavy lifting she asked for, but after our first couple years there really wasn't much of it, as the lawn care and hedging and the gutters and the snowblowing were contracted out, and though I could afford a housekeeper Rita ended up looking after the kitchen and bathrooms and the laundry and pressing, the only thing I did for her diligently being the food shopping, enjoying the early Saturday morning stroll down the aisles, ticking off items on the list she'd written out on the back of an old utility bill, rapt in the specter of that week's glorious meals.

One morning late in our relationship and maybe the thing that finally did us in, I returned from the supermarket to find her still in bed with her night shades on and aired some vague jackass comment about maybe getting something *done* today. She popped up like a viper and laid into me like she'd been itching to do daily for a decade at least, saying how the only time I ever did something for her or anyone else without grousing or complaining or with a sour puss on was when there was a distinct possibility of some benefit to me, how in that way I was maybe—no, definitely— the most trivially needy, self-centered person she had ever met, that if she were verily on her deathbed and it was the lunch hour I probably couldn't help but ask her how she prepared her special egg salad with the diced black olives and sweet pickles and then bring the mixing bowl into the bedroom for a full-on demonstration.

That kind of smarted, to be sure, and as I went into a tortured and convoluted defense about trickle-down beneficiaries of a person's self-interest (I'm no Reaganite, being rabid about nothing, but still the theory has a natural attraction for me, given that the trickling aspect is just my sort of "work"), she stepped out of bed and came up from behind, tapping my shoulder, and whacked me square in the face with her pillow as I turned to make a point. It didn't hurt so much, of course, being more a shock than anything else, but this suddenly bloodthirsty look in her usually nurturing huge brown eyes did stun me into silence, and I'm not so sure she wouldn't have wielded whatever she grabbed first that morning, be it a pillow or a bat.

And even though there's probably no better time to go kissing up to her than now, when she's just cut loose from Richie and knocking about the house alone and maybe against all good judgment thinking fuzzily about us, this present near future of me standing here on the rickety back stoop of Rita's shotgun house holds a potentially dangerous outcome, and not because I think she might haul off and bonk me again. The reason is that she might just be tempted enough to let me have another taste, the circumstance of which, if it can't sustain, will certainly leave me in a desolated state. Theresa in her own stubborn manner has allowed me to remain in the rare air of some seriously aromatic denial (for which My Declining Self has been grateful, every day and every minute), but there's another part of me that doesn't care anymore if I can't help but see the loose grit and grub of this life, and risk something more intense than irritation or annoyance. It's the question of participation, again, though this time I'm slotted to practice it in a form wholly singular, unbolstered, which you'd think would be the highest manifest pride of a full-blooded American guy like me but has long been my greatest dread, save final extinguishment itself.

I can barely press hard enough to ring the bell.

Nothing happens, and I'm going to ring again, but in the next moment I find myself mincing down the steps to flee before any flak bursts erupt, already thinking of how I'm going to be walking all night to get back home, when I hear Rita say in her loamy autumnal voice, "I'm here, Jerry, I'm here."

She is wearing a loose white cotton dress, with a pretty lace pattern at the neck, sort of South-of-the-Border style, the sight of this and her dark-hued beauty reminding me of those raven-haired señoritas in the westerns, not the lusty barmaid or wizened hooker but the starry-eyed young village woman who endlessly carries jugs of water and wears a big silver cross and though captivated by the stoic gringo gunslinger come to save the town remains loyal in the end to her long-suffering peasant husband. But I'm no hero, and neither she nor her people ever needed any help, and if I had a hat I'd be holding it out for whatever lowly alms might be given, a ladle of water, a crust of bread, a slip of time beneath the shade tree out back, to gather myself before at last moving on.

"I don't mean to bother you," I say, suddenly feeling ashamed of myself. "I don't know what I'm doing. I'll leave you alone."

"How did you get here? I don't see your car."

"Theresa dropped me off."

"But she's gone," she says, her voice riding a hard edge.

"I know. It's my fault. It was stupid and I'm going."

"I'll call Theresa at the house."

"She's gone on errands. She won't be home for a couple hours, at least."

"I can call you a taxi, then. I can do that for you."

"You don't have to."

"What, Jerry, are you really going to walk home along the Expressway? You'll get hit. You're not going to put that one on me. I'll call a cab now. You can wait right there if you want."

"Okay, then."

She steps inside for what seems a long time, and enough for me to look around and notice that her garden is overgrown, the ground-hugging tomatoes spidery and wild for not having been regularly pinched back, the string beans and squashes too big for good eating, the basil and parsley long bolted and flowery, what almost everyone else's plot looks like late in the season but never Rita's, who kept her patch in the far western corner of my property looking like one of those serene, ultramanicured Japanese gardens, a miniaturized Eden of gently tended plants with their ripened issue gorgeously shining and pendant. Every summer but this one I waded daily through those rows, eating the vegetables right there, my roving live salad, Rita hardly able to make a full dish for my culling, though never in the least minding. She enjoyed the plain hard work of it (like with everything else she does), which is why the present sight disturbs me so, as if having to deal with guys like me and Richie has steadily depleted her hardihood and forced her to run too long on low battery; in fact as I look around it's all a bit forlorn, the small paint-flaked stoop unswept of dead bugs and leaves, the flowerpots empty save for hardened, white-speckled dirt, and I can't help but peer through the screen door to the counter of the tiny kitchen, weedy with mugs and plates, and mourn for her a little, knowing that this should be the golden period of Rita's life, being fifty and still beautiful, when she ought to be tasting the not-so-proverbial fruit of her good character and labors with a man she loves and who loves her back and is wise and generous enough not to waste another moment of her precious time.

"There's no cab available," she tells me, through the screen. "One's going to come, but not for an hour."

"Thanks. I'll wait out front."

"You don't have to do that, Jerry. I don't despise you, you know."

"I know."

"Besides, you can help me pack up some things."

"Pack up?"

"My lease is up this month, and I don't want to live here any-more."

I can't believe it's been a year, though at times it's seemed like ten. "What are you going to do?" I ask, stepping inside the kitchen. It's dark and cramped but still smells good, of mint and lemons. She's just made supersweet iced tea (her sole addiction, in every season) and unconsciously pours me a glass, the small au-tomation of which would be enough to break my heart, if there weren't the uncertainty of where she might now go.

"I've looked at a couple places. They need experienced RNs pretty much everywhere, especially in the South and the West."

"You like Long Island."

"I thought I did. But why should I? I certainly don't like the crowds, or the roads. The people aren't very nice. I don't like to boat or fish. I'm starting to think it's the worst of all worlds, pushy, suburban, built-up, only shopping to do."

"But this is our world."

"Maybe yours, Jerry. I don't know. Kelly told me about Portland."

"In Maine?"

"Oregon. She said it's a nice small city, with friendly people, mild weather, mossy and woodsy. I checked. I could pack my clothes and throw a garage sale for the rest and get on a plane next week."

"You don't know a soul out there."

"Maybe that's better."

"Everybody is white."

"Everybody is white everywhere."

"But you have *family* here."

This stops her, for a moment, because of course she doesn't have anyone around in terms of blood relations, which has never seemed to bother her, but I think really has.

"I wish Theresa had stayed and visited," she says.

"It's my fault. She wanted to, but I told her I needed to see you alone."

"You said at Richie's she was in trouble. You never told me any details. Or was it just another Jerry story?"

"Maybe it was," I say, thinking how present matters (and the larger scheme, too) demand less complication, and not more. "But you should talk to her anyway."

"I will. How is Jack? I thought I saw him last week in that big black truck of his, driving out of the Lion's Den."

"That bar in Huntington?"

"I was meeting Kelly for lunch. I was parking, and I waved, and I thought he saw me, but he just drove off. Sort of wildly, in fact. He almost got into an accident."

"He's been out of whack, of late. Things haven't been so hot at Battle Brothers. You should really call him, too. But only if you want to."

"Of course I want to, Jerry!" she says, with due exasperation. "Don't you think it makes me unhappy, not to see them as much as I'm used to?"

"No one's keeping you away. I've never not asked you to come to something. Maybe I should have made sure I wasn't there."

"That would have helped."

"Okay, I got it. But Jack really needs you, I'm sure of it. He talks less and less to me. The last time he came by he was sort of drunk, so he said a few things, we yakked, it was pretty decent stuff. Maybe alarming, but decent. Otherwise it's pretty much hello and goodbye. Soon he's not even going to grunt at me, it'll just be all nods."

"What do you want him to say?" she says, though not in an accusatory tone.

"Maybe he could tell me how the business is falling apart. Or he could lie, give me a big cotton candy story. I don't care. Maybe he could tell me what those spoiled brats of his are up to, or what *objet* Eunice just bought for the house. He could tell me about my yard, which is what he did last time. Now, that was nice."

"Why am I not surprised to hear nothing about what you told or asked him?"

"That's not my job! And even if it were, what do I have to talk about? Nothing's ever different in my life, except for you and me, which he definitely does not want to discuss. He's the one who's young and in the thick of it. I had my turn of trouble. Or so I thought."

"You're always saying that, Jerry. Like you already had a lifetime of it with what happened to Daisy."

"I think that counts for a damn big share."

"Of course it does," she says, sitting down next to me at the half-sized corner breakfast table, close enough that our wrists almost touch. "But somehow you think nobody else has ever had similar difficulties."

"That's not true. And hey, I've never whined or gone on about it, have I?"

"No," Rita agrees. "You haven't mentioned Daisy more than a dozen times since I've known you, and maybe just once or twice referred to *that.* But everything you do—or don't want to do, more like—has an origin in what happened to Daisy, which at this point is really what happened to *you.*"

"It did happen to me!"

"But it's never ceased for you, Jerry. You look to spread the burden all the time. Everybody is a potential codependant, though with you they hardly know it. You're sneaky, that way. When I wanted to have a baby, what did you say to me?"

"That was a long time ago, sweetie. Who can remember?"

"I'll refresh your memory. It was my thirty-seventh birthday, and we were having dinner at The Blue Schooner."

"Gee, that was a fancy place. Huge shrimps in the shrimp cocktail."

"Of course you remember that."

"Okay. I don't know. Probably something about my being too old and tired to raise another kid."

"Not quite," she says icily. "You said *I* was too old and tired."

"Not a chance. I'm not that stupid."

"Actually you were trying to be helpful. It was your way of saying I should be enjoying my youth instead. Traveling a lot and dancing and staying out late. The thing was that I was already raising Jack and Theresa, which I was happy for and never felt bad about or regretted. I loved those kids even if they didn't quite love me."

"They loved you, and they love you now."

"Oh, I know, I know. The thing that makes me crazy is that I knew then that you weren't thinking of me, of my potentially lost youth. You just naturally wanted to ensure you had me available to go places with."

"Look, if you had insisted on having a baby, I would have agreed."

"Right! You might have said okay but you would have pissed and moaned all through the pregnancy and after the baby arrived been a total grouch every time it peeped. I should have left you then, because I really did want a baby, but for some reason I'll never understand I thought I would only have it with you. I'm a total bimbo fool."

"Don't say that."

"It's the truth."

"Maybe you loved me a little, too."

"Maybe."

"I'll make it up to you."

"What, Jerry, you're offering to knock me up?"

"Sure. Right now, if you want."

Rita laughs, though wearily, like it's the thousandth time from me she's heard it all. "Well you know how old I am, Jerry. And you're sixty."

"Nearly sixty."

"Nearly sixty. Together that's a lot of mileage on my eggs, and your sperm."

"A woman older than you just had a kid, she was, like, fifty-seven. They can work miracles now with the hormone drugs."

"That's a crime, not a miracle. Anyway, ours would definitely come out with three heads."

"As long as it's happy."

"Do you think that's remotely possible?"

"I think it's very possible."

Rita quietly sips her iced tea, as do I, the window fan around the corner in the living room sounding like a monk droning on in the misty, craggy-hilled distance. It's his only song, and he's telling me to keep still, to shut my mouth, to be bodiless and pure, to not spoil this moment with the usual spoutings of ruinous want and craving, my lifelong mode of consumption, to sit before this lovely woman of epic-scaled decency whom I desperately love and let the bloom just simply tilt there before me, leave it be in the light, undisturbed, unplucked. And if ever I could manage such a thing (if there be Mercy), it should by all rights be at the present moment, when I'm as conscious as I'll ever be of what Rita means (and not solely to me). But what do I do but corral her shoulder and supple neck and deeply kiss her, kiss her, like I've been imagining I would do for the last dim colorless half year, taste the soft pad of her lips, her perennially lemony breath, while in parallel process steeling myself for the next second's indubitable turn, the repulsed insulted shove-off. What happens, though, is exactly not that, for while she's not pressing into me she's also not quite pulling back, and when I sneak a peek through my bliss-shut eyes I see that she's closed hers extra tight, like someone who's about to get a flu shot, and maybe her heart's thinking is that she'll endure this unpleasant but soon invaluable inoculation, the little sickness that wards off the permanently crippling disease.

"Oh, Jerry, what are we doing?"

"We're making love."

"I don't think so."

"Give it a chance."

"I don't want to."

But she lets me kiss her again, and I don't have to be loony to think that she's kissing me the tiniest bit in return, reversing the flow, and then just like that we're standing back in the living room, her arms hanging straight down in a fast-diminishing wish of neutrality, with me holding on to her sides just north of where her hips jut out, my favorite spot no doubt because it was the first patch of her I ever touched; and who but all regular fellows like me (and the occasional Sapphist gal, too) can understand the achy bottoming-out feeling in your variety meats as I glean the gauzy cotton dress for the stringy banding of her panty, this bare narrow line of everyperson's dreams.

Rita turns her face away and buries it in my neck, as if she can't bear to meet my eyes out of shame and self-disbelief, such that I can almost hear her mind going *Idiot I am he's such a slime,* and so it occurs to me that I should hug her as tightly and chastely as I know how, which I do, and in mid-clutch she sort of cracks, literally, her spine aligning with the sudden gravity, and I pretty much carry her to the sofa before I ease her up onto it, hands cupping her thighs, head in her throat, rubbing my face in the heat-heavy spot of her wishbone, the tiny redolent dugout I've tasted thousands of times. And if I could remake myself into just that shape and size it's right here I think I would forever reside.

After a while she says, breathless, "The taxi's going to come."

"I'm on it," I answer, stumbling back into the kitchen. I pull a $20 bill from my wallet and flag it with a stickup note (*Sorry buddy!!*) and close it in the door.

"Let's stop now," she says, when I return.

"All right," I say, but already I'm all over her, making her lie back, her dress nicely crumpling, and after another while she's all over me, roughly, almost angrily, like a woman possessed. I know she's missed me some, too, because she's liberally using her mouth, the diverse songs of which of course I preternaturally love but which always ultimately lend for me a somewhat sorrowful undertone to the production (besides the depraved one instilled early on by my nun-based education), and I pull her up to kiss her and we wrestle out of our clothes. Soon we're in the familiar saddling of our bodies, girl on top but not yet conjoined, hers still amazingly youthful if definitely fleshier than I recall, thicker around the middle and the upper arms and thighs, while I, looking down at myself, am this odd-sectioned hide of pale and tan, flabby and skinny except for my gut, the only remotely vital thing being my thing itself, darkly hued, though only decently angled, in truth looking a bit like something trapped under plastic wrap, reduced for quick sale. Rita maybe senses this, for she grasps it like an old airplane stick, arcing us into a slow and steady climb, and I can't help but wonder aloud, "How was he?"

"Richard?"

"Yeah."

"What are you asking?"

I nod. "You know."

"Jesus, Jerry."

"I can ask."

"No, you can't."

"But you can tell me."

"Richard was twice the gentleman you are," she says, a spiteful cast in her eyes.

"And?"

"Okay," she says, gripping down hard. "Maybe only half the man."

I'm pretty sure she's lying, but it doesn't matter in the least, for this is an instance when it really is the thought that counts, and it shows, for suddenly I feel as if I'm giant, as if I have a one-and-only axis, ruddering me blindly to a star, and I whisper, "Do you want to?"

"A-hum," she barely whispers back. She kneels up and lifts herself, her breast sway more pronounced than I remember, showing a bit more travel, which is no awful thing at all. I take a heft of each as she guides us toward the cloistered inlet, our trusty craft hugging the shore, and it's no surprise I feel like I'm encapsulated in the moment, in this module of my dreams, knowing it's of little use or consequence to be still doggedly working the controls. For Rita is the one who's in command, suspending us now in an eddy, for which I'm actually glad, for even at my age I don't know if I can withstand that first quick plunge (it's been a long time, dammit), and it's telling that I wouldn't mind if we simply stayed in this most intimate contiguity, just hugging, which perhaps reveals the truth of what they say happens even to guys like me, that you go soft first and foremost in the mind, long before the rigging ever fails.

Rita stares me in the eyes. She doesn't want to know whether it'll be another story this time around, because of course in fact it won't be, and rather than some set of hard questions for me is what basic thing she sees she needs that I, in my chronic lack of empathy and wisdom, still somehow manage to provide; I fear I'm now present at the moment of some sober mutual recognition, which in my late reckoning is perhaps the surest sign of any lasting love. Rita grabs the back of my neck and lowers herself down, down, our fit familiarly cosseted and snug, and for a few seconds neither of us really tries to shift or move or start a rhythm. But then the doorbell rings, somebody's at the back, and this gets us going in a nicely syncopated time; it *ring-rings* again and I call out that I left some money and don't need the cab. The voice that I hear calling back sounds much like Theresa's, which I don't expect and so ignore. But she calls again and Rita, realizing who it is, quickly climbs off.

"It's your daughter, Jerry, go let her in."

I get up, but given my indecent state (the situation reminding me of those mornings when I had to wait out my wake-up wood beneath the covers while the kids jumped all over me and Daisy in our bed), I shake my head, and so Rita tosses my trousers onto me and quickly pulls on her cotton dress. As they greet one another with warm cheer and chuckles, my situation naturally wanes, and by the time they walk back to the living room I'm mostly dressed, tucking in the tail of my Battle Brothers logo polo shirt.

"Sorry to crash the party, guys," Theresa says.

"Of course you're not," Rita offers, almost motherly in her abashedness. "You want some iced tea, honey?"

"That'd be great, I'm parched."

Rita heads to the kitchen.

"What's the matter?" I say, searching Theresa's face. "You feeling okay?"

"I'm perfect," she answers. "But there is a problem."

"Okay."

"It's Pop," she says, a bit too softly. "I called on the way home and spoke to Paul. He said that Ivy Acres was trying to reach you, and after a little work he convinced them to tell him what was wrong."

"Okay."

Rita comes back and hands Theresa a glass. We stand there, waiting.

"It seems that Pop has run away."

"What do you mean, *run away*?"

"He's AWOL, I guess. They think since yesterday at dinner."

"They think? They haven't seen him for nearly a whole day?"

"I was wondering that myself," Theresa says. "I called them while I was driving back here, but nobody would talk to me, since they only have you as the stated guardian. But I know from Paul that they haven't yet called the police."

"I'm calling now," Rita says, standing at the hall phone. "I have a friend at the county sheriff's office. He'll know what to do."

"Where the hell could he have gone?" I say. "He doesn't even have a wallet anymore. How did he get anywhere? He can't walk more than a few blocks."

Theresa says, "Maybe there's a mall bus that leaves from there. If we're lucky, he's probably just sitting in a Banana Republic."

"Jesus, let's hope. We better go to the nursing home right now."

I stop and kiss Rita as we leave. I tell her, "Please don't pack. Please don't move. Don't do anything. At least not until I sort this out. Okay? Okay?"

Rita nods, not quite looking me in the eyes, and then gives Theresa a quick deep hug. Then she gives me one, too, with a little extra, and while this should do nothing but hearten and calm, I have the awful flash of an idea that this is the last I'll ever see her. Here we are, just brushed by passion, certainly back on my plotted-out course, and all I can think to do is take one mind-picture after another of her brown sugar eyes, and her brown sugar cheeks, and the uncertain tumbles of her thick, coally hair. Yes, here's a beautiful woman. And when soon thereafter my daughter and I are back in the front bench of the softtop, though now with me at the wheel, opening up the big-chambered engine, the old rumble so bold and booming you'd think we could fly, I have to ask, Why should this be? Why now? But there's no answer to that. Just this: here is the Real, all Jerry's, all mine.

t e n

I USED TO HAVE NEIGHBORS down the street named Guggenheimer, George and Janine, a couple right around my age with a bunch of kids and longhaired dogs. They moved in just after Daisy died and lived there for eight or so years. From my point of view they were a happy, sprawly, boisterous lot, always playing lawn darts or Wiffle ball, the hounds racing around and almost knocking over the kids, George and Janine constantly attending to their house (the same ranch model as mine), either sweeping up or landscaping. Despite what seemed their constant activity, the yard front and back (they had a corner lot) was always kind of a mess, pocked with plastic toys and dropped rakes and bags of Bark-O-Mulch and lime. It really didn't bother me at all, because after a while as a professional landscaper you get sick of the totally clipped and manicured look, and don't mind a guy who looks after his property himself, even if he does it half-assed and badly, which is how George Guggenheimer did it, though with obvious ambition for the place, given all the projects he'd start. There was the new paver brick walkway, and the hedge of arborvitae, and then undoubtedly the most difficult thing he tried, which was the koi pond in the backyard, spanned by a miniature Japanese-style bridge.

The paver brick walkway turned out okay, if you wanted to be charitable, mostly because you couldn't see it from the street. Up close it was completely uneven and buckled, some spots so high or low that you could hardly go the length without stubbing your toe and tripping. The arborvitae hedge lasted about three weeks after he put it in, about thirty ten-gallon plants, the victim of both too shallow planting and overwatering.

Naturally I'd given him some neighborly advice about both projects and he even wrote down some of the finer points but I suppose in the end it's about execution and attention to detail and George wasn't the kind of guy you'd let hammer a nail you were holding, or maybe even dig you a hole. This last skill was part of the problem with the koi pond, which looked great to start, with fat orange and pearl-colored koi and blooming water lilies and a faux-rock waterfall that played Hawaiian-style music whenever someone approached. It was George's finest hour, but only for about a week. The pond began to drain after one of his older boys tried to guillotine a koi with a garden spade, missing of course and slicing through the liner. I advised George to completely empty the thing and patch the liner when it was totally dry but he went ahead with some supposedly special underwater "glue" he found at a pool supply store and proceeded to kill all the fish (they bloated up and turned black in the face). This would have been okay had he stopped right there, but the younger kids were crying all day about the poor dead fish and Janine was pissy and probably withholding sex because of the moody kids, and George decided next in his know-nothing homeowner wisdom to cut out the part he'd glued. He ended up punching a hole in the underlying concrete shell he'd laid in too thin to begin with, discovering in the process a large sinkhole right next to the pond hole, where the old septic system had been and mostly still was. He would have done something about that had he not had the egregious fortune of having a wicked summer storm surge in that night, raging with lightning and thunder and three inches of rain. In the morning the sky was perfectly clear, the ceiling unlimited, though I knew something was awry because when I picked up the paper at the end of the driveway I could smell an epic rot, like some dirt of pre-history, and when I walked over there after breakfast a crowd of neighbors had already gathered at the back of George's house, all holding their noses, peering into what had been a smooth back lawn but was now a huge jagged trench running from where the koi pond had been all the way to the street, the Japanese bridge smashed in half and lying mud-soaked in the trench. Really, you could have filmed *All Quiet on the Western Front* right there at the Guggenheimers'.

George was down about it certainly but with extra mopiness, and after the crowd thinned out and the sewer guys told him the ballpark figure for the job he took me aside and said he might not survive this one. I told him to laugh it off and just write the check (just the way you would blithely say in any "nice" neighborhood with a bit of resignation and no veiled pride), that he'd fix the mess and get another koi pond, this one bigger, but he just shook his head and sat down on the wet lawn and in a real breach of sub-urban decorum began to bawl like a baby. I crouched down beside him and held his shoulder for a half minute until he piped down a little, and I told him the way I used to tell all my worried, scared clients (and there wasn't anybody who wasn't), in my laconic captain-of-the-squad way to pull it together because this was one we were going to win. I immediately regretted using "we" because he hugged me with his sloppy face and I think he assumed that maybe I'd get the guys from Battle Brothers over with a couple of earthmovers and backhoes and roll out fresh sod. Before I could say anything else or backpedal he said they were financially shot. I asked him what he meant by that because like everybody else it seemed the Guggenheimers were spending what they pleased and on what they wanted and so that automatically meant they were making the money, too, but he said it again, they were shot, fucking shot, the directness of which surprised me, as you never hear in neighborhoods like this how everything was about to fall apart.

I felt bad about it, which automatically meant that I would call him the next day to "check in" and commiserate from a distance and then promptly make myself scarce for two or three weeks, which is exactly what I did, your basic poor-fuck-but-damn-glad-it-ain't-me routine, but then it happened that the very night after the koi pond debacle George stopped for a gallon of milk at the Dairy Barn and bought a lottery ticket and won, won pretty big, not one of those mega-million games but a kind of jackpot they don't seem to offer anymore, where you get a set amount of money each year for as long as you live. It was promoted with a slogan like "Salary for Life," and was $100,000 a year paid with a wink every Labor Day, an amount that in those days wasn't just plain vanilla upper-middle-class living, and for the Guggenheimers it was a ticket to ride high. Like me, George had inherited his livelihood from his parents, in his case a couple of long-established dry-cleaning stores in Kissena Park, Queens, but he'd done a thorough job of running them into the ground, not to mention ignoring the new competition from all the Korean and Chinese owners coming in. The truth of the matter, as he told me the day before, was he'd been planning to sell the businesses and get into some other line (what that was going to be he didn't say), because he was out of equity and cash and was carrying a hefty debt on his ranch house and the cleaners, and was just about to step into the crosshairs of the collection agencies and banks, which is exactly the appropriate time in our good culture to throw away your last few bucks on a 20-million-to-1 shot.

There was a short segment about the Guggenheimers on the *Eyewitness News*, George and Janine looking sweaty and stunned as they held either end of a big cardboard check, the amount for which I noticed wasn't a number but a question mark followed by a lot of zeroes, the point being the sky was the limit. Right away they sold the dry-cleaning stores (to Koreans, of course) and did the smart thing and paid off their most pressing debts, consolidating the others through one of those sketchy New Jersey mortgage outfits, and then setting about to fix the sinkhole in their backyard. But soon enough the spending geared up. They hired Battle Brothers to bulldoze and clear-cut the property and plant and lay everything in totally fresh. George traded in his old cars for a couple of brand-new Mercedes convertibles, his (silver) and hers (red), and when they went out as a family they had to take both cars and jam the kids in each.

Janine it turned out was very much into modern art and design and began buying a lot of stuff from local galleries, sculptures of figures either really skinny or really fat as well as Cubist-style and Abstract-ed paintings featuring the same kind of figures, and furniture from Maurice Villency and Roche-Bobois that was sleek in form and always cold and uncomfortable, the program in fact not so dissimilar to what Eunice has done over at Château Battle. The house itself was completely razed and done over and in the end not so strangely it was almost an exact replica of the Guggenheim Museum, ⅕ scale, with a big circular parking garage–inspired turret dominating the massing and hardly any windows. The concurrences didn't in the least occur to Janine or George, as neither had been to the museum, nor by extension any surname irony, the facts of which made you pull for them all the more, as they were simply enjoying the found fruits of their good luck.

And maybe it would have all gone swimmingly, had George not been involved in a frightening little car accident just before another year had passed. While driving on the Southern State Parkway he was rear-ended, the front of his convertible accordioned in, too, when he was thrust into the car in front. George was banged up pretty badly and got forty stitches in his face and hands and spent a night at the hospital for observation of his concussion. After a few days he was fine but I suppose he got to thinking about his brush with death and what that would mean for his Salary for Life, and pretty soon you hardly saw him driving and then even walking in the neighborhood. He called me up one day and asked if Battle Brothers could put up an eight-foot chain-link fence around the entire property, which we did, and he had house alarms and cameras rigged up, and before long he was hardly ever outside in his own yard, fearing that he'd catch some deadly virus like AIDS, which was just coming into the news then and was still mysterious enough to keep you wondering. George even began to stay airlocked in his private bedroom suite (he'd moved out of the master because Janine was naturally venturing out to shop and ferry the kids around and see friends, and was thus a ready importer of contagion), and grew more and more distrusting and fearful of anything having to do with the outside world. So it came as no surprise that after a year of this Janine divorced him, taking the kids to what I hear is a nice gated golf community in North Carolina, where Janine looks after the central clubhouse. George still owns the house, I believe, though he moved out long ago, to where nobody knows.

Of course, I'm thinking about George at the present moment not because I had so much feeling for him (which I did, aplenty, in a knowing, down-the-street neighborly way that had to do with our shared existence of familial and realty responsibilities), but because I, perhaps like George Guggenheimer, am beginning to see this sprawly little realm as laden with situations not simply dangerous and baleful; it's the fact that no matter how fast or high you might keep moving, the full array of those potentialities are constantly targeting your exact coordinates, and with extreme prejudice. And while this is self-absorption in the classical mode, I must admit Rita was right, I did think I'd banked a life's worth of slings and arrows after Daisy, maybe even enough to safeguard the next generation, maybe to wash back, too, on the one previous. But Theresa's illness and now my father's almost magical disappearance are new instructions from above (or below or beyond), telling me in no uncertain terms that I cannot stay at altitude much longer, even though I have fuel to burn, that I cannot keep marking this middle distance.

I am not even mentioning the latest turns in Jack's financial totterings, which compared to these other potential calamities would seem downright welcome if they were the only things we had to consider and deal with, but, to be honest, something about his trouble pushes me right up to the very limits of my tolerances for what life can sometimes unsparingly orchestrate. With Jack it has to do certainly with the issue of legacy, namely the fucking-up of said thing, which if we come right down to it is what we secretly find most compelling about legacies (yes, even our own), not the pleasures of bestowal or some rite cycle of being, but rather the surprise diminution that in the not-so-fetching opera of our lives comes in the inglorious rushed finale, the wondrous aria by a brash new tenor, who can hit every soaring note except the one that counts. For there's nothing as deeply stirring as familial failure, cast across time.

And the skinny of that failure is this: Jack has sunk the ship. If I may be business-channel-like about it, let me say that he is accomplishing it with a highly effective one-pronged strategy of capital overinvestment. Namely, everything he has been buying for the company, from the new cube vans to the five-ton haulers to the mini-backhoes (equipment we always leased per job or week or perhaps for the season at most), he has been buying outright with the idea that Battle Brothers would be subleasing to itself (in the form of paper subsidiaries) in a complicated (and no doubt semilegal) cash flow optimization/accelerated depreciation scheme that he did not bother to vet with crusty old Sal, dealing directly instead with an offshore banking firm registered in the Caymans or Nigeria or Uzbekistan or some other such "republic" where generally accepted accounting principles are held in an esteem equal to whatever national constitution was drawn up for them by do-gooding wonks at the IMF. Not that I understand exactly what's happened, but the result is that with the long-anticipated slowdown in work (due to the sluggish economy, plus the intense competition of late, as every hammerhead and his ADD-afflicted, Dremel-wielding brother have gotten into the home improvement business in the last ten years), he's no longer able to pay off the debt service on the machines and getting no real or even "accounting" profit back, meaning he's sinking in shit both ways. This would not be so big a problem if he could sell the rigs anywhere near cost but everybody demands a huge discount these days and it's almost not worth bothering, except that there's a whole bunch of office equipment and technology and software and other high-priced gizmos that become obsolete a few seconds after you plug them in, which it turns out nobody wants at any price, and that Battle Brothers seems to own enough of to open our very own Staples store.

The other day, for a minor example, when secretly called in by Sal to look over the ledgers for myself, I happened to stub my toe on what I figured was a funky coffee table Eunice had ordered up at full suggested retail but was actually a gross case of five or ten thousand floppy disks, brand-new and still in the shrink-wrap, meant originally for backing up every last transaction of our business. They now have been superseded of course by compact disks that hold many multiples the data and will be cheaper eventually though not soon enough for us. Predictably I happened upon in the supply room gathering dust the floppy disk drives that were recently changed out, piled forlornly with their cables hanging out and tangled like the viscera you used to see troughs of at the butcher's, though all those sloppy kibbles and bits were turned into something somebody somewhere wanted, and duly *got*, eventually, whether they knew it or not. All of which makes you sort of worry if our wondrous civilization has evolved to the point that we've somehow abrogated that particular law of thermodynamics concerning the conservation of all energy and matter, as it seems that what we're coming up with now is made so that it can't possibly be used or reintegrated after the initial burn. It's pure by-product from the start, slickly marketed and apotheosized as essential for mass sale to a well-meaning guy like Jack Battle, and finally reposed as mere foot fodder.

I've already detailed the extensive corporate headquarters—style renovations to our once humble garage, costs that surprisingly were not mortgaged and amortized as they normally should have been but instead (for the purpose of a discount negotiated by Eunice) outlayed in cold hard cash, cold hard cash something the business is quite low on in reserves, so low in fact that our usually cuddly banker at Suffolk National has begun sending chilly missives concerning our insufficient and recently missed payments on the seven-figure note Jack took out shortly after I stepped down from the helm. Apparently Jack has been attempting to refinance this hefty note (okay, it's $3 million, twice as much as Sal suspected), but even in this age of before-you-even-ask-for-it credit he hasn't yet found any takers, partly because he spent way too much for a nicely treed four-acre parcel of land directly behind our property (he was itchy for a major expansion right from the get-go), though mostly because the property itself has come under suspicion of being an environmental hazard.

I'd always feared it was our original property that might go afoul certain green regulations and standards, but it seems the previous owner of the new plot had a big-time commercial photo-finishing business in Hicksville. For the past twenty-five years he dumped the chemicals and other liquid unsavories from interests he had in a string of instant-lube centers into an old well on the property, which he neatly bulldozed over and sealed and covered with fill and fresh sod. This would be bad enough except that the local homeowners whose properties abut in a ring this new one of ours are now filing a lawsuit claiming health problems (one of whom not so ironically being that girlfriend of mine from youth, Rose Cahill, who actually lives in that same house now with *not one but two* supposedly autistic adult sons), their experts and also now county and state and probably soon federal environmental safety inspectors drilling for soil samples and testing surrounding well water for heavy metals and radicalized chemicals and oils, such that our nice big little family business with its surfeit of plant and equipment is now, given the potential liabilities, worth pretty much zilch.

Though Sal, bless his randy old soul, insists this isn't quite as bad as it sounds.

Apparently there are certain protections having to do with de-claring bankruptcy that will shield us for a while from legal action and foreclosure, plus we now have our own representation, too, serving notice to both Mr. Mercury Water and our alarmist neigh-bors, namely (this time), mirabile dictu, Richard Anthony Coniglio, Esq., who was completely gentlemanly when I (ready to grovel, ready to beg) phoned him. Richie instantly conferenced me in on a call to his underlings, scrambling those fast jet associates Kim-ster and Kenton from the deck of the Fortune 50 multinational they've been defending (against the outrageous claims of some greedy supposedly ruined Micronesian fishing village) and vectored them screaming into our own modest fray.

The key now, of course, is to delay and delay and delay, and delay some more, let everything and everyone stew in the procedural stays that we litigious Americans have perfected into high performance art. Richie has even been so generous as to offer to bill us only for his associates' hours, and not his own, and though it's unclear *pro* exactly what/whose *bono* is inspiring him into such magnanimousness, I would like to think it's a feeling that we're alumni of sorts, brothers from the old neighborhood and even linked via Rita in that way men are when they do all they can to crush each other and only then intimately glimpse the reflection of their own vulnerability. Probably closer to the truth is that we're at the general point in our lives when almost all the heaviest lifting has been done, and you can finally begin to measure yourself not solely by the usual units of accomplishment but by the plain stupid luck of your draw in a macrocosm rigged with absolutely nothing particular about you in mind.

One might be wondering how it is that I've learned about these goings-on, given that I haven't talked at all to Jack since he came by the house last, which is certainly the case, and I could say that Sal has been the mostly disinterested informer and go-between and facilitator, which is also the case; but it should be no surprise to anyone who has been a father or a son, or for that matter born into any kind of real family at all, to hear that Jack and I haven't discussed said huge subject, or endured any lingeringly awkward moments because of it, or even plied each other with subtle, passive aggressions that would steadily accrue on the cellular level until one or both of us up and burst in a cascade of recrimination and vitriol. For all I can see, he's continued to show at work each day at 6 A.M. sharp and gone about addressing Total Dissolution with some help from Sal while making no attempt to hide from me what's been happening, knowing full well that I know full well, and not agonizing (at least publicly) about what any of us might think. Of course, I don't know what's going on in his head, or in his household (though I'm almost certain Eunice has no inkling, as she'd have been all over me with directives from her command-and-control center of a pearlescent white Range Rover); whatever he's thinking or feeling I do have to say, gotta say, that I'm kind of proud of the boy, goddammit, not for fucking everything up of course but for soldiering on as he has, for just trudging ahead with old-fashioned head-down dignity, plowing forward like one of those ice-breaking ships in the Arctic, whose prow is harder than it is sharp.

Too bad that what lies ahead in the visible horizon are just floes and more floes, with ice fields re-forming in his wake, supplies and fuel running dangerously low, and morale undoubtedly dwindling besides (the Discovery Channel, it turns out, does indeed corroborate with life on the ground); and although I've said I'm at a limit as to what I can stand to witness, the first question for yours truly must be why I'm not doing more to bear necessary heat upon this situation. Pop, in my place, would certainly rain fear and misery upon Jack's suppliers, and lay off half the crews and the entire office staff (except Sal, who would have to answer the phones, too), fire-sell anything that couldn't otherwise be used to dig a ditch or lay in brick or fix one of the machines, and then force-feed the Suffolk National guy and his wife double porterhouses and vanilla-y merlot at Ruth's Chris, instead of perching here as I am in my God seat and bemoaning, bemoaning. Truth is, Pop would be referring to this as Our Problem, Our Mutual Assured Destruction, Our Shit Sundae, and he'd be digging in with the same gusto he'd have for my mother's self-admittedly mediocre cooking ("*You're welcome to make the sauce*"), which he groused about nightly but always accepted seconds of, and even thirds; vis-à-vis Jack, even at his age he would have thundered with disbelief and anger but then stood by him and taken on whatever load needed bearing and generally gotten hopped up on the disaster of it all, because, unlike me, he could never stop believing in the significance of the enterprise, he could never look on that stolid grimy box of a four-bay garage and see anything but the shape of a glorious lifework which the Fratelli Battaglia literally put up one brick at a time.

Jerry Battle, it must appear, can let the mortar pit and crumble. He can stand by and watch the gutters overflow, the water pooling against the foundation. He can gaze yet a thousandth time upon the buckles becoming waves in the asphalt yard, only to pick up the phone and speed-dial ahead for his three-soft-taco lunch. And though all of this (semi-) metaphorical illustration is pretty much the bare fact of it, and frankly how I had always wanted it to be, duly punched out for the very last time, *no matter what,* I can't now loll around and let Jack sink lower in the icy water, and not because I give a hoot about Battle Brothers. I don't. I never did. Pop always knew that, but he didn't mind, because through luck and happenstance and my sagely ever-passive hand, business tended to get done. So it squarely depresses me now to think that Jack might have thought I *did* care, which has to be my fault entirely, and perhaps explains the lengths he's gone to trying to make the business worth more than it ever possibly could be worth. No doubt that I should have derided his interest when he was in college and asked to work summers for us; I should have mocked it as dummy's work, an idiot's errands, said anything that might have plumbed his core anxiety about himself, which he has always harbored, instead of letting him join and then eventually become foreman of one of the landscaping crews, and then hang out after they rolled back in at the end of the day and drink beer with the mechanics, when he was the boss's son but a regular guy and so maybe too readily accepted and admired.

And while I know Jack was never headed for a fancy law associate's position like Richie's Ivy League minions, or was an intellectual sort like his sister, I'm damn sure that he could have made a perfectly fine sales rep for one of those big pharmaceutical companies, or a valued young executive in some corporate human resources department, taken full advantage of his athlete's natural poise and fealty to the team for the cause of genteel and estimable profit. That would have been good by me, for sure, though I must acknowledge, too, that I never pushed Jack away from Battle Brothers too assiduously, namely because—surprise, surprise—I actually didn't mind the idea of his taking over someday, if that somehow meant Pop would get and stay off my back about The Future, thereby committing the sin of tendering one generation's dreams for the illusory expectations of another, which is no doubt a practice wretched, and shameful, if time-honored.

I'M NOODLING all this about at the moment, or trying not to and failing, sitting here on Pop's made-up bed in his room at Ivy Acres. I'm waiting for the head administrator to drive back in from his home in Cold Spring Harbor after normal business hours and explain to me how an eighty-five-year-old man with limited mobility walks off a twenty-acre campus without a trace and then isn't missed for an entire night and day. He's going to do so because I've threatened his assistant that otherwise he'll be speaking exclusively to a jodhpur-clad partner of Whitehead Bates in the morning, and the duly confused/impressed assistant immediately slipped off to a secure phone and called his boss.

Jack, meanwhile, has gotten it into his head that he's going to drive around the county checking the bus depots and diners and the dozen or so local Starbucks shops because Pop had their coffee once and thought it was a revelation and might now make some kind of crazy coot pilgrimage there, as if he were going to hire on as a barista before he kicked off, which after I considered for a second didn't seem that far-fetched a notion.

Paul has accompanied me to Ivy Acres for moral support, but after an hour of waiting here in Pop's room he's all but talked out on the incompetence of institutional structures and systems and turned on the television instead, switching with the jump button at the commercials between the Discovery Channel (Wild Predators) and HGTV (Before and After renovations). The combination, as you might expect, proves remarkably soothing to yours truly, as all I need to forget everything else is a good meaty nature channel show where the ants and the termites are about to wage total arthropodan war.

"I only like the Before," Paul says. "At least the old place had some wool to it. Some shagginess. Now everything looks as if it's been bikini-waxed."

"Most people like that."

"I guess. What bugs me even more is how they had no qualms about destroying everything, even the good stuff, like that great fireplace."

"That was a beauty."

"Sure it was. You know better than anybody that you can't buy that old brick anymore. And the newel posts of the staircase. Did you see how that guy took his sledgehammer to those? He found that pleasurable."

"He *was* loving it."

"No kidding," Paul says, getting excited, maybe even agitated. "There's no respect anymore. People want what they want and they want it now. Nothing comes before them, literally or in time. Everyone is Client Zero."

"Numero Uno," I say.

"Chairman Me."

"A Solo Flyer."

"Exactly," Paul says. "They think they can go anywhere and do anything, as if none of their actions has any bearing except on themselves, like they're in their own mini-biosphere, all needs self-providing, everything self-contained, setting it up like God would do himself. It doesn't matter that there are people on the outside tapping at the glass, saying, 'Hey, hey, I'm here. Look out here.'"

This stops me for a second, as he's striking closer to home than I'd prefer. Then I realize why Paul isn't quite acting like himself, which I assumed had to do with Pop being missing and all of us feeling anxious and moody. He's talking not about me but about his wife, Theresa, who, if you think about it, has done a pretty spiffy job of shutting out any chance of real inquiry, any real debate, who hasn't let by more than a few loose atoms of dissent, the only surprise here being that you'd think her seriously empathic prose-poet husband would have been asked to help steer from the beginning.

Theresa was feeling a bit tired, and so despite her wanting to come along I'd somewhat forcefully suggested she remain back at the house, just in case Pop managed to make his way there. In fact I scolded her, finally getting sick of her merely humoring my opinions. This I feel bad about, as she's looking washed-out of late, as though the blood isn't being fully pumped to all parts of her body. Her coloring is all wrong, her face appearing as if it were lighted from within by an old fluorescent tube, an unsteady flicker in her usually bright eyes. And I should really say she's been feeling tired all the time, though of course not breathing a word of complaint; I've just noticed her lingering a bit, in whatever arm-chair she's sitting in, or leaning with discernible purpose against the kitchen counter, or sometimes not showing up at all for break-fast, even after Paul goes back to their bedroom to let her know the herbed omelets are ready. In fact I would say she's not eating half the food she normally would, with Paul and me taking up the slack, as evidenced by our sudden fullness of gut and cheek.

Sometime last week I went into their bedroom after they'd gone out to shop for maternity clothes, as I was searching for some of the Cessna manuals in the closet, and noticed crumpled in the wastepaper basket a threefold informational booklet like the kind you see in plastic holders beside the magazines in the doctor's of-fice, though this one you probably got from the doctor himself in the privacy of the exam room. It was a general introduction and overview of symptoms and treatment of non-Hodgkin's disease, which is among the most treatable of cancers, assuming, of course, that it *is* treated, with some combination of surgery and radiation and chemotherapy, depending on the particular stage and expres-sion of the disease. But the thing that got me was a single-sheet insert that was also crumpled up inside the booklet, titled "Non-Hodgkin's and Pregnancy." This basically outlined what a preg-nant woman would normally do, with those in the first trimester advised to terminate the pregnancy and pursue treatment, with those others postponing treatment—and only if the disease were slow-developing—delivering early (32nd to 36th week) by cesar-ean, then immediately employing a vigorous regimen to attack the disease. Theresa is just now into her 22nd week, obviously making no plans for anything other than a full-term delivery. It isn't hard to figure out that she's doing none of the recommended above (no matter the progression of the cancer, which might be spreading to who knows where), and judging by how tightly the literature was balled up, is not about to stray from her self-charted course. If I think about it, this episode with Pop has at its best provided a diversion from my children's troubles, diversion being perhaps the most ideal state of existence.

"Perhaps the best thing," Paul says, looking nearly angry now, his fleshy cheeks ruddy with vim, "is that pretty soon we won't have any true Befores, only Afters, shiny and virtual Afters. This host won't have one decent thing left to destroy, and he'll have no choice but to cancel the show."

"Maybe it'll be called After the After," I say.

"After the After doesn't exist," Paul says grimly. "Not for me anyway."

"Sure it does," I say, instantly sounding a bit too much like I'm trying to convince myself of something. "Look at me. I've had a whole life of After."

"Is this when Theresa's mother died?"

"Sure. When it happened I thought everything else would fall apart. I had no idea how I was going to raise the kids and still run Battle Brothers. For a couple months there nobody wanted to get out of bed. We'd get wake-up calls from the principal's office at the kids' school. Then I met Rita, and she saved our lives. Rita was After the After."

"You were lucky, Jerry," Paul says. "My life's going to be too sorry to save."

"Look, son," I say, in the gravest in-all-seriousness mode I can muster, "she's not going to die."

For a second Paul's eyes desperately search me, as if I might know something he doesn't. But then he sees that of course I don't.

He says, "It's good of you to say that. You should keep saying that."

"You ought to, as well."

"I know. Keep reminding me."

"Okay."

"You're not exactly like Theresa always said you were." Paul says, "She's always complained about you a lot."

"Hey, hey, a lot?"

"Well, much less these days. Actually not at all, lately."

"But before."

"Yes. She griped regularly how you'd run roughshod over anybody whenever things got troublesome for you, or something got in your way or made you work harder than you had to. That you had this supernatural ability to short-circuit dealing with the needs of others, so well in fact that people generally avoided any attempts to involve you."

"She couldn't just say I was 'lazy'?"

"Theresa has her way. There was also the usual complaint about how you could never bear doing anything purely for someone else, unless there was at least some modicum of benefit to you, but that's not relevant, because what I was going to say is that Theresa is so much like the person she makes you out to be, really just the same except she's perhaps more forthright and aggressive in her stance than you are, which you'd think would invite more discourse and interplay but shuts it down all the same, and even more finally in fact. And I'll admit to you now this is pissing me off, Jerry. I'm sorry, but it really is. It makes me feel a lot of anger toward her that I certainly can't express to her but that I can hardly deal with anymore. Yesterday I made a whole spinach lasagna with this nice béchamel and I browned the top of it a bit too much. Normally that would be acceptable but you know what I did? I took it out of the oven and walked to the back of your yard and I just chucked the whole thing, glass casserole and all, as far and high as I could, and it cracked into at least fifty pieces on a pile of logs."

"I was wondering why we ordered in."

"I went to clean it up this morning, but some animal had eaten the whole thing. I just collected glass, and the episode made me angry enough again that I cut myself picking up the shards. I bought you a new dish today, just so you know."

He shows me a bandaged finger, and says, "I'm losing my grip here, Jerry."

"That's okay."

He says, "Maybe the truth is I don't want to know anything."

Here's surely something I can relate to, but it's not the moment to let him give in to the Jerry Battle mode of familial involvement, that ready faculty of declining, my very worst strength, and I have to say, "You're not built like that, Paul. Whatever you're thinking of late about your writing, I know you can't accept being in the dark or on the 'periphery.' I've read every word you've published and even if I haven't really understood the half of them I'm pretty certain you're a guy who can't stand not being part of what's happening. I don't need a Ph.D. or square-framed glasses to see that it's killing you to just stand by and let Theresa make all the decisions about what's going to happen. It's her body and I'm sure she's got all kinds of rationales and constructs about that to throw at you, but it's your life, too, and you probably can fling some funky constructs right back at her, plus the fact that you're miserable. Let her know that—show her. Lose your shit if you have to. We Battles only really respond to fits and tears and tantrums, the more melodramatic the better."

"Theresa sometimes talks about how bad her mother got, which I think really scared her. She sometimes still has nightmares."

"Really?"

"She had one last night, in fact. Her mother was a very intense woman, huh?"

"Really only at the end," I say, realizing that I'm instantly defending myself, and trying to forget the picture of my daughter at the tender age of five, sitting at the dinner table with cheesy macaroni in her mouth, too fearful to even chew as Daisy chopped cucumbers for the salad furiously at the counter, white-and-green log rounds bouncing all over the floor.

"I'm sorry I'm so focused on myself, Jerry," Paul says. "Here I am talking to you about your not-so-well daughter, and now your father is missing."

"I'm doing all right."

"It must seem as though things have taken a strange turn."

"They're both going to be fine."

"Yup." Paul smiles, nodding with hollow vigor and optimism, all welcomed, and I join in as well, and it's enough good gloss between us to make me feel that I can believe whatever either of us might say, or propose. For while Pop is presently MIA, I have this strong conviction that he's not in any real trouble, that the old gray cat isn't so much wounded or confused or fighting back feral youth in whatever cul-de-sac or strip mall he's lost in, but rather delighting in the open possibility of the range, perhaps in fact sitting in a coffeehouse lounge, chatting up some willowy chai-sipping widow. The only detail gumming up the works is that it doesn't seem that he left with anything but the clothes he was wearing, save for his Velcro-strap black orthopedic walkers, his last outfit being his polka-dot pajamas, which you'd think the sight of in public on an unwashed and unshaven old man would prompt any number of citizens to alert the authorities.

The home show ends and I browse channels. Paul excuses himself to get some tea from the dining room. I find an animal program that I've seen before, about the lions of the Serengeti: the "story" is of a crusty old male lion they (the producers, the native bush-beaters, the cinematographer?) named Red for the color of his mane, which, apropos of nothing, is exactly the hennaed hue of Kelly Stearns's last self-dye job. Red has long been the dominant male of the pride, showing his appreciation of the hunting prowess of his lionesses by serving them sexually whenever they are in heat and then spending the rest of his time power-dozing and snapping at flies and sometimes chasing off the younger upstarts or killing some death-wishing hubristic hyena who thought he could carry off a cute cub and get away with it. Red has apparently ruled this lair for a long time, but is now being challenged by a very large mature young male newly arrived on the scene, named Nero (for no specific reason), who is making forays into Red's territory, sniffing at the females, and generally making a show of himself as an electable new king.

Red, of course, hitches himself up and out from the sorry shade of his acacia and charges the interloper, driving him off, but only temporarily. Nero comes back that night, and although there's no footage of the battle, the next morning we see that Red has been badly mauled, his right hindquarter slashed nearly to the bone, his mane matted with his own blood, a deep gash in his jowl. He's limping off to an old den, maybe the one where he was born. Nero, meanwhile, is holding court by the tree, spraying it liberally with his stud juice, receiving unctuous groveling licks from the males and females, and brusquely mounting most of the latter. The King is dead. Long live the King. The last we see of Red, he's lying on his side, slowly panting in near-death, too weak to even shoo the multitude of flies who swarm about the huge hind wound in a teeming shiny quilt of black. Before nightfall the pack of vengeful hyenas picks up his scent, and by the morning Red is but a rickety boatshell of ribs and hide; he's not even an appetizer for the scrawny young jackal who's scampered by too late, and later on birds will take the scattered tufts of that arrogant hennaed mane as thatching for their nests.

Maybe Pop really is in trouble.

Maybe he really is lying face down in a roadside ditch.

But if he is, I have a feeling he's only doing so because he's hiding from state troopers patrolling the roads for him, which they're presently doing (this definitely not the standard operating procedure for missing persons but courtesy of Rita's highly placed sheriff friend), Pop ducking at each spray of headlights so he might enjoy a few more hours on the lam. And instead of feeling sorry for himself as I expected he would (as I no doubt would be feeling for myself), at least he's goddamn doing something about it, even if it is completely stupid and dangerous; at least he's taken hold of the moment angling away from him and typically wrenched it back his way.

I used to hear stories from my uncles about him when they were young, how they'd get into some serious rumbles where they lived up in Harlem against marauding gangs of micks and kikes and niggers, everybody using whatever was at hand, broomsticks and chains and tops of garbage cans as shields. My uncle Joe said it was like a fucking Wop Coliseum in the alleyways up there around 135th Street, these barbaric knock-down brawls where it seemed somebody was definitely going to get killed but the worst thing that ever happened was when Big Anthony Colacello slipped on a pile of horseshit as he was about to clock some poor Irish kid and hit his head on the curb and didn't wake up for two whole days. When he did he was exactly the same except he'd lost his sense of smell, and they'd play pranks on him like spreading limburger cheese on the back of his collar as they were on their way to skipping school.

Apparently Pop was the best fighter of their gang because he didn't mind getting hurt and had no fear of anyone. He would just lower his head (thus becoming Hank the Tank) and take whatever punishment he had to as he pushed in and waited for the guy to tire before counterattacking with a viciousness that surprised the crew every time. Pop I guess was a lot angrier then inside and out for the usual reasons of privation and poverty and general mis-treatment by family members and people in the street and at school and by the authorities, which these days you'd call racism and discrimination but then was known as the breaks, how it was, your miserable fucking life. No doubt these days they'd have identified him and his brothers and cousins and the rest of their street-clinging crew as "at risk" youth and placed them in special programs with teams of sociologists and educators and therapists evaluating their intelligence and home life and probably diagnos-ing them with all kinds of learning and emotional disorders and prescribing medicines and skills-building regimens, finally buoying them up with grand balloons of self-esteem that they might float high above the rank fog of their scrounging dago cir-cumstance, to land somewhere in the sweet-smelling prosperous beyond.

Pop certainly did, as did almost every last one of his genera-tion's Battaglias, with the exception of his cousin Frankie, who died of a freak heart attack at nineteen, and then another named Valerie, who from the age of eleven smoked like an iron smelter and came down with lung (and liver and brain) cancer a month af-ter her nuptials and was in the grave before she could even con-ceive a child. For if you took an accounting of all who proceed us, our alive and semi-alive relations from Forest Hills to Thousand Oaks to Amelia Island and to everywhere else they've rooted themselves with a vengeance, you'd have some kind of portfolio of golden twentieth-century self-made American living, all those spic-and-span houses and Gunite pools and porcelain- and crystal-filled curio cabinets and full-mouth braces for the kids and the double wall ovens set on timers to bring the roast rosemary chicken and casserole of sweet-sausage lasagna to just the right crisp on top as Dad pulled the white Lincoln up the driveway, their contribution to our Great Society being the straight full trickle-down to my generation of Battaglias and Battles and Battapaglias and the rest of us with the sweetheart deal of a Set-It-and-Forget-It existence. Like everybody halfway decent and useful I of course recognize that one's character should rightly derive from privation, crucibles, pains in the ass, and so I guess my only semi-rhetorical question is from what else does it come, if there's always been a steady wind at your back, a full buffet as your table, and the always cosseted parachuted airbagged feeling of your bubbleness, which can never brook a real fear?

Pop's pop was one of those stumpy big-handed gray-haired fellas in coveralls you still spot every once in a while shimmying up on a neighbor's roof to repoint the top of the fireplace chimney, because guys like Pop and then me didn't want to learn the skill and they could never retire because there was no one else who knew how to do the job and they could never not take the call. In fact maybe Pop and I have more in common than I know, because really he had little interest in building garden walls and cladding Manhattan townhouses in limestone or doing anything like what Nonno was doing, whom I know he loved like a God but considered not a little backward and ignorant and lucky that he had him as a son. Growing up, Pop was smart enough to see how everybody was moving to the suburbs into their own houses with big yards and patios and pools and paved driveways, and he knew that the owners would be working too hard in their regular jobs to come home on the weekends and want to take care of it all. So against Nonno's wishes he moved the business out here to the suburbs, mostly dropping the bricklaying part (only stick-built, clap-boarded houses out here) and shifting the focus to landscaping and yard care, which for a good many years was a veritable gold mine for the Battles, because he kept his early clients and moved along with them to bigger and bigger places right up until they died.

Pop was pretty magnificent then, this when I was a kid tagging along in the summers and he was in his prime (Bobby was just an infant). He'd stand there at the start of the day on the bed of his truck, hands spread atop the roof of the cab, calling out the jobs and saying who'd be working on them and with what foreman, exhorting the guys to do the job right (because if you do it right you don't have to remember to be honest) and then giving out a few loose bucks to those who were making the grade, cracking jokes the whole time and praising everybody and being the studly captain of the crew. When everybody had their marching orders he'd slap the cab and say, "All right, fellas, let's roll 'em out." The trucks would start up in a sweet dieselly cloud and he'd lead them out of the yard in a column like he was fucking Field Marshal Rommel. On the job I'd watch as he glad-handed the customers and was tough on them, too, and I'd have to say that whatever I know about common commerce and people I know from him, how he'd convince some guy to line his pool with real tiles instead of the cheaper rubber liner for the sake of standards and posterity, appealing to what pushed the guy out here in the first place, which was an idea about the destiny of the good American life and how each of us had a place in it, guiding it along. If George Guggenheimer had been his neighbor he would have been his best customer; Pop would have had him put in two koi ponds instead of one, with a waterfall in between, and then maybe an entire authentic Japanese garden, with a Zen sand pit and a manicured bamboo "fence" and a couple of those baby red maples that look so delicate and weepy, never for a second allowing George to entertain the idea of doing anything himself but feeding the fish (and maybe not even that), and definitely going over there after the lottery win and slapping some sense into him about not being such a pathetic, fearful, neurotic twitch of a man.

With the women he dealt with Pop was a natural charmer. He'd always compliment them on their clothes or hair even if they

were just standing there in their housesmocks, and they'd often offer him coffee or if late in the day a cold can of beer. He'd always—always—accept, and if he felt particularly good or if there
had been a problem with the job he might sing a few bars from
Puccini or Verdi for them, his brassy tenor voice reaching me outside as I waited on the stoop or in the truck if it was raining.
Sometimes, of course, I'd have to wait a very long time. Once I
wandered around the back of one property to see if there was a
swing set or basketball hoop and I saw Pop and the lady of the
house balling away on the deck lounger by the pool Pop had just
put in with Spanish blue tiles laid on the bottom in the shape of a
schooner, Pop's big pale ass bobbing up and down between her
doughy, stippled thighs and her heels (she was wearing brown
spikes) digging holes into the cushion, where she was trying to get
some traction. I was too young to think too much about it, and to
be honest it never bothered me as it might have. I wasn't angry for
my mother's sake, because she seemed as though she knew, and
maybe because Pop didn't make a big deal of it or try to sell me a
story. All he did was buy me a special high-flying kite I'd been asking for, The Big Bombardier, which I flew whenever the wind
kicked up the littlest bit or a summer storm was blowing in.

I sure loved that Big Bombardier.

And maybe if you asked him Pop would proudly say he was the
colonist, the pioneer, the one who had to clear-cut the land and
fight tooth and nail with the natives, and that I'm the settler, the
follower, the guy who grooved the first ruts in the road, the one
who finally overflowed the outhouse shithole, who has presided
over the steady downward trend of our civilization perhaps just
now begun its penultimate phase of entropy and depletion. And if
you're Theresa or Jack or Rita or anybody else (or even me for that
matter), you could easily extend the argument to include the other
collations between us, our frank father/son successions, that he's

the racist to my apologist, the sexist and womanizer where I'm the teaser, canonist to popularist, stand-and-deliverer to recliner. And if I'm obliged to bring in the customary automotive metaphors, Pop must be one of the last of the great American sedans, those wide-body behemoths, possessed of egregiously wasteful power, overarmored, fuel-hungry (ever-desirous), picking off on his way to the store every doe and dog and rabbit and squirrel without showing as much as a dent, when I'm doing everything I can to prove that I'm something other than an early '80s model from a fallen Detroit, something big and bulky on the outside but alarmingly cramped within, with scandalously poor gas mileage and rickety suspension, though trimmed in buttery leather throughout, and with an AC system that could cool Hades. And in this sense, maybe Jack is the last hurrah of our golden Pax Battaglia, the burly all-terrain multitasking machine that will go anywhere it pleases, but it looks more and more as if he'll soon have to retrofit himself with fuel cells and narrow bicycle tires, shrink down the sheet metal into one of those pint-sized helmet-on-wheels jobs that are sadly the norm in London and Paris and Rome.

And if I may for a moment jump back to the previous metaphor and the (de-) moralizing story of Red I will say it is not Pop's story and in fact probably not even mine, but rather Jack's and Theresa's and Paul's and maybe yours, because it's the jackal and birds with whom we departed, skittering over the dust-dry plains after the great lion has roared and we hyenas and buzzards have split up the rest, and what is there left but the merest shaving of the splendid, just enough of a taste to pang the knowing belly?

Paul returns with his tea, as well as with the Ivy Acres administrator, whom I met on the first day I deposited Pop and have seen in the parking lot a couple of times since, a guy named Patterson. Patterson is a sleepy-eyed, semi-balding, mid-forties white guy in no-wrinkle khaki trousers who could pass for a lot of us out here, fed a bit too well on big Australian shiraz and rotisserie chickens and super-premium ice cream, who buys shelled pistachios only and snacks on them in his big Audi out of sheer crushing boredom, who'll go down on his wife as long as she's just bideted, who is easygoing except when it comes to the bottom-line expediency of his life, which, to nobody's credit, he can usually find in peril everywhere, at home or at the mall or here at work.

"Good evening, Mr. Battle."

"What the hell is going on here, Patterson?"

Patterson makes as if he can't hear that particular register, and just stands there a second waiting for the air to clear. "It's good that you and your son-in-law have come in."

"Good? I want to know how you let this happen, and what you're doing about finding my father."

"Why don't we sit down, Mr. Battle. If you please," he says, ushering Paul and me into chairs, while he sits at the foot of the bed. "Let me inform you of what's transpired so far, and the actions being implemented."

I'm annoyed by his sneaky tactic of cutting out any culpability in this mess, keeping it all in the passive, and then backing up the conversation, which is of course what I myself would do with a customer whose job we'd maybe messed up. But despite recognizing this I don't call Patterson on it, mostly because I understand that Pop's run is not Patterson's fault exactly (if at all), and that he's had to drag his flabby ass out of the lounger and tape the rest of whatever jackass-glorifying TV show he wasn't closely watching. I even almost feel sorry for him because his is just the dicey situation our litigious scapegoating civilization tends to put you in, when you've been installed at the big controls just long enough to absorb the most serious trouble, while bearing no real power at all.

Still, some chump's got to *represent,* and be punching bag for the rest, and so I say, to get the discussion snapped back on terms of my liking, "Look, Patterson. You had better start doing more than some good informing, or you're going to have a major action on your hands. My attorney's Richard Coniglio, senior partner at Whitehead Bates, who has constant wood for this kind of thing."

This seems to freeze up Patterson, like he's actually heard of the firm, for he breaks into a wide why-me smile and clears his throat and kind of hitches himself up, balls to gut, like some pitcher down 3–0 in the count.

"There's room for calm here," Patterson says, collecting himself. "Our experience leads us to believe that your father is likely fine, if what he's done is just wander off."

"Your *experience*? How often does this happen?"

"Almost monthly, Mr. Battle. Ivy Acres is not a holding facility, a prison. Sometimes people forget that fact. We consider our community members to be adults, and as adults they're free to move about, come and go on the shopping shuttle, take outings with friends and relatives, really do as they please. We're talking, of course, about our members housed in the main part of the facility, and not those in Transitions, who aren't as independent or mobile."

"I thought you had a pass system."

"We do. But it's only so we know where members are and how long they'll be out. When people don't come back we wait twenty-four hours and almost always they were at a niece's house and stayed over after dinner, or they just lost track of the time and missed the last shuttle and checked into a hotel. It has been very rare during the time I've been here that there have been *issues*."

"I think you should tell us about those," Paul says. "Just so we're aware."

"That's privileged information, I'm afraid."

"Well, everyone tells me I'm a privileged guy," I say, without the scantest levity or irony.

This doesn't intimidate Patterson, certainly, but I can tell he is beginning to plot out the best course for himself, trying to calculate whether he ought to toe the company line and say nothing more or maybe turn a little state's evidence right here and now, see if he can't ride the fine middle course and slip through this thing without any serious damage. I'm wondering, too, whether this might be one of those moments that I as an American of obvious Southern Italian descent might take advantage of (given the cultural bigotry/celebration concerning certain of our neighborhood associations), and suggest to Patterson that he'd do well to tell us whatever we want to know, lest the firm of Whack, Rig & Pinch arrange a special late-night deposition for him, dockside or alleyside or maybe right in the garage of his Cold Spring Harbor colonial, when he's just about to roll out the garbage container to the street. I really shouldn't, in deference to Pop, who can't stand any such talk, despite and perhaps because of the well-known fact that the Battaglia brothers got their start paving and walling the properties of certain connected guys at their second-home mansions in Brookville and Lake Success, but I warn Patterson he'd better start plain "wising up," and "stop being such a punk." Patterson now clears his throat again and says, "Unfortunately the two people involved clearly intended to leave the campus. They took specific measures."

"Like what?"

Patterson ahems. "One of them ground up three bottles of sleeping pills and mixed them into a milkshake at a diner, where he was found dead in the men's room. The other was a woman who took our shuttle to the mall and shopped for most of the day. But instead of returning on the bus she somehow made her way up to the roof and jumped off the top of Saks."

"Christ . . ."

"Besides those instances, Mr. Battle, we've had only success. Now, you wanted to know what we're doing about finding your father. The police have been notified, of course, and we've also hired two private investigators, who are out searching for Mr. Battle right now. The lead investigator called me as I drove in, and so far they can confirm a sighting of an older man of his description."

"Where?"

"At the Walt Whitman Mall. In fact this very morning. A security guard apparently escorted him out, as he wasn't appropriately dressed."

"Escorted him out where?"

"Just out. I asked this, too, but the guard didn't note where the man went."

"Did he say what *the man* was wearing?"

"I believe it was trousers and a pajama top."

"Fucking great. That was Pop."

Paul says, "At least he was fine as of this morning, which means he got through last night on his own."

"It's a whole other night tonight," I say, thinking how good it is that Jack is driving up and down the Nassau-Suffolk border scouring every park and playground and strip mall for his grandfather. As I've noted, the thing about Jack is that he has never been in the least lazy in his life; I can't remember an instance when I asked him to clean the gutters or shovel the driveway or set the dinner table and had him groan or shuffle his feet or do anything but get on the job, the same as if I'd suggested that we throw a football around, or maybe go to Shea Stadium, which we did only once, when a customer of mine gave me a couple of playoff tickets in 1973 (Jack was thrilled because he got Rusty Staub's autograph). Jack's trouble has been of course that he tends to respond not wisely but too well, like a cricket that jumps whenever you touch him; it doesn't matter that he might be perched on the edge of some chasm. This is not my way of intimating once again that I think Jack isn't the brightest bulb on the tree, because even if that were true it doesn't matter in the least. Let's face it, for most of us in this more-than-okay postbellum Western life, smarts really don't count for a tenth as much as placement and birth, the particular trajectory of one's parturition, and if there's a genuine flaw to Jack's character it's no secret he gets too focused and purposeful for anybody's good, and especially his own, for it would never occur to him to lift the hatch and just bail out before the groundrush stops everything dead.

"Maybe Jack will find him," Paul says, as usual reading my mind. "I'll call and let him know about Pop being sighted at the mall."

He doesn't know Jack's cell number (nor do I), so he takes my phone outside the building to speed-dial him while I reacquire Patterson, who appears a bit sodden all of a sudden, like he's just come off a chartered fishing boat on a chilly, mist-spritzed day, like he'd pretty much give anything to get back home and pull on his flannel pajamas and crawl into bed. And though in fact I have zero interest in suing anybody ever, and can't think of what else to have him do save piss away his time keeping me company while I fret about Pop in my backslidingly diffuse and scattered manner, I say, anyway, "You're going to make this come out right, Patterson, or I swear once my attorney gets busy you'll be lucky to run the nut-and-candy cart at Roosevelt Field."

To this Patterson is mum, his lower lip pressed up tight against his half-exposed top teeth, so that he looks like a big bald, worried rodent, and I'm ready for whatever sweet load of sunshine he's going to try to blow up my ass, thank you very much. But presently Paul appears in the doorway, and then Jack, bearing what looks like a pile of dirty laundry in his arms, laundry with sneakered feet. I realize he is carrying Pop, wrapped up in a soiled—and very smelly—bedsheet.

"Pop . . ."

"He's not dead," Jack pronounces, evidently responding to my expression.

Pop moans with trenchant exasperation, as he always does. He's alive.

"He's pretty out of it," Jack says, laying him down on the bed. The top of the sheet flops down, revealing Pop's face, which is sunburned and badly peeling. "He told me he didn't sleep for two days."

"Where did you find him? At a mall? A park? Not at *Starbucks* . . ."

"Right outside here," Jack says. "I was parking the truck and I saw something move in the pachysandra by the duck pond."

"What the hell do you mean?" I turn to give Patterson a look, but he's already gone, yodeling something from the hallway about finding the house doctor.

"He was back over there, where that other section of the home is."

"*Transitions*," I say, picturing him grimly looking in at Bea from the window.

"He's probably very dehydrated," Paul says. "And in shock."

Jack says, "I pinched his skin, and it's pretty bad. I asked him and he said he had been drinking water. But I didn't see any bottles. Maybe from the sprinklers. Or the duck pond."

"Oh Jesus," I say. "Is Patterson getting a doctor?"

"I'll go find him," Paul offers. He runs out, leaving the three of us in the room, posed like in one of those neo-Classical deathbed paintings, the acolytes deferentially arrayed at the great man's torso, his mouth twisted in the last mortal coils of agony, his eyes cast upward to the Maker . . .

"Can you two give a guy a little room here?" Pop hoarsely blurts out, hacking up some very gluey spit. Jack cups his chin with a tissue and Pop spews it out. "And instead of trading all your medical theories, how about a goddamn glass of water?"

While Jack fetches one from the bathroom, I try to take the dirty sheet from him, but he won't let me.

"Come on, Pop, it's filthy. And so are you."

"I like it this way."

"You smell like cat piss. And other things."

"I don't care. It makes me feel alive."

Jack gives him two glasses, and he bolts both down, which is probably not ideal, and hands them back to him for more.

"What the hell did you do these past two days?"

"I walked by day," he says, intoning not a little prophet-like. In fact he seems too tranquil, and steady, for what he's obviously weathered.

"I guess you didn't get very far, with your legs bothering you."

"Just to the gate," he says. "I was just going to take a short walk at first. But then some kid drove by and asked if I needed a ride, and I told him I did. He dropped me off out in Easthampton."

"You went out that far?"

"That's where the kid was going."

"Didn't he wonder why you were wearing a pajama top?"

"Hey, he was wearing a shirt with cuts all over it, like it got run over by a combine. Plus he wasn't too swift."

Jack brings the glasses back full and hands them to Pop. "So what did you do out there?"

He bolts them down, again. "Like I said, I walked. I walked on the beach, all the way out to Montauk Point."

"That's got to be fifteen or twenty miles at least. You really walked all the way?"

"Well, I almost got there. I could see it, that's for sure."

I ask, "Did you have any money? What did you eat?"

"Of course I didn't have money. I was just going out for a little walk, remember? Plus I'm kept a pauper, so I have no freedom. And if you want to know, I panhandled."

"You begged?" Jack says, crinkling his forehead, like his mother sometimes did.

"It's not below me," Pop replies, glancing at yours truly. "Nothing's below me."

I say, "So you begged on the beach in the Hamptons."

"Yeah," he says. "Most people wouldn't part with any dough, but they were decently generous with the food, which I ate but didn't like. Sushi, some other rolled thing they called a 'wrap.' This is what people bring to the beach. And how come everything has to have smoked salmon in it? Nobody appreciates an honest ham sandwich anymore."

Jack asks, "Did you sleep on the beach?"

"Oh yeah. It was real nice, sleeping outside. It wasn't too cold either. In the morning some cops gave me a ride to town. After I got together enough for a doughnut and coffee, I hitched a ride back from a guy in a Jaguar. I think he thought I was some nutso billionaire like Howard Hughes. When I got back here I didn't want to go inside right away, so I lifted a sheet from the laundry service truck and camped out."

"You could have told somebody, you know."

"What, that I was going to sack out with the ducks? The jerks here would have called you, and you would have called some shrink, and all of you would have gotten together and sent me to a place where they have metal grating on the windows."

"I wouldn't have," Jack says, most unhelpfully. "Next time, you can come stay with us. I'll set you up on the deck with a pup tent."

"I need the open air."

"Fine, then, anyway you want it. Better yet, you can come stay with us now if you like."

"Oh yeah? You mean it?"

"Why not? You have a month-to-month lease, right?"

"Ask Mr. Power-of-Attorney. Hold on, I gotta use the head." We help Pop out of bed, but he bats away our buttressing and goes into the bathroom.

"Of course it's month-to-month," I say to Jack. "But shouldn't you talk about this with Eunice?"

"What makes you so sure I haven't?"

"I know you."

"You think you do."

"Well, have you?"

Jack says firmly, "She'll be fine with it."

"But you ought to make sure, don't you think, before getting him all excited? Besides, I don't know if it would be the best thing for him."

Pop calls out, "I'll take the guest room with the big TV, okay, Jack?"

"Sure thing, Pop."

"Are you hearing me, Jack?"

He stares right in my eyes. "The best thing for Pop, or for you?"

"For me? For him to stay at *your* house? Christ. I don't know what that means. I really don't. And I'm thinking about you, kid, especially you. You've got a wife, and kids, and a big house to run, and a business to . . ."

". . . You know, the one with the big *tube* TV . . ."

"Sure, Pop, sure," he says, and then to me, "To what?"

"What?"

"*To what.* A business to what?"

"You know what."

"Tell me, Dad."

"Forget it."

"Come on, let's hear it."

"I said forget it."

Jack gives me a look—or actually, he doesn't, which is a look in itself—and for a scant moment I feel myself tensing my neck and jaw for what I'm intuiting will be a straight overhand right, popped clean and quick, and I actually shut my eyes for a breath. Of course nothing comes, nothing at all, and when life flips back it's just Jack gazing straight at me, his mouth slightly open in his way, with that resigned enervation, like he's waiting for a train that always runs late.

"Well, don't worry about it," he says. "It's going to be okay."

"I won't," I say. This sounds as empty as it is untrue, but like most men we accept the minor noise of it and try to move on.

But presently we don't have to, as Paul and Patterson and a light-brown-skinned guy with his head wrapped in a bright purple cloth—presumably the doc—enter the room in a rush, though they're momentarily frozen by the sight of the empty bed; Jack points to the bathroom, where we converge, Jack first. He knocks, calling for Pop, and then opens the door. Pop is sitting hunched on the edge of the tub, grasping his arm.

"What's the matter?" I ask.

"My arm hurts. And my neck. It's like clamped inside."

"Please let me in," the doc says, pushing through. But just as he does, Pop sharply groans and pitches forward with sheer dead weight, and it's only because of Jack's quick reflexes that he doesn't smack his face on the hard tile floor. He and the doc gently turn him onto his back, and the doc gets to work, 100 percent business (definitely a welcome change of pace), checking his vitals, trying to track the pain, with Pop wincing as fiercely as I've ever seen him, tiny tears pushing out of the corners of his eyes.

"What's wrong with him?" I ask, all of it in sum beginning to spook me. "Shouldn't we call an ambulance?"

Paul says, "It's already coming."

The doc tells Patterson to alert the hospital to ready a cardiac team.

"He's having a heart attack?" Jack says.

"Possibly," the doc answers. "But we won't know how bad it is, or even what it is, until we get him to the hospital." He asks Pop if he thinks he can swallow some aspirin, and Pop nods. Patterson is sent to get some. When he returns with them, Pop takes two, crunching on them like children's tablets, and lies back. The doc now regards him more generally.

"Why is he in such a miserable condition?"

Patterson says, "This is the gentleman who left the premises."

"I see."

"Can't you do something for him?" I say.

"There's nothing else I can do. We simply have to wait for the ambulance."

But now Pop sort of yelps, and claws angrily at his neck, like there's something ditch-witching its way out of him. Jack holds him steady and then eases him back down, and for a moment he seems to calm, but then all at once his whole body becomes sort of warped and rigid, like a sheet of plywood that's been soaked and then too quickly dried. He rests again, his eyes shut. And then it starts again.

"Steady him now," the doc says, he and Jack quelling the new tremor. "Steady him. Steady. He'll make it through."

Paul is nodding in assent, but in fact it looks to me like Pop's going, really going. Going now for good.

eleven

I REMEMBER, from the time I was old enough not to care so much, Pop liked to say to me, with a put-on twang, "You're okay, Jerome, but I'd like you a whole lot better as a nephew than a son."

And I'd say to him, "Likewise, Uncle Hank."

We'd have a chuckle about it, our little hick routine, and often we'd play along that way for a while, through whatever we happened to be doing, driving in the car or painting the fence, and talk about stuff that we normally wouldn't talk about, which was pretty much everything, though this was of course only when Bobby didn't happen to be with us. When the three of us did go out together I was happy to sit in the back and let them shoot the shit and razz each other and just focus on my books on flying aces of WWII. It's no great shock that after Bobby went to Vietnam we didn't play the game anymore, and not because I was getting too old. But it was sort of fun while it lasted. Maybe we'd be driving out east to buy shrubs for a job and Pop would ask me about my girl and whether I'd finally gotten my fingers stinky, to which I'd make like I was hoisting my rig and say, *If my big one counts,* and we'd stupidly yuck it up like that all the way to the nursery, yakking like nimrods about women in the street and the latest car models and the merits and demerits of certain brands of beer. It was all a dumb joke but it was easy and comfortable and it doesn't take an advanced degree in psychology to figure out what we were doing, or why, or that those times were probably in fact when we felt closest to one another, most like a father and son.

I recount this with less nostalgia than a kind of wonder that we played the game at all, though at that moment in the jostling ambulance with the sirens *wop-wopping* and the sturdy EMS gal barking in Brooklynese his sorry vitals ahead to the ER, when it was clear that this was Pop's last careen on our side of oblivion, I thought for sure that I heard him try to drawl some avuncular sobriquet to me through the misty oxygen mask, some snigger to ol' Jerry-boy to check out the lushly ample hindquarters of the lady paramedic. But it wasn't that, of course, rather the muffled gasp of a death throe, in equal parts pissed and terrified, punctuated by his grasping my hand so tightly that I had to squeeze back as hard as I could to make him relent, actually crackling the little bones in his hand. Pop then kind of wailed and the butch paramedic possessed of these huge caramel-brown eyes noticed us holding hands and said with a fatalism and tenderness that walloped me deep in the chest, "It's really all we got, huh?"

I guess I blurted a yeah, not thinking much about what she was referring to, and it's only now, a few weeks later, when things have settled down and I'm finally up here again in sleek *Donnie,* Theresa serving as my copilot, cruising at a smooth altitude above this familiar patch of planet, that I'm able to peel away to the fuller meanings.

I should note without further delay that Pop has not been lowered into the ground, or sifted into an urn, or shelved away in a granite wall cabinet, nor is he otherwise in any way closer to the netherworld than he was when rescued from the Ivy Acres ground cover, but ensconced in the lap of Jack and Eunice Battle luxury, *bain en suite,* satellite TV clicker and walkie-talkie in hand, so he can squawk down to Rosario and order up a Bloomin' Onion or other microwave treat whenever he feels a lonely hollow in his gut. He is convalescing in style after the combination heart attack and mild stroke (an extremely rare occurrence, we're told, both to experience and then survive, particularly with no extreme ill effects). Eunice I hear has been especially solicitous, turning down his bed herself while he receives his daily bath from the hired home nurse (female, untattooed), and then fans out the dozen or so journals and magazines she replenishes weekly for him on the west end of the king bed, pillows fluffed and propped, the forever-blab of Fox News on the big tube awaiting his scrubbed pink return. Jack, too, is being extra helpful, keeping Pop up at night with a special subscription to an adult channel, his favorite program being the *Midnight Amateur Hour,* in which we are introduced to the porn star aspirations of excruciatingly ordinary middle-class folks, one couple Pop swears featuring the head cook at Ivy Acres. Even I have been going over there every other day, bearing gifts of guilt-larded fruit like biscotti and Sambuca and twine-wrapped soppressata or other such items that might bolster his memory of another time in his life when things weren't any better or worse but when at least most of his family and friends were still alive. Maybe it should be no surprise that it takes a serious brush with death to really land oneself in Nirvana, which in this case for Pop—and soon enough me, soon enough you—is a convening of family predicated not so much upon either obligation or love as on a final mutual veto of any further abandonment.

And if *family* is the "it" the ambulance gal was talking about, the all-purpose F-word for our times, *really all we got,* like anybody else I'm not sure whether that's an ultimately heartening or depressing proposition, though perhaps that's not the point. I will confess that at the very moment I thought Pop was a goner, kicking the bucket, croaking for good, I didn't much *feel* love for him, even as I *had* love; I felt intellectually sure, is what I'm saying, which is no excuse. What this might suggest about families in general or ours in particular or just sorry old me is that while prophets tell us we're innately bestowed with enough grace to convey righteousness and bliss to entire worlds (much less one person), we mostly don't, at all, just pure potential that we are, just pure possibility. And the people who most often witness and thus endure the chasm between our exalted possible and our dreary actual are the ones we in fact love, or should love.

This is why Pop is in fact so lucky now, so very lucky, which has nothing to do with his being alive. (We're all alive, aren't we?) And for a host of reasons I doubt this attention lavished on Pop will be duly lavished on me when my time comes due, the primary one being that unlike Pop I'll probably be pushing hard for special treatment, and thus receive none in return. I should wise up and probably start getting chummier with Jack's (and eventually Theresa's) kids, besides just appearing in the doorway of their double-height foyer with the Disney videotape of the week, waving it like Fagan might a piece of bread above the dancing urchins. In addition I can't bear to tell Pop that his only grandson and bearer of the Battle Brothers torch will soon have to relinquish several lifetimes of accrued capital for a final grand blowout liquidation sale, which even then won't cover the various notes come due. I can't bear to tell him that our sole recent investment in the property is a fix for the section of cyclone fence that one of the guys accidentally ran through a few years ago with a backhoe, and only because Suffolk National Bank ordered us to secure the grounds and garage. Richie Coniglio tells me that Battle Brothers will be pretty much stripped, but assures that Jack himself will be safe, if safe means still owning the big house and big cars but no longer possessed of the salary to maintain it for too long.

Lately Theresa has been accompanying me on my visits to her brother's, and to my happiness has been exceedingly warm toward him and Pop and also toward Eunice, who has taken the news of Battle Brothers' demise quite hard. After Pop had his trouble Jack suddenly came clean and opened the books to her, and apparently for a week or so she didn't do anything different, quarterbacking the household offense as always with Rosario blocking upfield, picking through the various ladies' lunches and kids' pool parties with that austere English-German efficiency, even audible-izing an impromptu single-malt scotch tasting at the country club followed by a raclette party back at the house. But then the next day while waiting to pay at Saks, somebody allegedly nudged her and she pretty much freaked and actually started singing a pop song, quite loudly, all of which she couldn't remember, and then bent all her credit cards in two and had to be escorted out to her Range Rover by mall security. She's been seeing a counselor twice a week since, and appears to me to be calmly, perfectly okay, though perhaps calmly, perfectly okay is a worrisome drop-off for someone accustomed to rolling forth at full throttle and being all-time 4WD-engaged. Though we don't know whether she is on medication, Theresa has recognized the imbalance as potentially serious, and has taken her, without a whiff of irony, on a couple let's-just-be-girls outings, including a longish session at the fancy new Korean nail salon on Deer Park Avenue and an even longer one at the all-you-care-to-eat Brazilian meat palace, where at least Eunice thoroughly ruined her manicure clawing and gnawing on char-grilled short ribs and baby backs.

Theresa, I'm sure, practiced her current form of all-you-care-to-eat, as she did earlier this afternoon at the marina restaurant near Bar Harbor where I ordered us each a two-and-a-half-pounder with drawn butter and dinner rolls, she barely touching her meal. We're heading back now along the seaboard, our flight path taking us past the southern beach suburbs of Boston and over Buzzards Bay, to cross the Sound at its wide mouth and then follow the northern shoreline of the Island, until the final turn to MacArthur Field. Having Theresa along is an unusual circumstance, and one she initiated. In fact, I'd normally never fly on a day like this, when the weather, although supremely fine on the journey up, holds the chance for an inclement change. At present, we're approaching the start of the Cape and I can see far off in the distance and probably still southwest of New York City the broad white cottony mass of the approaching system, nothing like dark thunderheads fortunately but to this exclusively fair-weather flyer material stuff all the same, and a sight I've never seen, at least from up here.

At breakfast this morning Theresa was in an expansive mood and talking about how she was starving. Paul instantly whipped together some French toast from day-old challah bread, which was excellent but she couldn't eat, and then after Paul sort of slunk away deflated she expressed an intense hankering for lobster and asked me if we could fly to Maine. I called the weather service for the forecast and told her probably not, as a low front was moving rapidly up from D.C. and could make for uncertain conditions on the return. I offered to pick up some lobsters at the fish market instead but she insisted and said she was finally feeling hungry for *something* and I figured who was I to say no to her. Paul thought it would do her (and clearly himself) some good to get her out of the house, and so we drove to Islip and went through our checks and got *Donnie* right up, riding a strong tailwind to Maine in what had to be record time.

On the bleached-cedar dining deck of The Peeling Skiff the

sun was undiffuse and brilliant, both of us sporting baseball caps and sunglasses, Theresa's hand aglitter with the ring Richie bought for Rita and that I attempted to give back to her and that she and I quickly agreed to put to better use, by bequeathing it to the next generation. With the fat candy-store rock on her finger and her Yankees cap, Theresa was looking particularly girlish, and for a moment I felt a strange blush of accomplishment, for no other reason than that I had known her for the entirety of her years, now not so few, which is no great feat, of course, but still the sort of stirring that can make you almost believe that there might not be any more crucibles ahead, just this perennial interlude of melody and ease. When our plates arrived she got all excited and quickly tied on her white plastic bib and took the cracker right to a meaty claw, but after forking out the chubby little mitt she just sort of nibbled on it like it was her second or third lobster and after putting it down chewed idly on a couple of the small legs before neglecting it altogether. I didn't say anything because I wasn't that mad and really what was there to say that wouldn't be completely fake or depressing. After I finished mine, she pushed her plate over and I ate her lobster, too, even though I was already full, solely because I couldn't bear it slumped there unrequited between its lemon wedge pillows, staring up at us one-armed, thoroughly wronged.

"Hey, what's that?" she now says over the headset, pointing ahead to a strip of small islands off the Cape. "Is that the Vineyard or Nantucket?"

"No, no, they're over there," I say, motioning farther out. "You're looking at Naushon, I think. Or Pasque. Those are old-money hideouts, where I think they choose not to have electricity. They boat in ice and candles."

"Ice and candles?"

"That's what I hear."

"Sounds kind of kinky."

"Definitely not."

"I guess that's class."

"Yeah. Class."

We nod to each other, for emphasis, though neither of us is caring to make much of a point. This is how we talked on the way up, too, with her asking about a certain geographic or urban feature, to which I'd offer a bit of trivia about the nuclear submarine yards at New London or the history of Portuguese immigration to Providence or mention a surprisingly excellent fish-and-chips place in Buzzards Bay, where they brew their own malt vinegar. Conversing over the headsets is never like a real conversation, the overlaps and separations and pauses and canned feeling of the sound making for brief information exchanges at best, not to mention the constant pulse of the motor buzzing every nook of your being, which is not a bad thing at all if you want to feel as if you're busy just sitting there. This used to frustrate Rita sometimes, that we'd spend a whole day in the plane and seemed to have chatted nonstop but not about anything remotely personal, which suited me okay and in the end perhaps suited her as well. And why shouldn't it? Because when you're up here and aloft and all you're really trying to do is figure a word for the exact color of the sky, or count the whitecaps risen in a certain square of sea, or make sense of the almost infinite distance between yourself and the person driving his car on the lonely dead-straight road below, you don't want to engage in the familiar lingering intimations, allusions, narratives, all that compacted striated terra-firma consideration, but instead simply stir with this special velocity that is in itself worth the whole of any voyage, this alternating tug and weightlessness of your constant departure.

"What do you think is going to happen with Jack?" Theresa says, speaking of terra-infirma.

ALOFT

"Jack? At some point he's going to have to sell that house. And probably a lot of that stuff they have."

"Eunice does love that house."

"I don't think Jack does, or ever did."

"Where will they go? They have so much stuff. Not to mention Pop."

"I don't know," I say, instantly picturing the movers bubble-wrapping and crating him right there in the bed, propped up with clicker and Hot Pocket in hand.

"I can't see Jack and Eunice in a rental."

"You can get a real nice condo these days. They'll do fine."

"But there's no more Battle Brothers."

"Jack will get something going again."

"Are you going to help him?"

A loud rasp of noise squelches the end of her question, and I pretend it got lost in the wires.

After a moment, she says, "Well, are you?"

"Am I what?"

"Are you going to help Jack?"

"I'm retired, remember? And I'm not rich. At least not enough to start a new business."

"You should still *help,*" she says, with clear alarm, her emphasis actually squawking the sound. "You have to."

"Of course I will," I say. "It's just not yet clear how."

"I can tell you how, Jerry."

"Okay."

"Why don't you invite them to live with us?"

"Are you nuts?"

"We have plenty of room."

"Plenty of room? There are three bedrooms, last time I looked. Jack and Eunice would need one, the kids another, and unless Pop is willing to go back to Ivy Acres, which I doubt, then one for him.

That still leaves you and Paul, and then me, the owner of the house."

"You can convert the study to another bedroom for yourself, and Paul and I can move downstairs."

"Downstairs? That's the basement!"

"Maybe Jack can build some walls. There's already a half-bath down there. Besides, we're not going to stay with you forever."

"What are you talking about?"

"You forget I'm on leave. I'm going to have to teach again."

"What about extra maternity leave?" I say. "Isn't that the *law* these days?"

Theresa says, "I suppose so," though without much conviction, and not because she's someone who doesn't keep up on her worker rights and benefits. There's not been much pessimism in the house, if at all, the only indication of worry and trouble being that Paul sometimes has to excuse himself from the room or take a stroll around the neighborhood, probably so his heart doesn't suddenly shatter into a thousand jagged pieces; but by the same token there hasn't been any talk whatsoever of the future, or of any future past a few days out, which I can say over the last couple months we've been together has been a pretty liberally bestowed mercy among us, and judging from the sudden panicky hollow pinging in my gut, one I haven't appreciated near deeply enough.

I say, "You should take unpaid leave and stay longer. Paul can finally finish his book. When you have the baby you can take the master bedroom. There's an old crib in the basement that I'll clean and move up for you."

"That sounds nice."

"No problem."

"But what about the others?"

"What about them?"

"Come on, Jerry."

With the light shining from behind her sunglasses I can see her eyes searching me, perhaps not so much looking for the desired answer but rather the glimmer of a character somehow more wise and generous and self-sacrificing than the one that I for some fifty-nine and fifteen-sixteenths years have come to possess. Being who she is, Theresa would never have cared for the kind of father with whom she could discuss fuzzy intimacies, talk interspersed with full-on hugs and remembrances of previous challenges righteously met and overcome, all at a pitch of loving confirmation muted only by the wistful minor-key note that we couldn't always be together every moment of our lives. Then again, I don't know if she would have even wished we were that rare pair who could take turns riffing, say, on the Lacanian imbrications of contemporary family life (another few words I've learned this summer), or talk fast and loose in slick jump cuts between our favorite neo-Realist films and hip-hop marketing and the sinister global triumph of capitalism. No doubt things could have been different between us, much different, and maybe there's no actual alternative reality that would have proven any better than what we have now, or at least that we could practically abide. We are consigned to one another, left in one another's hands whether we like it or not, and perhaps the sole thing asked of us is that we never simply let go.

Still I say, "Jack won't want to come back to the old house."

"That's not what Eunice tells me," Theresa answers. "She's ready, too. All you have to do is call."

"You're kidding, right?"

"Nope."

This confounds me, even thrills me, but still, I say, "What about Rosario? There's definitely no room for her."

"She could come three times a week, to help tidy up, until she finds another full-time job."

"Who's figured this out already?"

"Take a guess."

I look at my daughter, lightly touching her controls. I say, "The house will be a zoo."

"We'll all have to pitch in. Including you. Including me."

"Myself I can see," I say. "But you're doing fine."

"Come on. I let Paul do everything."

"Which he's pretty damn good at, if you ask me."

"Doesn't make it right."

"It does at the moment. Besides, if he didn't work so hard, he'd go crazy."

Theresa starts to say something, though her mouth must have come too close to the headset microphone, because the reply is distorted with noise. We're quiet now, just the steady blenderizing of the 150-horsepower Lycoming engine. She's gazing off to the northwest, over toward Hartford, or Albany, where there's still clear sky overhead. To the southwest, where we're headed, it's definitely going to be a bit soupy, which is plenty alarming, and it's probably good that I've already decided to fly back on a pretty direct route, in the hope that we'd somehow cut a few minutes off the trip, a few minutes maybe proving the difference between a cloudy or clear touchdown. The specter of not seeing the field for the landing is one I've often imagined, nosing down into the murk and trusting only the instruments, hoping for enough daylight between the mist and the field to get a comfortable sighting before the final approach, for which I have some practice but not enough to make me happy. This is no pleasing challenge for a guy like me, who likes very much to see where he's going to step next, especially when life is a Paris street, fresh piles of it everywhere.

"Pop is going to be tough. But I suppose I have to heat and cool the whole house anyway," I say, disbelieving the Real as now embodied in myself. Which must always be a sign of deep trouble. "We can try it for as long as people can stand it."

"Okay, Jerry," she says without a note of congratulation. "Maybe you can call Jack when we get home."

"Can't you call him? You could just tell Eunice, couldn't you?"

She waves me off with a flit of the hand as a mother might a too-old child begging for a nostalgic piggyback. I want to tell her that she's not quite understanding this one, that even though she thinks it's about my laziness and long-practiced avoidance of appearing tender and loving before my son, it's really about Jack himself, that he should be spared the ignominy of having to hear and acknowledge such an offer, which, as modestly as I might play it, and I will, naturally abounds with all sorts of subtle and excruciating indications of shame and failure. Or maybe I'm not giving Theresa enough credit, maybe she knows this to be the case and thinks Jack should face the paternal demonhead straight on, just accept whatever that minor if terrible god will extract of his vital masculine juices and afterward get on with the quotidian work of replenishing.

"You two have plenty to talk about anyway," Theresa says. "The business notwithstanding."

"What now? Is he having trouble with Eunice?"

"There's tension, but only because of the money troubles. They're actually pretty devoted to each other, beneath all the nickel plate and granite."

"That's good," I say, "because it's only Formica and chrome from here on in."

"It's just time to call him, okay? He's shaky."

"Yeah, okay, but he seems the same to me." This is mostly true, at least to my perception, everything about his manner and dress unchanged, save for the odd sight of his unwashed black truck, the alloy wheels grimy and the usually mirror-shined body splattered with dried work site mud and dull all over with a toffee-hued grunge. He's cutting back, which is necessary, as I know he always had the truck washed once a week on Saturday mornings for $22.95 (the #4 Executive, with double polycoat and tire dressing), for I'd meet him every other month (and spring for the #1 Commuter, at $8.95) and have a big breakfast at the Pit Stop Diner next door. And yet on this one I kind of wish he weren't economizing, because at certain times you really do want your loved ones to keep up appearances, and for all the worst truth-blunting reasons. If I had a personal voice recorder I'd note to myself that when I do call as Theresa recommends I'll offer to treat him to the #4 Executive, plus blueberry pancakes, this very weekend.

"He even mentioned Mom the other day."

"Daisy?"

Theresa nods, taking off her sunglasses, as the sun has now dipped behind a high bank of clouds, many miles in the distance. "Actually, he was talking about the day she drowned."

"Oh yeah?"

"Yeah," she says, squarely looking at me, and not in the least somberly. "It's amazing. It turns out he was around when it happened."

"What are you talking about?" I say. "You were both at your day camps. When I got home there wasn't anybody but Daisy."

"I guess that's true," she says, "but Jack was there before."

"He was at lacrosse camp. You were at music camp."

"Drama camp," she corrects. "I was at mine, but Jack told me he turned his ankle and got an early ride home. Do you remember that he was limping?"

"No."

"It's funny, but I don't either," she says. "I really don't remember anything, which I'm happy about. But Jack says he was there. He has no reason to lie."

"Why didn't he say something then?"

"I guess he was upset, and scared. Besides being a little boy."

"So what else did he say?"

"Just as he got dropped off, someone was coming out of the house. A delivery man or something. Except this guy was drinking from a bottle of beer, and Jack remembers feeling angry toward him, though it was nobody he knew."

I don't answer her, because I don't know how much Theresa recalls of that part of Daisy's life and I'm certainly not interested in educating her here and now, but she says, "I assume he was there to see Mom. That's right, isn't it?"

"Probably so," I say. I suddenly remember all the empties in the house that afternoon, almost a whole case in all. Of course it wasn't the first time I'd come home to find that she'd been drinking heavily, though she mostly drank her sweet plum wine when she drank and the party-like litter of beer bottles had seemed unusual. I'd figured she'd been entertaining, a fact that wasn't so terribly hurtful to me at that point, the literal mess of the house more pissing me off, which really says it all, and after finding her suspended near the bottom of the pool the likely fact of some random guy having been there simply dissolved away among the thousand other details and duties that follow any death, and it never seemed important to mention to the cops who came around later that day that Daisy hadn't been drinking alone. But still the flashes of that day quicken my breath, and all at once I feel as though I'm flying at 50,000 feet, or maybe 150,000; it's like the air is thinning so rapidly we're in danger of floating up into the exosphere, right out into the black.

"Anyway," Theresa goes on, "Jack went inside and saw a lot of beer bottles in the kitchen, but not Mom. She wasn't in your bedroom, either, but while he was there he saw the bed all messed up and her underclothes on the floor. And more empty bottles. That's when he saw her out in the back. Jack was going to step out the sliding door of your bedroom and say he was there but I guess he didn't. He just watched her for a while. She was standing naked on the edge of the diving board, drinking a beer. He told me she looked very beautiful. Like a Roman statue, before any ruin."

"Jack said that?"

"I'm quoting verbatim," she says, unwistfully. "But he said he was scared, too. And I guess still angry, though he didn't really understand why. You can imagine what a bizarre and sexual sight it was for him. So he's just standing there watching her, and he realizes all the pool floats have been taken out of the water. The tubes and the swan raft and then that big pink doughnut she always used."

This was true, and something I didn't really think about when I got home. I'd assumed the pool had been cleared out by the cops or ambulance people, though it was an odd sight to see all the floats neatly lined up on the concrete deck, like the audience for a swim meet.

"So what did he do?" I ask.

"He said he ran," Theresa answers. "He just ran out of the house, as fast as he could. He went to the playground, he was so scared, and went on the swings, for like an hour."

"Oh, Jesus, Jack."

"So when he finally comes home it's all over. He knows exactly what's happened. The driveway's full of police cars and fire trucks and the ambulance, with its lights going. That's what I remember."

"Why didn't he say something?"

"I'm sure he thought he was responsible."

"I guess so," I say, remembering now how he kept asking if little kids were ever sent to jail.

"But of course nothing happened to him. And then you were so efficient afterward."

"What? Because I had her cremated? That's what Daisy wanted, you know."

"I didn't know, no," she says, finally a little bitterly. "And I'm not talking about cremation. I'm talking about how you managed everything so quickly after that. I'm mean, come on, Jerry. It was a world speed record for goodbyes. I didn't think it then but it was like a freak snowstorm and you shoveled the driveway and front walk all night and the next day the sun comes out and it's all clear, all gone. And then the fact of our not even being allowed inside the funeral parlor."

"You were there, but Nonna kept you two in another room."

"Yeah, Jerry, I know. We sat in the back of an open-casket wake."

"Jesus. I didn't know that."

"I'm sure you ordered her to keep us away."

"I didn't say to go to somebody else's funeral! Anyway, don't you think that was the best way? You were little kids, for chrissake. I don't care what anyone says. Kids don't have to mourn. And now that I know what Jack saw and had to deal with, all the better."

Theresa turns to her window. "You're probably right," she says, after a while, and tries to smile. Genuinely. I try to smile back. But none of it's any real solace to me. For I could say that I'm still reeling, that I've not yet begun to process all this new information, but that would pretty much be an outright lie. Wouldn't it? Not because I had any knowledge that Daisy's death wasn't wholly an accident, because I didn't, but you'd have to be a complete innocent (or maybe a kid) to imagine such a thing *not* happening, that her drowning in the pool wasn't somehow foreseeable, given the way she was raging and downfalling and the way I was mostly suspended, up here before I was ever up here. And if any part of what I'm saying is confessional, it's not *re:* Daisy but rather the kids, who I knew years earlier would almost certainly end up witnessing some excruciatingly awful moment.

Outside the air is getting a bit choppy, the *d-dump d-dump* as if we're cruising in a speedboat on a rippled-surface lake, the meter even and steady. I can see the weather coming together maybe 50 miles directly ahead of us, not thunderstorms, thank goodness, but odd high-hung batons of cottony haze, odd because you'd normally encounter such a thing in the early morning before the sun rose and burned it off but rarely if ever now, in midafternoon in late summer. Because of the change in weather I've called Mac-Arthur for an instrument approach, the new routing duly given, and taken us down to 5000 feet, and we've just flown over Westerly, R.I., passing over the mouth of the Pawcatuck River, and are now approaching Mystic and Noank and will fly along the northern shore of Fishers Island right down the line to Plum Island and then Orient Point, tracking in along old Route 25, hitting Southold and Cutchogue and Mattituck before buzzing the big outlet mall at Riverhead, where I'll pick up the Expressway and take it on in before banking south for my home field, the route so ingrained in my head and hands that I could probably fly it at night with shot gauges, just the long ropes of the car lights to serve as my guide.

But now the turbulence ramps up, the invisible pockets hitting us hard and fast (like speed bumps in midair), the up and down severe enough that I tell Theresa to tighten her seat belt and brace herself, just not on her control wheel. It's raining on us now, or better we're in it, and I hope like heck that we're not heading into a so-called embedded thunderstorm, surprise shit that no pilot wants ever to see. I glance over and Theresa's curled up a bit, and I can see she's already a little green about the gills, that sloe-eyed open-mouthed pant. I reach back behind her seat to where I keep the coffee bags for getting sick in and hand one to her. To my surprise she immediately retches into it, not a lot, because she didn't eat any lunch, but enough to make me worry that it's not solely airsickness. She folds it up and wipes her mouth with the back of her hand.

"You okay?"

"Yeah," she answers, leaning her head against the window. "I'll be fine."

"We don't have long to go," I say, "but it might get rougher."

She half-smiles and gives me a thumbs-up full of irony and goofiness and cool, and for a mostly happy instant I think I can see almost every one of us in her, Battles and Daisy both. But suddenly I feel she's very young and I'm very old and I can't believe I've ever allowed her to come up here. For a while I considered keeping a parachute in the back for Rita but she hated the idea and now I'm wishing like crazy I had, so I could strap it on Theresa just in case one of the wing struts now fails, before she's trapped with me in the metal-heavy groundrush. And no sooner than I finish the thought does *Donnie* get a deep frontal wallop, *Whomp!*, and then another, *Whomp!*, the force of each rocking us in our hard cockpit seats, violently enough that my sunglasses fall off and land somewhere down near the pedals. The rain is fearsome. Theresa's headset has rotated forward on her head such that the band is in front of her eyes, and I reach over and pull it back into place. She's wincing, and suddenly there's a blot of blood glossing her lower lip.

"Theresa!"

She touches her mouth and inspects the smear. "It's okay, I just bit my . . ."

Whomp-Whomp!

Donnie bucks, then feels like she's yawing straight sideways, and for a long, long second I lose hold of the wheel and accidently push the rudder pedal, and we dip hard to starboard like we're on a bombing run, diving to 4 o'clock, the airspeed indicator boinging inside the crystal like a fat man stepped on the scale; *Donnie*'s motor screams, the wings shuddering right down to the rivets, the airframe racked to its outer tolerances from pulling a G or two more than it was designed to pull, and you finally understand in that continuous pregnant second what people are talking about when they hold there's a nano-fine and mostly philosophical distinction between falling and flying. Or fearing and fighting, which perhaps explains how despite my overwhelming impulse to curl into a single cell I not-too-consciously manage to right her, get her level and steady, only to see we've lost 1000 feet, an entire skyscraper, which is absolutely fine as long as there's no more funny business.

"Are you okay?" I ask Theresa, who is canted forward a bit awkwardly. "Hey, talk to me."

"Yeah," she says weakly. "I've had enough of this, though. I want it to stop. Okay, Jerry? Make it stop."

"Okay, honey. We just . . ."

Whomp!

". . . we just have to get out of this damn pocket!"

Whomp-Whomp!

"Shit!"

Whomp-Whomp-WHOMP!

This set is nearly concussive, and produces in me what must be the dream of a boxer as his clock is being supremely cleaned, the wash of giddy relief that this is not yours truly but some other chump caught in the klieg lights of ignominy. As the beautiful dream dissipates, though, I can feel that my neck is already stiffening, the little bones fusing, with everything else that's jointed, hips and above, feeling distinctly unhinged.

"Theresa, honey," I hear myself say, my eyes probably open but not really working, unwilling to witness what will no doubt be the *coup de grace,* "hold on, honey, hold on!"

But the final wallop doesn't come. The *whomp* just doesn't

whomp. The rain has stopped. And all we have is the alto hum of *Donnie*'s prop, the rpms in the key of A, a drone that's as sweet as any Verdi tenor crooning of a singularly misguided love.

"Theresa, baby, we're clear, we're clear."

She nods to me and even smiles but there's a look she's manifesting that I have seen plenty in the mirror, and on Jack, and Paul, and even Pop of late, but never on Theresa Battle—namely, this face of deferral—and I say, "What the hell is wrong?"

She glances down to her lap. And there, between her tanned legs in black Bermuda shorts, on the red vinyl seat, is a shiny pool of wet. She lifts a knee and the clear liquid dribbles over the white-piped edge.

"Please tell me you peed."

She shakes her head.

"Oh shit."

"It's too early," she says. "The baby's much too young to be born. We're only at twenty-five weeks."

"Do you know how much time you have, before it gets dangerous?"

"No." And then, with the alarm of a hard fact, "I have to get to the hospital. Now."

"It's going to be twenty minutes to the field, maybe more."

"To what field?"

"The field we came from! The only one."

"You have to fly me to New Haven, Jerry," she says. "That's where my doctor is, at Yale–New Haven. I can't go anywhere else. Not now. Please!"

"I don't know. I've never flown there."

"Does it really matter?"

"It shouldn't. But this doesn't seem the time to experiment."

"Can't you use your chart?"

She reaches back and hands it to me, and I don't want to waste any time looking, but now that I'm really flying again I can see we've strayed from our flight path in just the direction she wants. This fact isn't material; even though I can't see much for the thickening haze, I know we're in fact much closer to New Haven than we are to Islip, which is probably twice the distance from here and definitely shrouded with the same weather. So I flip through the charts as quickly as I can while we remain on our due-east heading. And I see that there in fact is a field, which of course I knew some time before in a normal frame of mind, called Tweed, in East Haven, just a few miles from her hospital.

"All right," I tell her, "we'll go where you want. How you doing?"

"I feel okay I think."

"Are you sure?"

"Owwww . . . !"

"What the hell is wrong?"

"Something hurts," she says, suddenly breathing short and fast. "Oh shit . . . shit . . . owwww!"

"We should be there in ten minutes, if I can do it in one run. Let me try to call the tower now so I can ask for an approach, and an ambulance."

She nods, her eyes closed tight with the pain. When I get on the tower frequency for Tweed and explain the situation to the controller he rogers me for an instrument clearance for immediate landing on a south approach, runway 2-0, and places the other traffic in a holding pattern. At least the airspace and field will be exclusively ours. I'll head west over the Sound for a minute and then veer northwest overland before banking back for the landing. The problem is that it's now cotton candy up here, the visibility diminishing fast, and the guy in the tower warns me that it'll probably be a few feet as I'm approaching, which means I won't be able to see any landing strip lights until just before the wheels touch down. I know Theresa can hear all this but between the rapid lingo-laden technical instructions and sketchy audio quality and the astoundingly equable tones of our aeronautical exchange she probably isn't fathoming the potential peril ahead of us. When I finish talking with the tower and give her a thumbs-up I'm heartened to see that she shoots me one right back, no matter what she really knows.

But as I make the turn inland the vapor steadily thickens, puffy batts of mist moving quickly past the windscreen and thus reflecting what seems our now inhuman speed, the ground wholly invisible below, the last blue patches of sky fatefully receding above, and I'm seriously beginning to wonder why this should be the moment of payback for my years of exclusively fair-weather flying, why I couldn't have simply been torn apart all by my lonesome in a nasty gray-black thunderhead à la Sir Harold. Why I couldn't enjoy your basic heroic romantic disappearance from the radar and been interred and eulogized *in absentia*, which really ought to be my fitting end.

Theresa says weakly, "Thanks, Jerry. For taking me flying."

"Are you kidding? I can't believe I let this happen. It's all my fault."

"I'm the one who wanted lobster."

"Doesn't matter. I'm your father."

"So?"

"I should have said no."

"Maybe you're right."

Theresa laughs, or screams, quite volubly, I don't know which.

"Are you comfortable?" I ask her. "What can I do? Are you cold?"

"I'll be okay," she says, tightly cradling her still gently mounded belly. "Just fly, Jerry, okay? Just fly."

So I do. The tower takes me over what must be land, and then has me turn 180 degrees for the runway, adjusting my heading as he lines me up with the field, and I check my airspeed, my altitude, my localizer, my glide slope, every indicator a go, and I take us in. And the air down here isn't rough, not rough at all, in fact it's the lightest meringue and we're a clean, sparkly knife, which is exactly what I'd hoped, for Theresa's sake. But what it is also is totally blanking, we've been swallowed up whole, the world outside gone completely opaque; I can't see the wings, or the struts, I can't see the damn nose. It's pure whiteout. I could be flying us upside down, or on our side, or pointing us straight toward the ground, and despite what the gauges posit my surging instinct is to pull up sharply and break off what is surely a doomed course, for whoever these days can fly blind and still so faithfully true?

Not Jerry Battle, for sure. But as we descend the floating cross-hairs in the crystal magically align, literally right on the dot, and I take a hand off the wheel and grab hold of my daughter's unperturbedly cool fingers and palm, and at the last moment I actually shut my eyes, clamp them as tight as the engine housing, because what does it matter when there's nothing to see anyway, no real corroborative signs? And in the strangely comforting darkness I see not some instant flashing slide show of my finally examined and thus remorseful life but the simply framed picture of Theresa's suggested grouping not in the least difficult to delimit or define, all our gentle players arrayed, with scant or even nothing of me in mind.

I'll go solo no more, no more.

A skidding bump, the back-tug of the flaps, and we're here, running at neighborhood street speed on the field. To the port side, parked next to the terminal, an old-time ambulance is waiting in the fog, its lights silently spinning.

"We're here, baby," I say, my eyes giddy with tears. "We're here!"

But when I let go of her hand to turn and taxi *Donnie* back to the terminal it falls limply between us. I look over and her head is thrown back, her eyes closed, the band of her headset scraping at the side window, and for a second it feels just like that one summer when I was taking us home at the end of her failed runaway junket, when after the first couple of hours I truly wasn't angry at all, and was even secretly pleased, in fact, to be driving down the straight-shot highway as I watched her sleep the beautiful sleep of her at-last-exhausted adolescence, the bronzed arid palettes of the Dakotas rushing by at eighty-five.

"Baby?"

And when I look once again, I'm confused, for her face and throat, I think, are surely not cast in such a light-shaded stone, or wan papier-mâché; they can't be that null newsprint color. When I undo the seat belt and pull her over she slumps sideways on me with such a natural drape that I'm almost sure everything will be perfectly fine, my girl's just tired, and as we jounce along the paneled tarmac, it's like both of us are now guiding this little ship in, both of us at the controls.

twelve

L IFE STAYS THICK AND BUSY, on the ground.
Rita, my sweet never-at-rest, stands at the stove making today's lunch of grilled ham-and-cheese sandwiches (and ones without ham for the kids) while I set the dining room table with plastic
utensils and cups and paper napkins and plates. She's already prepared the cucumber and tomato salad, and a tray of homemade
brownies for dessert, and for my contribution to the meal I've
emptied a bag of rippled potato chips into a bowl and opened a
fresh warm jar of gherkins (the pantry closet, unfortunately, run
through with hot-water pipes). Along with the brats' juice boxes
and raspberry seltzer for Rita and Eunice, and because it's an unusually mild October Saturday, and because I simply wish to, I'll
put out a six-pack of light beer for us guys, which I'll have stowed
in the freezer for a short stretch before, so that the first sip feels almost crystalline, like tiny ice pops on the tongue.

Pop, not amazing to report, wasn't wild about this at first, but
he's grown into a fan. He puts in cans for himself now, though half
the time he forgets and plucks one out of the nonfreezer section of

the fridge and instead I have to throw away the burst ones regularly. But I don't mind. You could say we've all had to come around in the last few weeks, dealing with one another's daily (and especially nightly) functions and manners and habits and quirks, which in themselves of course are thoroughly inconsequential, and one hopes not half as telling of our characters as are our capacities for tolerance and change. Perhaps from this perspective we blood, relational, and honorary Battles should be considered a pretty decent lot, for we've been mutually permissive and decorous and even downright nice, if nice means being mostly willing, mostly communicative. This doesn't preclude of course the periodically pointed communication, as Eunice aired earlier today after breakfast while she was cleaning the bathrooms, her self-appointed Saturday chore. As the kids were settling in to a solid four-hour block of *Nick Jr.* on the tube and Jack showing Pop the work going on outside, with me heading down to the basement to finish constructing the wings on a balsa-framed model of *Donnie* (a hobby I haven't taken up since youth), Eunice marched out to the kitchen wielding a wet toilet brush in her yellow rubber-gloved hands and called for a conference on the Problem of Hair. Apparently with just two bathrooms for the seven of us we are steadily shedding enough of it to weave a hallway runner, which, though not as disgusting as dried pee on the toilet seat (a snuck glance by her at Pop), has resulted not just in a furry feeling underfoot but a serious clog in the sink and tub drains. Jack piped in about people not winding up the water hoses, and I added a note on the strange desire to illuminate empty rooms, and it was only when Rita arrived bearing grocery bags of foodstuffs and asking if she'd just missed Paul (Yes, ma'am) did we all clam up and retire to our respective tidier-than-thou corners.

Paul, who despite my protests insists on sleeping in the basement behind a sheet pinned to a clothesline and so tends to stay out of our hair, as it were, would probably not partake in the colloquium anyway, as he has more serious things on his mind than prickly domesticities. Just before Rita arrived for her Saturday visit to cook and clean a bit and then take me away for a night, he departed as he does each morning for St. Jude's Hospital, where in the preemie unit his son and my grandson, Barthes Tae-jon Battle, all 4 pounds 8 ounces of him, sleeps inside a clear plastic boxed crib. Twice a week I'll make the trip with him, but of course he goes every day, sometimes returning home and going back at night, and from what I can see and hear talking to the nurses, he has the same routine each day. He'll stop by the cafeteria first and get a large tea, and if the baby is sleeping or in a state of "quiet alert" he'll read aloud from the pile of books he brings in his knapsack, hours and hours from volumes of poetry or novels or the literature-studies journals containing critical essays of Theresa's, these last of which I can hardly understand but like to listen to anyhow in the same way I suspect the baby is not knowing but still listening intently, the purely plucked tones of Paul's calm writerly voice like an incantation, like a spoken dream. He'll read until the baby wakes, and then rock him and play with his unworldly tiny fingers and toes, small and tender enough to appear nearly transparent, hardly seeming to qualify as bone, and then get the boy suckling from an equally diminutive bottle, which the kid has always taken to quite well, voraciously in fact (indication enough that he's ready for Battle).

Whenever I'm accompanying, Paul will hand him over to me for a stint, and though without fail I'll play the ham-handed dolt for the cute, hefty nurses there's zero chance that I don't know what I'm doing. When I cradle his body in hardly two hands it seems to me I'm holding a refinement rather than something premature, too young or too small, a perfection of our kind that needs no more special handling than an unwavering attention, which might be object lesson enough. Each time I'll examine him closely, and I'll note that his pixie face is distinctively un-Caucasian, not much of a beak to speak of, the eyes almost like stripes in the skin, and the only thing that makes me pause for a half second is not that he doesn't look anything like me, which is how it has to be, but that I can't quite see his mother in him either, not yet, anyway, as he is an exact replica of the infant Paul's parents have shown us in pictures from his baby album. But maybe it's better this way for Paul and the rest of us, and that she's somewhere there, but not there, maybe mercifully good that in this one expression she's presently demurring.

But then the sweet runt will cry out (more like intensely mewl), or loudly crap in his diaper, and I'll know some opinion's afoot. For some weeks now the baby has no longer been aided by any breathing apparatus or fed intravenously, but for another couple weeks will still be monitored round-the-clock for steady vitals and the right mix of blood gases and sugars. Then, if all looks cheery and flush, and he puts on weight with the formula, Paul will finally bring him home.

Naturally, the all-agreed-upon plan is to ensconce Paul and the baby in the master, Jack and Eunice to sleep on the pullout in the family room for however long it takes for the second master bedroom addition to be completed, which by then should be close. Jack has been directing the construction, the final project in the books for the venerable firm of Battle Brothers Inc., est. 1938, and which promises to be a sizable loss. But no mind. I told Jack to build it the way he wants, with the grade of finishes that will make him and Eunice happy and comfortable, and that whatever Richie Coniglio couldn't slush into the larger write-off of the business, I'd absorb. Jack, however, has done the whole job straight off the shelves at Home Depot and Lowe's, Eunice ordering the sale fabrics and furnishings from Calico Corners and Pottery Barn, the sort of floor-sample fancy just about anyone should be able to appreciate, and certainly counts as deluxe for me.

On this score I'm damn proud of Eunice, for it seemed like she was constantly wincing at the start of construction as she flipped through the catalogues of mass-produced and marketed items but is now (perhaps with regular bathroom duty on her mind) celebrating availability and easy-care use as her primary design considerations. She was pretty depressed to have to move out of their house at Haymarket Estates (Jack found a Danish corporate executive on assignment to take a three-year lease on the place for $6000 a month, fully furnished, which will cover the mortgage and taxes plus), but she's no dummy and as Theresa said is genuinely devoted to Jack, duly remaking her bed minus all the silk shams and throws. The plan, I suppose, is that they'll use the time to regroup and reload and maybe in three years return to the château, assuming Jack is back earning. But I'm hoping things will go well enough here at our busy little ranch and maybe they'll have refigured their aims and priorities and decide to stay on longer, just renting their mini-mansion out again. The truth (which I'm sure Jack and Eunice already know) is that the chances of Jack's making the kind of dough he was paying himself are as slim as some homeowner adding a 20 percent tip to a Battle Brothers contracting invoice, and why I was the one first championing the bedroom addition, to make it as easy as possible on them to stay, my secret plan being that not too far down the road Jack will take over the house permanently and still have room for their kids and Pop and Paul and Barthes, and that I, with whatever luck is left to me, will find my closing digs elsewhere, such as Rita might desire.

Slim chances there again, champ.

At least this is what Pop tells me after lights out. With the kids in the third bedroom, we're bunking together, the space between our twin beds just wide enough that we can't simply reach over and nudge/hit each other. This is a good thing, I suppose. The other night he was snoring again with such a tortured, bestial rage, as though his body were trying to force his tonsils out through his nose, the wracked growls alternating with nearly minute-long cessations of breathing (Rita says it's sleep apnea), that I had to toss a slipper at his hulking mass, and wake him.

"Do you know what time it is?" he said, like I was the one who'd been sawing away.

"It's late."

"What do you want, Jerome?"

"You think I should put up another headstone out there?"

"What?"

"You know, out there."

"There *are* stones out at the cemetery."

"I mean one for Daisy."

"Oh," he said, scratching at himself down low. "I was wondering why there was that space in between your mother and Theresa."

"I think it all looks pretty good. But Daisy's spot just seemed kind of lonely."

"Maybe to you."

"Still. I should put another one up."

Pop rolled back away from me, onto his side. "Well, I thought that from the day she died. So did your mother."

"Really? Why didn't you say something?"

"She was your wife."

"But you both loved her. You had a say."

"You think you would have listened to us?"

"Yeah," I said. "I probably would have."

"Well, maybe that's why we didn't say anything. Now let's get some shut-eye."

I thought about that for a while, as Pop almost immediately started rattling the windowpanes with his two-stroke, how in fact after what happened Pop didn't seem to bother much with me as he'd always bothered before, instruct me to do exactly this or that with the customers or the business or the kids. He just kind of receded in an un-Pop-like way, which I attributed to my mother telling him to back off for a while and just lend me whatever hand I might need. Which they both did, my mother especially helpful around the house and Pop, too, at the garage, where he came by a couple of times a week to keep the mechanics in line by replenishing their dented metal cooler with cold beer and sandwiches. It never occurred to me back then as a presumably long-minted adult that he might have finally decided it was time to let me stew in a holding tank of my own, be it eye-high with shit or honey, and not, as was his wont (born out of ego-fied generosity and expedience), to keep giving me things anymore, foremost opinions and advice. I suppose this would normally be my moment to be expressing gratitude to him, for the usual (if tardy, extra-subtle) parental relinquishment, but I still wish he'd naturally intruded and called me a cowardly coldhearted fool and went ahead and ordered up a customary funeral and headstone for Daisy, as I wouldn't now be staring at an oddly unbalanced plot of sod whenever I visit the cemetery with Paul, following a day at St. Jude's.

At the gathering at our house after Theresa's funeral, in fact, among the countless other miserable happenings of that day, Sal Mondello (who is officially retired now, after the bankruptcy filing) came up to me afterward and extended his condolences and then added, "It's a shame her mother can't be with her." If the randy old geezer hadn't actually looked so brittle about the chops I'd have busted him one solid and wrung his neck with his own Major Johnson. But I didn't, and just nodded and accepted his old-country gesture of an envelope, then received the scores of her friends and relatives and other sundry people who came out, some of whom I didn't even recognize. But of course her high school friends, Alice Woo and Jadie Srinivasan, were there, in black-on-black dresses and hose, clinging to each other like there was a fierce ill wind blowing, crying their eyes out from the pew to the grave, and then those who obviously came out for us bereaved, like Richie and his associates, and Kelly Stearns and Miles Quintana, who despite showing no such indication were clearly there *together* (the Movietone story of how this happened I later learned from Miles, and it involved a final Parade parking lot altercation with Jimbo and the subsequent mutual realization by a maturing white Southern woman and her young brown urban knight that they had more in common than simply a love of enabling their respective constituencies to temporarily exit the dreariness of life through mid-budget holidays). The supporting presence of these friends and associates didn't comfort so much as reveal for me a surprisingly pernicious secondary gloom over the already near-suffocating pall of woe, the knowledge of collective mourning initially soothing but soon enough all the more depressing, such is the idea that no one completely escapes.

Paul, to his credit, didn't try to keep it together for anybody's sake. He lost it at the house that morning, and on the car ride to the church, and literally a few words into his remarks at the pulpit he simply stopped and stepped down and sat down next to us and bawled as loudly as he could. I was proud of him. At the lowering of the casket Jack had to hold him up, lest he stumble and fall into the hole, and back at the house afterward he had an attack of sharp pains in his belly and chest, which Rita and one of our doctor friends attended to, successfully treating with a dose of Pop's antigas tablets. That night, after everyone else had gone to sleep, while sharing the last $150 bottle of a boutique cabernet that Jack had brought over and opened unbidden and somewhat oddly insisted the two of us drink, Paul thanked me for getting up and finishing his eulogy. I said it was no problem, an honor and a privilege. So we drank to those, and to a few other puffed up et ceteras, even chuckling a bit, and soon thereafter we polished off the plump, inky wine. Because he naturally couldn't handle it and was completely grief-exhausted besides, I had to walk him to his bed, where I'm sure for the first time in days—certainly then and perhaps since—he slept an intractable, unfettered sleep.

I didn't, quite, and lay in bed for a long while staring up at the ceiling, tracing paths along the mottles and cracks, of course only inviting a dreadful circularity. I began to feel as if I were lying in a box and naturally didn't want to continue on that line and so I stepped outside onto the patio in the cooling night air and sat slumped in a deck chair beneath the moonlit sky, the distant, big-hearted-river sound of the Expressway filtering through the dry leaves of the trees. The sky, despite the half-moon, was still brilliant with celestial lights, and when I looked back over the roof I thought I saw a glinting streak fall to the horizon. There was another, and another, though appearing lower in the sky each time, and to see the next ones better I went around to the side yard, where I kept the gutter-cleaning ladder, and quietly leaned it against the gutter. Then I climbed up onto the roof, walked atop the house back over the kitchen, and sat down and waited.

There was nothing then. And I was trying my best not to remember the day but kept thinking anyway how I had finished up reading Paul's speech, which came right after Pop's, and then Jack's. It was beautifully somber, serious, elegantly lyrical stuff, and not just heady with its quotations from Heine and the Bible and the I Ching and Blake but also marked by earthy and detailed remembrances of her and their life, and even though they knew it had been written by Paul a number of people complimented *me* on the moving, heartrending words.

Though I'd told him he could take a pass, Pop insisted he was fine, and was clearly bent on saying a few words; but he only spoke off the cuff for a minute or two at most, coughing between words to suppress any burgeoning gasping or tears, and talked respectfully of her tough spirit and independent views, though he ended somewhat gruffly and inappropriately, mumbling that he hadn't seen her much of late at "the home." Jack, on the other hand, left little unmentioned in his sheaf of prepared remarks, moving quite slowly and for some reason nonchronologically through this or that scene from their childhood and teen years, noting in most every instance how his brawn had been neatly trumped by her brains. At one point he had to pause for an awkwardly long time because he was physically shuddering at what seemed surely the end of his talk, but then held it together and continued some more and didn't quite arrive to any concerted finish but instead mostly just stopped.

I was supposed to speak next, Paul slated to go last, all this outlined in the printed program. But after Pop and Jack went, Paul turned and nodded to me and then just popped up from the front. And while it wouldn't be right or fair to say that Pop's and Jack's speeches were failures exactly, because nothing expressed (or not) in such a circumstance can be anything but painfully singularly real and thus in its own profound way absolutely truthful and worthy, there hung in the silence of the church after Jack said his piece a distinctly off-kilter note that seemed desperately in need of some harmonizing response, which automatically summoned the poet in Paul to rise from the bench.

When Paul then took his turn and thereby preempted me I wasn't in the least offended or upset. I was feeling lucky, even glad. Even though I surely had in mind a thousand modest, authentic things I could have said, among them how I'd always liked the loose windblown way she wore her all-black clothes, or didn't dig how she'd often hug the yellow line when she drove, or could mention, too, if it were the least okay to do so, that while she never did regain consciousness in the ambulance after her placenta detached and bled out in a manner that, I swear, I swear, I would not describe if even my life depended on it, I was almost certain that her hand's grasp on mine kept tightening with purposeful assurance and not that she was dying or already dead. No, no, I didn't have any words, lofty or not, to offer the broken-faced throng.

No, none.

And why not? I don't know. Maybe it was old-time unreconstructed denial, or that oft-documented lazy-heartedness of mine, or else what might simply be a pathological fear of sadness. None of these of course is any good excuse, which I can mostly handle, except what does disturb is the thought that somewhere up there (I hope and pray, *up there*) Theresa Battle has had to pause in free mid-soar and grant pardon to an utter terrestrial like me.

That night I sat for some time on top of the house, and then, seeing nothing else falling in the sky, stood up to go back down. But when I checked my footing on the shingles I noticed it, the faint shade of the wide X I had inlaid, which strangely glimmered now more vividly in the moonlight than it ever had in the day. And after I locked the sliding door inside and checked on Paul and Jack's kids and climbed back into my empty bed, I thought no matter how much I wished to disappear sometimes, to fly far off and away, I really couldn't, and maybe never did. Or will.

Rita says, "The sandwiches are almost ready, Jerry. You better call everybody."

"Maybe I won't just yet," I say, my fingers tapping on her hip the first few bars of a majestic unknown song of love. "Maybe I'd just like to stay here with you."

She leans back into me. "It's a lot of sandwiches."

"We can manage it."

She kisses me, but quick and light. "Just go."

In the den I inform the kids that lunch is ready. They hardly nod at me as they momentarily stop sucking with fury on their thumbs, their action cartoon at full-bore climax, worlds exploding in a cataclysm of galaxial smoke and fire. They wait in silent, fearful awe until the hunky robot hero reappears and then cackle like the damned. I tell them again, and with their free hands they wave me on to the adjoining laundry room, where Eunice is plucking clothes from the dryer.

"Thank god for Rita!" she says when I mention lunch, handing me a stack of folded dish towels. "Take these back to the kitchen, will you? And please put them *away*, okay?"

After I comply I head outside and see Pop coming from around the side of the house, where the bedroom addition is going up. He's wearing a ratty sweatshirt and jeans, a leather tool belt loosely wound around his ample waist. He's been eating well since leaving Ivy Acres, and he's been pretty energetic besides, walking daily around the neighborhood and even helping Jack with the construction, only superlight-duty stuff of course, like measuring and cutting pieces of cedar siding.

"How's it going today?"

"Like always," he says, patting his tape measure. "Guns blazing."

"Is Jack back there?"

"Tell me it's chow time."

"A-huh."

"Good, I'm starving. Where are you going?"

"To get Jack."

"He's not over there."

I stop. "So where is he?"

Pop says, "Look in the hole."

What Pop is calling the hole, of course, is not quite that. It's a 20-by-40-foot pool trench, dug by Jack himself a couple of days last week with a backhoe from one of our former competitors, who was more than happy to rent him the machine at half the regular rate as a going-out-of-business present (Pop later told me, as it was being loaded on the truck for return, that he'd taken a nice long whiz in the gas tank). Jack figured that with all they'd given up, the kids could at least have a pool, and I wasn't one to argue. He's done a pretty nice job, given that he probably only had fifteen or twenty hours on such equipment before this, and the only associated mishaps were a couple crushed terra-cotta planters and a deep gash in the corner of the garage from the shovel, damage that looks truly horrid but definitely isn't structural. Jack pretty much dug out what had been filled in all those years ago, and the excavation proved to be unexpectedly archaeological, as we uncovered some of his and Theresa's rusty yard toys and some rotted sneakers and dolls amid the fill and gravel, and as he plumbed each side of the old pool you could sift about and find a few of the original decorative tiles, like it was some ghostly ruin of Pompeii.

I now see that Jack is indeed just climbing out, having probably made some final checks of the depth and grade. It's crazy, but we're going to try to do the finish lining ourselves. I tell him lunch is on and he gives me a nod.

"Is it ready?" I ask.

"Ready as ever," he tells me. "Maybe Monday, we'll give it a go?"

"Okay."

He shows me the soiled palms of his hands and heads for the side door to the laundry room, where the utility sink is. But instead of going in too, I step down the ladder to the bottom of the hole. Unlined as yet with concrete and tiles, it's a huge dark shoebox, the earth cool and still moist in the corners and along the deep end. And as scary and unnervingly quiet as it is to be even this far below ground, I do like the smell, which is loamy and fat

acknowledgments

I would like to thank the John Simon Guggenheim Memorial Foundation and the Hunter College Research Foundation, for support during the writing of this book.

I also wish to thank Frank and Richard Branca for the helpful aeronautical consults, Richard Purington and Ann Dickinson for the quiet, cool writing cottage, and my colleagues in the Council of Humanities at Princeton for their friendship and inspiration.

I am indebted, as ever, to Cindy Spiegel and Amanda Urban.

And to my sweethearts, Annika and Eva, for being just as they are.

and sweetly vernal, not at all of extinction, and I breathe in as deeply as I can bear. I've found myself coming down here at least once or twice a day, standing and sitting and then leaning back against the steeply ramped dirt, gazing up at a perfect frame of firmament for flights endless, unseen.

Now where's Jerry? somebody says, the barely audible sound traveling just above and far enough away from me that I don't immediately answer. It's okay. No problem. They'll start without me, you'll see.